USA _TODAY_ BESTSELLING AUTHOR

DALE MAYER

A Psychic Visions Novel

EYES TO THE SOUL

EYES TO THE SOUL
Beverly Dale Mayer
Valley Publishing Ltd.

ISBN-13: 978-1-988315-69-0
Print Edition

Books in This Series:

Tuesday's Child
Hide 'n Go Seek
Maddy's Floor
Garden of Sorrow
Knock Knock…
Rare Find
Eyes to the Soul
Now You See Her
Shattered
Into the Abyss
Seeds of Malice
Eye of the Falcon
Itsy-Bitsy Spider
Unmasked
Deep Beneath
From the Ashes
Stroke of Death
Ice Maiden
Snap, Crackle…
What If…
Talking Bones
String of Tears
Inked Forever
Insanity
Soul Legacy
Coveted

Boxed Sets and Bundles
https://geni.us/Bundlepage

About This Book

Even when a person can *see* something, it doesn't necessarily mean he should *look*…

Celina Wilton is technically blind, but, given the alternative of being dead instead, she's learned how to adapt to a condition she finds far from ideal.

Leader of a community of psychics, Stefan Kronos is often asked by the police to help out on special cases where his unique abilities assist with investigations. When he's called upon to consult on a case, Celina falls squarely on his radar. For a long time, he's wanted to get to know Celina better, and the only reason he's gotten as far as he has around her walls is by proceeding in unusual ways. He's had to cautiously watch his every step…and now, in order to protect her, he has to watch *hers* as well.

But, to unravel the threads tangling their lives with a vicious killer, Celina will need to trust Stefan enough to let him inside her barriers.

This stalker is like none other Stefan has encountered. Before long, he realizes he's not the only one with eyes into Celina's soul…

Sign up to be notified of all Dale's releases here!
https://geni.us/DaleNews

CHAPTER 1

ET ME SEE.

No. Celina Wilton shook her head, then immediately stopped. He couldn't see her. And no movement was going to stop the voice in her head. The cruel, cunning voice of a predator. One who'd found his prey. And like most predators, he loved to torment his victim.

It was unthinkable. She – a ghost-whisperer of today – herself now haunted in the very worst of ways.

Let me see.

No. She refused to give him what he wanted.

I won't go away. You know that.

And I won't let you see. No matter how long it takes.

Soft, mocking laughter filled Celina's head. She trembled. Who was this evil soul? Why was he doing this? She'd asked, but he hadn't yet answered. He had something else on his mind. Plans. She desperately wanted to know what they were, but didn't dare give him the satisfaction.

It will take forever…and I have more time than you.

Not if I have anything to say about this. But did she?

She hoped so. But she hadn't found a way to change the situation yet. She needed someone to help her. Only there wasn't anyone in this world that could. She'd been caught in a web of her own making, thinking she knew what she was doing – until this evil found her. And taught her a major lesson — that she really knew nothing. That being able to see a ghost or two did not make her a pro. That she was an innocent in a world she thought was safe and easy, only to find predators lurking in the shadows. It was a sign of her own naiveté that she hadn't known predators *could* exist in this ghost world.

She wished she could turn back time to when she'd seen her first ghost and ignore him. If only she'd treated him as the fantasy figure her friends had all said he'd been.

Except then she'd have missed communicating with Caslo, her childhood friend. Her dead best friend.

She felt so alone.

Like she'd always been alone.

Right now she was surrounded by people as the orchestra broke up for the last practice before the new show opened. Chairs were shuffled back and cases opened, voices raised in laughter.

Celina waited for the noise to die down.

"Celina, are you coming out for a drink?" Jacob Coburn, friend extraordinaire, asked from beside her.

"I was thinking that an evening at home would be better. I could use a good night's sleep before the big performance." She reached for her purse behind her chair and double checked the clasp, her hands sound and sure. She'd been living without her eyesight for so long that this was normal. Natural. She stopped just short of thinking *comfortable*. There was nothing comfy about this.

There also wasn't anything natural about people's responses to finding out she was blind, the pity in their voices.

She was blind. Not deaf, regardless of the often hushed whispers, nor dumb, even though many friends instinctively jumped up to answer for her. Being used to others' behavior didn't make it easier.

And Celina hated being called disabled or *worse* – differently abled. That was not her. Would never be her. Her condition was a stumbling block on the pathway of life and for – her – a handicap. She was handicapped regardless of politically correct terms. Besides, she wasn't *completely* blind.

She could see shadows sometimes, but not always and only if she strained her eyes.

"Come on. One drink won't make a difference, surely." He hesitated then added, "Besides, I want you to meet a friend of mine. He's planning on joining us."

She paused, closing her violin case before choosing her words carefully. "Where are you going?"

"To Chico's."

She stilled. Why there? It had to be a coincidence. They couldn't know. She didn't dare tell them. Their sympathy would be more than she could stand.

"I'll drive you home afterwards. Just one drink to celebrate all of our hard work," he said in a coaxing tone.

She could hear the smile in his voice. Jacob knew her too well. Knew how to get her cooperation.

"Opening night is tomorrow, and after that we won't have a chance for weeks," he said. "We've got this. But it took tons of effort – team effort – and the team wants to celebrate…"

"And I'm part of the team," she finished for him. There was no arguing the logic. And one drink wouldn't hurt her. In fact, it might just ease her tension for the coming night. Then again, all nights were tough these days. But why Chico's? Any place but there.

As if hearing her thoughts Jacob added, "Chico is putting on a special deal for us. He's expecting us."

Crap. Of course he was. That old man was generous to a fault.

"Fine. One drink," she said, giving in with a gentle smile.

Bruce walked past, clanging metal to metal. "A big drink then, if it's only one." More metal clanged, letting her know he was busy collecting the music stands to carry off to one side. Bruce played the drums and could have played with the best rock bands in the world, but the classics had stolen his heart.

"I'll be done here in a moment. Mind if I catch a ride with you two?" Bruce asked, his voice fading slightly as he walked away. "I'll take a cab home afterward."

"Sure thing," Jacob said to Bruce, and to Celina, "I'll go lock up your harp."

"Thanks." Chico's? Well if she had to… she could do this, like she'd done so much before. With a deep breath, she put on her sweater, grabbed her purse, walking stick and stood. Bruce snagged the chair as she left it. "Don't sit back down. There's no chair any longer."

"As always." She smiled. "You're always stealing the chair out from under me."

"I wait for you to stand," he protested, but the smile in his voice was that of a young boy playing tricks. Still his words reminded her that he was always careful to tell her when he took her chair.

"You do. Barely," she teased.

"Complain, complain, complain. Good thing you're so beautiful, with alabaster skin, that jet black hair. And those eyes…" He gave an exaggerated swooning sigh then added, "Not to mention having a voice like an angel, otherwise we might not put up with you." Bruce walked back toward her, his shoes echoing in the almost empty hall. He laughed. "Who am I kidding? With just one of those qualities we'd still be hanging around like smitten puppies."

Celina snickered. "As if. You all have the women sniffing around you now. There's a different woman in your bed every night. Just because I'm blind doesn't mean I can't see."

"How the hell you do that I don't know." Jacob protested, his voice moving closer to them. At her side again, he added, "Besides, *I* don't have a different woman in my bed."

Celina leaned closer and whispered, "That's because it's a different guy instead."

Jacob gasped, an embarrassed pause filling the air. He whispered in a shocked voice, "How the hell would you know?"

"The different men's aftershave that clings to you. Men usually stick to one kind. And you're often surrounded by different ones."

"Damn, really?" His voice full of chagrin as he said, "I shower every day."

"Yeah. Those goodbye kisses must be dynamite."

Jacob's lusty laughter rolled through the almost empty music hall. "Oh, they are – they are."

"Besides," she added because she couldn't resist. "Your voice also deepens when you're around an attractive male."

"Oh no." Bashfulness colored his voice. "I had no idea."

"Most people wouldn't notice," she reassured him. "But my senses are sharper than most people's."

"Ugh," Jacob grumbled. "Still, it's a little unnerving to consider anyone being able to notice such mannerisms."

A heavier footstep walked toward them. Jacob leaned closer and whispered, "You won't tell anyone, will you?"

"I haven't yet." She reached out a hand and patted his

shoulder, hitting him somewhere around the collarbone. "The world is a little more accepting now…"

"But the music world is very small. And not that accepting."

"I won't say anything," she promised. "Of course, my silence might require a drink to seal it."

"Blackmailing me, are you?" His voice was overly hearty as Bruce walked over.

"What's she blackmailing you for?" Bruce asked. "Maybe I can get in on this deal."

Celina's laugh tinkled freely across the spacious room. "Go find your own deal to make. This one is mine." With that she walked toward the exit.

"Wait for us," Jacob called out, the clipped sound of his footsteps echoing as he raced to catch up.

She put out a hand to grab the large square handle on the big double doors when Jacob said, "I've got it." The heavy door whooshed open. Cooler air hit her in the face as she walked through the small entrance room to the exit. She waited, a small smile on her face, for Jacob to open the exterior door for her.

The fresh air rushed to greet her. She tilted her face slightly into the breeze, loving the wash of coolness. Portland street sounds and smells greeted her. Gasoline. Car engines, people joking and laughing. The hum of an everyday evening.

She tilted her head, straining her senses, searching for something, anything other than what was on the surface. A habit she couldn't break since her accident.

And found nothing. Thank heavens. She had no idea what she'd do if she ever did – it hadn't happened yet.

"Are you all right?"

She started, then relaxed. "I'm fine. It looks like a beautiful night out."

"It is, but how you could know that I'll never understand."

With a smirk his way she stepped out into the night.

THE BAR WAS hopping. Celina didn't need to get any closer than the curb to hear the music flowing out of the pub in front of her. Lights flashed and bounded behind her eyelids as she faced the building. "Surely they don't have an old disco ball in there, do they?" She laughed as the colors flashed her way again.

Jacob approached from the right, his steps tired, heavier on the weaker left leg, his laughter bright regardless of his obvious fatigue. Excited. Almost too excited. She tucked that away inside.

"They do indeed. This place hops all the time. Come on, let's go find the others." Jacob grasped her elbow gently and tugged her toward the noise. She couldn't explain the instinct to pull back. Jacob's touch? Or the destination? She'd been to many a pub over the years and several of those same ones since her accident and subsequent eye surgery.

At this time of night the pub was loud, as in it was possibly too much of a good thing. She'd prefer a glass of white wine in the corner by a fireplace listening to live music. This felt like tequila shots being egged on by everyone in the room.

She sighed inwardly. She only had to stay for one drink, and hers wouldn't be a shot of anything. She'd have a Baileys and coffee if she could. Although caffeine wasn't the best thing at this time of night either.

"Just one drink, then I'll take you home." Jacob said quietly from her side, as if understanding her reticence.

"And I'm going to hold you to that," she muttered as Bruce opened the door and she was hit by the full blast of music and people spilling into the entranceway. Jacob tightened his grip on her arm and half-led, half-dragged her forward through the ruckus.

"Celina's here!"

A cry went up to her left as Jacob nudged her into the large group.

The fun was infectious, loud – and, as it included her, irresistible. She was grabbed and hugged, her cheeks bussed as people talked to her, over her and around her.

She recognized most of the people by their voices, some by their hugs and others that just felt the need to keep a hand on her.

That was another thing she didn't understand. Once she became blind, so many people seemed to feel that her ability to recognize them would be enhanced by physical contact – at least she assumed that was the cause. They were right, but not in any way that they'd understand. With her eyes closed and her sight gone, she couldn't see the bright colors that filled the pub. They were still there, she knew – she'd seen enough of them over the last several decades – and to a certain extent she still saw a pale ghost of them now.

The bright colors were one of the things she missed most about not being able to see. The vibrant, moving ribbons of sound – especially when she played. They used to fill her eyes with tears; then she realized that she was the only one who could see them. It was such a disappointment to have lost the brilliance of those colors with the loss of her eyesight. That she could see them at all now was wonderful, but... it wasn't the same. She'd thought of herself as both a musician and an artist, controlling the colors as they danced to the notes she played. She made artistic creations in the air while her music was art for the ears.

It hadn't taken her long to accept that the visual art was a gift even if she was the only one who could see it – and was still a gift in faded form.

And with so few gifts in her life, she'd been happy to have what little there were. Although she'd had a few low spots in her life, she'd also been blessed.

She needed to remember that.

"What took you guys so long?" Cindy asked beside her. Cindy played a wicked trombone and couldn't sing a note, much to her chagrin.

"Just cleaning up behind you," Bruce teased. "Everyone raced out so fast no one took the time to clean up."

"Ah, well. What would we do without you?" Cindy moved something that tinkled – ice in a tall glass – past Celina. "Here, the first drink is on me as thanks!"

Jacob laughed. "Well, in that case…" He took a long drink. Celina could hear him swallowing. He was that close to her.

"Celina, what will you have?"

She started at Cindy's question, the word *nothing* on the tip of her tongue. Bruce spoke up before she could and said, "She'd like a glass of white wine."

"I do, do I? Maybe I want something else," she said. The instant spark of anger felt odd inside. She didn't want to be here and really didn't want people answering questions for her – even if they were decent answers.

What was wrong with her today? She shouldn't be so waspish. He was only trying to make it easy on her. Like everyone tried to make everything easy on her. There was just no making this…easy.

I can make it easy. Just let me see.

No. Never.

I can do it without you, but it would be more fun with you.

No. Killing people is not fun.

Oh, it so is.

That dry dusty chuckle reverberated inside her head. She trembled.

Especially when no one knows who I am, the nasty voice whispered. *Or what I can do.*

I don't even know what you can do. I don't want to know, she cried silently in her mind. How had her life come to this?

That's easy. You wanted me here You wanted to have your eyesight back – so I stepped in to help you.

No. No. She shook her head.

Oh yes. See, you still don't believe me. Or understand why. That's funny. I'm so going to enjoy your reaction when you do find out about me. He laughed. *Maybe a little proof is needed.*

What? No. She shook her head, not caring if other people stared at her strangely. She knew she'd become odd this last year, but who could blame her? She'd lost her fiancé a year ago from an aneurysm. She'd been involved in a serious car accident three weeks later. And it had been bad enough she'd ended up with several busted ribs and a head injury, with her eyesight compromised by the trauma that even surgery hadn't been able to fix. Then to top it all off, she had somehow collected a vengeful ghost. One who wanted her to believe he could do so much.

She was being haunted. If such a thing were possible.

No proof. Please, she whispered in her head. *I believe you.*

No. I don't think you do. So give me a moment. I've been

planning something like this for a while. It's the perfect time. This way you'll know for sure.

The weird blackness left her mind. Thank heavens. She needed help. Someone who could understand what she was going through. But it wasn't exactly something she could go to a doctor for. And a psychologist would have a heyday inside her head. Weren't there enough people in there already?

Bruce lifted his glass beside her, the ice smaller, softer, clinking softly along the glass. "Another. I want a couple of tequila shooters," he cried. His suggestions brought on screams for shooters.

Celina sank back into the booth beside Jacob. She wanted to leave. She didn't know what kind of proof this evil thing inside of her was going to offer, but she wanted no part of it.

"Are you okay, Celina? You look ill."

"I'm not feeling well. Please, I know I haven't finished my wine." In fact, she hadn't touched it. "But I'd really like to go home."

Cheers broke out beside her. Instinctively she turned. "What are they doing now?" she asked.

"Just tequila shots." The tone of his voice sounded slightly odd. She stilled, her mind racing to turn the suspicions and fear squeezing her chest into something calming. She had to get out of here. Now. Urgency had her lurching to her feet. She struggled to find the entrance to the pub. She stumbled into one person and bounced off another. "Sorry," she said. "Sorry, I'm sorry. I'm just trying to get some fresh air."

"Celina, wait."

But she couldn't. An inner drive propelled her forward

to the entranceway, only she was jostled from one side to the other with no room for her walking stick. And the entranceway was no longer where it should have been. She hit a wall. Hands out, she scrambled back as far as she could down that wall.

Under all the loud music and laughing a roar built. No one appeared to notice. She tilted her head, listening as the sound rapidly grew.

In the background, as if in a movie on slow motion, she heard the first screams. Then more.

Then the sound of a huge roar. A crash. Panicked cries. Glass shattering, sprinkling down on everything and everyone.

Finally silence. The horrible, deafening silence.

Celina waited, shock, fear, terror holding her locked in place. She couldn't see. She could only hear. She bowed her head. Fatalistically, she turned ever so slowly to stare blindly at the blank chaos in front of her. She could only imagine the scene.

A woman screamed. And screamed. A man groaned. Then another one off to the side started to cry.

"Help me," a woman whispered close to Celina. "Please help me."

Celina reached out a hand in her general direction and was jerked forward as the woman clutched at her and tried to pull. "I'm here. But I don't know what happened."

"I don't know." The woman started to sob. "Help me, please. I'm hurt."

Instinctively Celina crouched at the injured woman's side, patting her hand gently. There wasn't much she could say, but she knew comforting sounds were coming from her mouth.

People moved slowly amidst the cries of pain and the weeping. Something dreadful had happened but she had no idea what could have taken place.

A man in front and off to the left of her said, "A large truck drove into the front of the pub. He's halfway inside the damn room. He's hit dozens and probably killed half of those."

Oh no. Her heart seized as she turned to face the chaos. "Jacob? Bruce? Are you okay?"

There was no answer.

"Jacob!" she screamed. "Where are you?"

She couldn't hear any response over the building noise as people cried out for help and still others wept for their friends and family.

She tried to control her panic. *Oh God. No. Please, not my friends.*

She didn't dare try to find them in the mess. She gazed in the direction of the injured woman, her hand gently patting her on the shoulder. She'd never felt so helpless. How had this just happened? And why? And did the predator have anything to do with it? Her heart pounded in her chest and she could barely breathe. And that's when she heard something else.

Silence – from the woman whose hand she held. Silence, where moments before there'd been raspy breath. Silence, where moments before there'd been broken weeping. Celina stroked up the woman's arm to her throat and pressed two fingers against her sticky skin.

And bowed her head. The woman was dead.

No, her heart screamed in denial. This couldn't be happening. They'd just come for a fun hour of celebration. Not this life-changing disaster.

She'd already survived one of those. She wouldn't wish anything like that on anyone. And never twice.

Underneath her sorrow and budding grief, she heard that hateful laugh inside her head.

What do you think? Was that enough proof?

She froze. *Oh God. No!*

Oh yes. Do you believe me now?

CHAPTER 2

STEFAN KRONOS BOLTED awake and out of bed. He was halfway across the room before he realized it. Panicked, he spun, searching for the danger. And stilled.

He was alone.

In his own room.

He rested in place, his heart slowing, listening. Reassured that there was no immediate danger, he ran his fingers through his rumpled hair and growled, "Now what?"

He'd barely slept an hour. And not for a lack of trying.

But as was so often the case, his wants weren't important.

Timing was.

The more he tried to force the information of what was wrong, the further back the elusive knowledge in his conscience slipped. Out of sight. Out of his mind. Out of his reach.

He strode to the tall floor-to-ceiling windows and stared out into the night. What the hell had woken him this time?

Instinctively he sent out a silent probe searching for the direction of the distress. He knew it was a cry for help. But it was one he didn't recognize. At least not in this form. It came raw, terrified, and coated in other energies.

Unless it was another psychic like those that had been filling his house and cluttering up his life lately. He loved them all, but there was no doubt that the landscape of his life was very different than it had been a decade ago.

Then he'd been alone and unknown. Now the opposite – in both cases – was true.

He stared out into the dark sky, watching as the clouds played peek-a-boo with the moon. Something was wrong somewhere. Then again, something was wrong somewhere every minute of the day. Unfortunately. He dropped his forehead against the glass, relaxed his guard and sank deeper into his soul to let his senses roam free.

His energy slipped outward, upward into the midnight of the sky, looking, tasting, *feeling* the wrongness. Behind him the television turned on. He stilled but didn't turn around. He'd sent out energy in all directions with too much force again. Some of it had turned on his electronics. Not unexpected. Not normal, though. And better than what could have happened; he often fried the electronics.

"We bring you breaking news. A full-size truck has driven into the popular nightclub Chico's downtown on Robstown Street. Reports are still coming in. There are ambulances on the scene. We do have a report that several members of the Portland Orchestra were in attendance celebrating their new season." The newscaster paused. Stefan slowly turned. He stared, his heart frozen, his energy thinning as it swirled in shock.

Celina.

"This just in…we have established that several members of the orchestra have been injured," the newscaster continued. "Two fatalities are confirmed. We'll bring you more as we get the details."

Stefan collapsed to his knees. *Oh dear God. Please, not Celina.*

Surely he'd have known if she were dead. Then he remembered the cry that had woken him from a deep sleep. Could it have been her? He should have recognized it if it had been, although the distress signal had been coming from the same general direction.

To find out for sure he needed to get to the scene. To the hospital. Where he could find her. Help her. Locating her wouldn't be a problem. He already sensed her thin, wispy energy from here. He'd visited her enough on the etheric level to be able to find her anywhere in the world. But he wasn't sure he could stand the thought of finding out she was injured and in need of something beyond his capabilities. Of all his friends Dr. Maddy was the only one that might be able to help if she was seriously injured.

And we need to find that out first. Don't panic until we know. Dr. Maddy's warm, compassionate voice slipped into his mind. *I'll make the calls. You wait for me. Don't rush down there. You aren't family or friends, and you won't be allowed in to see her. Think, Stefan. She doesn't even know you.*

Stefan tilted his head back to stare up at the massive glass dome above his head. No, she didn't know him. Not who he was now at least.

Dr. Maddy slipped out of his mind, for once leaving him feeling bereft. He'd been blessed to have so many talented friends to call on.

And there'd always been *her*. The love of his life. And now that life may have been cut down before he had a chance to see her in person.

He knew his thoughts made him sound like a madman. And he'd done a lot to keep the others in the traditional world from finding out about his crazy mind. He'd spent time in a place where he was *supposed* to get help. Oh, he'd gotten help, all right – just not the kind he'd needed. Thankfully he'd quickly learned to keep his mouth shut. He'd left there as fast as he could and had never looked back.

Dr. Maddy spoke quietly inside his head. *She's injured, but not badly. Cuts from glass as she was trying to help the victims. She's already been checked over. She's emotionally traumatized but not physically. She will be fine.*

Thank you, he whispered in a prayer-like voice. *Thank you so much for finding out.*

Now rest. She has a lot to deal with. Send her some loving energy, but don't go to the hospital – you'll only be in the way.

Understood.

And she left.

Stefan stood up, ran his fingers through his hair again and tried to take stock. He was still shaky inside. He wondered if that had been her fear he'd felt earlier. There'd been no reason for her to call out to *him*. She didn't know him. Or had she been transmitting blindly to anyone who'd listen? She'd have to be a strong transmitter for that to happen. Due to her blindness, Celina's other senses would likely have become stronger to compensate. She might have picked up on his energy and sent out a call for help. He'd love to think it had been on purpose, but he had no reason to go there.

He'd been the one checking in on her, not the other way around.

It had always been Stefan peeking into her life to make sure she was doing okay, to connect in the only way he could. Still, he should have been able to recognize her energy if she had been the one calling out to him – at least he thought he would have. But context was everything. In a traumatic setting she'd have called out for anyone. The energy pathways he'd forged would have made it easier to get her message. And depending on her psychic abilities, she might have been coated in bits and pieces of those she cared about, completely changing the look and feel of her energy.

There'd been a sense of violence surrounding that cry. Like an attack of some kind.

He mulled over the accident. Could the fear have been one last cry from the driver of the truck before he'd smashed into the pub? Had he survived the crash? If so, Stefan wanted to talk to him. He would have to wait and see. As his senses returned to normal and he got a clearer understanding of why he'd been pulled awake, he realized there'd been some movement in the universal energy. A tear in the structure of life. A violence done on the etheric level.

He frowned, his senses stirring. As everything was connected, so too was this connected to the fabric of their lives. Everyone's lives. There was evil out there. He'd seen the proof of it. Once he'd known, there'd been no going back. Innocence was no longer an option.

The boogeyman did exist and in his world, he lived on many different planes of existence.

Stefan walked over to his computer and turned it on. Still dressed in his pj bottoms he sat down to check the news. Maybe they would provide the clues he was looking for. He knew one thing for sure: there was no going back to sleep tonight.

SAMANTHA BLAIR GASPED, then groaned as she burst through the vision. That was all her newly learned control would allow. Her intentions were simple. Sink into the vision, grab the information she needed – if any – to help the dying person to let go and step out. Easy, right? It was when Stefan had explained it. In practice? Not so much.

Be in control, Stefan had said to her during one of their training sessions. *Remember, Sam, this is your energy. Don't let fear stop you from controlling it as you are meant to control it.*

Consciousness broke through and Sam's eyes opened. She shuddered, a film of sweat forming on her skin. So much better with a bit of control, and yet so much worse – she still couldn't do anything about these visions.

A warm arm slipped across her ribs and tugged her up close to a familiar broad chest.

That was one thing that was so much better. Brandt Sutherland. She'd been alone for so long. Now…she had a man who loved her. He understood what she went through on a regular basis with her crazy psychic abilities. Who could possibly want to connect with victims while they were being murdered?

A cold nose nudged her cheek.

"Hey, Soldier. I'm okay, boy," she murmured softly, reaching out a hand to stroke the huge dog's muzzle. Moses, her other dog, stood at Soldier's side and whimpered in the back of his throat.

"Sorry, I didn't mean to wake you guys up."

"What about me?" Brandt's warm voice drifted hot against her neck. "Did you mean to wake me up?"

His lips trailed up her throat before drifting over to explore her ear. Sam smiled, love welling up from deep inside.

"I'm always happy to wake you up, my love."

His arms clenched around her. She rolled toward him and reached up to meet his lips with a deep, soul-stirring kiss of her own.

God, she loved this man.

CELINA SAT IN a daze. The hospital bustled around her, the noise overwhelming her. The pain. The suffering. The grief. She tried to block out the shouts, cries, and incessant weeping. She understood. She really did, but there was no way to survive the onslaught of pain without closing herself off. No way to find the peaceful core she so desperately needed to keep oriented in her physical space. People who could see didn't understand how hard it was to be blind and upset.

She got turned around, misjudged distances, and misunderstood certain sounds. She needed to be grounded to do anything and even more so to take a trip. One more reason why she didn't travel as much as she could.

She also didn't have a guide dog, although many friends had suggested it. But getting one meant accepting that her condition was permanent. And she couldn't do that. Wouldn't do that.

Her doctor also wouldn't sign off on her condition. As far as he was concerned she should be able to see. He'd done everything right. It was only Celina that wasn't doing what she needed to be doing.

And he was so right about that. She didn't dare do what she needed to do.

Plus, there was no way she could explain why.

"Celina, are you doing okay? Are you sure you want to be here and not resting at home?" Gordon, the ex-manager of the Myrtle Auditorium, home to the orchestra – and a very good friend – stood in front of her. "Let me call a cab and get you home." His hand brushed down her cheeks, the warmth of his palm and fingers sending off sparks. "Please, Celina. You can't do anything. The doctors are working as hard as they can to help our friends."

"I feel like I need to be here," she whispered. "I know I can't help, but if there is anything I can do in any way then please let me know."

Gordon's voice deepened, a long heavy sigh escaping before he said, "I will, but I wish you'd go home."

She smiled up at him. He was such a good man. She might not be able to see much, but she could see a color with everyone and Gordon's pale blues were lovely. That said a lot about him. "I know you do. But I'll sit here quietly for a little while. If you hear anything let me know."

"Will do." She listened to hear if his footsteps faded away. But a large noisy group of people moved past, making it impossible to separate all the sounds. There was no plausible reason for her continued stubbornness in staying here. She'd been offered several chances to go home but she hadn't been able to leave. Cindy was dead. Bruce was dead. Jacob was fighting for his life and was currently in surgery. How could she leave him to fight alone?

People walked past her in a continuous wave. She had no idea if they were friends or family of the injured or if they were here for unrelated events. She was so tired, but she couldn't let go of the fear that whispered through her veins, flowing on the river of her blood, making every breath that much harder to get out.

Her fingers clutched the soothing rock she'd hung onto for years. It felt right in her hand. Held special meaning in her heart. And had become her comfort in times of great stress. She carried it everywhere, all the time.

"Are you okay?" A quiet, deep and – oh God – smooth-as-chocolate voice spoke from beside her. She'd been so lost in all the traffic she'd disappeared into the quiet of her mind and hadn't noticed the stranger sitting down beside her.

Her nostrils flared at the man's cologne. She'd never smelled it before. She was sure of it. There was nothing about it she recognized, but…there was something familiar. The answer darted into her mind then disappeared before she could grasp it.

She was losing it. Confused. Disoriented. It had to be from the chaos she'd been through tonight. This was not a good place for her to be. Not that she'd tell him that. "Yes," she said quietly. "I'm okay."

"You looked to be having a little trouble," that rich voice said with a gentleness that touched her. Except she didn't need his pity. Or anyone else's.

She tilted her lips at the corner politely and straightened. "I'm fine." She firmed her voice and added some strength to the tone. Maybe he'd believe her this time and leave her alone.

"Good."

He slumped down in the chair, his knee accidently brushing her as it slid past. Sparks leapt between them. She jumped. He leaned forward. "I'm sorry. Did I scare you?"

She tilted her head, letting that smooth, silky voice wash over her. God, it was magnetic. Making her want something…something more than what she had. "No, you just surprised me. I'm a little jumpy, that's all."

"No wonder. If you were in this tragedy at the pub then you have good reason."

She winced. Her instinct said to keep her mouth shut. This man could be a reporter. He could be an insurance investigator. She had no idea. He was a stranger…and yet not a stranger. And that "not a stranger" part disturbed her more.

"No. I wasn't." She offered the white lie without a qualm then settled back and closed her eyes. "Now if you don't mind I'm going to rest a bit."

And she shut him out.

"STEFAN, ARE YOU at the hospital?" Brandt asked.

Stefan frowned into his cell phone. Damn psychics. Was there no privacy? "Why," he snapped, "would you ask such a question?"

Brandt laughed. "Because everyone knows how attached you are to Celina. And the psychic grapevine tells me she's been in an accident. How is she?"

"How would I know?" Stefan said moodily as he stared at the dark beauty beside him who had already shut him out. She appeared to be fine, maybe shaken up a little. He wanted to talk to her but couldn't find an opening. Talk about frustrating.

He stood and walked a few steps away so he wouldn't disturb her. Why he'd come down here he didn't know. He was obsessed with her. And damned if that didn't make him angry. Though he knew she was his natural mate, it didn't make a damn bit of difference if she didn't acknowledge it. At the rate they were going she wasn't going to let him close enough to acknowledge anything.

That was the problem with his psychic knowledge. He knew too much at times. Waiting for Celina to find him, to know him and really see him had been hard, but now that the time was getting closer… it was almost impossible.

He was doing what he could to help breach the gap between them, letting her get used to his energy. Sitting beside her, so close – and yet there might as well have been oceans between them. Except he could see tiny energy flares flicking his way. Easing down his own guard, he let her energy flares mingle with his, tentative, then interested, questing but reserved. Always reserved.

Maybe an instinctive reaction to strangers? Maybe a reaction to him?

He hoped not. The road ahead was already turbulent.

"I need help. And you need something else to focus on." Brandt's voice turned brisk and businesslike. "If you're at the hospital we're close. If you can meet me outside, I'll swing by on the way home."

Stefan frowned. "I'm not sure I'm recovered enough to be much help." He ran his fingers through his longish hair. Time for a cut again. Where did the weeks ago? Oh yes, that last case with a psychic killer – yet another one – had wiped him out.

In spite of himself Stefan felt his flagging spirits lift. What did that say about him that a series of cases, probably death and destruction, interested him? He'd been doing this work for too long. He needed a break.

A real rest.

He turned to stare at Celina. As if aware, she turned those blind eyes his way. He'd already sent out a probe to see if he could touch her aura. She'd rebuffed him immediately. That wasn't good. She needed to let him in.

But then, since she didn't know him, why would she let him in? Then again, she rebuffed his energy like a pro – and how did that work? Was she psychic? He'd often assumed any partner of his would be, but had contemplated the joys of one that wasn't. He had enough upsetting nights, edginess with energy flares and disturbed dreams for several people. Being around non-psychic people was calming, soothing in a way. At the same time they didn't understand him or his work or what he could be going through at any given moment.

"Hey Stefan, snap out of it, will you? Sam's going through some weird stuff. I've done some research but I could use your take on it to help sort through this mess. Can we meet or not?"

"Fine. I need to go home too." He stared at his watch in disbelief. He hadn't once considered the time when he'd thrown on clothes and rushed down here to be with her. "Can't believe it's after two in the morning already."

"Meet me in the parking lot in five." Brandt hung up.

Stefan stared at the horrible pastel walls, hearing the muted sobs in the background. He hated hospitals normally and wouldn't come willingly. Had actually shored up his own defenses to come in. As the foreign energies buffeted him on all sides he realized it was past time to leave.

With a last lingering look at Celina he started to walk away when he felt something odd. He spun around, but the hospital waiting room was empty other than Celina and… a few ghosts. She sat in the same place, her head now resting back and her eyes closed. A simple fog of energy floated toward him. From her? From someone else? He reached out a hand and the fog retreated. He stepped forward and the fog dissipated. Instantly.

The hairs on the back of his neck lifted. He stared at Celina but she never shifted.

Instinctively he backed up a step and then another. What the hell – or who the hell – was that?

He glanced around the room a second time, reassured himself that the ghostly visitor was no longer there, and turned around and left. Sometimes he saw too much.

HE SHUDDERED, THE weakness spreading throughout his being. He didn't know where he was. Who he was. Or maybe *what* he was. That was a better way to say it. His existence had spread so thin, his mind so weak, his strength so nonexistent.

It was getting harder to keep his thoughts together. But clarity was elusive. There and gone again. Solid then vaporous. And always worse after he focused everything he had and managed to execute one more step in his plan. The massive effort draining his reserves, as if the shock was too much for his system and he needed to reboot.

He needed to grab onto something – someone – and focus again. Likely, onto her. She made a great target. He could do more. Say more – be more when he was with her. But after he left it was as if he closed in on himself – worse off than before. As if the effort to be there in that form took more out of him than anything else. This reaction was lessening the stronger he became, but there was still a weakening of his senses when he left her. As if she were taking something from him.

Which added to his hatred.

This existence was not what he'd wanted. Not what he'd thought would happen to him. It was good and it was really horrible. How could he survive with so many fragments of reality? How could he pull this disjointed existence into something stronger? More coherent? He desperately needed to. This couldn't last. *He* couldn't last. But now, more than ever he wanted to. There was something he needed to do. Someone who needed to pay. He had to survive long enough to see his plans through.

This life was empty and yet overflowing at the same

time.

He was dying. One little bit at a time. Not like death in the normal way, but a strange, slow, drifting way.

There had to be a way to cut off the deadwood pulling him in all directions – and faster than the slow-ass method he'd been employing. It was taking too long given the weakness and lassitude in his mind.

If only he could think clearly.

There were moments of clarity when he could speak out. Then times when the world was so muffled any action was impossible. Even as he worried on the issue, an answer drifted closer then drifted away. But he'd seen just enough to remember the plan. The plan he'd already been undertaking.

Now he knew what to do.

He hoped.

CHAPTER 3

"CELINA, DO YOU know who that man was?" Gordon asked, walking into the small waiting room, his voice odd, muted.

Celina opened her eyes, a reflexive habit, and said, "No."

"Hmmm." Gordon didn't sound convinced. "He was looking at you pretty intently."

"He was just being friendly. Whoever he is he got a phone call and left."

"As long as he wasn't bothering you. I came to tell you that Jacob came through the surgery just fine. He's lost a lot of blood and they will keep a close eye on him overnight in the ICU, but they're optimistic about his chances for a full recovery."

"Oh, that's wonderful news." She jumped to her feet, her hand instinctively going to her chest. She beamed up at him. "Is there any chance of seeing him?"

"No, not tonight." The relief in his voice shaded her disappointment. "He needs to rest. Come on, let's get you a cab."

"Wait, I have to grab my purse." She turned back and bent to the floor for her larger-than-any-purse-should-be tote and straightened. "Now I'm good to go."

"I can't imagine what you carry inside that thing. It's big enough for you to almost crawl inside and have a nap."

"That's my secret to staying alert all day." She stumbled and righted herself. "Sorry," she muttered. "I hadn't realized how tired I am."

"Comes from sitting here all night while still in shock yourself. A good night's sleep will help."

"I'm fin–" A big yawn caught her by surprise. She moaned lightly when her mouth finally closed. "Sorry, that one almost hurt."

"Like I said."

She walked at his side, grateful that she could follow his colors since she hated being led around. Jacob had always ignored that preference, telling her she was being stubborn and too independent. She sighed. At least Jacob was going to be okay. She'd known him for a long time. More than a friendship, they shared music in their soul. Like any creative person, finding someone else to whom the expression of that art meant the same thing was like finding a soul mate without all the highs and lows of a sexual relationship. Yet in a way it was creation at its best. Supported and shared. The lead ball of fear in her stomach broke into small pieces and started to dissolve – finally. She walked taller, straighter, as the weight of this horrific night slipped off her shoulders. She couldn't help her dead friends, but if there was anything she could do for the others she would be there for them. So what if she was blind? She wasn't helpless. However, as she collapsed into the back of the cab, she realized how exhaust-ed she really was. A decent night's sleep and she'd be just fine.

Not likely.

She stiffened, her defenses that she'd let slip in her fa-tigue slamming back into place. *Go away.*

Why would I do that? This is the fun part. The aftermath.

All the angst and remorse. See, you could have prevented this.

She gasped.

"What's the matter?"

A rush of air brushed past her cheek. Was Gordon that close?

"Did you forget something?" He asked from right in front of her as if leaning in close.

"No," she said quickly. "Sorry, I was just thinking of some things I needed to take care of earlier." Like hell, but she didn't dare let on what was happening. Besides, who would believe her?

"Tomorrow is another day. You'll have lots of downtime now. The show is cancelled until further notice." He added as he backed away, "Go home and rest."

She closed the door and the cab slowly pulled away.

She hadn't considered that. To lose the show wasn't such an issue, but to not play – that was a big deal. It was her healing. Her outlet. *Stress release* was what some would call it. A connection to the rest of the world in ways she couldn't explain.

A friend of hers had once suggested her music was so powerful it was magic. She'd laughed at the time, but had often wondered at the joy that coursed through her soul when she played. It healed her. She didn't think anyone else received the same benefit though. Too bad.

The cab pulled up to the front of her secured apartment building. She opened her door. "Thank you so much for the ride."

"Do you need a hand in?" the driver asked.

"No, thank you though. I'll be fine."

"Well, if you're sure," he said doubtfully.

She dredged up a confident smile and said, "I'll be okay.

Thank you."

And she turned and faced her apartment building. Of course she'd be fine. What else could go wrong this night?

STEFAN WALKED OUTSIDE into the clear, sparkling night and stopped for a moment to stare up at the twinkling lights. It was truly beautiful and so mysterious. Like so much of the world. He took several deep breaths of fresh air, waiting for the tension and soreness along his back to ease. A holiday would be good. Except when he took a break his damn ghosts went with him too.

He continued to the parking lot and reached his vehicle as Brandt arrived. He waited for his friend to get out. "You should be home with Sam, not here working on more crazy cases."

"Sam is waiting for me now. If I'd never been called out you couldn't have pried me from her arms." Brandt grinned, leaving Stefan no doubt how loving those arms would be. "But as long as we're both here…"

Stefan smiled slowly. He loved to see his many psychic friends partner up and grow and mature into the type of loving relationships everyone dreams of having. Sam had been one of the most tormented psychics he'd ever met. And one of the most talented.

"How are her lessons going?" Stefan leaned against his car, the light from the lamppost shining on his face.

"She's doing really well." Brandt's face lit up until he caught sight of Stefan's face. His smile fell away. "What's wrong? You don't look so good."

Stefan shrugged. "Life has been a little rough lately."

"And yet life has been pretty smooth and easy these last

few days – until tonight."

"Maybe too smooth." Stefan's lips quirked. "Too easy."

Brandt's gaze sharpened. "Is something stirring?"

"Always," Stefan responded. "More than usual? Maybe. It's a little too early to say."

Brandt crossed his arms and rocked on his heels. "Then I'm glad I brought this file. These are cases *possibly* connected to Sam's current visions. She's having weird attacks but isn't ready to talk about it yet. She *says* she's not connected to any person at this time – thank God – but she said something weird."

Stefan leaned forward. Anytime Sam had something weird to say he wanted to hear it.

Brandt continued, "She said someone is walking in between."

Stefan frowned. "I may have to call her about that. There have been more tears in the energy fields. I don't have a cause for them."

"Big tears?" Brandt asked carefully. "As in something evil coming across to raise some major hell?"

"I don't know," Stefan said. "It's strong, it's focused, but they are all small events. I can't even say they are connected. But the more of them there are the more concerned I get."

"Right. If you're concerned you know I'm terrified. Keep me posted, and please do call Sam. She needs her rest. Maybe talking to you will help."

Stefan nodded. Sam was a beautiful person inside and out, and her talent taxed her physical body worse than anyone else he knew. He asked, "Now why am I here when I could be home in my own bed?"

"For one, I want to make sure you're okay. For you to go to a hospital and remain for longer than a few minutes, something must be going on. And from what I understand the energy you have to expend to stay there is brutal, and that means you're not only exhausted but also very connected to someone involved in that nasty accident. Celina, of course."

Stefan stared at him, wondering how his life had become cluttered with so many friends. Caring friends. Dare he say *loving* friends? "True. But at this point I think I'll head home before I drop."

Brandt grinned. "Sounds like a plan for both of us." He turned around and reached into the front of his truck, pulling out a brown manila envelope. "This is the file I mentioned a moment ago. I can't connect the cases but…they are the closest I can come to matching up Sam's information of these visions. You know how iffy that can be." He shrugged. "Take it. Have a look at it tomorrow."

"Now you're talking." Stefan stood up and felt the parking lot shift and sway. Damn. He needed to get home. "Tomorrow. I'll take a look then."

Brandt handed the thick envelope over. "Are you sure you should be driving?"

Stefan shot him a look, snatched up the envelope, and walked to his car.

HIS FOCUS WAVERED a little more. His thoughts blurred and he had a hard time hanging onto them. Brain fog set in. He shuddered. He was losing it. Again.

It was worse this time. And it shouldn't be. It should have been better. Easier.

He couldn't let go of the idea that there really was an end to his life.

His mind screamed *no* but the evidence was undeniable. He'd done everything he could but the facts were facts. He was struggling to maintain any kind of existence. And his moments of clarity were too important to waste. But afterwards the effort set him way back. Almost to the same distorted, broken-up beginning again. He hated that. It always took so long to pull himself together.

His energy was spread so thin he had to wonder if that in itself wasn't the problem.

He really wanted his focus in only one place.

To do that he needed to focus on pulling himself together. He almost laughed, as that was the last thing he could do. Still, if he was spread too thin then it would take up too much energy to keep going on all fronts.

It was time to cut out some of those fronts.

Clean out the not-so-much fun debris in this life and keep the stuff he enjoyed, or at least the ones he had more strength to control. It was an amazing journey, but he'd taken so little time to enjoy it.

And that needed to change.

Determined, he set about analyzing the deadwood in his life. It was time to take a chainsaw and free himself.

CHAPTER 4

CELINA WALKED GRATEFULLY into her apartment, turned on the light from habit and locked the door. She leaned against it and closed her eyes. Traveling was always stressful, with arriving home a huge relief. After a moment of rest she walked, a little shakily, into her bedroom. She knew it was going to be a bad night. How could it not be?

Once ready for bed she sat cross-legged in the center of her down comforter. She took a deep breath, then another. Using old esoteric techniques she'd learned from her friend Mimi before she died, she slowly worked some of the tension out of her shoulders and spine. She often played music before bed, but tonight she was too tired and too full of sorrow.

"It was bad, wasn't it?" Mimi asked, her disembodied voice soft and thin.

Celina smiled, wan and weak, but it was a smile at least. Not that her ghostly friend would care. She'd seen her at her best and at her worst.

"Yes, it was bad," Celina whispered. She kept her eyes closed, letting in the wispy images of her friend from behind her closed eyelids. She always saw Mimi in a light purple cloud. Mimi had been eighty when she passed and had embraced the theme of purple for the bulk of her last twenty years. She'd also been a yoga instructor, a professional florist, and a lover of men. She'd often make the comparison of men to flowers. *They both have a short shelf life*, she'd say with a twinkle in her eyes and a wink for punctuation. She'd lived large. Of course she'd never let go in death.

Celina had tried hard to get her friend to cross over into the light. Mimi had laughed and said she'd go when she was damn good and ready. And not a moment earlier. If there were things to experience on this side first, then she was going to experience them. And all that hollering could stop because she wasn't listening. Most people had known her to be quietly refined. But around Celina she was ribald and bawdy. Maybe death had loosened the reins on her inner soul.

"You look like you're dead. Hell, even I look better than you."

Celina stretched her arms above her head and said, "You *always* looked better than me."

"True," Mimi preened, adding, "But I had to work at it. Why the hell did you stay at that hospital? I could have told you there was nothing you could do. In fact, I tried to tell you just that."

"Yeah, well sitting in a hospital where I can see ghosts – not just you but plenty of others – is not fun so I shut all my senses down. I refused to see anyone." Not that it did much good when she had to keep peeking out to see if her friends appeared, the process exhausting her even more.

"Besides, you can't see anyway, can you?"

Celina sighed. She went through this issue with Mimi on a monthly basis. "Not the same way, no. I see ghosts, but not in human form like I used to." When she'd lost her sight she'd thought she'd lost the ability to see ghosts. For an instant that had been a relief. Then she remembered all the wonderful souls she'd met and helped go home. When she saw her first one after her accident it had brought tears to her eyes. At least she could still see them. Her secret hobby. According to Mimi she was a diehard do-gooder, and those types of women *never* got the man.

Not that she was looking for a man. Her fiancé had been dead just over a year now and she'd done her damnedest to contact him. He was the one ghost she'd never had a chance to see. Unfair, but that's the way it was. Maybe she'd tried too hard. Cared too much. If there were rules to these communications she hadn't figured them out.

She'd also lost her first love – then again, she'd been just a kid so most people would call it a crush. But Caslo had left an indelible impression on her. She'd loved that guy. Idolized him, really. Then he'd been thirteen and she only eleven.

The two of them had been neighbors, inseparable friends for years. Until he'd left, taken to a special program for gifted kids. He'd been gifted, all right. Like nothing she'd ever seen since.

She'd tried to stay in touch but had never heard back from him. Then she did – in one of the most unexpected ways.

In fact, he'd been her first ghost. A heartbreaking first.

She hadn't wanted to believe it. Had cried and screamed and refused to believe it. So had he. He'd told her over and over again he wasn't dead. She knew better, and finally she'd convinced him.

The only good thing about your best friend being dead was they could still spend time together. He'd been a mainstay in her life for several years. Every once in a while she'd half-heartedly try to convince him to go to the light and move on. He always gave her that beautiful soft smile and told her he was where he wanted to be and had no plans to leave anytime soon. But the status quo had changed. Had needed to change. For his sake. She missed him even now. In fact, he'd given her the soothing stone she carried with her everywhere.

"So why did you stay?" Mimi repeated. "You knew it would take all your strength to be there – so why?"

"I had to," Celina admitted softly. "I had to make sure that if any of my friends died and were at the hospital that they would know I was there for them."

"And did you see any of them?" Mimi asked, curiosity in her voice.

"No," Celina said. "I didn't." And that part bothered her – a lot. What was the point of being able to do this if you couldn't help the people you cared about when their time came?

"Well, you know it can take time. That's why I don't understand. There was no point in being *there*. I can talk to you anywhere."

Celina smiled but didn't answer. That was the thing about ghosts. They thought they knew everything when, in fact, the longer they stood on this side of the veil, the more their focus narrowed to a few of their favorite subjects.

"Sleep, child," Mimi said comfortably. "I'll watch over you."

And that was as good as it was going to get. Celina slipped under her covers, rolled over, and curled up.

She fell asleep instantly, the smell of lavender drifting across her nose.

STEFAN TOSSED THE file onto the countertop and moved on to his bedroom. Restless and edgy, he stripped down to his boxers, dropped into a deep yoga position, and slipped out of his skin.

In energetic form he stretched and straightened. With every little inch he could feel the tension and muscle aches dropping away. He'd been doing too much for so long without any relief. He knew most men would go and find a partner for a night. He wasn't most men. He was no longer interested in other women. He needed Celina. Had always needed Celina. Even though he'd kept a watchful eye on her over the years waiting, hoping, she still wasn't ready for him. He couldn't help himself from zipping a tiny bit of energy in her direction to make sure she was adjusting to the shifts in her life.

He was surprised but happy to find her sleeping soundly. Several other energy forms were huddled in the room. He didn't stay. He checked to make sure none of her guests were malevolent then, with a soft brush against her smooth cheek, he left. She slept, and although they weren't angels she had people who cared watching over her.

She wasn't ready for him but that didn't change the fact that the time for them was soon. Just that thought alone was enough to energize him. He'd loved her for so long. While the right time had been years away he'd dated, more out of loneliness than looking for a long-term relationship, and though he'd met some fascinating women over time he hadn't had a whole heart to give anyone.

The people he really cared about were his close friends, but not one had been his lover. They'd all found lovers of their own, and although joyous for them the long wait for his own love life had created an inner black pit of isolation inside. Loneliness was one thing; to pine away yet another. He couldn't afford either. Such negative emotions disturbed his focus, tore his energy ragged and stopped him from concentrating. It didn't help to calm that sense of something off, something brewing, something toxic in his space.

Whatever was wrong wasn't in his personal space; it was in the spaces he considered his. Like Dr. Maddy's place – the children's hospital he did so much volunteer work in – and with his friend Tabitha's Exotic Landscape reserve. He worked with many people on many projects.

But out there something was stirring.

He rose to his feet, shook his legs, and walked to his studio. His restlessness needed an outlet. He picked up a blank canvas and placed it on the always ready and waiting easel. He turned the lights to low, picked up his palette, brought out a mixture of purples and lavender and began.

HE DIDN'T FEEL so good. He knew he was running out of time, his energy weak. He'd been delighted to have this opportunity to do so much more than he'd thought possible. He still clung to the hope that something, somehow, would allow him to heal long enough to find another way, but knew inside his heart – if he had one any longer – that it was past time that he was done with this. He liked games. In fact, he loved them. But there wasn't the same satisfaction when he wasn't using his own hands. This "one step removed" crap just didn't give him the same sense of accomplishment.

He'd have to pick his next few victims a little more carefully. He didn't want to run out of them before his time on planet Earth ran out too.

But if he cut out the deadwood maybe the others would

be easier to keep alive. Play God, so to speak.

He smiled. Not a bad gig if you could get it.

IN BANGOR, MAINE, Bernie Governor hopped into his Dodge truck, waved goodbye to his beautiful loving wife and headed into work. He was a lucky man. He'd survived the accident eight months ago, came through the surgery with flying colors, and had managed to return to his wife of twenty-seven years. They'd been together longer than that, and he could only hope for many more. They'd been awesome years. She'd given him two great sons who'd both married and given him two grandsons. All he needed was a little granddaughter and his life would be complete. Hell, it was complete now, but everyone always wanted that little bit more.

It was human nature.

He didn't want for much now. He had his job and he knew he was lucky there, but then he'd been driving the same fuel truck for Best Fuels for years. That rig was his baby. He got to travel around and take care of business. He knew most of the customers in this area and they all knew him. It was a good way to live. He had their back and they had his. He knew the younger generation didn't have a hope of getting anything like what he'd spent the last twenty years with and he was sorry to see that. In his day family and friends meant everything. Now, not so much.

He took the right lane and headed down Main Street. He was looking forward to getting behind the wheel of old Bessie. He'd been driving that same old girl for a lot of years now, and he sure hoped his boss had fixed that gear shift while he'd been recuperating. That shifter was a might bit troublesome before. If they hadn't taken care of her she was going to be downright cranky to downshift on those hills, and that wasn't good.

Keeping that in mind he drove carefully. There was nothing like being in a bad accident to make you more road aware. He'd not been at fault when his old pickup had been T-boned by another truck, and he'd sure like to live the rest of his life without a repeat experience. He made the last few turns and pulled into the yard and parked. As he hopped out his phone buzzed.

Mary, his wife. A simple text that warmed his heart. "I love you." He stopped, smiled, and sent back a response, the same response they'd been making back and forth to each other all those years. "I love you too."

He walked into the office prepared to start the day.

"Hey Bernie, nice to see your old ass back in here."

"Glad to have this old ass still intact and here as well." He grinned. "I sure am ready to see old Bessie. Been sitting at home and watching TV for far too long. What have we got on the slate for today?"

"A couple of nice easy deliveries to start your first day back."

"Good." Great, actually. He'd been raring to get back to work, but he wasn't sure how he was going to handle a full day's work after being off for so long. He tired faster and he wasn't sure how he was going to get used to not having his afternoon nap. Still, he was glad to get back into the swing of things. He was way too young to retire. Maybe another ten years and he'd see. He liked being home with Mary just fine, but being an invalid wasn't the same thing as being retired. Mary had fussed until he'd been ready to lock the door between them every chance he'd gotten. He'd quickly reversed that strategy when he'd been strong enough to lock her in the bedroom with him. To his delight she'd stayed more often than not, too.

The time home had been a wonderful reinvention for his marriage. Even now he could feel a silly smile breaking out on his face.

Life was good. He grabbed the schedule and the keys from Connie, the receptionist, and walked out to old Bessie. Damn, she looked fine. He patted her front grill. "Are you happy to see me, old girl?"

He hopped up, ran through the basic checks, and smiled when he realized the guys had her filled, fueled, and ready to go. "Gonna make it easy on me for the first day back, huh?"

Brady, one of the servicemen on staff, waved at him from the side of the lot. "Drive carefully."

Bernie honked lightly and headed out on the first run. He had to pass a school and several parks. Worked for him. He headed down the main street and pulled off to the side street to take him down and around the main traffic. He geared down and took the corner, then headed up Hurricane Hillside. Getting up wasn't so bad, but going down the long, slow corner on the other side – that was the bitch.

He crested and slowed, and then Bessie picked up speed. He geared the truck down, smiling as she responded beautifully. "Good on you, Brady. Glad to see you treated Bessie right. She's tuned up prime."

At the bottom of the hill on the side were the high school and the big ball park. It was full today. He frowned, trying to remember who was playing. "Well, it's a great day for it."

He downshifted again and smiled.

Nice to see the community doing so well.

He was picking up speed again on the long, slow slide to the bottom when he felt it hit.

Heat. Not a nice warm heat, but a crushing density of power and pain and…burning heat in his chest.

His heart. God, it hurt, like a fire inside the actual organ. Like a hand reaching inside his chest and squeezing. He groaned, feeling heat then ice racing through his body. His ribs locked and he couldn't breathe. He hit the brakes, desperate to pull the big rig off to the side of the road. He didn't know what was wrong, but he couldn't think for the blackness in his mind.

The rig turned, finally following his command. And he realized he'd pulled it in the direction of the massive playing field. The crowded playing field.

No. Bessie, no! His foot slammed on the brake hard as he shifted down. Too hard. His foot was on the brake, his hand on the emergency brake, and neither was working properly. His big body had always been a source of pride and joy – until the accident that had changed so much.

Bessie started to take on a life of her own.

Bernie tried to save Bessie. He tried to save the park full of people. He already knew it was too late to save himself. Death didn't appear to be done with him.

Well, he refused to take a mess of happy, bright kids with him. He'd take out the power lines and that damn building before he'd go out doing this kind of damage. With a superhuman effort, he yanked at the wheel as the black mist crept into his eyes.

Just then, his beloved Bessie hit the guardrail, flipped on her side, and slid across the road. He blinked and tried to focus, only he could see nothing but a reddish black mist.

The effort pushed him over the edge and he knew no more.

CHAPTER 5

CELINA OPENED HER eyes and bolted upright. She stared into the cloudy gray world of her room. Normally she saw enough to see blurry shadows with light and dark playing games with her mind. Right now there wasn't even that much going on, but the hair on the back of her neck was standing straight up and shivers rippled down her spine. Something was wrong. Fear reached up and grabbed her by the throat.

Damn. This odd warning system had only gotten stronger since her blindness. Before it had been a purely peripheral sensation. Now it was an instant prodding in her psyche. She just didn't know what to do with it.

She closed her eyes, swallowed hard, and tried to relax. And thought she heard something. Like a heavy breath. Her eyes flew open, her gaze darting around the room helplessly. She held her breath and listened. But there was no movement. No more breathing. Nothing shifted except for the ice hardening in her stomach. She sat up again. "Hello?"

She tilted her head at the eerie silence. She swore she'd heard someone. But who? And why?

Her chest expanded in a huge gasp as she realized she'd been holding her breath again. She took a second deep breath. She couldn't hide her presence. If someone else was here, then they knew she was too. She slipped from her bed and snugged up against the wall, her breathing low and shallow. She carefully walked the perimeter of her bedroom and then moved out into her small apartment. She knew the person was gone. Inside. But her mind and psyche weren't on the same page. She'd never be able to go back to bed until she knew for sure.

It took a good ten minutes to check the nooks and crannies of her apartment before she made her way back to her bedroom. She slipped under the covers but couldn't relax her mind. She checked the time. It was four in the morning. A horrible thought struck. She grabbed her phone and called the hospital to check on Jacob's status. He was doing well, but another member of her group hadn't done so well. He'd died less than an hour ago.

James. She knew him, but not as well as other members of the group. He played trumpet and had an online company with his wife.

That there'd been yet another fatality in that stupid accident really bothered her. When would this be enough? The driver of the pickup was also dead. Then again, there was a good possibility that he'd been dead before he'd hit the pub. He'd possibly had a heart attack before the crash. She certainly didn't blame him, but she wanted to blame *someone*, anyone, for the senseless loss of life. James was a young man. Bruce was older but full of life, and had so much more to give.

Cindy. She'd been a blessing to be around. Always with a smile on her face and in her voice. She had a ready wit that often caught people unaware.

Celina had been blessed to know these people since before her accident, and she knew their faces. Cindy had been beautiful inside and out.

Before she realized it tears were rolling down her cheeks. She sniffled them back. Heavy emotions sent her energy even further off track, and those ghostly friends in her life tended to know instinctively when she was upset. Both physical friends and ghostly friends, although there weren't many non-ghostly friends left. Jacob was one of the few.

"Damn right we know. What's upsetting you now?" Mimi asked. She'd become the spokesperson for a less-developed group of ghosts.

"Another friend died tonight from the accident," she whispered through the tears.

"And as we keep telling you – and you more than most should know – death is not an ending."

"It is for him – and me in a way. I might be able to see his ghost, but that's not a good thing. Like you, he should move on."

She reached for a box of tissues sitting on the corner of her night table. "So it is an ending. And one that didn't need to happen." She crumpled up the tissue and wiped her eyes. Half done, she lowered the tissue. "It's all so senseless."

"Unless you believe in karma, or God, or fate. If you believe in a grand plan at all, then you have to accept that this happened for a reason."

"I won't accept that," Celina cried. "Bruce didn't need to die like this. Neither did Cindy. Or any of them."

"You don't know that. It's not for you to know. It's for you to accept."

"I don't want to accept it." That was the core issue. She was losing friends all over the place and she wasn't ready to accept that. And underlying all that was the knowledge that she wasn't ready to accept her own state.

A weird blankness filled the room.

Mimi gasped and poofed into the air without warning. Celina already knew what was wrong.

The cold creeping into her soul told her she had another visitor.

That's easy to fix, came that horrid, smug voice. *I've told you time and time again. Let me see.*

Never. She rolled over, pulled the covers up over her shoulders, and blocked that hateful voice out of her head.

STEFAN WASHED HIS hands, but the very effort of cleaning them was almost too much for his exhausted body. The painting was behind him. He didn't bother looking. This painting had been an outlet for his frustration and nothing else. And it had done its job. Tension no longer rode his shoulders like a steel bar. He was physically tired but mentally calm. Now he'd take a quick glance at Brandt's file and deliver answers in the morning. He picked up the file and walked upstairs to his bedroom. He dropped the file on his bed and headed to the shower. Feeling clean and refreshed, he collapsed on his bed and opened the file.

Five minutes later sleep was the last thing on his mind.

He reached for the phone and called Brandt. A sleepy voice answered. "He's not here, Stefan."

He glanced at the clock. It was six a.m. Damn, where had the night gone?

"Sam?" His voice gentled. This woman who'd gone through so much was a kindred spirit to Stefan's soul. She was small, gentle, with an inner core of steel. She needed the steel to have survived the horror in her life. "I'm sorry, I thought I called his cell phone. I didn't mean to wake you."

"It's all right," she said, the smile in her voice warm and

caring. "The dreams have been tough lately. I'm glad you pulled me out."

"Brandt mentioned you were having trouble sleeping. What kind of dreams?" he asked, his voice surprisingly sharp. He immediately apologized. "Sorry, it's been a long day and night. Something is happening but I can't pinpoint what."

"I'm just getting snippets myself. Not strong enough to see who or what, just lots of blood. But not any one scene. One time it's a car accident – at least I think that's what it was. Another time it seems to be a surgery happening. Then it's a suicide. Honestly, I have no idea what's going on. Tonight I felt as if my chest was so hot it was like it was on fire and I was gripping a steering wheel from a big truck." She sighed. "It's weird to connect to accidents or suicides. That's so not me."

"Maybe your skills are changing again," he suggested, "now that you're learning more control."

"Great. Not." She yawned again. "Sorry, I've been trying to sleep for a couple of hours, and it looks like I'm ready to try again."

"Then do. I'll call Brandt at the office."

"Good night," she murmured, then it sounded to Stefan as if she dropped the phone as she fell off to sleep.

He smiled. At least she'd sleep. Like himself, Sam often found sleep hard to come by. He redialed, getting Brandt this time.

"Thought you were going home."

Brandt snapped in disgust, "I did and got called back in. Did you sleep?"

Stefan snorted and walked to his studio in the back. He flicked on the light and stared at the massive bloody heart in the middle of his canvas. "I painted a bloody valentine scene tonight when I came home from the hospital. I'm trying to figure out if this is related."

"Why would it be?" Brandt asked. "I'm sure any shrink would have no trouble associating the painting to Celina being in an accident tonight."

"Except I spoke with your lovely wife about her dreams and now I'm wondering if my painting and her visions are connected. I need details. And how did you get all this information on the different cases anyway?"

"Grant."

Stefan nodded. It's what he'd expected. His FBI friend was always on top of the weird and wonderful cases.

"And how did he know what to look for?"

"I was trying to find something to match up to Sam's nightmares. She's so much stronger now that she's learning to control her abilities. It makes my job much harder. Now the victims can be anywhere across the country – or in different countries."

"And that had been my initial interpretation. Except… damn it." Stefan leaned closer and said in outrage, "Someone else painted a scalpel into *my* picture."

Brandt gasped, then laughed and laughed. "Oh my, is that Alex's sister messing around in your life again?"

"Probably." Stefan turned around to find his pixie of a ghost, the sister of a dear friend, sitting crossed-legged on his paints. "Did you do this?" he growled at her.

She frowned. "So what if I did? It needed something."

He rolled his eyes. "I wasn't doing anything specific. This was an exercise in stress relief." He paused and eyed her carefully. "Why a scalpel?"

She shrugged. "It looked like the heart had been cut out, so I figured a surgeon's knife was the perfect accompaniment." With a glare at the painting she added, "But I didn't do a very good job, did I? I keep trying to be as good as you, but it's not the same look at all."

He shook his head. "If you want to paint, then I'll get you a canvas of your own and you can paint all you want. Just please leave my paintings alone."

She straightened, obviously offended. She glared at him and when he sighed heavily and was about to apologize, she poofed into thin air.

"Damn," Stefan snapped at the empty space where she'd been. "Stop running away when I'm talking to you."

"Did she disappear on you?" Brandt snickered. "She's a cheeky kid, isn't she?"

"That she is. It's like she's moved right in and taken over. She says she's needed." He groaned. "Not sure what I'll do if she decides to take up cooking."

Brandt went off in gales of laughter.

"Glad you think that's funny." Stefan glared into the phone. He didn't get why his teenage ghost Lissa was such a source of amusement to everyone but him. He cared about her, but she was a ghost for crying out loud. She was supposed to go home. Instead, she said that now that her sister Alex, one of Stefan's psychic friends, was fine then Stefan was her next mission. Maybe after he finally got his life together then she'd consider leaving. For now she was having too much fun to go.

Stefan wanted to throw his phone across the room. Ghosts weren't supposed to haunt him. But in her case it was out of sisterly love that she stayed, and honestly Stefan didn't quite know what to do with her. And therefore did nothing.

"So why did you call?" Brandt asked. "If I remember correctly none of these cases involve hearts."

Stefan pulled his thoughts together. He'd seen something in the files. "Is there any correlation between the victims all being in some kind of accident? Several mentioned that they were in rehab or physiotherapy."

"Hmmm." Brandt said, his voice deepening. Stefan could see Brandt's frown in his mind's eye. Could hear him tapping away on a keyboard.

"One had a car accident," Brandt added helpfully. "Another went crazy at three thousand feet in a small plane and opened the door. So that hardly counts."

"And what makes you think these men had anything hokey about their cases?"

"Sam. Yet I can't find anything to connect these cases. There are a few others that I have sent for more information on but I'm still waiting. Can you pick up anything?"

"Not yet." Stefan shook his head as he walked to the back of his studio. "Keep adding to the pile if you think more are involved. In fact, better widen the search."

"So you do think there is something wrong here?" Brandt said in relief. "I *knew* it."

"Well, I don't *know* it. But I'm willing to keep that door open with both Sam and I triggering to hearts today."

He hung up and stared at the picture he'd had sitting in his studio for several weeks now. It was one that had been causing him a lot of problems and he didn't know why — except it was unfinished. The violent scene of a car accident was painted on the same day that one of the victim's in Brandt's file perished in a horrific accident of his own.

Stefan's painting was an exact match to the photo in the file.

Yet for some reason he hadn't been ready to share that eerie fact with Brandt.

In Stefan's world timing was everything. And there was no such thing as coincidence.

CLARITY. HE NEEDED more clarity. Each time he managed a step in the right direction he slid – not as much as before – but still too much. He needed to focus. He didn't know how much time he had. How much effort would be required to complete his plan. And he couldn't help but feel like he was running out of time.

Out of energy.

Maybe each step was cutting off a piece of deadwood and allowing the rest of him to regroup, but maybe it was also diminishing his energy.

That couldn't happen.

He was supposed to grow stronger by doing this.

He *needed* to be stronger. More powerful. He needed to do more – just so he could do one thing.

Revenge – at all costs.

He had to hang on to that anger.

It was all he had left.

CHAPTER 6

SOME MORNINGS SUCKED. Celina woke to a gloomy heart and an achy soul. Her head hurt, her eyes burned, and every time she shifted under the duvet her body screamed. She'd forgotten to take something to relax her muscles and now they'd locked down. She hadn't been badly injured in last night's accident, but her body was still crying in protest of any movement this morning. She'd love a hot bath, but likely only had time for a shower.

Then she remembered that the concert was no longer happening tonight. That meant all the practice and preparation and rehearsals weren't happening today either. Damn. A wave of grief for her friends washed over her.

Maybe that bath was the answer after all. She slipped out from under the covers and reached for the clock. She pushed the button and listened to it read out the time. It was past nine in the morning already. She never slept in, always careful to go to bed well before midnight. She hated the hour between midnight and one. That's when the weirder things in her life had happened. Or at least it was when more of the uninvited ghostly visitors decided to stop by. She stood slowly and winced as her back protested. She'd start the bath running and do a few stretches while waiting.

She walked to the bathroom and as she reached the open doorway a horrible stench hit her. Her hand went to her chest. She couldn't breathe. She barely managed to stop herself from gagging. Didn't want to take another breath – she choked on that smell. She knew that smell.

She knew it deep inside. It was the smell of blood. Lots of blood.

She stared down at her hands, fingers splayed wide in front of her. And could see nothing. Of course. She shuddered at what could be in front of her. Something someone else had done. Something someone had left for her to find. Only she'd never be able to see it.

Let me see. Anticipation licked along his nasty voice.

Never, she whispered in horror. *What have you done?*

Nothing much. Nothing that didn't need doing. And nothing here – maybe.

She shuddered, in fear, in revulsion, at what she'd find in her so-private space. Her invaded space. This was her home. She needed it to be exactly as she left it, day in and day out. She knew how many paces from her bedroom to the bathroom, from her bathroom to her kitchen counter. Blindly she reached out to the closest wall for support.

Someone had defiled her space. The who and why eluded her. Nausea clung to the back of her throat. She daren't go inside the room. Who knew what had happened here? She tilted her head to one side and listened hard. There were no sounds, no breathing, no water dripping. Just silence.

Just like in the middle of the night.

Her breath coming out in panicked gasps, her emotions tumbling in circles, she retraced her steps to her phone.

An hour later Celina, now fully dressed, huddled in the corner of her kitchen. She was completely surrounded by chaos. Her apartment was awash with strangers, horrible noises, and conversations that were guaranteed to set her teeth on edge and made her wish she was anywhere but in here listening to the voices going on around her as if she were deaf, not blind.

"She's blind – she couldn't have done this."

"Blind doesn't mean stupid. It wouldn't have taken any strength to do this."

"But she'd have needed to see. It's only blood. But the way it's written…"

"Besides, she's not covered in blood. It's not like you could stay clean doing something like this."

"She could have cleaned up in the kitchen."

"The techs checked. The sink and drain tested clear for blood."

Celina sank deeper into herself. So far no one had asked her about anything specific. She opened the door, pointed to the bathroom, and then she'd lost control of the situation. She buried her face in her hands. She didn't know what had happened in the last twenty-four hours, but she'd had enough already. She wanted normalcy back.

Whatever that meant.

Since her accident and multiple surgeries there'd been no such thing.

Sure there has been. I'm just your new normal. It's so nice to have found you. To talk to you. Seriously, it's a great comfort.

That oily voice of evil slid into her mind and wallowed in place. She systematically walled him up and blocked him out. If only she could figure out how to get rid of him permanently. She'd tried to mention it to her doctor, and he thought she was just having trouble dealing with the reality of her new state.

Sure she was, but she was also dealing with voices in her head. She'd didn't dare mention the ghosts. She so wasn't up for a mental health session. But she might have to be.

"Miss, if we could speak to you for a moment?" The apologetic voice interrupted her deliberations.

"Of course," she said softly. "I don't know what you found. Please explain."

"That's what we need to talk to you about. First off, you called us yourself – is that correct?"

She nodded her head. "Yes, I went to go use the bathroom and stopped at the doorway because the smell was so strong."

"And you knew it was blood how?"

"I didn't know," she corrected. "I suspected it was. I spent all last evening waiting in the hospital, and there was a lot of blood at the pub first. That's not a smell you forget easily."

"You were at Chico's last night?"

She nodded. "I was, then I went to the hospital to be treated for minor cuts," she said soberly, "and stayed until my friend came out of surgery."

She could hear him scratching down notes on paper. She wanted to tell him to get a tablet, it would be faster, but she wasn't going to interfere. In truth, she just wanted this issue cleaned up and the men out of here.

"Do you have any enemies?"

The question came out of the blue, blindsiding her.

She straightened and tried to school the look of shock off her face. Then realized that something terrible must be in her bathroom. "What's in my bathroom?" she cried out, her voice rising. "Is there a dead person in there?"

"No." The policeman rushed to reassure her. "Not at all. I'm sorry. The person left a message on the mirror, that's all."

"A message," she said blankly, her mind racing. "What kind of message?"

"It says, 'Be careful, it's not what you think.'"

She sat back and stared in his direction. "But that makes no sense." She shook her head helplessly. "It's obviously a warning of some kind. *Be careful.* That's easy. I'm always careful. But to say it's not what you think – that doesn't make any sense." She turned her gaze to the doorway and the new arrival waiting and asked, "What is not what it seems?"

"That's what we're hoping you can answer," said a higher-pitched voice.

She shook her head, bewildered. "Are you sure there wasn't more, maybe elsewhere in the bathroom, like…" She threw up her hands. "I don't know, maybe on the shower curtain."

"The shower curtain?" the doubtful voice asked, just shy of implying she was nuts.

"I don't know," she muttered, "Why would anyone write a message on my mirror? Why not tell me directly? It's not like they had a problem sneaking into my apartment while I slept to write a cryptic note."

"Are you sure you locked the door?"

"Yes, and the doorman saw me coming in late last night. I woke up in the night thinking there was an intruder. I searched the apartment but there was nothing."

"What time was that? And tell us exactly what you heard."

She explained, listening to them scribble notes on paper around her. "Then I fell back asleep and didn't wake up until I had to go to the bathroom this morning."

"We're almost done." He cleared his throat. "Is there anyone you suspect of doing something like this?"

She stared, her eyes open and blind, directly at him. And said forcefully, "No. The people I know make beautiful music for others, not cryptic scary messages on people's mirrors in the dead of night."

"Right." He straightened. "If you do think of anyone who might want to scare you or hold a grudge against you, please let us know."

Sounds of material shifting and papers sliding across one another shifted through her ears. She could almost see him pulling a card out of his pocket. Just then a hard piece of paper was gently laid in her hand. "Then call me."

She nodded, her fingers closing over the card. "I will."

"By the way, who has keys to your apartment?"

She listed off the people who came and went when she needed help. There were only two – Jacob and Bruce.

"Also, did you use that bathroom last night?"

She nodded. "When I came home."

"And what time was that?"

"Close to three a.m."

"And you found the bathroom like this when?"

"A couple of minutes before I made the 911 call." Her mouth moved, but her body had frozen into unnatural stillness.

"Good enough. We'll be in touch if we need anything else."

She waited. She just wanted them all gone.

"By the way, it might be a good idea to change the locks."

She shrugged. "What's the point? The two people who had the spares are either dead or severely injured, so obviously the intruder was neither of them."

STEFAN GLARED AT the phone in his hand. He'd been awake for precisely five minutes. He clicked to answer it and said, "Three times in twelve hours is too many times."

"You're right. But you're going to want to hear this one."

Stefan listened in shock as Detective Brandt Sutherland gave him an update on Celina's night. "I was looking for an update on the pub incident and her name came up after she called 911. I just got off the phone with one of the responding officers as the file isn't yet complete. He said it was the damnedest thing."

Brandt's voice changed as if reading off a written piece. "She opened the door, let them in, pointed to the bathroom then sat down in the kitchen. When they came back out it was as if she hadn't moved a muscle. She was fully dressed but sitting like a stone in one place. He said her head was downcast and the stillness was odd. He said it was like she was waiting for a blow."

"I imagine that would be a hell of a blow. Think about it. She can only imagine what horror might be in her bathroom." He frowned not wanting to think of what she'd gone through.

"True enough. She didn't ask the officers to search her place for the intruder, although they did a certain amount of searching anyways. But the blood was contained to just the bathroom."

"And it's been confirmed to be blood?"

"Yes. Human blood. We're looking for a match right now."

"Enough blood to suspect the person who lost it might be mortally injured?" Stefan's voice was sharp. Inside he was stunned. What was going on in Celina's world? "Can I see the crime scene?"

"Why?" Brandt asked. "What can you do? I doubt a dis-embodied entity or a ghost could smear blood all over a wall like that." Brandt stopped. "Could one?"

"I've never seen one do that," Stefan admitted, frowning, thinking of the roomful of ghosts he'd seen. "Then again, Lissa is painting, and who'd have thought she could do that? I know Celina has an affinity for ghosts. Maybe one of them saw something. I might be able to find out."

"Hmm. I can't just open up her house without reason, and neither can I have you as a paid consultant on this case as there is no way to warrant your–"

"I'll do it for free."

"Hell, of course you will." Brandt fell silent, thinking.

Stefan stayed quiet. "That would make two incidents involving her in what, twelve hours?" Stefan said calmly, too calmly for his churning gut, but control was important. He wanted to rush to Celina's side – and that he couldn't do. "That's two too many. I'm thinking that's no coincidence here."

"You think the crash at the pub and this blood on her mirror are related?" Brandt added slowly, "It could be a family member of one of the deceased, angry that she's alive instead of their loved one."

"Or maybe the driver of the vehicle knew she was going to the pub and thought to settle an old score."

"And missed her? So he came back from the dead to threaten her?" Brandt held his amusement back. "That's hardly possible, is it?"

"I no longer know what is possible – if I ever did."

A thoughtful silence filled the line. "I'll talk to the guys and see what their take is on this. If there is anything odd, then maybe I can get you to do a walk through. There's no way to know if there's anything paranormal about this mess."

"Not yet. But there will be soon. The sooner I see it, the easier it is to trace the energy."

"Trace the energy? So if you see the energy, can you track it back to the person responsible?"

"Not necessarily, but there is a chance I'll recognize the energy signature. And I'll certainly recognize it again if I ever see it."

He held his breath. Then added quietly, sincerely, "Please, there's no time to lose."

"Can you check in on her bathroom psychically?"

Stefan started in surprise. "Yes. What I might be able to find depends how many energies are moving through the place and have messed up the scene."

"Lots, unfortunately. They didn't find any fingerprints. Or anything else, for that matter," Brandt added. "And because there are lots of other energies there, does that mean you won't be able to pick up any of the energy from the scene even if you are there in person?"

"You know it's stronger when you're right in front of it." He needed to set up a psychic guard around Celina's place. He should have done that already. He hadn't seen the necessity, and his energy was always being forced in too many directions. But she needed him now, and he'd tap whatever reserves he needed to get this done. It was paramount that she stayed safe.

"I need in." He stood up and walked out to his studio. "Do what you have to do, but I need in." And he hung up the phone.

JACOB LAY IN his bed, hating that he was here. It hadn't taken too long to realize his life was completely screwed up. But how and why he didn't understand. He knew he was in the hospital. And that he was in poor shape. But he had no recollection of what had brought him here.

A sense of urgency had ridden him since waking up. He'd needed to tell someone something. But he couldn't remember what. Or even who he was supposed to tell.

He'd seen something. Heard something? Something important. But what?

And why couldn't he remember? He stared at the white curtain divider. He could barely move because of his injuries. Still, from the bits and pieces he'd heard, he was the lucky one.

At least he was still alive.

CHAPTER 7

ANY MOVEMENT HAD Celina groaning like she'd hit her senior years overnight. Decrepit and worn out, like a clock that had worked long past its warranty date. She knew she'd hit a crossroads. Something bad was going on. God, she wished she had help. Again.

Her friend, Jillian, was beside her. Both were quietly drinking tea. In the years they'd known each other, Jillian had never mocked, laughed at, or appeared to be disgusted with anything Celina had said or done. That kind of acceptance was priceless. Then again, she didn't know everything about Celina.

She'd been a passenger in the car accident that had taken Celina's sight just three weeks after she'd lost her fiancé.

"You didn't hear anything?

Celina shook her head, then voiced a fear she'd been quietly nursing. "Maybe I did it while I was asleep." She winced as she heard the words out loud. "No, I couldn't have, surely?"

"I don't think so," Jillian said, her voice barely above a murmur. "But what do I know? Is there anyone you can ask?"

Celina smiled a little. "I wonder if there's a help line for stuff like this."

"Maybe. You see and talk to ghosts; maybe one of them

can tell you what happened?"

"That's the trouble. I haven't seen any of them since I woke up this morning."

"As in whatever happened might have scared them, too? That doesn't sound good."

Celina's chair creaked as she settled back. She hated the restlessness in her soul. Hearing a better understanding of the situation than she'd have thought from her friend, she asked, "Have you ever seen ghosts?"

Jillian hadn't shared much of her family history. A private person, she also had an eclectic group of friends that she was seriously closemouthed about. Celina didn't mind. She knew Jillian needed these people to keep her sanity. She was also a musician and was driven to compose, yet never shared her music. She said it was secret. Special. Personal. Couldn't give it to the world. Actually, she'd said something one time that Celina had puzzled over. She'd said, "It's not mine to give to the public." After that she'd refused to answer any more questions about it. She often looked tired, worn out. As if she was battling demons of her own. And knowing Jillian she probably was. She'd always been one to cheer on the underdog and defend the underprivileged or help those in need.

And as warm as she was, she wasn't one for physical touch. Celina had reached out many times early on but Jillian always stayed back, avoiding contact.

"Forget about me and my nightmare." Celina leaned closer, worried about her friend. "How are *you?*"

"As always, I'm fine."

Celina smiled at Jillian's offhand comment. "But you aren't always fine. You are often very depressed and try not to let others know."

"Except you," Jillian's voice lightened with wry humor. "You always seem to discern my feelings at a level I don't myself."

"A side effect of losing my sight," Celina said lightly. "I'm more sensitive to nuances in people's voices."

"When do you go back for your next checkup?"

"Coming up soon. I'm trying to forget about it." She stared ahead, her thoughts consumed with dread at the thought of going back there. The last thing she wanted to do was to have the doctor repeat that there was nothing wrong with her. He wouldn't say that in so many words, but the message would be the same. "If I go, that is."

"Of course you need to go. Who knows what he might find?"

She lowered her gaze to stare at the table and the cup she could feel in her hands. That was the problem. She was petrified to hear what the doctor would find. But for all she could tell Jillian, she hadn't yet told her about the voice – it was hardly the same element as her friendly ghosts like Mimi.

"We'll see," she compromised. "At the moment I'm not so sure what to do. The last thing I want is to be here with that," she waved her hand in the direction of the bathroom, "but neither do I want to leave my space. I hate trying to navigate strange places."

"And you don't have to. You could always get a dog. You are allowed a small one in the apartment complex. A service dog would be ideal. A dog to help you get around and for companionship."

Celina loved the idea of a dog, but not because of being blind. And that went back to the idea of not accepting her condition. She didn't *want* to be blind. A seeing-eye dog would be permanent. And she refused to accept that her vision would never return.

Jillian's fingers brushed the top of hers. "Easy, sweetheart, you're going to break the cup."

Celina released her death grip. She flexed her fingers several times. "Sorry. I'm still a little tense."

The doorbell rang once, and then a second time. Celina's stomach sank. Great, here was round two. "That's the cops. A different group," she muttered, pushing her chair back to stand up.

"Ugh," Jillian said.

Celina called back, "I know you can't stay for long. If you want to take off now while they are here, you could always come over later."

"Will do."

Celina opened the door and frowned. Heat and power radiated toward her. "Hello?"

"Hello," said a calm, masculine voice. "I'm Detective Brandt Sutherland and I have Stefan Kronos, a consultant working with the department, with me." He hesitated. "May we come in? We won't be long, but we'd like to see the crime scene."

She stepped back and away from the entrance. By rights she shouldn't even be here, but it wasn't like she had any place to go. She motioned in the direction of the bathroom. "Help yourself."

"Thank you." Two men walked past her. The second one caught her attention as he moved past her. She lifted her head and sniffed gently. She recognized that aftershave...and there was just something else about him...she recognized him...or maybe it was his name.

Celina waited at the door but the consultant didn't say

anything. She wracked her brain as to why his name rang a bell in her memory.

Jillian stepped closer and whispered in Celina's ear, "Oh my God, they are both hunks."

Celina's lips twisted. "Really? Well, their looks don't do anything for me."

"Maybe not, but wow." Then her voice changed. "I feel like I should know the first guy but can't place him."

"Hmm. I thought I recognized the consultant's name, but I don't know from where."

"Think about it, and be good while I'm gone."

"Like I have a choice," Celina muttered as she closed the door behind her friend. She really needed to give up her self-pity and get on with her life.

"Like hell," she said to no one in particular, then realized how odd she must look standing in the hallway talking to herself. She made her way back to the kitchen where she sat down with her tea and waited. She lifted her cup ever so slightly when she felt it – almost a ghostly poke.

It was a weird, snaky, sneaky feeling. She frowned and lifted her face in the direction of the doorway.

"Did you want to talk to me?"

That deep milk chocolate voice that promised a million midnight dreams spoke, his tone curling her toes and making her drop her cup. She knew that voice. Oh dear God, she did. "You," she whispered. "What are you doing here?"

"Do you know me?" the consultant asked. "From where?" The smile in his voice sent shivers down her back.

It was stupid, but she felt she'd touched this man before and had been touched by him. Finally, forced by a compulsion she couldn't understand, she whispered the truth under her breath, "From my dreams. I've seen you in my dreams."

STEFAN STARED AT her. He didn't know what to say. Was she serious? She'd spoken in such a soft voice he wondered if she'd realized what she'd said.

He hadn't seen her in any of his dreams, but he'd walked in and touched on hers many times. Had she picked up on that? Or was it something else?

"Pardon?"

Her gaze widened and she flushed. "Sorry, just muttering to myself."

Damn. He didn't want to pry, but he'd love to know a little more. He could do some investigation on his own later, but it wasn't the same thing as her admission. He wondered again if she was psychic and if she knew. Many people didn't know they were. She had a room full of ghosts, but then he suspected she'd had a lifetime full of the same thing. He studied her energy, seeing the embarrassment and discomfort. He wanted to check her energy out deeper, but she had walls up. Serious walls. He could scale them, but not without her permission.

"Did you find out anything new?" she asked suddenly, motioning behind him.

"I haven't looked yet. Brandt is in there first. I thought I'd ask you a few questions, and I do realize that they are likely to be ones you've already answered."

"Then why ask again?" she said in a reasonable tone.

And because it was a reasonable tone, he answered honestly. "Because reading a report is not the same thing as getting the information firsthand."

She tilted her head, her silvery gray eyes sharpening with intensity. He leaned forward suddenly. There was something in her gaze. Something lively. Could she see? Doubts filled him. Yet if she could, why would she pretend to be blind? It made no sense.

Then she answered with a light laugh, "That makes sense. Fire away."

Shaking his head at his fanciful thoughts, Stefan focused on the issue at hand. He went over the questions he knew she'd already been asked about living alone. That the door had been locked. Did anyone have the keys? Had she woken up in the night? What had alerted her to something being wrong in the bathroom?

At that last question her energy, which up to then had been comfortable and easygoing, even reserved, suddenly pulled up tight and close. The color shifted to a darker purple and the softness disappeared. He frowned as he watched the hidden walls become instantly visible.

She had some deep protective instincts. His interest deepened. He knew so much about her – her energy that showed no subterfuge, her innocence in many ways, the charm and beauty of her aura. She was a good soul, and he'd known that for a long time. He couldn't imagine being attracted to a woman who wasn't. In the work he did it would be a basic requirement for his survival.

And he'd been attracted to her for a long time.

In a soft, distant voice, she said, "The smell of fresh blood."

That was the part he didn't get. He hadn't gotten any smell from the bathroom. Then again he hadn't been allowed to get very close yet. A clue, but one he didn't understand.

"Have you had reason to have smelled fresh blood like that before?"

She snorted. "Are you asking if I've ever killed anyone?"

"Not at all," he said quietly. "I was thinking of a bad accident, a job in the healthcare field, or something similar."

Her bristling eased, and she dropped her hand from her chin to stare in his general direction. As always, he found himself studying that gaze. Something about her eyes, her physical blindness, bothered him. He just didn't know why.

Her odd silvery eyes were clear and direct. Her eyes didn't smile, missing the mobility of a person with sight. Something he'd thought he'd seen earlier. Maybe he'd been mistaken.

He could see so much other energy around her that he knew some of it was her ghostly friends, but not all. There was something dark lurking in there. Held secure by her walls. Secrets? Evil? He wondered if she had any idea they were all there, in her space, all the time. She had to know on a subconscious level, but he wasn't sure she had any conscious awareness.

There were also bits and pieces of her friends clinging to her – or ones she clung to. A couple she held tucked in close. From the protective way she was caring for them, he knew that they mattered to her. They were also a huge drain on her energy.

He'd never seen anything like it.

There was a tiredness around the corners of her eyes, the droop of her lips, and the slump to her shoulders. Of course waking up to find something nasty in her bathroom had to be one hell of a shock. Add to that not being able to see exactly what was wrong, and anyone's fears would be sent into hyper drive.

His gaze whispered over and through her energy again and saw something he hadn't noticed before. One of the energies that she was keeping close looked familiar. But it was half-hidden. Tucked in tight, he couldn't get a clear view of the signature because it had almost completely morphed into the other energies. He frowned, not sure what he was seeing.

"What?" she asked.

"Sorry? I didn't say anything," he murmured.

"No, but you frowned."

He straightened in surprise. "How would you know?"

"Something shifted in the way you were looking at me." She smiled. "Then you pulled back. I'm very sensitive to small movements and the energy around me because I can't see. My other senses go into overdrive."

Bemused, Stefan lifted a hand, and even though it was childish he moved his hand gently in front of her. She didn't move, and her facial expression didn't change in any way. He lowered his hand.

"Satisfied?" she asked softly, as if aware of what he'd done.

His eyebrows shot upward. Then decided to be honest. "Yes."

She made a slight movement of her head then turned her gaze to the doorway.

"Stefan, can you come here please?" Brandt stood at the doorway to the kitchen.

Stefan stood up. "Sure." He walked over to Brandt. "My turn?"

Brandt nodded and led the way to the bathroom.

Stefan stopped at the doorway and his mind instantly recognized what he was seeing. Dried blood decorated the sink, the floor, and dropped down off the mirror at every letter of the message.

And he realized something else. Whoever had done this

had the same energy signature as the bit of energy that Celina cradled so gently in her aura.

TALK ABOUT FUN. He didn't know how far he could make this go, but then again he'd had no idea that he could have gone this far. Talk about a bonus. He was feeling slightly better today. His training practice was a little stronger.

It couldn't last. He knew that. He'd wracked his mind for a way to keep this happening, but at some point in time body parts wore out. He knew the end was coming. He could only hope and pray for more time.

He really wanted to maximize the damage. And it wasn't like he could just build a bomb or organize a major terrorist attack. He was limited in so many ways. He could manipulate people into doing stuff his way and doing things he wanted done, but he was still restricted in terms of the skills of the other person. And so far he hadn't been lucky enough to find anyone with major SEAL training or survivalist skills. Both would be fun. But the very nature of both occupations made it unlikely for them to come into his sphere of influence. At least not through the general way.

What he needed to do was connect to the weaker parts of himself. Then he could find out how to get rid of them. He had found many of them but had much less control over them.

What he needed was her.

CHAPTER 8

S TEFAN WALKED OUT of Celina's apartment building, his mind consumed with the implications of what he'd seen.

"Stefan, you're awfully quiet. What did you find?"

Stefan glanced over at his friend, wondering how much he should disclose.

"Yeah, and no secrets please." Brandt snorted. "I know there's lots you can't tell for sure and that you don't have a clear picture and that you don't really understand anything yet, so let's start with first impressions."

Stefan laughed. "Nice to work with someone who knows me."

"Oh, I know you. That's both a blessing and a challenge."

Stefan glanced at him sharply. "Are you struggling with me or Sam?"

Brandt gave a sharp bark of laughter. "Both. You are challenging people. And I love you both," he said calmly, "but you are definitely frustrating at times."

"You mean all the qualifications with everything I say."

"Yes. You and Sam both say nothing is clear or straightforward. Everything is ambiguous and couched in warnings. Even after all this time."

"And that's because, even after all this time, you want to

jump on everything we say as if it's the complete truth."

"It usually is."

"Usually is not the same thing as definitely."

"How can you deal with definites when you speak in possibilities?" Brandt walked to the truck and clicked the unlock button for Stefan to get in. "I don't get that."

"Shall we continue this philosophical discourse on the nature of psychics and their fear of being wrong, or shall we return to the topic at hand?"

"Oh please, let's get back to business." Brandt hopped in and started up his truck.

In the passenger seat, Stefan leaned his head back and closed his eyes. Marshalling his thoughts he said, "I found the energy signature from the bathroom to be the same as one of the many energies in Celina's personal energy space. It's one she knows and holds dear."

"Huh. So a friend of hers did this?" Brandt drove onto the main street, away from her building. Shaking his head, he said, "That would explain the access to her apartment. They likely had a key."

"Possibly."

"'Possibly'? What are you not telling me?"

"There could be several other explanations yet. It's too early."

Brandt slapped the steering wheel. "See, there you go again. I know it's too early. I know it's not clear. But there is something in there besides the little taste you offered. What is it?"

"I'm not sure." Stefan rolled his head toward his friend in time to see him glare at the inside roof of the truck. "Honest. At this point I can't say what's odd here. But there is something."

Brandt sighed. "Fine. Be that way."

"Besides," Stefan straightened, "didn't you hear her say that both her friends who had keys were either dead or dying?"

BEFORE THE MEN had left they'd told her she could clean up the mess now.

She had taken cleanser and several cloths and starting at the doorways, she'd cleaned everything in her pathway from floor to ceiling and wall to wall – and then had done it all over again.

She hadn't dared call anyone else in to help her. The shocked questions would kill her to answer, and she needed to know for herself that this was cleaned up.

And that meant she had to do it herself.

Now she was beat. And sore. And scared.

Celina walked slowly back to her bedroom and carefully lay down on the bed.

A huge sigh of relief at being back in bed swept through her, followed by an even heavier, deeper one at finally being alone.

Except you're never alone. You know that.

I want to be alone though, she said quietly. Too tired to be angry. The blackness inside her was too big to deal with. Resigned, she thought, *You could leave.*

I could. But what could that do? You'd be all alone, and that's no good.

I just said that's what I want, she retorted, temper flaring. *Haven't you haunted me enough?*

There was a pause, and he laughed and laughed. *Oh, that's rich. You're worried about me, but you didn't recognize the consultant that was here this morning was the same guy who sat beside you at the hospital for hours last night.*

Her mind danced around putting the pieces together, and now that she knew she easily made the connection. Her eyes flew open. He couldn't be allowed to know. She tried to cover up her lapse. *Yes, I did. And so what if he was there at the hospital? He's a police consultant. There were lots of other police there, too. There were a lot of people there from all walks of life. Or maybe he knew someone involved in the accident.*

Maybe, and maybe he's stalking you. The male laughter had a hard edge to it. *Wouldn't that be something?*

No, she snapped. *It wouldn't be.*

Thankfully the voice in her head disappeared. Yet the implication he left behind disturbed her.

A thin layer of ice filmed over her skin, and unable to help herself she crawled back under the covers. It wasn't much comfort given her horrible morning, but she'd take what she could right now.

Alone now, she wanted to let down her guard even just a little bit. But it was hard. She spent so much of her life behind walls, it almost seemed normal. It was difficult to loosen up. But what a stressful way to live.

Some people she couldn't keep out, and some people she wasn't sure she wanted to keep in.

She didn't do well with relationships. College had seen her survive several rather rambunctious ups and downs and several short-term relationships. She hadn't been so odd then. But she'd been intense. Something guys hadn't liked. Except in bed.

It wasn't until her last year in college that she'd met Peter. The relationship had been hard and fast, and they'd been engaged within four months. She'd lost him from a brain aneurysm barely three months later. Devastated at the time, she'd spent months trying to make contact with him in the spirit world. It had seemed like she'd lost everyone important to her. Then she'd been involved in a car accident and lost her sight. Yeah, her life sucked big-time now.

She preferred to make good friends instead of trying out different lovers. And the man in her dreams – what had possessed her to whisper that in his presence? What a fool. And where had that even come from?

She was a little put out that she hadn't recognized that voice last night. Had he spoken to her? She couldn't remember. Surely she'd have recognized him even if he hadn't. Then again, why would she? She'd been a mess. A walled-up, isolated island of pain. Of course she hadn't wanted to talk to a stranger.

Yet this stranger was so familiar – like the many times she'd woken up from vivid dreams, as if she'd met someone special. But in the morning there'd only been a sensation, not a memory or a vision to hold onto.

So either her tormentor was wrong – and wouldn't that be nice – or something was different about the man this morning. Or about her, she admitted. And that was more likely. Last night she'd been in physical pain and emotional torment. She'd just been through a horrific accident and had lost several friends. She'd been focused on sending positive, loving energy to her injured friends, not the cool stranger at her side. There'd been many strangers in that room last night. He'd been just one more.

This morning the circumstances had highlighted his presence and that voice had slipped into her consciousness, grabbed her by the throat, and made sure she paid attention.

She smiled wryly. "Great," she said out loud. "Now he's got my attention. So what? Last thing he'd want would be a neurotic blind woman in his life."

"You don't know that," Mimi said softly. "You're always knocking yourself down. You've got to stop doing that. There are a lot of good men out there that wouldn't mind your physical condition in the least."

She smiled at Mimi. Ghosts came and went, usually unannounced. "No, they'd accept it, but they'd prefer a woman who was whole."

"Is there such a person? Everyone has scars, injuries, defects. Just some are more visible."

"Is that what my blindness is, a defect? In a way I guess it is."

"No, it isn't," Mimi said stoutly, "but that's how *you* see it."

"Did you see who wrote that message on my mirror?"

"What message?" Mimi asked.

Celina sighed. Of course she hadn't. That would be too easy.

"Damn. I hate days like this. I need to go and do something." Celina smiled. "I'll go to the hospital and visit Jacob and the others, then maybe go to an art museum, walk through the gallery, and soak up the ambiance. I miss that place. I might not be able to see, but that doesn't mean I don't enjoy being there." In fact, being at the gallery helped her find peace inside. Gave her hope. She used to go all the time; now she went when she could sneak away.

"Yes, do that. Get out and have fun."

She called the hospital, but that had only added to her depression. Jacob wasn't doing as well as they'd hoped. He was still in the ICU and wasn't allowed visitors. Feeling tired, sad and vulnerable, she had Porter, her doorman, call her a cab to the museum.

Walking up the stairs to the large, imposing entranceway

she allowed her memories to fill in the missing elements that she could no longer see. This had been one of her favorite haunts, and one of her greatest sorrows was that she could no longer see the beautiful exhibits.

"The same bench, Miss Wilton?" asked the guide standing just inside the front door. "It's a quiet day today. Would you like me to show you to one of the new chairs we have placed around the rooms?"

She smiled. "If it's new you'd better show it to me before I find it the hard way. If there is one close to the new exhibit that would be lovely."

"There is. The artist is new to the West Coast but is fast making a name for himself here."

"Lovely – what does he paint?"

"His wife."

JACOB SAT UP and stretched. Damn, he felt good. He threw back the covers and hopped out of bed. He stood tall and arched his back, shifting and rolling his shoulders. What a great night's sleep. He was grateful those bizarre nightmares seemed to have finally stopped. It had to have been caused by the drugs. Nasty things. Although they beat living with that horrific pain. He knew he'd been in an accident of some kind and vaguely remembered going to the bar with Celina, so he could only presume they'd been hit on the road. At least he felt decent now.

Raring to go, in fact. That weird brain fog was gone, and the air around him looked normal. For a long time he'd wondered if he'd ever be able to get out of that ghastly drugged state. If that's what being in a coma felt like, his sympathies went to those currently in that situation. What a horrible way to live.

Just then a nurse walked into the room. There were four other beds in the room. He couldn't see most of the other occupants because of the curtains surrounding them. Several curtains were open, but he didn't want to pry by walking around and checking to see if he was alone. Most likely the room was full.

He smiled as a nurse entered and went to the first bed.

Maybe the doctor would be in soon and he could get out of this place.

The nurse walked to the second bed and he waited. When she left that bed and came toward him he grinned and said, "Good morning. I feel great today. When is the doctor available? I'd really like to go home."

She had a tablet of some kind in her hand. He waited, wishing the nursing staff could actually dredge up a personality. It was one of the reasons he hated being in here. They were either cranky or run off their feet or super talkative, and you learned way too much about their boyfriend's ex. He sighed and shifted. Her face twisted as she clicked through the screens.

Uh oh.

He couldn't help it. He sidled closer and tried to peer into her screen. The angle was just that little bit off so he couldn't read the text. It was his file though. Nice to see the medical system moving forward with technology. He glanced up at her face. "So what's the verdict? Will I live?" he joked.

The nurse sighed. She tugged the open curtain over to hide his bed slightly. He frowned.

"Hey, what's going on?" He turned to face his bed. And saw a body lying still on the bed.

His body.

CHAPTER 9

AFTER RETURNING FROM the museum Celina needed to connect to her own creativity. There was nothing like seeing passion in someone else's work to inspire her own. She was blessed with the ability to play several instruments, the harp and violin being her favorites. Right now she wanted to feel her bow in her hand. She opened her father's old violin case, picked up his and now her beloved instrument, and drew the bow across the strings. The moaning sound matched the fear and pain in her heart. Her life had swung out of control and she didn't understand how or why. She wanted this asshole gone from her mind, her friends alive, and she wanted her old normal back again – the normal from before her accident.

She knew it was never going to happen, but that didn't stop her from wanting more or wishing it could. Her bow stroked back and forth in a haunting melody as a warm up. A tune of woe and a tune of hope. A melody she'd written that serenaded her emotions, honoring them, while giving her a chance to release the pain and replenish her soul with joy.

Tears formed in her eyes as her fingers moved and her arm swung and dipped. She'd been through so much this last year. And she couldn't see a way forward. She needed someone to help her deal with the craziness in her world.

She'd have to let go of her fear and pride and talk to a counselor or a psychologist. She was terrified this voice was a part of herself. And she was desperate to assuage this fear that she'd hurt people somehow. That she was responsible. She didn't know how she could have, but the dread persisted. A concrete, festering awareness that maybe there was something seriously wrong with her.

"What song is that?" asked a voice in the living room.

She frowned at the ghostly interruption but refused to stop playing. "It's not really a song, I'm just jamming." She smiled at the old phrase. She was playing for herself. That was all.

"It's beautiful."

"Thank you."

She ignored the ghost, noticing a twinge of familiarity, and had to wonder if she was just getting more comfortable with so many of them. After all, she saw or sensed plenty of them on a day-to-day basis. And did her best to keep them at bay. She could only handle so much, and lately it was much less. She was surprised this one was here. It wasn't like she'd left a psychological door open. The more she thought about it, the more it bothered here. "How did you get in here?"

There was a moment of startled surprise. Then he said in a soft voice, "Your music called to me."

Her fingers faltered, and then she recovered. Her music had called to him? That was new. She didn't know if she liked that idea or not. She said lightly, "I don't think my music has ever done that before."

"Oh, I'm sure it has," he said. "Do you play other instruments?"

"Several."

"Lovely for you."

Her fingers continued to play as her mind dwelled on his words. And realized it *was* lovely to be able to do that. She moved from instrument to instrument as her soul required. Each instrument offered her something different at the moment. She loved the harp. Sometimes, like this concert that was supposed to start tonight, she was doing a special with her fiddle. It allowed her to stretch and grow as a musician. And that allowed her to stretch and grow as a person. "Who are you and why are you here?"

"I'm a friend, and I'm here to enjoy your music."

Such ghost-like answers. So often they couldn't even give their own names.

"Then enjoy," she said, smiling. And closed her eyes. She let the emotion pour through her strings and let her heart soar. She played until the need in her had drained and the stress and tension had moved from her inner core out to her trembling arms. She lowered the instrument with a long sigh. Then she shook out her arms, straightened her back, and rolled her stiff neck.

"You play beautifully. Thank you."

She started, having forgotten her visitor. "No problem."

"Do you make those colors happen on purpose?" he asked.

She froze. And for the first time she opened her eyes. Her ghostly visitor was a pale blur to the left of her, his features indistinct, his glow faded, weak. "You can see them?" she asked.

"Yes." He said it so simply, as if to say *of course, can't you?*

Celina frowned. "Not many can."

"I'm sorry to hear that. They are beautiful." He shifted slightly. "Do you make the music and the colors are secondary, or do you paint first and the music is secondary?"

She laughed. "I have no idea. I had hoped that they worked together, and they do, but the pictures aren't quite the way I'd want them to be."

"Then maybe you should try to make the paintings in the air and see what music comes from that."

She raised her eyebrow in surprise. "Interesting suggestion. Thank you."

The smile in his voice couldn't be missed. "No problem. I like art in all forms."

She tilted her head, realizing her ghost was very subdued. He was also alone in her room. Often she could sense several ghosts at the same time. More often than not they couldn't see each other. "Have you seen any other ghostly visitors here?"

"Not at the moment."

She frowned. "Meaning you have before?"

"Once I stopped in and saw there were others and I left soon after."

She nodded. Ghosts were just as contrary in death as they'd been alive. If he'd been a loner in life, chances were good he'd be a loner in death. That saddened her. Everyone needed someone.

"Then as you appear to enjoy my music, I hope it made you happy."

"It did. Thank you."

She returned her violin to her case and turned around to see Mimi in front of her. Mimi said, "That was lovely, dear."

"Oh hi, I didn't realize you were here." She scanned the room but realized the pale ghost was gone.

"There's been no one else here, my dear child. Are you feeling all right?"

Celina laughed. "So because you didn't see or sense someone, I must be ill?" She shook her head. "The world does not revolve around you, Mimi. Sometimes other people see things you don't."

"Maybe," Mimi said comfortably. "But my world revolves around me, and that's all I'm concerned with."

"Oh, the simple life of being a ghost."

"It is simple," Mimi laughed. "No cooking, no cleaning, no job, no bills to pay."

"What a way to view death." Celina shook her head. "What are the things you miss doing?" she asked curiously. The more she dealt with ghosts, the more she found their perspective to be a refreshing take on the life she often took for granted.

"Hugging a child. Making love. Being held by someone who cares. Family." Her voice faded, as if the words were too hard to get out. She disappeared in front of Celina's eyes. Or rather, from the back of Celina's eyes.

Slowly Celina stood, thinking about Mimi's words. Given that Celina had lost or hadn't known most of her family to begin with, she already missed much of what Mimi did – and she hadn't died yet. Sure, she had a few friends, but she was closest to her ghosts. How sad was that?

Sometimes it really bothered her. The artist she'd met at the gallery today came to mind. A man so in love with his wife, Shay, that she was his sole subject. She'd desperately wanted to see the huge paintings when the artist had stopped by unexpectedly. He'd been kind enough to sit down and described his work to her in great detail. For that moment he'd given her a stunning insight into what she'd once been able to see – art. He'd been blessed in so many ways. The other good thing to come out of that had been that he'd obviously known it.

And it made her life seem so much emptier.

Tired and depressed, she walked to her bedroom, wishing she had more friends. Wishing she had someone to join her for a bottle of wine tonight. She really didn't want to be alone.

Her phone rang. She laughed. Good. Maybe someone heard her silent call.

Instead it was her eye specialist's office.

"You had an appointment today. You didn't show up. We've rearranged this appointment several times. Dr. Jorgensen needs to see you."

Celina listened to the tirade in silence and winced. Jillian had even asked her about that appointment this morning and she hadn't even triggered to today being the day. "I thought it was next week," she admitted, massaging her temples.

"It was today – booked on a Saturday as he has another specialist here to see you. I left a message on your voicemail," the reception said, vexed. "This doctor has some different techniques. She's only here this weekend."

Celina frowned. Damn. A different specialist? She didn't know how she felt about that. "What time is it now?"

"It's four-thirty. Why?"

"I just wondered if maybe I could catch a cab and come and see her."

"Just a moment." The receptionist held the phone away and there was muttering going on in the background. "They will be leaving soon. Can you come right away?"

Celina's mind raced. Maybe the specialist would be the one to finally give her answers. She'd been remiss in not going back to Dr. Jorgensen, but after all she'd been through she didn't need to listen to more frustration on his part. But he'd taken the next step. For her. How could she do any less?

"I'll be there in twenty minutes."

SITTING CROSS-LEGGED IN the afternoon sun, Stefan opened up his senses and slipped free of his body, stretching for only a short moment before flying free. There were so many things on his to do list. He almost laughed. How many other people had lists like he did? As in first leave body, next float over to Celina and make sure she was doing okay, then check out the hospital.

Floating easily, he moved through Celina's apartment. Celina's empty apartment. He frowned as he zipped through the space. Where the hell was she? The question had no sooner filled his mind than he caught it back. He was *not* amused at his possessive reaction.

He checked out the energy of her apartment. Instinctive-ly he sent out a wide band of questing energy, searching for anomalies. The energy was frazzled but calming. Nothing extreme, and no new upsets that he could see. There were yesterday's multiple energies still clogging up the space. He shook his head. Celina might have a lot of experience with ghosts, but she had no idea how to handle foreign energies in her space. That was something he could do for her.

He spent a moment cleansing the apartment of all the strangers. When he was done the place would feel like home again. It took longer than he thought. He could feel the pull on his own energy resources as he mentally catalogued many of the strangers, seeing the signatures and their actions for what they were. The police doing their job. Then there were ghosts that were sliding through the different planes, touching base with her in and out of their existence. It was one of the mysteries of the ethers that everyone who died could create the space in which they existed to be what and where they wanted it to be. At the same time, they appeared to stay within the parameters they set.

Lissa, his friendly teenaged ghost, appeared unusual in that she was owning her space and expanding it. She stepped forward to greet other souls caught in this fractured existence on her own. Like a personal greeter.

He smiled. Lissa was a jewel, and there was no way death could dull her brilliance. She hadn't had much chance at a physical life, but once she'd gained a foothold in the etheric world she'd taken charge of her existence and now lived it. Which sounded odd, because of all the things she was, alive wasn't one of them.

He paused to survey the room and realized there were strains of something that had come and gone. An energy that frayed sparks with each movement instead of moving smoothly with control. A new spirit who'd just crossed over, or one newly connected to Celina. It looked similar to what he'd seen in the bathroom but it was different. And that difference concerned him. The bathroom had been overrun with strangers, and that could affect the look of the signature – he hadn't been here soon enough after the event to identify the energy. Being the hunter he was, he understood this was connected to the incident.

He purged that trail from the apartment, leaving her space clean and renewed.

Then he shifted to the hospital. The energy buffeting against him shot his guards into place. Damn. He hated hospitals. He closed in his energy, zipped up his aura, and moved cautiously through the hallways. He floated above the moving throngs of people. This place was always busy. He wasn't sure what the drive had been to come here, given that it was the last place he wanted to be. Yet he couldn't shake the connection from the orchestra incident to the warning message in Celina's apartment, and that meant checking out the driver of the truck that had slammed into the pub. He had hoped to speak with him, but as the man hadn't survived the crash Stefan hoped to gain some insight from his corpse. Nice thought. Not. First he needed to see the surviving orchestra members.

He drifted through the various rooms, seeing the energy, the healing, the disease, the sickness, and the thick blanket of heavy emotion. Grief, sadness, and bright flashes of anger dominated.

All normal. All to be expected. He reached the floor where the injured orchestra members were and moved through the hallway, seeing the little bits of connecting energy between several rooms. They were there. He stopped at one doorway, recognizing the energy. Interesting. He sent a mental note to Brandt. Heard the other man's shocked denial and then closed the mental door. He needed to concentrate here.

He popped into another room to find a woman sleeping, bandages on her head and her right arm in a cast. Nothing was amiss in her room or energy – at least in a negative way.

Going from room to room, Stefan was unable to shake the feeling that he was looking for something and would recognize it when he saw it. But he wasn't finding it. Frustration rode him as he zipped through the massive building.

He closed his eyes and saw the morgue in his mind's eye. When he opened them he found himself in the right place.

Techs worked in systematic fashion in the large room with several full tables, autopsies in progress. He shifted his gaze to the large wall of cabinets at the end of the room. He drifted closer, searching for links to the orchestra. There were two here. At least two.

Stefan studied the energy coming from the cold, clinical room. Instead of it being empty of color and form, the place seethed. With anger, pain, loss, denial, grief, and most of all that sense of regret. Regret that they hadn't had time to say goodbye, regret for all the loved ones left behind. Regret for the things they left unfinished. There were so many that they rolled in together, creating a morass of seething turbulence.

He had seen many a person pass on and just leave. Those were the easy cases. More often than not the ones he saw – and he'd admit it was his affinity for violence that likely kept the natural selection this way – were full of unresolved issues.

Many people couldn't leave when death came to them. And that was too bad. No one was ever prepared for death when it was their time. Unless they'd been dying for a long time or had made peace with their death. He'd heard of people crossing the river that divided the two planes of existence and coming back, but he wasn't one of them. He walked the gray area between those planes and could often speak with those that had crossed over and somehow came back, or those that had never left and were even now grabbing for a foothold into the craziness of life that they weren't ready to leave.

He wished he could tell everyone to let go and let death be your friend. But he couldn't. It wasn't his place. Nor was it his truth. He hadn't been there, so it couldn't be. And he could only speak his truth.

He slipped closer to the big metal drawers on the one

side with computerized door locks. The morgue was more advanced than many. Anything that dignified those in death made it easier on everyone. He shifted along the wall, searching for anything that would make sense of this. He strengthened his barriers against the energy vibrating at a level he'd prefer not to access. It helped dim the noise somewhat. He wasn't sure why the energy was so extreme today. Two men entered the room. He eased his barrier slightly to hear their conversation.

"Man, what a night. Talk about gang wars. What have we got – seven dead and three more upstairs? The ones out on the street are rioting even worse now."

That explained it. Young anger, anger of the righteous, vigilant anger, and the anger of losing in that war were all clearly flying around him. A gang fight had sent many members from both sides to lie in a relative calm side-by-side in the morgue. There would be no more fighting in here. At least not against each other. Hopefully. He shifted his focus and took a moment to separate the energy, and realized a half dozen screamed louder than normal. If these young men had fought this loud and this strong while on the streets, they'd probably done a fair bit of damage to innocent bystanders as well.

He shook his head. Talk about bad karma. When would humanity learn? One paid for every misdeed – if not here and now, then later. And he'd met enough of those people to know that fact for sure. No one ever took heed because payback could take decades.

He shifted back again, drifted around the two men who were shuffling carts full of bodies. Some into drawers, some lined up to go to autopsy, and some needing paperwork. He wondered at the human capacity to deal with death every day. Did it affect these men? Or did they see it as a necessary service that they could do for mankind? He'd likely never know.

As he turned to drift toward the autopsy room, he caught a tiny thread of... something. Something odd. Something off. Again.

He followed the faint thread of energy out to the autopsy room, to where a man lay nude on the table, a big Y incision on his chest, his ribs open, while someone in a gown muttered over him.

Stefan couldn't hear him clearly, but there was something wrong. He slid down to the far end and tried to see the name on the chart. Owen Dugar.

"Poor bugger. You didn't know what had happened, did you?" the doctor said. "Looks like your heart just cooked itself. Beyond weird. Well, let's take a closer look."

As Stefan lifted his gaze to study the heart in the man's hand, he realized he'd never seen anything like it. The heart looked like a hunk of oozing, burnt meat. How the hell had that happened?

The doctor stared.

Stefan stared.

That was when he realized something else. Even though dead, there were foreign energies on this man's heart.

He studied the dead man's open chest. There were scars on the man's belly, but with the chest open he couldn't see if there were other scars to indicate earlier surgery, like bypass surgery. Although Dr. Maddy would likely be able to get the information for him, he didn't want to wait. He continued to listen, hoping for more.

"Even with everything they'd done to you, you still didn't make it," the doctor said to his dead patient. "I've never seen anything like this one. I'm going to speak with your cardiologist. See what he might have done different with you, and if he had any idea what might have caused this."

With that he placed the heart on a scale to weigh the blackened mass.

Armed with that information, Stefan closed his eyes and retraced his pathway home. All he could think about was how long a surgical team's energy would stay in a body after surgery.

Thankfully he had someone he could ask.

"You know, I don't think I have a conclusive answer for that," Maddy said thoughtfully. "There are too many variables, such as the level of caring in the surgeon, if there were any type of complications that would require multiple people to step up, or if the patient died and had to be brought back. Depending on what the surgery was there could be any number of other people involved in the process."

Maddy shifted in the straight back desk chair, wishing she were back in her own comfy office rather than in Dr. Jorgenson's office and rubbed the back of her neck slowly to ease the tension.

As for Stefan's current question she added, "Give me a day or so and I'll see what I can find out with my own patients. Several have other surgical issues. I can check and see." As she thought about it she had to wonder. "You know, one of the first things I do is clean out the energy, release the blockages, and work on any of the system's imbalances. I don't care who or what or why the problem exists, I just go and clean them out."

"Meaning?" Stefan's tired voice slipped through the phone. "Meaning you don't have anyone on your floor with a recent or old surgery that you haven't cleaned out yet?"

"Exactly. But..." she let her voice trail off as she thought about it. "There will be many of them at the children's ward."

"Right." Stefan's voice perked up. "Why didn't I think of that?"

"If it was anyone but Celina involved you'd have been all over this," she said warmly. "There's nothing like a personal involvement to throw your thinking off."

"Ha, my thinking has been off for months," he growled.

She smiled, remembering the concert they'd all gone to where they had seen Celina for the first time. "Actually about a month. As long as you help from a distance and give her some space..."

"She's got big trouble riding her back. She gets a day or two and that's it."

Maddy couldn't help herself. She laughed. "But you have to let some things happen as they were meant to. The road to heaven and all that..."

"Hell," he said in disgust. "At the moment there isn't a road going anywhere but into the nearest sewer." And he hung up.

"ERIC?" LILLIANA MOORE walked over to her eight-year-old son and bent down to him. He lay curled into a tight ball on the hospital bed. His face was scrunched in pain with beads of sweat rolling down his forehead.

"Honey, can you tell me what's wrong?"

He shook his head and tugged the covers higher.

She settled on the side of the hospital bed and reached out a hand to gently stroke his shoulder. "It's the leg again, isn't it?"

He still wouldn't speak. She frowned, thought about it, then understood. "No, not the leg – the new bone piece, right?"

His head barely moved, yet it was enough. He'd started protesting about the cadaver bone implant as soon as he'd woken up from surgery. She didn't know who had told him that bone had come from a dead body, but because of the wild imagination and fearful mind of an eight-year-old it was the worst thing anyone could do. She'd like to wring that person's neck. Eric hadn't been the same since he'd woken up. He said odd things, hated to be alone, and now had a horrific fear about the boogeyman – even worse, he had a morbid obsession with death.

And he wanted that damn bone out. Something that wasn't likely to happen – especially given that the surgeons were delighted with the results of their handiwork.

She didn't know how to help her son. He needed to talk to a counselor, but she was hesitant to bring another stranger into her son's world. She wished there was someone here who could help.

She didn't even know who to ask.

CHAPTER 10

GIVEN THE TRAFFIC in Portland on a Saturday after-noon, it was nothing short of a miracle that Celina made it on time. Breathless, she made her way to the specialist's office, her walking stick a reassuring tapping tool as she strode down the hallway. Third doorway on the left. She dragged her stick along the wall until it hit the first door, then the second, and then a third. Standing outside for a moment, she tried to control her ragged breathing. This was too important. She needed this visit. Needed to find out if there truly was something else wrong with her eyes or…

See, now I'm going to be interested in finding that out too. She shuddered as the same insidious, poisonous voice crept through her mind.

Go away, she snapped. *This has nothing to do with you.*

Ha. We'll see about that.

She mentally took that gargoyle image that she always saw in her mind and poured cement on top of him. It always worked – for a moment or two. Then he somehow managed to break through and return. Often though, he became really angry that he couldn't control her and would take off, looking for new ways to torment her.

She waited a moment longer to make sure she was alone, then reached for the doorknob and walked inside.

"There you are." The woman's voice on the left was quietly relieved. "I'm so happy you made it."

Celina laughed. "I almost didn't. That downtown traffic is deadly at this time."

"I know," the woman commiserated. "Let's hope it will be worth it. We aren't used to working weekends, but we've had patients in and out all day and they've been saying variations of the same thing."

Celina smiled politely. She stood in the middle of the room, not quite sure what she was supposed to do.

"I'll take you right into the examining room and let Dr. Jorgensen know you are here."

Relieved, Celina let herself be led to an examining room. There were sounds in the other room of an animated conversation going on. She smiled, loving the sound of the woman's voice. And she'd never heard her eye doctor sound quite so alive before. The door opened to tinkling laughter that was so infectious Celina couldn't help but smile.

"Here she is." Dr. Jorgensen moved into the room in his usual short, hoppy movements. He was a small man and clipped his shoes on the tile floor as he walked. It made it easier to keep track of his whereabouts as he moved around her.

Celina smiled. "Good afternoon. I'm so sorry for missing my appointment. I completely forgot about it."

"Not to worry. You made it and that's what counts."

He shifted to face someone who stood in the doorway.

Celina opened her eyes, and damn if she didn't see something greeny gold in the doorway. Interesting. Either one of her ghosts had decided to come and visit her here – which would be odd but not unheard of – or this specialist had something odd going on so Celina could actually see her. She saw ghosts in colors and energy forms all the time but not people. And that would be incredibly unusual as well. But it gave her hope.

She nodded acknowledgement to the now silent woman standing still at the entrance. "You are the specialist Dr. Jorgenson wanted me to meet?" she asked.

"I'm Dr. Maddy." The woman glided into the room gently, carefully, as if feeling her way. Celina tilted her head, her eyes open as she watched bright yellow and green colors stream and twist with the woman's movements. She'd never seen anything like it. With or without her sight.

"Hello, Dr. Maddy. Thank you for seeing me."

Dr. Maddy said, "Hi, Celina. Dr. Jorgensen has told me so much about you."

She could hear the smile in Dr. Maddy's voice making her respond in kind. "That's probably not a good thing." Celina shrugged. "He can't figure out why I can't see."

"I've seen your medical records and the surgical reports. According to what I've read the surgery to reduce the pressure on your optic nerve and reattach the optic nerve in your left eye was a complete success."

"How can it be a success if I can't see?" Celina countered.

"That's why I'd like to take a look." Dr. Maddy approached. "May I?"

Celina nodded. "Go ahead."

For the next half hour Celina went through every eye test she'd already had done many times over. She waited in silence while the two doctors carried out minimal conversation. Then Dr. Maddy stepped around Dr. Jorgensen to stand in front of her. "May I explore your head?"

Dr. Jorgensen took that moment to step out of the room.

Curiously Celina nodded. "Of course."

What followed was a systematic search of her head as Dr. Maddy's long fingers glided and stroked from front to back, from side to side. At one point she said, "Interesting." But she didn't elaborate.

Celina had no idea what her skull shape might have to do with anything, but she was willing to be checked over for anything.

After it seemed Dr. Maddy had done everything she could do, Celina asked, "Well, did you find anything?"

"Maybe, but I need to perform a couple more checks. I'm going to leave you here for a few moments." And she left. The door shut, leaving Celina alone. She wanted to get up and move around but something stopped her. She didn't feel like she was being watched, but neither did she feel like she was quite alone.

As she sat there, a strange lassitude filled her limbs. A warmth like she'd never experienced before crawled up her legs. She'd have cried out in shock but it felt good – so good she didn't want it to stop. She whimpered in delight as the heat reached the aching muscles from last night. She probably should have mentioned the accident to the doctor, but he would likely have tut-tutted her to death and not been able to help anyway.

The heat continued to climb up her hips and spine. Celina leaned back and moaned lightly as her body let the stress drain from her neck and shoulders. Heat spread to all corners of her body, making her almost writhe with joy. Peacefulness filled her as she shifted into the heat, to the places that were missed. It continued to climb higher and higher, easing into her neck and whistling through her veins.

She shivered, then shuddered. That felt so good. She had

never felt anything like it. She wanted it to last – forever, if possible.

Then it shifted into her skull and heat flashed and danced through her brain. She reached up a hand to her forehead to see if the warmth she was feeling inside was emanating outside. But it wasn't. Her forehead was cool. So was her neck. Bizarre. Yet there was no fear attached. There was a sense of joy. Release. Peace. Lord, it felt wonderful. She didn't know if Dr. Maddy was responsible or not. She hoped so, because she'd do a lot for a repeat session.

And then the heat hit her eyes.

She groaned. The warmth turned hot and achy inside her skull. What had been a comforting heat now sent flares of spitting shocks into her skull. She slammed her hands up against her head and she cried out.

Instantly the pain stopped.

The heat stopped.

And the flares inside her head stopped.

The comforting warmth washed over her, sweeping her body gently in long, soothing strokes from the top of her head down. She shuddered as her body eased back again in relief as she realized the pain was not coming back. She didn't know what had happened, but it had been brutal. So fast and so deep, with such cutting pain. She hadn't had time to do anything but react.

She'd gone from being in a euphoric daze to being in agony.

Slowly the panic eased back. And peace was again filling her insides. If nothing else she was starting to feel better. She opened her eyes, willing them to see something. At least a little bit. Enough that she could get around to do what needed to be done.

Just not enough…

Not enough for me to see? Is that it?

She stilled, the benefit of the smooth healing instantly evaporating. "What do you want?" she hissed out loud, hating that he could understand when she spoke to him in her mind or out loud.

I want to see. Let me see.

"No."

You're here now. Fix it. Let me see.

She slammed her eyes shut and swore softly under her breath.

Her nasty visitor laughed, that same horrible sound that gave her nightmares and woke her up in a cold sweat.

No. I will never let you see.

MADDY SAT CROSS-LEGGED in Dr. Jorgensen's office. A ripple of aftershock still wracked down her own spine, even as she gently stroked Celina's spine back to peacefulness again. Shaken but quickly regaining her sense of balance, Maddy left anchors in place for further work. And there was further work required. But not the same type of healing work she was used to.

All the energy issues she saw came from different emotional issues or physical causes. That she hadn't come up against one like this before didn't mean much – especially given the millions of different scenarios that people came up with to hide. Nothing was protected more than one's deepest, darkest secrets. And she had no way to know at this point what Celina might be hiding or was indeed trying to protect.

Taking a deep breath, she slowly eased out of her meditative state and pulled her energy back into her body. She opened her eyes and stared at the plain, simple office, her thoughts churning. She needed to come up with something to say to Celina, and then she needed to connect to Stefan… and fast.

STEFAN SAT OUTSIDE on his deck, a pot of healing tea at his side. The late afternoon sun had slipped lower behind the trees, setting up a kaleidoscope of rays peeking through the branches. He loved this time of day.

Stefan.

He smiled. *Hello, beautiful. What's up?*

I just did a session on your Celina.

At the concern in her voice the smile fell away. *What's wrong with her?* He couldn't keep the alarm from his voice.

That's the thing. I couldn't get to the correct region of her eyes to find out. I came up against some major walls that immediately attacked me.

Attacked you? he asked incredulously. *Why?*

I have no idea. And no, before you ask, I've never seen it before. She took a deep shaky breath. *It was a little unnerving.*

Sounds like it, he muttered. *Are you all right?*

Yes. She rushed to reassure him. *I'm fine. I'm not sure what to say about Celina.*

Is she healthy in every other way?

Yes, in remarkably good physical health. Not in energetic health. She's stressed and bleeding an incredible amount of energy to her injured friends, keeping her ghost communications functioning, and the anger, guilt…she's feeding that with energy she doesn't have to spare.

Anger for what? Stefan asked cautiously.

I don't know. You'll have to ask her.

He snorted. *And how do you recommend I do that?*

There was a long silence. He shifted in his position like a child caught in a lie.

She smiled, the mirth rippling through his mind. He flushed. Damn it. Was nothing ever secret?

I'll leave you to answer that question all on your own, she said, laughing. *I need to do some more research on Celina and that blockage. I left anchors in place to make it easier to track back.*

Does she know what you're doing?

Not clearly. She did agree to see me as a specialist. She was aware subconsciously of my actions as I worked to balance her chakras and smooth the blockages in her meridians. She's very responsive. But it's not like we had a discussion on energetic healing.

Excellent. And it was. It made a person easier to work with, and they healed faster if their energy ran smoothly. It also showed an affinity for energy work. That would also explain her kinship with ghosts. Energy was energy – on both sides of death's door.

JACOB STARED AT the nurse. She wavered in front of him. He squinted hard. He didn't know what was wrong. He'd thought he'd seen Celina earlier. Thought he'd heard her music, but couldn't remember clearly. As if he was in a fog.

He'd tried to speak to her, tried to leave her a message, but nothing worked. He didn't understand it. He couldn't be dead because he could see as clear as anything. He could walk, breathe, smell even, but no one seemed to see him or could hear him. Except there were one or two people that maybe could. At least they looked at him as if they could. He hated that. They looked at him, through him, and around him as if he was there but they never said a word. Why? Frustration ate at him. He desperately wanted answers, but there seemed to be no one that could help.

He turned around and found himself in a beautiful garden. Shock slammed into him. What had happened to the dismal hospital room? Not that he cared. This was so much better. He spun in a circle arms wide open, grinning as he stared at the sky, the flowers, the grass. And came to a stop.

A young woman sat cross-legged in front of him.

He held his breath.

She looked at him and smiled. "Hi, I'm Lissa. I'm going to take a wild guess that you're lost."

CHAPTER 11

CELINA OPENED THE door to her apartment and barely made it inside before she knew she was going to crash. She didn't know what had happened at the doctor's office, but that wonderful feeling had disappeared – as in long gone. Like someone had pulled a plug in her big toe and all the stuffing had drained out – was still continuing to drain. She couldn't remember ever feeling so empty. So lacking in bone and muscle she could no longer stay upright.

She didn't like it.

Throwing her bag onto the table beside the entrance and staggering into her bedroom, she kicked off her shoes and managed to get her jacket off before she dropped face-first on the bed. She groaned in relief. She'd made it.

"What is wrong with me?" she groaned to the empty room.

Mimi answered, "What's happened?"

"No idea. First the stupid appointment I'd forgotten about, then a weird session with the specialist." Celina rolled over slightly. "Followed by a strange experience that ended with an excruciating headache."

"Are you feeling better now?" Mimi asked.

Eyes closed, she considered the question. "I feel better all over as if I'd had been at the spa all day, but I'm also exhausted. That pain though…talk about scary. It was like someone hit a tumor in my head. The pain is better now but it's not completely gone. More like it's waiting to rear up again at the slightest warning."

She shifted on the bed, and damn if that pain didn't start to roll toward the front of her head. "No," she gasped. "That can stop any time."

"Is it the headache again?"

"Yes." She groaned. "It really hurts."

"Try to relax," Mimi said, "Maybe it will ease back."

"I'm trying." She twisted in pain, wishing her ghostly visitors away, no matter how loving and concerned they were. They were dead.

In a gentle voice, Mimi said, "If you could mentally try to release the pain…"

"Ha, that's easier said than done." Celina shuddered as another greasy wave rolled through her. Could she make it to the bathroom and find something for the pain. She hated drugs, but there was no doubt they were a godsend sometimes. Right now was starting to look to be one of those times.

With any luck a painkiller would let her fall asleep for a couple of hours. She wanted to drop out of her life and come awake to being someone else. She knew it was childish. It didn't change anything.

"Stop being an idiot and get up," she muttered to the empty room.

"You're not being an idiot," said Mimi.

Mimi had the ability to appear and disappear at will, she thought a little wistfully. Why couldn't Celina?

"Your life will get better," Mimi said gently.

"Yeah? When?" With that she forced herself to sit up. And pain slammed into the back of her head. She cried out and fell back onto the pillows.

She lay gasping for breath as she waited for the booming in her head to lessen. When it started up again she shuddered slightly. A light film of sweat had risen over her skin.

"What's going on?" she whispered. "Why is this so bad?"

It's bad because you wouldn't listen. That same evil voice twisted through her head. *And if you try to send someone else in here to get rid of me your punishment will be much worse.* His voice promised retribution she knew she could never handle.

"I didn't send someone to get rid of you," she cried out. "Honest. I didn't even know that was possible." And now that she did… she immediately squashed that thought in case he could hear it.

You must have. There's no other way that person could have gotten in here without your permission. That means you let them in. That means you wanted them to get rid of me.

Accenting his anger, pain stabbed through her skull to rest just behind her eyes. She screamed, her back arching, her fists grabbing handfuls of the bedding beneath her. She twisted in slow, painful attempts to move away from the pain. Suddenly it stopped and she collapsed to the bed again, weeping. "Why are you doing this to me?" she cried out.

Behave yourself and I won't have to.

And he was gone.

STEFAN WATCHED IN horror as Celina twisted and cried from a pain she couldn't bear, seemingly coming from inside. He could see no outside injury and no change in her energy. Who? Why? It made no sense. If someone was attacking her then their energy should be clear enough for him to see. It wasn't. He was only here in his etheric form, true, but he'd never had a problem seeing invasive energy before. Or seeing the energy connected to whomever she was talking to – he had to assume someone was there. Someone who had a way to keep their presence hidden. As in behind walls. Strong walls.

And damned if that didn't just piss him off. He needed to keep Celina safe, and that was not happening in any easy way. He could see the anchors that Dr. Maddy had placed. There were no black blobs or encroaching dying energy. He couldn't begin to see what was going on. Because he couldn't, he felt helpless.

It was something he hadn't felt in a long time. He wanted to jump into her mind and find out for himself if someone was in there. Then again, the intruder could possibly make Celina pay in even more painful ways. Any added pressure right now would likely knock her out cold. Although if she were unconscious he might be able to get a clearer picture.

He watched her as she struggled to the bathroom for a painkiller then back before collapsing into bed again. Within minutes she slept, no longer fighting the pain but instead letting it take her under. Good. He sighed. She needed to rest. He didn't know what the story was, but she looked physically worn out and mentally exhausted.

Yet he found himself hesitating to enter her mind. A stranger's mind, no problem. But this was Celina. His beloved. His natural mate who had no idea who he was or what she was to him. Too bad he couldn't just up and tell her. But the universe didn't work that way.

She had to see him for her partner all on her own.

If she were to understand afterward what he'd done

without her permission then it could damage something between them. Though there wasn't anything there yet, there wouldn't be if he crossed personal boundaries. That made him tread a little lighter than he might have in other cases.

Plus he didn't know this parasite and what he could do. The last thing he wanted was to give him a reason to hurt Celina again.

Too bad she didn't know him. He could offer his help or to talk to her about her abilities and current difficulties right now, but he didn't think she was ready. He could use mind suggestion as a technique to propose she do something that she wouldn't normally do, but again that breached a line he couldn't cross. So what the hell was he going to do?

Then he got it. He could visit her dreams.

CELINA RAN THROUGH the endless darkness. There was nowhere to go. Nowhere to hide, and yet she didn't know what she was running from.

She staggered to a stop under a tree and leaned against it, trying to catch her breath. She walked a few steps and shook out her legs. The sky was dark, she was outside in the woods, and yet she didn't know why she was here. Or why her dreams would put her here. She didn't recognize the area at all.

A twig cracked behind her. She froze.

"Celina?"

She frowned. That voice almost sounded familiar. Almost. She slipped behind the tree and peered into the darkness. A golden glow formed off to one side. She shook her head and squinted. Surely that wasn't…a ghost?

No. She leaned back against the tree. Dreams were bizarre a lot of the time. Dark ones like this – always. But to see a ghost in her dream? Was that possible? No. She was manifesting him for some reason.

At least in her dreams she could see – mostly. And that was a relief. It was also a pleasure. She snorted. It helped her to live her life of darkness when she was awake.

As she leaned against the damn tree, she had to wonder if this dream was a metaphor for someone chasing her in the darkness of her life. Maybe she had a stalker who wanted to taunt her instead of attacking her? Like the evil voice in her head. Although he attacked her plenty. The reminder made her sick. Indeed, she leaned over and took several deep breaths, willing the bile back down her throat.

"Celina," the voice called again, only closer this time. And more familiar.

Who was he? She wasn't scared of him and that had to be a good sign. "Who are you and why are you a ghost in my dreams?" she asked. "That makes no sense."

He hesitated, and then said in a voice tinged in humor, "If you know it's a dream, why are you still running? Why not just change the dream?"

Say what? She twisted so she could see his golden glow clearly. "How is that possible?"

"If you're aware enough to understand you are in a dream, then you are aware enough to change the dream by just creating a different reality."

She straightened and brushed the back of her jeans as she thought about his words. "You're saying I can just change anything I want?"

"Within reason. This is lucid dreaming, and some people can exert a great deal of control over the dream."

"Yeah, well." She half-turned to look into the dark

woods. "Apparently I can't. I'm not some people. In fact, I'm not remarkable in that way at all."

He laughed. She turned to glare at him but her attention was caught by the light shining over the area where she stood. She spun around, realizing the dark, scary woods were now being swamped with bright morning sun. In the light, the scenery reminded her of an old place where her family had gone camping many times over the years.

It wasn't a full recreation, but it was enough to make her smile with the good memories. "What happened?" she asked.

"I lightened the tone for you."

She stared at him then cocked her head. "Sorry? You changed *my* dream? How does that work?"

He smiled and walked closer. "As I said, in a lucid dream you can make things happen the way you want them to happen."

"But I didn't make the sun come out. You did."

"Because that's what you wanted. I couldn't have done it otherwise."

She shook her head. "Who are you that you can do this?"

"I'm the man in your dreams," he said, his voice just short of amused.

And it clicked. "You're the police consultant."

And she woke up.

Dry-eyed, she stared at the ceiling mulling the impossibility of her dream. Resolutely she rolled over, determined to go back to sleep.

CHAPTER 12

T HE NEXT MORNING Celina woke up slowly. It took a moment to realize the pain was gone and her body lay relaxed and at peace. She'd actually gotten some sleep – thanks to the knockout pills she'd taken. She checked out her body and realized that all in all, she felt pretty decent. Not sure why, but she'd take the gift. As she sat up and swung her legs over the side of the bed, her muscles moved smoothly and freely. No aches or stiffness from the horrible accident.

The thought reminded her that she hadn't checked in on Jacob. Maybe she could visit him at the hospital today. Eagerly she stood and headed to the bathroom. The closer she went, the slower her footsteps. She lifted her head and wrinkled her nose. It smelled sweet. Normal. She stepped inside. It felt right again. She cocked her head and wondered. For some reason her apartment had that old homey feeling to it again. It no longer felt like her space had been violated.

Happily she headed to the shower. It was an odd feeling being in there, but there was no scent of anything wrong. Still...she made a quick job of it. When drying off she thought she heard a noise. Her towel moved slower over her wet body, head cocked to one side as she listened carefully. Nothing. Briskly she wrapped a towel around her wet hair, grabbed her robe, and returned to her bedroom. Halfway there she saw Mimi. She smiled. "Hey, was that you making that noise?"

Mimi snickered. "Not likely, but I wish I could. Just think of all the fun I could have."

Celina shook her head and continued into the closet to pull out clothes for the day. She stood and stared blankly, wondering what color she wanted to wear. And realized black jeans and her favorite long red sweater would be perfect. It took her just a moment to find the items in her extremely well-organized closet. It was the only way she'd know to be able to find the right clothes when she needed them. When it came to spring cleaning, yes, she enlisted friends to help her go through her closet and find the clothes that were too worn to be good, or the ones that had slipped to the back of the closet where she'd forgotten about them.

"That color looks lovely on you."

Besides, Mimi's taste was excellent.

"For a ghost you're very observant," she said, but there was a smile in her voice. She had instinctively dressed in her walk-in closet outside of her room. She'd been seeing and talking to ghosts for a long time and it was natural, familiar, but there were just some things that didn't feel quite right. Walking around nude in front of them was one of those things. Mimi was forever commenting on her clothes, having been a clotheshorse in her lifetime. For that reason Celina often used Mimi's eyes for picking out clothes. Even in her case Celina didn't completely undress. Ghost or not, she preferred her privacy, and some ghosts didn't appear to understand that.

She placed a quick call to the hospital and found out that Jacob still wasn't faring well and only family would be allowed to visit. With tears in her eyes she put on coffee, wondering if there was anything she could do for him. He'd loved music. She wished she'd be allowed to go to the hospital with her small harp and play for him. Maybe it would make him sleep easier.

She stared in the direction of her musical instruments and realized that was something she could do regardless.

She ate a simple breakfast, mulling over the vagaries of life and decided that she'd sit inside this afternoon and work on that score she'd been trying to write. Jacob had been the one to challenge her to put it on paper. She smiled. Maybe he had the right of it after all. She didn't want to leave this earth without leaving behind something that expressed her years here on the planet. Something to justify her usage of the food she ate and the air she breathed. It was a different concept, but it felt right to her. In fact, as she washed up the few dishes she'd used, she had to wonder if that wasn't a gift she could give to Jacob when he woke up.

Writing that score would require a little bit more of herself than she'd given so far. Jacob would appreciate her making that effort.

Empowered, she walked into the living room and sat down with a notebook at her side. A habit she'd yet to break. She'd never learned Braille – another bit of defiance on her part. She'd turned to audio books when her sight had disappeared.

She turned on her laptop then opened her file. She loved that she was still connected to the world digitally. She took notes through her voice-recognition program and always recorded her music on her laptop as well. She had a special keyboard and software all donated by the Society for the Blind. Accepting it had been difficult, but she hadn't wanted to be completely cut off from the world to the extent of not having a computer.

The speakers didn't offer the best sound, but hearing her music playing back meant she had the ability to tweak the notes to make it perfect. She listened to the recording of what she'd written so far and had to admit that it wasn't half bad. Now if only she could finish it.

She picked up her harp and drew her fingers across the strings, a smile lighting up inside, the graceful, haunting notes filling the room. In her mind's eye she could see the purple notes rippling through the room. She deliberately added a red, then a turquoise, and followed it by several white strands, watching as the colors rippled and played as her music lifted and fell with their actions. She knew the colors were the music and the music was the colors, but sometimes it seemed they had a life of their own. She couldn't always tell which came first. She just knew together they created something special. She struggled to work on the composition the way she had it, but her mind wouldn't let go of the colors.

Finally, she put down the harp and thought about it. "Maybe it *is* better to let the colors come first and see what I can design, ignoring the music, then listen to the playback and see how bad it is."

With that decision, feeling a little silly she let her fingers ripple across the strings, pulling the combinations she already knew would bring forward the specific colors she wanted and let them dance and play in the air in front of her. She gave herself over to the joy of creation and let the colors slip, move, and dance as they seemed to need to do.

Eyes closed, relishing the joy of color, she lost herself in her art.

A long time later, her arms aching, her lower back sore

and grumbling from being in the same position for too long, she pulled back and let her fingers slow. The same haunting refrain she'd started with drifted across the room, a ghostly accompaniment to her music. A fitting end. She bowed her head and a shudder rippled down to her toes.

Straightening, she stretched her arms over her head. "Now let's see how that sounded."

She lowered her arms and her fingers danced across the keyboard, sending the recording to the beginning. She hit the play button and sat back to listen.

The same haunting refrain filled the room as the first part of the tune played from her laptop's poor speakers. "Not half bad. Not brilliant, but…"

Then it shifted. The tempo became lively, energized, then skipping faster and faster into a crescendo of joy. In her mind she could see the same colors as she'd originally played them with her music. She sat in wonder for the first time, really being able to focus on the colors, and realized the shades were beautiful, but the music that had created them…was absolutely brilliant.

"Oh my," she laughed, clapping her hands together. "What would Jacob say?"

"He'd say it was perfect," said the weird pale ghost she'd seen yesterday. His features were indistinct yet glowing.

She was surprised he was still there. "What's perfect?" she asked, wondering just what he saw, if anything.

"Both," he said. "The music and the painting."

He looked at her in a way that made her think he understood. "And I'd have to agree with Jacob."

She shook her head. "I don't understand. How can you see the colors?"

"Why shouldn't I be able to?"

"Huh? Because you're dead?"

He hesitated, then murmured in a gentle voice, "Am I?"

And just like that he winked out.

She stared where he'd been in shock. She'd had similar conversations with many ghosts.

Please let that not be Jacob. Her hand instinctively went to the phone in her pocket. She almost didn't want to call in case he had died. She sat back, her phone in her hand, and remembered she'd had that conversation with Caslo several times as well. But he'd been dead for decades.

Just to be sure she called the hospital. And smiled. Jacob was still fighting the good fight.

Determinedly, she picked up her laptop to listen to the music again when the phone rang. It was her eye doctor. A few minutes later she hung up, wondering if this was good news or bad news. The specialist wanted to see her again. In her office. That part Celina didn't like as it meant travelling to a new place, and she wasn't sure what to think about seeing the specialist again. She remembered both the wonderful inner sensation she'd experienced – if that had been Dr. Maddy's work – but she also remembered the horrific pain.

If the pain had been the result of something the specialist did Celina wanted nothing to do with her. Neither could she forget the threat from her nasty voice in her head. He could make things very ugly for her. She had to get rid of him. But how?

STEFAN DROPPED INTO bed. He'd been grabbing two-hour stints of shut-eye for days now. He needed so much more. Celina was a pressing issue that dominated his thoughts. He was desperate to have her safe and healthy again. Hell, he was just desperate to have her in his life.

Just as he closed his eyes his phone rang.

He glared at the ceiling then realized who was calling. He picked up the phone. "What's up, Maddy?"

"I have Celina coming for a second appointment tomorrow morning at nine. I think you should be here to see what I see."

Bolting upright, he hopped off the bed and paced his room. "Is that a good idea? She only knows me as the consultant for the police."

"And whose fault is that? Do you really want to avoid her or do you want to be able to get to know her on a different level? She needs your help, Stefan."

He winced. "I'm not sure I'm the person to help her," he said honestly.

"If you aren't, I'm not sure who else could. There is a blockage in her head that's causing her great pain."

"Is the blockage hers? I've seen her walls. She has an impressive self-defense system."

"Yes and no. There is a foreign feel to it, but I don't sense another person in there."

"Hmmm." He waited but realized there was no other option. Besides, there wasn't much he wouldn't do to see her again. "I'll be there." And he hung up.

He lay back down and slowly worked the stress out of his system. His mind relaxed. He yawned once, then twice, and rolled over.

And was dropped into a vision. A young mother worked in a kitchen prepping food. Two toddlers ran around her kitchen. One was screaming and one chasing. Within seconds the screams turned to laughter and the two boys reversed roles to run back through the kitchen in reverse.

Stefan studied the image, trying to see his purpose into this window. The woman eased a hand down to rub her lower back. She stood still for a long moment, her head bowed. She appeared to be focusing on her breathing.

The light into the kitchen vision had a dim look as if faded. He'd often understood that to mean a past vision rather than the bright clarity of something happening currently. As he tried to make sense of it the woman reached for a cloth and ran it under the cold water. Wringing it out, she folded it into a square and placed the cloth against her lower back. She gasped several times and a sheen of sweat broke out on her forehead. She collapsed against the sink, the noise of the boys completely dominating the sad, desperate scene. There was black surrounding the region of her liver.

Stefan understood what was coming next. Nothing he could do but watch and try to see the details. He'd tapped into this for a reason, but which one?

The woman reached into her pocket and pulled out a cell phone even as she did a slow slide to the floor, her hand still holding the cloth in place. At least he could now see her face. And the pain that ravaged her gentle features, the gray cast to her skin. Whatever was wrong, it wasn't new. She'd been ill for a long time. He frowned as she appeared to send out a text. She leaned her head back against the cupboard.

One boy saw her and recognized that something wasn't right. He ran to her and crawled onto her lap. "Mommy, what's wrong?"

The other boy came running behind him.

She grabbed them both and held on tight.

Stefan snapped back to his bedroom and closed his eyes as a shudder wrapped around his heart.

He had no way to know what the woman was experiencing except potentially a burning sensation in the lower back.

However the vision was just a little too close to one of the files Brandt had given him.

Therefore the odds of her having survived this trauma were not great.

SAM SAT AT the end of the dock near the lake. This was their home now. Brandt and the Carlsons had come to an agreement over the price and the papers had been signed yesterday. She couldn't believe the difference such a thing made in her life. She felt grounded here. Needed, but at rest.

Now if only the weird visions would ease up. She sat, head tilted to the afternoon sun, Soldier and Moses at her side.

And screamed.

No warning. From one instant to the next her lower back caught fire and unbearable heat slammed into her right side. She cried, her eyes open, staring out over the cool water but couldn't explain it. Any of it. Soldier jumped to his feet, a low, deep growl in the back of his throat. He walked closer and nudged her gently with his muzzle.

She managed to reach out a hand and hold onto his huge head. She gasped as the heat built higher, hotter, stronger… and then just like that – it stopped.

She shuddered and burrowed her face into Soldier's neck.

Another one. Another insight into someone else's pain… Another person suffering with Sam being unable to help.

Then she burst into tears.

YES! IT WAS working. He was gaining strength every day. He

had no idea how far and wide he'd been spread, but pulling the plug on a few of the more major ones had helped a lot. His recovery was almost immediate after each session, and that made it so much easier to keep his focus. He didn't want to take all the pathways out, but given that he could think so much clearer it made this a doable option. And he had only so many that he could control. Most were only little bits and pieces and he could sense them out there in a fog, but it wasn't enough to grab onto and do something with.

And he wanted to do something. If this was his current existence, he wanted to be in control.

Not the other way around.

JACOB SAT AS still as a ghost and almost laughed at his own joke. There was nothing funny about this situation. As far as he could figure out his body was in a coma and he was lost outside. He'd been worrying about how to get back ever since he'd first recognized what had happened. He couldn't be dead because the machines at his bedside continued to beep and nurses came and went on a regular basis. There were also a few regular visitors.

His brother had popped in to glare down at his still form, and if he hadn't seen the fists clenched Jacob would have assumed his brother was angry. Instead, he'd taken it to mean that his brother was frustrated at his inability to help Jacob. And that would fit. His big brother had been looking after him for eons. This wasn't going to be easy on him either.

His mom had been a mainstay at his side, and that had brought nonexistent tears to his eyes. He'd been a trial for her for a long time. That she still came was a sign of something he just now understood.

Real love. Love that went beyond the physical. Love that went beyond the relationships he'd experienced thus far in his life. He'd loved his mother, but like so many families they'd all drifted apart. He was saddened by that now. She hadn't heard from him in weeks, and as he cast his mind back he realized it was really months. Many months.

He winced. Why was that? He loved her. Loved to spend time with her, so where had all the time gone? He stared around the large room and wondered at the other coma patients in there. There were three others. But he didn't see them wandering the halls like he was. Or if they were, they were at a different vibration or something. He'd heard something like that mentioned before but had thought it was all hogwash.

He wanted to see that young woman who'd popped up and scared him shitless, then disappeared as if the joke was on him. And there was no doubt about that. Her name was Lissa, she'd said. But he'd been too freaked out to talk to her. She'd been like seriously see-through. What was with that? What was with the change in scenery?

Then she'd disappeared – as in poofed into a puff of smoke – and had taken the whole outdoor garden scene with her.

He closed his eyes and leaned back, the seat rest poking through his head.

This was the most incredibly scary, most horrifying experience he'd ever been through.

And now the loneliest.

And there she was again.

"Ha. I thought you wanted to stay isolated in your little world, so I left you alone." Lissa gave him an impish grin. "How about now?"

CHAPTER 13

CELINA DRESSED CAREFULLY the next day. She had a long morning ahead. The changing seasons were both a blessing and a curse. The morning temperature in no way matched the afternoon temperature, and it was easy to freeze or boil out there. She'd heard the forecaster calling for sun but hadn't been able to feel any heat in the rays coming through the window. Maybe he'd meant later as in *much* later. She'd be home by then.

Collecting her purse and phone, she took the stairs down to the main floor hoping the cab would be waiting for her. Thankfully it was. The driver hopped out and came around to open the door for her. She thanked him and gave him the address to The Haven, where Dr. Maddy's office resided.

Surprise in his voice, he said, "No problem. That's quite the place. I sure hope you're going to see Dr. Maddy. If anyone can help you it will be her."

"Really?" How odd that he'd mention the one specialist she was going to see. "That is who I'm going to see, but I hadn't realized she was that well-known."

"Oh, she is!" The cabbie laughed. "She's got magic fingers. My brother's boy was badly broken up after a major accident. Docs said he'd never walk again and likely never be able to use his arms after all those breaks, but she got a hold of him and that's what she did – pure magic." He shook his head. "My nephew walks and plays video games now. He's never going to be a running back for his school, but he's planning on heading back up the mountain this winter to learn snowboarding."

The admiration in his voice surprised her. Celina had no idea the specialist had such a reputation. It did make her feel better about going to see her.

Maybe Dr. Maddy could help her after all.

Too bad she couldn't help her with the ghost problem.

At The Haven the cabbie parked and opened her door, then walked her inside and straight to the wall of elevators. He asked, "Are you okay from here?"

"I'm fine. Thank you for being so kind."

"Hey, I'm happy to bring anyone here. Are you sure you don't need me to wait?"

"I do need a ride home, but I don't know how long I'll be."

A business card was pressed into her hand. "No problem. Give me a call when you're done. I should be able to get back in time to pick you up."

She paid him and with a smile stepped into the elevator.

"I've punched the button for Maddy's floor. You're alone in here, so stay on until you get to the right floor." And then the elevator doors closed and he was gone.

She mused about the kindness of some people. Many cab drivers wouldn't have left their vehicle. This one had escorted her into the elevator. A nice man. The elevator went straight up. She listened to the computer voice count off the floors until it stopped. She laughed when the elevator computer said, "Maddy's Floor."

"Someone has a sense of humor," she said under her breath as she stepped out.

Using her stick she took several steps forward, expecting to hear the sounds of an office. Someone on a keyboard and someone else on a phone. There was only a gentle breeze blowing at her from the right. She turned in that direction, wondering about the strong wind when she sensed something else.

She stopped. Her head turned to the left and her nostrils flared. Her heart slammed against her ribs. She hadn't seen him since her weird lucid dream. And yet here he was. His presence felt right. And that just meant she was losing it. She said, "Stefan Kronos?"

And felt his surprise. She grinned.

"Yes. You have great instincts," he said.

"And you have a great aftershave." One she hadn't thought she'd smell again. Still, he'd made such an impression on her she willed his effect to be less strong today. And couldn't. This man, whoever he was, commanded the space around him. She'd love to be able to see him in reality. She wasn't into fantasy men, but dreaming about gorgeous males, at least gorgeous according to Jillian, had to be good for her heart and soul.

Surely.

"You here to see Dr. Maddy?"

"Yes, but as this is my first visit I'm not at all sure where to go," she confessed.

"Then let me help you." He picked up her hand, tucked it into the crook of his arm and led her forward. "Maddy's office is right here."

"She might not be ready to see me," Celina warned. "Isn't there a dragon secretary guarding the door?"

"No dragons here." he said.

A booming laugh broke out of him and she had to smile.

What was it about this man that made him so comfortable to be around and so familiar, yet so unique and so… right?

She didn't take to strangers. And that's where this situation deviated. He was no stranger. She just didn't understand why not.

STEFAN WALKED CELINA down the hallway toward Dr. Maddy's inner office. He loved this place. The ambience was hushed with love and healing. Surely no one could miss the extraordinary atmosphere. He watched Celina lift her head slightly and relax a little with each step. Her smile loosened, and when she took a deep breath and released it slowly he knew she was accepting the benefits of being surrounded by strong healing vibes. He liked to visit to get his fix too. The wing at the children's hospital was the same. Both places functioned like a micro ecosystem for healing. Each location required a tremendous amount of energy to maintain, although as the people healed they in turn added that positive healing energy back in. Each new patient had to go through a specific regime to get in. And each place could only accept so many at once. The energy level needed to be raised to accept the new lower-vibration additions so that the energy of the whole area balanced out in such a way to remain equalized for the other patients.

And the system was working. The children's hospital had some incredible results. Then again, children were so much more open to energetic healing than adults.

Stefan slid a sideways glance toward Celina, loving the way peace had settled on her classic features. High cheekbones, huge silvery eyes, and a wide, mobile mouth. He forced himself to look away. He was a long ways from being able to kiss her, and that fact drove him into frustration every damn time he saw her.

"Problems?"

"No." He glanced at her again. "Not at all."

"Oh. It just seemed like you were pulling away. I know I make some people uncomfortable."

"Not me," he said quietly. "You could never do that."

"Oh." This time humor tinged her voice. "Why is that?"

"I could say you're too beautiful, and it would be the truth, but chances are you wouldn't like hearing that."

She gave an indelicate snort. "It's not my looks that people see. They only see that I'm blind."

"And they are missing out on seeing something very special." He knew his voice had dropped – despite his best efforts – but hoped she didn't hear the longing in his voice.

When she stared directly at him, her brows together in a small frown, he knew she had. Whether she'd understood the emotion was a different story.

"There you are." Dr. Maddy's voice intruded into the arcing energy between him and Celina. Damn. Crappy timing. Still, Celina was here to see Maddy.

"I was just showing her to your office," Stefan said with a smile, stepping back slightly.

"Thank you." Dr. Maddy waited for them to pass inside before she stepped in and closed the door.

Celina cocked her head to one side. "You have a beautiful place here, Dr. Maddy. I don't think I've ever been to another place with a sense of peace as there is here."

"Thank you. We do good work here." Dr. Maddy shifted to her desk and sat down. "Celina, there is a chair on the left hand side – please sit down. Stefan, I'm going to ask you to wait outside for the time being."

He nodded and walked to the door.

"For the time being?" Celina asked. "Why is he here at all?"

Dr. Maddy laughed. "For lots of reasons. I'll explain in a moment."

And Stefan knew he'd been dismissed. Hating to, he stepped out into the hallway and closed the door behind him.

MADDY STUDIED THE troubled young woman in front of her. Celina had recognized Stefan as she'd expected, but as Stefan was so much more than a consultant in a field that she likely had little knowledge about, she didn't know how to start.

Then she remembered something Stefan had mentioned earlier.

"Celina, this question is likely to come out of the blue, but I do have a few reasons for asking so please answer as honestly as you can. And no, I won't judge you for your answers or withhold treatment if you think they are wrong. I just want the truth."

She watched Celina straighten and a protective shield drop down over her aura. Stefan scored a point there. Her defenses were impressive. So Maddy took a deep breath and said, "Can you see ghosts?"

"OKAY, RANDY, WE'RE going to change your diet and tweak your meds slightly, then I want to see you back in a couple of weeks."

The doctor wrote something on a pad of paper, ripped

the top sheet off, and handed it to him.

Randy stared at the new prescription, wondering when this nightmare would be over. He understood he was alive because of the surgery, but was it a life worth having? He'd been in pain ever since the transplant. He'd wanted to live desperately when it looked like he wasn't going to, but now that he was, he wondered if he'd cheated death and was paying for it.

One of the medications was giving him horrible nightmares, and he woke up in a cold sweat more often than not. Every time he came to explain the various problems his doctor just changed the drugs.

As he stared down at the paper in his hand, he wondered at what point in time a person had enough.

He'd lost his own wife a couple of months ago, and every day he wondered if this kidney that had saved his life wouldn't be better off saving someone else's.

You know what to do.

He did.

If he'd listened to that voice he'd have done it already. Now he realized the voice was correct.

He stared down at the prescription and couldn't help but think that if he took the whole bottle his pain would finally be over.

Do it, the voice urged. *You know it's what you want.*

That he did. Feeling better than he had in long time, he headed to the pharmacy to get his prescription filled. This was the answer. One he could live with – or not.

CHAPTER 14

CELINA FROZE AT the question. She wanted to bolt as far and as fast as she could away from there. Yet the lure of what Dr. Maddy might be able to do for her kept her glued in place.

"Why would you ask such a question?" she protested.

"Because I think you do, and I know someone else who does."

The smile in Dr. Maddy's voice had Celina instinctively smiling back. How did that work? "You're joking, right?"

"No, I'm not." And she waited.

Celina grimaced. "And what bearing does that question have on why I'm here?"

"Because although I don't see dead people per se, I do see energy. Maddy's Floor is an energetic healing project."

Maddy launched into an explanation that had Celina's jaw dropping. She gaped. How could she not? This woman was a doctor. Had numerous degrees. Appeared to be a smart, beautiful woman who cared. And here she was talking about something so esoteric, something so far out there, so foreign to Celina that the talk of ghosts slid into being a minor side discussion.

She couldn't help her head moving from side to side.

Dr. Maddy laughed, a joyous sound that held Celina entranced. There was no way she could call this woman crazy, and it was obvious it came from her heart, but this…she couldn't help but turn toward the exit.

"A bit much, is it?" Her beautiful laughter twinkled around the room again. "And I'm not crazy."

A wave of heat washed over Celina's cheeks. "I'm sorry," she muttered. "It's just so…" She stopped and shrugged helplessly.

"Energy is energy regardless of the form, and I make good use of it here. Now I'm not trying to convert you to our way of doing things, but healing happens in wonderful ways. I think the doctor who did your eye surgery is correct in that everything went well and there is no physical reason why you can't see." She smiled.

Celina stilled. This was what she'd come for. She held her breath and waited.

"When I saw you last," Dr. Maddy continued slowly, "I ran a quick scan of your energy and saw a blockage around your eyes."

"A blockage?" Celina leaned forward, her unseeing gaze intent on the doctor. And damn near thought she'd caught the doctor smiling.

"I don't understand what you mean by a blockage. Surely there'd be a lot of pain if I had a blockage?" She frowned and eased back slightly. "And Dr. Jorgenson would have seen something as destructive as that, wouldn't he have?"

"Exactly." Dr. Maddy beamed.

Celina felt warm, as though waves of benevolence were coming towards her. She had no idea what was going on, but it was starting to feel like she'd dropped into another world. She wanted to be open and able to receive whatever good things Dr. Maddy had going on here, yet this was starting to go way past her comfort zone.

"He would have. So would I. However, I can see a level most doctors can't. For instance, I can tell right now that you're feeling extremely out of your depth. Wondering if I'm a little off and whether you've wasted your time coming here. You have hopeful energy about being here, but that's been cut back by over half since I started talking. I can also tell you that you are draining a lot of much-needed energy to old friends, as if you are the one that can't let go. That you are holding a few people, special people, very close to your heart. As if in the very act of protecting them you can save them from harm."

Celina listened in shock. She swallowed hard. She wanted to refute the words as they flew her way, but for the most part the doctor was right on. "Look, I don't know how much of this I believe. The real issue is this blockage. If it's there… can you remove it? Is it stopping me from seeing? And if you remove it, will I be able to see again?"

"All good questions. The answers are…I don't know. I can't say why for sure. I've never seen anything quite like your case before." She said it with such honesty that Celina believed her.

"Then what do you know?"

"I know that I can go in and—"

"Go in?" Celina asked in alarm. "More surgery?"

"No, not at all."

Celina listened to Dr. Maddy's hair swish about her shoulders as she shook her head. There was something light in here, something…almost joyful. She was desperate to stay, but didn't know why. The place just felt right.

"There will be no surgery at this time, likely not at any time. I'm here to see what that blockage is and why it's there."

"Can you do anything about it?" Celina asked.

"Absolutely. Remember last time, when I did a sweep up toward your eyes?"

"That was you?" Celina gasped, remembering the horrible pain…and then the threats. She didn't know what to think. Except… she didn't want the asshole back. At all. But she definitely didn't want him to feel like she was trying to get rid of him.

"And that brings us to ghosts."

Celina, her mind locked onto the ghost that had been terrorizing her since forever, almost missed Dr. Maddy's comment. Then when it registered she had to wonder if the woman hadn't read her mind. Did she know about her haunting? Could anyone see that? Was that predator one of the people she had in her space or one she held close to her heart – her mind immediately dismissed that – or was he connected to her eyes? She'd been arguing with him for so long about seeing, but she'd never imagined he could have a physical impact on her ability to see. Not really. She'd been denying him, but as she hadn't been actually able to see she couldn't do what he wanted anyway.

Still, she didn't know what he could do with what little she had.

And he didn't believe her.

Or he wouldn't believe her.

Then again, she was trying to give a ghost a reasoning brain, and they didn't have that as she'd long since found out. They had a narrow focus that narrowed further the longer they walked this plane. He was locked on her sight, or lack of it, and couldn't leave the subject. It was driving her crazy.

"Celina?"

She started. "Sorry, I was just…"

"Thinking about the crazy idea of energy and ghosts. I thought if you saw ghosts you would have a more open opinion to the concept of energy being in different forms in a way that so many people couldn't understand."

"I do. And I don't."

The chair squeaked across from her. She winced. "I do see ghosts. Or I used to. Now I think I just imagine them. Because I can't see anything anymore."

She sighed. "At least not like I used to."

STEFAN KNEW HE shouldn't be listening in. But his senses were super jacked where Celina was concerned and Dr. Maddy had opened the door between them, letting him hear the conversation. He was happy that Celina had admitted to seeing ghosts, but the latter part of her comment worried him. He'd seen too many psychics unable to understand or to handle what was happening in their world. Too often they went quietly insane. Or if they sought out help and got the wrong kind, they spent the remainder of their lives in a drugged stupor. That Celina was afraid she was imagining ghosts was the same thing, just in her own quietly tortured way.

He felt for her. For all that he'd checked up on her, he'd been unable to reach out and help her. Something he'd always regretted. He'd been in the camp of "leave alone what wasn't his to touch," and he'd followed it religiously. But he might have been able to make her last year so much easier.

Still, she'd always resisted letting him get any closer, even after all this time. It was all he could do to stand back and let it all be. It was her body and her physical space. That meant it was her call.

But he could help her.

If she let him.

If Dr. Maddy let him.

"SO, ERIC, I hear you are having some problems."

Eric looked up at the doctor and his minicomputer. He'd like a little computer to play on but he didn't like the doctor. Any of them. No one understood. No one cared. They all thought he was making the monster up. He wasn't.

"Your mother says you aren't sleeping well. Now that's too bad," the doctor said in a too-happy voice. "You need rest to heal."

Eric stared at him, waiting for the usual heart-listening, back-listening, head-patting, writing on the tablet, and leaving. It happened every day around the same time.

And every day Eric didn't say anything. The monster had told him what would happen if he did.

The monster would do something horrible to Mom.

MADDY SHIFTED POSITION. She was in the corner of her office with Celina sitting in the chair as she had been before. They'd gotten to the point of Celina allowing her to take a look inside. She needed to make this fast for everyone's sake, especially Stefan, who paced outside.

Maddy closed her eyes, took a deep breath, and jumped free of her body. The process worked so easily now that it was almost a mind switch and she was out. She moved toward the quiet woman and, using the anchors she'd placed inside before on her previous trip, found herself back inside the base of Celina's skull. She hadn't blended with the energy this time. Instead, she opted to get a better view of the blockage.

She needed to see what was behind this problem.

With that in mind she slipped closer slowly, trying not to enter Celina's mind but stay separate psychologically and move between the organic structures to see the physicality of the blockage. Moments later she realized that there was none.

There was no physical impediment surrounding her eyes. If there was a blockage it was on either a mental, emotional, or energetic level.

Or most likely – all three.

"HOW ARE YOU?" Jacob asked Lissa, his see-through visitor. He was so damn grateful to have anyone to talk to he was afraid he'd say the wrong thing and she'd disappear. "I don't understand how you know me."

"Oh, I don't know you. Hadn't met you before you went into a coma," she said with a bright, translucent smile. A smile he could see right through.

He hated to ask personal information, but he really needed to know how to get out of this situation and hopefully back into his body where he might be able to wake up.

"Are you in a coma too?"

She laughed, a bright tinkle of sound that floated throughout the small room. "No, I'm not in a coma. I'm dead."

He swallowed hard and stared at her. "How can you talk to me if you're dead? I'm still alive." He motioned to his body, lying beside them. "I'm trying to figure out how to get back inside my body."

"You still have that option, but I don't. I died a long time ago. I kept trying to contact my sister after I'd died, but it took a while to sort things out. I refused to leave until I could though."

"As you are still here I presume you never managed to contact her."

"Oh, sure I have. It's great fun to be able to catch up with her. I love her very much."

He frowned. "So why stay now, then? Surely you're supposed to move on."

Her face twisted. "Maybe, and maybe not. I found that I have something to offer people while I'm here, so I do my best to learn and grow. I don't know what comes after this stage, and I'm not sure I want to know," she said with honesty. "I like my life here and I am learning to do more and more things. It can be lonely at times, which is why it's fun to meet people like you."

"Like me?"

"Sure – people caught in between. I've met a few ghosts too," she said in a commonplace tone of voice, "but they are often more zombie than alive."

He didn't want to ask too closely what she meant by that zombie comment, and his mind kept returning to her caught in-between comment. "Is that what I am? Caught between life and death?"

She studied him. "You tell me. This is your experience. You created this. Are you alive?" Lissa motioned to the form on the bed. "If you call that alive," she continued, then swung her arm toward him. "Or are you dead?"

Jacob winced. "I want to be alive."

"Then what's stopping you?"

He stared at the strange girl and her easy grasp of a situation that would drive him insane. She was so accepting. So complacent. "I don't know how to get back into my body."

"Pssshhh. Sure you do. It's easy. Just go lie down. Your body and soul know what to do naturally. The problem here is that something is stopping you from going back. That's the issue you have to solve before you can return."

There seemed to be an inkling of truth to her words, but he had no idea what problem he would possibly need to solve.

"Don't worry about it," she said with a smile. "You'll figure it out." She started to fade in front of his eyes. "Or not."

"Wait…"

And she was gone.

Damn it. He stared at his body and tried to figure out why he wouldn't want to go back to his old life.

CHAPTER 15

CELINA SHIFTED UNCOMFORTABLY in her chair. She understood in theory what the doctor had said she was going to do, but it still sounded like a sci-fi movie. Her mind couldn't let go of the concept of a blockage. If there was such a thing, then was it possible she'd get her eyesight back?

Her stomach wiggled. It's what she'd desperately wanted, but wanting didn't mean anything.

As she pondered whether she could be so lucky, a knife slashed out across her brain. She cried out. And the pain stopped. She gasped for breath, waiting for a return of the attack. When nothing happened she relaxed and waited for the doctor to continue. She didn't feel anything. She frowned, wondering if she should turn around or wait. Dr. Maddy had said not to move.

She waited. And waited. Then unable to help herself, she turned in Dr. Maddy's direction and realized the other woman's breathing had changed. Become deep. Slow. Too slow.

Celina bolted to her feet and raced over. She reached out her hand when the door opened and Stefan raced in. "Don't touch her," he cried.

Her arm froze in midair. She stared in his direction, hearing him drop to the floor. Then nothing. No movement. No sound. What was he doing? "I don't know what happened to her," she cried.

"It's all right. I can help her. Just sit back and let me work."

Confused but grateful, Celina fumbled her way back to her chair. "Is she going to be okay?"

"Yes, but I have to bring her back. Please sit down in your chair and don't move. I'll talk to you in a few moments."

And he went quiet.

Deadly quiet.

Celina waited nervously. She didn't know what was going on, but Stefan seemed to have it in control. But he wasn't calling for help. In fact, he'd gone so quiet himself she had to wonder if *he* was okay.

A weird hum filled the office. She searched the room for the source. And found nothing. Just a weird noise to go with her weird visit at the weird specialist. The noise grew louder and louder.

Then it stopped, just like that. She closed her eyes for a few seconds and prayed that both people were going to be okay. She opened her eyes and froze. Two figures stood before her. Two bright, glowing figures. Not ghosts. Or at least if they were ghosts, they were like none she'd seen before.

One male and the other female.

And damned if she didn't suddenly get it. "It's you two, isn't it?" she cried. "I can see both of you. But you look...so different."

A light musical laughter filled the room... or was it her mind? Celina didn't know. She didn't care. She couldn't believe what her eyes were seeing. "Really, it's you?"

"It's us. What do you see?"

"Two figures. Both of you more like glow sticks with shapes, and as you move there are bits and pieces of your colors floating off behind you."

Stefan laughed. "That's very good. What colors do you see?"

"Dr. Maddy is a luminescent green and you are all gold," she whispered, both entranced and horrified.

"Are you…" and she stopped, having trouble getting the rest of the sentence out of her mouth. She gulped. In a rush the words poured out. "Are you both dead?"

And damned if they didn't laugh again.

Stefan shook his head, wisps of energy drifting off in all directions. She was fascinated. "If you aren't dead, why can I see you?"

"That's a very good question. What you are seeing is our energetic forms. Do you recognize that your eyes are closed? You opened your inner eyes."

Her hands reached up, gently touching her eyelids.

Her eyes shot open. They were right. Now she couldn't see them. She spun around and searched the small office in case they'd moved on her. Slowly she turned back and deliberately closed her eyes…and she saw them inside her mind. Or against the back of her eyelids. She didn't know how that worked.

"How is that possible?" she asked in wonder. "This is how I see ghosts, true, but you look different." She struggled for the right words, knowing they were looking for more of an explanation. In the end she could only say, "You look… alive."

Dr. Maddy laughed and said, "Good. That's the way we should look. We'll come back now, and then I can go over what I saw in your head."

Her words had Celina freezing in place. Dr. Maddy had been inside her head. God. How could any of this be possible?

She reached out for her chair, stilling when a male hand reached out and directed her hand toward the left. She followed his lead and sank into her chair with a sigh of relief. She whispered, "Thank you."

His fingers stroked down hers and lingered for a long moment before finally drifting away, his touch as soft as a summer's breeze but as caring as a lover's kiss. She was deeply touched. Who was this man who could walk in energetic form and be a consultant for both the police and Dr. Maddy? How his role here worked she had no idea.

But she wanted to know.

She wanted to get to know him better, except he already seemed to know her – a little too well. Yet that in itself was intriguing. Disturbing but... intriguing at the same time. Like a fly drawn to the shiny web in front of her, she was taking steps that in her heart she knew she probably shouldn't but couldn't stop herself from doing so regardless.

She sighed and turned her head to the muted conversation going on at her side. Coffee – they were discussing coffee. Hesitantly she asked, "If coffee is an option then yes, please."

Dr. Maddy said, "It definitely is. I'm going to make myself a latte – will you join me?"

Celina brightened. She'd expected a simple drip system. "That would be lovely, thank you."

"I'll make them," Stefan said. "You two can discuss the recent events."

"Yes, what happened to you?" Celina asked curiously. "I thought you'd had a heart attack or something equally horrible. Then Stefan came racing inside and next thing I know you're in that weird energetic form that I could see." Celina tilted her head and waited to hear the answer.

"I was trying to observe the blackness in your head and was able to determine that it wasn't organic like a tumor, but energetic, as in a non-energy mass." There was wry humor in her voice as she added, "That's the good news."

"How is that good news?" She couldn't stop herself from reaching up to brush her fingers over her temple and eyes. "It sounds horrible."

"It's interesting. The next thing, and something I wasn't able to determine, is whether you have put this blockage in place or if you have allowed someone else to."

"Allowed?" she cried in outrage. "I'd never allow someone to do that."

"Actually," Stefan interrupted, the sounds of a milk steamer going on behind Dr. Maddy, "in order for someone to have done this they had to have your acceptance at some point in time. It could potentially have been a long time ago. But somewhere along the line you agreed."

She shook her head. "I'd never have agreed."

"That's the thing," Dr. Maddy said. "You might not have agreed to this, but you agreed to whatever this started as."

"That's horrible," Celina whispered. "I'd never have agreed if I'd known."

"Don't be too upset, as we don't know what this is yet," Stefan said.

She couldn't help but stare toward him. "That's hardly reassuring. Whether I know or understand any of this, to know that I have something going on inside my head is horrifying."

Stefan silently finished making the coffees and delivered the drinks.

Lifting the cup to her mouth Celina took a tiny sip, trying to marshal her thoughts. She couldn't get her mind wrapped around what they were trying to tell her. How real was this blockage? She really didn't know anything about this type of work. And that was something she had to rectify. She'd never blindly believed anyone. Still, she couldn't doubt that there had been a horrific pain that she also couldn't explain. She'd had no physical reason for that pain. The eye surgeon had said everything looked good. She'd been through a ton of tests originally and they'd found nothing. No one had ever found a physical, tangible reason for her blindness. Now she was faced with the intangible reasons.

And if all else doesn't make sense, then what's left must be true.

She sighed. "Okay. Tell me more."

STEFAN HATED TO hear the overwhelmed tone in her voice. He knew this was tough for most people. He felt for her but knew he was limited in what he could do at the moment.

"What do you want to know?" he asked.

She turned toward him, narrowed her gaze – as if she could see him – and said, "What does any of this have to do with you?"

He grinned. "I should have realized. I'm sorry. I left you my card but as it's not in Braille…" He kicked himself for not having made it clear before. "I work with energy. In all forms. I also work on the energy dome surrounding Maddy's project here. She's a specialist in healing energy. I don't have her skills in that way, but I can see and do a lot in other things."

Her silvery eyes locked on him. He could almost see the wheels turning in her head as she mulled his words over.

"I'll leave that for the moment." She turned to face Dr. Maddy. "You said this blockage could be something I did to myself. I can't understand how or for what reason I would do this. Can you?"

Dr. Maddy shifted closer in her chair. Stefan leaned back against the coffee counter and watched her move smoothly into her healer mode. She was so good. Such natural, warm instincts. Waves of soothing blue and healing green and light pink for joy wafted toward Celina. He watched as the energy ribbons stroked over Celina's ruffled aura, easing back her stress and lightening up her depression. It was so subtle that for some it would be the same effect as a warm, caring hug. In Maddy's case, that hug could do so much more. She was truly gifted.

He watched Celina shift back in her chair and relax as her own energy eased up and let some of Maddy's into its space. Together the energy warmed and worked on soothing the frayed edges of her emotions. She had to be feeling better.

He tuned back in to the conversation. Dr. Maddy was going into a light variation of how people we cared about could stay behind.

"Meaning that someone I care about could be doing this?"

Dr. Maddy hesitated. "That's possible. It's also possible that the person you care about is not who they are on the inside. Time and conditions can twist anyone."

Celina's lower lip trembled. Oh shit. Stefan cast around for something to add to the conversation when Maddy said,

"It could also be someone that you cared about and is long gone."

The lip firmed and Celina's gaze sharpened. She leaned forward and asked, caution in her voice, "Are you saying the person doing this could be dead? As in a ghost?"

At the affirmative answer Celina sank back and closed her eyes for a long moment. "You know this sounds really crazy, don't you?"

"It can't sound any crazier than some cases I've been involved with," Stefan said. "Cases that involved the dead or disassociated, and yes, ghosts."

Startled, she turned that stunning gaze on him. "I find this all so strange."

Yet her energy wasn't showing shock. In fact, there was acceptance and some understanding filtering through her aura.

"But not really." Dr. Maddy smiled. "You already see ghosts. You have contact with the recently deceased and with the not-so-recently deceased. This is just one further step."

Celina took a deep, shaky breath. "Given that this is all a tremendous amount of information to absorb and I can't possibly get a handle on it all right now, maybe we could just continue and you could tell me what happens next. What are we going to do?"

This was where it got tricky. Stefan knew she wouldn't like the answer.

"There is no clear-cut answer that we can give you. You are the one that needs to do some research into why this might be happening." Dr. Maddy frowned. "I can tell you that the couple of times I've come close to this blockage it has slashed out in an incredibly strong reaction and caused both you and I a great deal of pain."

Celina winced. "I remember. But I can't just go on with this in my head." Her voice rose at the end, alternately shocked and pleading, but ending with a tinge of anger.

"There are some things we can do," Stefan interrupted. That gaze pivoted his way. He asked her, "At the time that Dr. Maddy came close to the blockage, did you feel anything other than pain? Did you hear anyone talking to you? Did you notice anything different?"

Oh wow. He straightened up and watched in amazement as her aura immediately locked down, kicking Dr. Maddy's and his energy out and away from hers. Not just out, but pushed away. He could see both of their energies now drifting a good foot outside the edge of her aura.

"I guess the answer is yes," he murmured.

"Pardon?" The frown on her face deepened. "What do you mean?"

Stefan looked at Maddy to find her staring back at him.

Did she just do that and have no idea? she asked.

I think so. I think her defenses are so ingrained this is a natural response to any questioning that makes her uncomfortable.

Dr. Maddy turned to study Celina's energy. She was doing this but was almost disassociated from it. As if she set it up a long time ago and had forgotten about it.

"Are you two whispering?" Celina frowned. "What's happened?" she said in a sharp voice. "What's different?"

With a raised eyebrow at Maddy and her nod, Stefan said, "Remember I can see and work energy? And remember that a few moments ago you could see both Dr. Maddy and I in energetic form? Well, a few minutes ago our energy, which was soothing yours and helping to ease the tension in the back of your neck, was immediately kicked out of your aura – after I asked you that question."

Confusion rippled across her features. "Kicked out? Soothing the tension in my neck? I don't understand."

Dr. Maddy said in a gentle voice, "Maybe you don't consciously understand, but you have a strong defensive mechanism. It was totally fine for me to work on removing the knots along your neck and muscles, but Stefan's question triggered this defense, and in order to distance and detach yourself from the answer, your system locked down."

Silence.

"So the real question is…" Stefan paused then added, "What answer are you too scared to give?"

BRANDT WALKED INTO the cabin and called out, "Sam?"

No answer. He walked back outside and along the long deck. He had a few more case files to show her, hoping that something might trigger more flashes. He hated to do it to her because he knew these odd visions were causing her major trauma. If he could solve the problem and let her get some much-needed rest, then he'd do anything he could. He'd worked hard to put some extra flesh on her tiny frame and had watched in disbelief as it had all disappeared over these last weeks.

She shouldn't be getting these visions. They couldn't be connected to a single murderer. Most were surgical failures or accidents. But she'd insisted that they were both – connected and victims of a single murderer.

She hadn't been wrong as long as he'd known her, so he had to trust that she was right in this instance.

Not finding her inside the small cabin they both called home, he walked down toward the dock and whistled for

Soldier. The dog barked twice from the right. He traipsed through the small brush to find Sam curled up on a large rock under the waning heat of the sun.

Asleep.

Soldier and Moses were standing guard, one on either side.

His heart, a mushy part of him when it came to Sam, melted. He crouched beside her, debating whether he should wake her up or join the guards.

She murmured restlessly as he watched. He leaned closer, head tilted, wondering if she was trying to say something. After a moment he sat back on his heels and studied her. She didn't appear to be sleeping easy. Her breathing was shallow and the tiniest of frowns marred her beautiful face.

He reached out to cover her hand with his when she bolted upright, her face to the sky and her eyes – blind.

Then she screamed.

Joey Brown walked toward the diner. He couldn't wait for his meal. The diner made the best liver and onions he'd ever tasted. Considering he'd hated the stuff until a few months ago, he couldn't believe he was anticipating this meal. Before his breakup he'd never touched a lot of things that he really loved now. Green apples, sweet potatoes, garlic, and liver were just a few of them.

His buddy Steven joked that he was tossing off the old favorites and trying on new ones – the same as he was doing with the women in his life.

Steven could joke. The guy was tall, muscled, and still had hair. Joey had a bigger beer gut than his butt, and the only hair left on his body was everywhere but on his head.

His chances of finding another girlfriend right now were not great.

And maybe he was okay with that. Lorelei had been a crappy cook. If she'd been better he wouldn't have had a beer or two with every meal to wash the food down. It's not like he could suggest she take lessons or anything. She'd have hit him over the head with her frying pan if he had.

She might suck at meals, but she'd been the damn best baker he'd ever been lucky enough to hook up with. And so typical of women she'd bake a double batch of chocolate chip cookies, have one and then say she was too fat and he should eat them up to save her waistline. Then she'd want to bake again and would hassle him to keep eating the damn cookies because she wanted to try out some new cheesecake recipes.

And all that obliging had obligingly stuck around his waistline. But she'd stayed trim and he grumbled.

Now he was a fat ass, single, and heading to meet Steven and his latest girlfriend at the diner for liver and onions.

Who knew?

He rubbed his beer gut, wishing the damn burning would die down. It had been just bugging him enough that he was getting right pissed off. So pissed off that he was starting to get angry at everything. Damn Lorelei. She didn't have to leave him. They could have worked things out.

Hell, he deserved a chance just like every other guy. Fucking bitch. They were all bitches. Every last one of them. The burning in his gut heated up. He glared around at the busy street and the milling crowds. Everyone was partnered up. The whole world lived as a damn couple.

Well, he used to belong. But not any longer.

God damn it.

Now the rage bit in deep, bringing up old hurts and re-sentments, like his ex-wife who'd taken off with his kids. And his two daughters who couldn't be bothered to answer a damn email. Then there was his hag of a mother. The rage grew and grew. He could barely walk for the tension knotting his muscles. He cast his gaze around, looking at the large group of giggling women waiting for the street light to turn so they could cross the road.

All dressed up in heels, ready to lure the gullible males.

Well, maybe it was time for the tables to be turned on those unsuspecting women.

He passed the grocer who was outside moving out new carrots onto one of the heavily laden tables under the awning, a big knife in his hand. And Joey smiled.

Perfect. The grocer turned to help an older female cus-tomer at his side. He placed the knife down. Joey sidled over, picked it up, and slid it along one leg and carried on. The clouds moved in front of the sun just then, lending a dark, malevolent energy to the scene. Perfect.

He reached the unsuspecting group in less than thirty seconds.

Then the screams erupted.

CHAPTER 16

THE INSIDE OF the car was excruciatingly loud in its silence.

After Stefan's question, she'd professed to know nothing and had asked for a cab to be called so she could go home. There'd been a slightly uncomfortable pause, then Stefan had insisted on driving her home as he was leaving anyway.

It would have been churlish to refuse – even though she'd wanted to. But he'd led her down to his car and they'd been driving ever since.

He pulled the vehicle over and turned off the engine. She opened the door and brought out her stick. As she exited the car she said, "Thank you."

But he wasn't listening. She heard his door open and close and his footsteps as he strode to her side. Of course he was going to be the gallant kind of male.

"I don't need your help," she said brusquely. "I can manage just fine."

"Of course you can. But you don't have to."

And damn if he didn't pick up her hand again and place it on his arm as he had before. She wanted to snap at him for touching her, and at the same time wanted to ask him to hold her close and fix whatever the hell was wrong. But he couldn't do that. Apparently she was the one that had to. And how that was supposed to happen, she didn't know.

She kept up her silence until they reached her door. Be-latedly she realized he'd already been here.

She unlocked the door and turned to keep him out.

"Let me in," he said quietly.

"Why?" She tilted her head, listening for lies and decep-tion. Something she could use against this man who saw too much, knew too much, and could come to mean too much.

"We need to talk."

She gave an indelicate snort. "More talking? I'm pretty well talked out."

"Not about this." He waited, the smooth chocolate voice deepening as he added, "I can help."

A broken sob escaped. She bit the second one back be-fore it could follow. The dam was close to breaking.

And he seemed to know it.

"Let me in," he repeated, his voice gentle yet implacable.

"Why?"

"Because you want to."

She didn't have an answer for that. She was afraid he was right. And if he could see her energy and read it – maybe it told the truth. She stepped back from the door and made her way to her kitchen table. There she put her purse down against the wall and draped her coat over the back of the chair. "Do you want tea?" she asked.

"Yes, please."

She busied herself with making the simple pot of green tea and brought the special dragon pot and matching cups to the table. That she managed the simple task swiftly and easily without spilling anything said much for the amount of practice she'd put into this pastime.

She pulled out her chair and sat down. Realizing he still stood like a guard dog watching her, she motioned to the chair in front of him. "Please sit."

The chair scraped backwards then creaked as he dropped his weight into it.

"Now tell me, what do we have to talk about?"

"Many things, but the important one is why you don't want to talk about whatever is bothering you. I can't help until I know what the problem is." And as he spoke, colors rippled and played throughout the room, around him. So bright. So brilliant. They twisted and turned and expanded with his tone of voice.

She couldn't help herself – she reached out and grabbed one of the colors. Her hand went right through it. Of course it did. It wasn't like the colors were solid. They were only energy, after all.

And she froze. *They were only energy, after all.* How true, and it matched everything that Dr. Maddy had said to her. So it was all just energy.

"Is everything energy? You, me, the ghosts?"

"Yes. And because everything is made of the same things, certain rules apply to everyone and everything. So if someone is bothering you, human or ghost, then there are restrictions holding them back too."

She stared toward him, her voice quiet as she asked, "Are you sure?"

He leaned forward, his hand reaching out to wrap around her tightly clenched fists. "Absolutely." He squeezed her hands and murmured, "Tell me."

She winced, but her gaze once again caught on his hands, the colors wrapping and weaving with her own.

Her own as she'd never seen them before. She wanted to ask him about the colors. Ask him if he was doing it on purpose. They were so much brighter than she'd seen before.

If she could only see hers because of him. If such a thing was possible. She didn't think he could be doing that, but he'd said he worked energy so maybe that was a big part of it. She wanted him to be doing it. In her black world, she was desperate to see anything – and colors were extra special.

Fascinated, she watched the colors move and shift with the energy. She just didn't know what the energy was that formed it or what the energy wanted to do now that it was out and moving around. She realized his energy was retreating slightly, snugging up tightly against his hands. She wanted to shout *stop* so the energy would continue to play around her hand, but realized it went with his mood. As did hers, and hers was running back up her arms. Fascinating.

"Celina."

She nodded, opened her mouth, and explained. "About a year ago I had a horrible multi-vehicle accident with a couple of friends from the orchestra. There were several fatalities. My friends had only minor injuries but my injuries were more severe. I had a head injury, the same that injured my eyes. I had eye surgery to repair an optic nerve and within weeks of waking up afterwards – it's like I've been haunted. I don't know who this person is or why he's attached to me. But he says he can do horrible things. And he always tells me to show him. To open my eyes so he can see."

A shuddering breath escaped. "And I always refuse."

STEFAN SAT BACK. So this was the truth. Or at least as much as she was willing to share. It was enough for the moment. He thought about what the voice said. "Do you recognize the voice in your head?"

Her eyes widened, an odd light coming into her gaze. As if thinking on the answer she paused, then shook her head. "No. I don't think so."

He nodded and filed that reaction away for future pondering. "No idea who this person is?"

She shook her head immediately. "No idea. I've deliberately withheld from asking him very much. He scares me," she finished, her voice tremulous. She took a deep breath, her fingers locking so tightly the knuckles turned white then blurted out, "He caused the accident at Chico's."

"What?" Stefan leaned forward. "How?"

"I don't know," she cried. "He said that I needed proof and he'd do something to prove to me that he was there and not imaginary. Up until then I'd been afraid the voice in my head meant I was going crazy. As long as it didn't come too often I could deal with it. Hold the fear at bay." Tears formed in the corner of her eyes. "Within minutes of him speaking the truck slammed into the front window."

Stefan cradled her hands, his mind spinning with her words. He'd seen some impressive feats of possession and learned the extent of desperation that a soul could go through to continue its existence. But was that what this was all about? And if not, then what was going on?

"You've been afraid to tell anyone, haven't you?" he said, his voice gentle but his gaze intent. When a tear slipped down her cheek, he was lost. He stood and walked around the table to take her into his arms.

She snuggled closer as if she knew that was where she belonged.

Except she likely had no idea. Still, she was scared and needed someone. He was that someone.

For a long moment they stayed where they were, then

she pulled away. He wanted to tug her back into his arms but refrained. He didn't want to do anything to scare her. She was already terrified.

She reached for a tissue, and he was once again surprised at the confidence in her movements. He didn't think she had any sight available, but if her home life was this comfortable, this secure, how difficult it must be for her to leave this safe space.

He walked over to the tea kettle and plugged it back in. He could use a coffee at this point, but as he didn't see a coffee maker on the counter he assumed she didn't drink it on a regular basis. He didn't either, but there were times…

"You're awfully quiet," she said in low tones.

"I'm thinking about where to go next."

"Maybe you could at least tell me that I'm not crazy," she said half-humorously and half-hopefully.

"You are absolutely not crazy."

She brightened. "Really? You aren't just saying that?"

"No. I have seen some things that if I even tried to explain them, you'd think I was crazy. Believe me, I'm not crazy and neither are you. For anyone outside of this work, it's too hard to comprehend and they can't accept any of this. It's too far out of their scope of realism."

He walked back to the table and sat down, studying her. "That's fine for them. It's not going to work for us. Keeping our eyes closed, blinders on, or just trying to ignore that this stuff exists doesn't work."

"I want it to," she said petulantly.

He laughed. "I did way back when too. Not now."

"How long have you been doing this?"

He loved how she tilted her head when she asked a question. As if she could hear or sense the truth behind his words.

And maybe she could. "A long time. I don't remember much of my younger years – thankfully it's all a blank – but from my earliest memories I saw things no one else did. I knew things about other people that others wouldn't have wanted me to know. I spoke to people who weren't there and learned early on when to keep my mouth shut." He worked at keeping his voice neutral and even, but there was something about that intense gaze that told him he'd failed. He shrugged self-consciously. "Before you ask, yes, I was hospitalized for a short time because I hadn't guarded my tongue. Being young and aggressive I wasn't much good at following rules."

She smiled. "I understand. I'm glad you were eventually released."

He snorted. "Yeah, I learned to give the right answers very quickly." He didn't add that it had been the one time he'd used energy to affect another person to do his will. He'd promised to never do it again if he could just get free of that doctor's control.

It had worked, and he'd never forgotten his promise. He'd never done it again. If it became a choice of life over death he would do so again, but if there was any way to avoid it he'd take it. There was something deadly addictive about influencing someone like that. Given the wrong personality, it was easy to see how quickly and easily it would be to continue doing such a thing to make everything happen the way you wanted it to.

And psychic or energy criminals were the results. He'd been exposed to one or two, but thankfully they were in small numbers. He didn't think that was what was happening here but he'd learned to not assume anything. Those people were skilled and often desperate. That made them very dangerous.

MADDY WALKED INTO her office, dropped the last file onto her stack, and had just sat down when Stefan contacted her.

Maddy, Celina opened up. And Stefan filled her in on the conversation he'd just had with Celina.

Maddy sat back in her chair and considered the information. *It could be someone who is controlling her — or rather wanting to be able to control her and is frustrated that he can't. But that doesn't explain why he'd be able to have made that accident happen. That energy could be from someone deceased…* She pondered the options. *Or maybe this person could be able to see the future and when he saw the accident about to happen, pressed his advantage home and manipulated her a little more.*

I hadn't thought about that. Stefan's voice hardened. *Can't say I like games like that, either.*

They all play games, Maddy said. *Most are innocent, but in this case we need to understand the predator and try to see what he wants.*

If he's not alive then he wants continued existence.

And if he is alive — is he just playing mind games? What does he get out of this?

Maybe watching her spin with emotional turmoil and having her believe she's going crazy, Stefan said. *I hate to think of her being tormented like that. Not to mention believing that she might be responsible for the accident because she couldn't stop him.*

No! She isn't. Maddy groaned. *But it's so typical of people. She's very caring. That's going to be an instinctive reaction on her part.* She stared at the painting on the wall in front of her as she thought about the little bit of that energy she'd had a chance to observe. *I did sense a strong relationship between this energy and her – a dependency type of relationship.*

As if he's dependent on her for his continued existence?

I'm not sure about that. I just know that there was a strong sense of need on both sides.

I want to read her energy and see who these other personalities are that she's holding close.

See if she's willing to release them. They are all draining her system, and she can't afford to lose that amount of energy.

I'll talk to her.

I presume you are there with her now.

Yes.

Then be careful. If this entity has a twisted attachment and does have the ability to make things happen, you could become a target.

Stefan snorted. *Bring it on.*

She smiled as he disappeared from her mind. She wished him well. She liked what she'd seen of Celina. That the woman was full of secrets matched much of Stefan's life. She doubted he'd shared much of his life with many people. Celina had lots of walls to deal with herself. Chances were good they'd have some interesting times ahead.

And they'd be all the better for it.

She'd seen the energy arc between them. The twisting, eager energy on both sides reached as one for the other. Thank heavens – but there was so much more needed for a real relationship.

She could only hope they'd make it. Stefan was an extraordinary person and he needed someone special just for him.

Celina didn't want anyone in her life. Or thought she didn't want anyone in her life. She'd let Stefan in only so far, then those walls would go up and he'd get shoved out.

Maddy laughed. She'd bet on Stefan any time.

BRANDT HATED TO be called into work on weekends, but murderers didn't give a damn. His cell phone rang just then. The ring tone telling him who was calling. He smiled and reached for the phone. Good – she was awake. Hopefully she'd gotten some rest first. With the visions coming one on top of the other right now, she could barely function. "Sam? Are you okay, sweetheart?"

"Yes." Except her voice was faint, almost a whisper. "I just heard on the news something about a stabbing downtown?"

"Hmmm. I heard something about it, but not the details." He frowned and his voice sharpened. "Why?"

"I think it's the same thing."

"Sorry?" Brandt shook his head. "Same thing as what?"

"He was one of the victims – same as the other cases." She paused then added, "I could feel an ugly burn in my lower belly. Not just a pain but a horrific heat, and the hotter it got the angrier I got. I caught bits and pieces of his thoughts. He was angry at his doctor, at the accident he'd had, at his ex-wife, at his girlfriend who'd just left him and how bad a cook she was and what a wonderful baker she was. How his friend Steven had yet another girlfriend but he was too old, too ugly, too bald to get another girlfriend. And his anger went from his girlfriend to ex-wife to mother to women in general. Then he saw the women. I don't think he even thought about what he was doing, but he picked up a knife and started slashing."

Her voice died away, leaving a painful emptiness on the

phone. The tears that clogged her throat made him blink the moisture back in his own eyes. She went through so much trauma with every vision. Not to mention the frustration and sense of failure that she couldn't do anything to stop it all from happening.

"Did you see him actually stabbing anyone?" He clicked on the windows of his computer, trying to bring up anything that would give him the information about the incident. It had only just happened from his understanding.

"No. I jumped out," she admitted.

"Is there a chance he survived?" He wished the people she connected with would survive these attacks, but she only connected with the victims as they were dying.

"Possibly. I didn't hang around long enough to find out."

"And yet he was a murderer in this scenario?" How did that fit anything? He had a large file of disconnected cases now that made no sense. All he had to go on was a mess of unrelated incidences with no similarities. Except Sam.

And that was his best clue. She'd never been wrong yet.

"I'll see if I can find out more. I'll bring it home tonight."

"Thank you," she said, her voice stronger as she distanced herself from the vision. "I'll be waiting."

"I'll only bring it if you have a swim and try for a nap later today."

"I planned on it." She laughed. "I'm fine, you know."

He grinned. "You, my beloved, are more than just fine."

And with that he hung up, her laughter still ringing in his ears. God, he was blessed. The smile fell off his face as he returned to hunt for any information on her latest vision.

JACOB FELT LIKE an idiot.

He was lying on top of his body, sprawled like a lumpy blanket. And no matter what position he tried out he couldn't get back into his body. He remembered Lissa's words about needing to find the reason why he wasn't in there, but for the life of him – and didn't that phrase made him wince – he couldn't come up with a good reason.

He loved playing for the orchestra. He loved his friends. Sure, he had some problems with his family, but nothing major. He was close with Celina, and that brought him up short. He'd taken her to the restaurant that night. Had she been injured? He hoped not. She had enough to deal with. He couldn't remember anything about the accident.

There'd been something important then. Something important.

What was it?

CHAPTER 17

A WEARINESS CELINA hadn't felt in a long time swept over her system. She knew Stefan's sharp eyes would notice. Fine. She was too tired to care.

"Why don't you lie down?" he suggested.

She smiled. "I plan on it after you leave."

A slight whoosh of air drifted toward her as he said, "Except I'm not leaving."

She froze. Damn that smooth voice of his that made everything seem so reasonable. So easy. But not this. And not this easy. Keeping her voice light she said, "Why?"

"Because I can see energy, and I want to see what goes on here while you're asleep. You have several ghosts in here now but they are distant. Wanting to communicate but not able to."

Ouch. She wasn't sure she liked him being able to pick up so much.

"Tell me why they are there in that state." His voice, so soft, was controlled and determined.

She shrugged. Well, it wasn't a big deal. "I was overwhelmed. Somehow with the accident it seemed like any and every ghost could call on me at will and I couldn't handle it. I closed a door and let only a few in. And no, don't ask me how I closed it. I just did." She gave a small shrug. "As it was, several still managed to get in."

"Were they persistent?"

"No, I just think they were more capable." She turned to look around her room, knowing where everything was and where her ghostly visitors usually were. "It's an odd thing to consider that some ghosts are more conscious, more adept than others. But it's the same with people. I just hadn't considered that the same traits would show up between ghosts." She stood up. "This conversation would have normal people running for the hills."

"I'm not normal people." There was a hesitation in his voice.

Celina stopped and waited for him. When he didn't speak again she said, "What?"

"Nothing. It's stupid."

"What's stupid?" she said, frowning.

"I was going to ask if you need any help, but you are obviously very competent and don't need it."

She paused, hearing a note in his voice that said he'd like to help regardless. As in he wanted more from her than she was giving at this point. She had to think about that. Her life was a mess. She really didn't need anyone else adding complications. She opened her mouth to make that clear.

She sensed his indrawn breath, as if waiting for her to say something he wasn't going to like but damn it, the words wouldn't come out. Because in spite of all the problems, in spite all of the people in her life, real and ghostly, she didn't want to go it alone. Didn't know if she could. But she knew this man would never want to be anyone's crutch. He'd want a partner. In every sense of the word.

Could she be that for him? That was the dream she'd had with her fiancé. And that had gone up in a puff of smoke.

She couldn't sense any eagerness or pushiness in his voice or actions. In fact, she had to wonder if she'd imagined his tone. She'd shut down so much of her life after Peter's death that it was impossible to know if she were interpreting the signals correctly. She really wished she could see the answer in his eyes. The truth on his face when she asked him.

The thing was she was interested herself. And too damn afraid to go down that pathway.

Tired and frustrated with the constant double questioning, she made her way to her bedroom. "I'm going to lie down. You do what you want."

"I'll stay then." The humor in his voice hit her as she entered her room.

Inside she leaned back against the closed door and shut her eyes for a long moment. *Thank God he was.*

HE COULDN'T IMAGINE a more prickly character to have fallen in love with. Not that he had any choice, of course – but still it was the universe's way of making him work for what he wanted. He'd just once like to have something come easy. So many people saw his gifts and ignored the pain and difficulty they'd brought him over the years.

For years he'd been dealing with women's unwanted attention. A man should be so unlucky. But as he could see the women's energies he knew what was behind their actions. And that was a huge turnoff. He didn't want to sleep with a woman who wanted the cachet of sleeping with a psychic or that came from sleeping with a person with certain notoriety. Too often his looks were the reason for the instant attraction, and that was difficult and often made him – almost out of necessity – blunt as he brushed them off. The last thing Stefan needed was someone who judged by the cover.

Celina was refreshing that way. His looks meant nothing to her. But he'd very quickly realized that her blindness was something she endured on sufferance, and was making no attempt to learn to live with it beyond what she had to. She'd rather see with her eyes than her fingers, and given that it wasn't an option at this time she'd prefer to do neither. An all-or-nothing girl.

He settled into the living room in his lotus position and slipped free of his body. He could do a lot of his work from here. Good thing, as his days were too busy and nights lately had become even worse.

Opening his eyes, he could see the room come alive with colors and energies. He searched to see if there was anything off and found everything calm. Normal. Next he checked the security measures he'd put up, and again everything appeared fine. More confident now he slipped into her bedroom to hover over her sleeping form. She needed rest. These last couple of months – years – had been rough on her. In fact, as he looked at the old energy moving restlessly, entwined with the newer, he figured much of the last few years had been tough.

On instinct he headed to the hospital and checked out the other survivors of the accident. He needed an eyewitness. Someone who'd heard something. There had to be a reason behind the accident. He wasn't prepared to listen to the claim of Celina's predator as the cause just yet.

He closed his eyes and willed himself to the morgue.

The icy chill hit him first. Opening his eyes, he found himself at the same part of the large, connecting rooms as he'd been in last time. The same lineup of sheet-covered bodies before him. Different bodies, he thought, as several were young women. New arrivals, considering the conversation going on around him.

"Stabbings at the street corner. What is this world coming too? That guy there, Brown," one of the staff pointed to a large, middle-aged male off to one side, "up and attacked without warning. He killed these three women and knifed two more. They are still upstairs."

"So autopsies on all three?" Gurneys were rolled forward and backward, shifting the order of the work to be done.

"The boss is doing the guy."

The other man nodded, not seeming to care either way. "Let's hope the doc finds a medical reason for going off half-cocked and killing those women."

And that's why he was here. Stefan watched as the same black energy he'd seen in the morgue before on yet another body drift around this Brown character. He had no idea how long this man had been dead, but that black mist was still here, dissipating but thick enough that he could see the layers on the body.

He needed to be here during the autopsy if possible, and if not he needed to see the autopsy report. Somehow this man was connected to Celina's troubles.

That meant he had to contact Brandt.

He smiled. No time like right now. He popped over to Brandt's office to find him at his desk, pounding away on the keyboard. *Brandt?*

Brandt's gaze shot up. "Stefan?"

Yes. I need to ask you a couple of questions.

"Well, I'm alone, so go for it. What's up?" Brandt's voice reverberated oddly in Stefan's head. Brandt had come a long way and his telepathic skills were getting better all the time.

He just couldn't keep doing so for long periods of time, so they didn't talk that way unless they needed to. *You've got a guy in the morgue I'm interested in.*

"Yeah, well, we've actually got a lot of guys in the morgue. Which one are you talking about?"

A man who just stabbed several women.

"Interesting. I should have guessed," Brandt said, busy clicking away.

Guessed what? Stefan asked.

"Sam contacted me earlier. She'd connected to him and led me through the vision right up to the point he'd grabbed up a knife from the grocer and started stabbing."

What else did she say? Stefan asked, his voice sharp. *I need to know everything she said.*

Brandt walked him through what he remembered. "If you need more than that you'll need to call her yourself, but leave it for a bit. I keep hoping she'll finally get some sleep one of these days."

She's still not sleeping? Stefan didn't like the sound of that.

"No. Too many visions. That's a problem. If there was a chance of a serial killer being involved here, there's no way he'd be as prolific as this. There has to be something else going on here," Brandt said. "The visions are wearing her out. In the beginning it seemed like the connections were weaker, but now she says they are getting stronger. She can now hear their thoughts and feel their emotions. She said this stabbing guy was burning up in pain, and rage was fueling his actions. She said it was a horrible rage. Deep-seated and very old."

Of course. Emotion is one of the best ways to gain a hold into someone. And one he hadn't considered. *You should be collecting a few more of these cases to add to the pile I have.*

"I have them," Brandt said. "Just haven't gotten them to you yet. I could run them by your house today on the way home if you want."

I might not be there. I'm keeping an eye on Celina right now.

"As in keeping a watchful eye or keeping a physical eye?"

A physical eye, Stefan said, hearing the humor in his friend's voice. *Glad everyone is having fun at my expense, but Celina is a long way away from having a relationship.*

"Too bad, I feel for you," Brandt said with just enough honesty that Stefan relaxed.

Thanks.

"She doesn't live that far out of my way. I'll run by and drop the stack off if that helps."

That would be good, Stefan acknowledged. *I can study them here. How long are you going to be?*

"Leaving soon. So I'll print off this extra information and add it to the growing pile and be there in…" he paused, checking his watch, "in about fifteen minutes."

Okay, come upstairs to the apartment. I'll be waiting.

Stefan zoomed out of town to check in on Sam, planning on questioning her further only to find her fast asleep on the couch, both dogs ever watchful at her side. He sent some soothing energy down over both dogs' backs, letting them know he was here. Both whined and wagged their tails.

It's all right, guys. I'm going to work on Sam's energy a bit to help her sleep better. As he looked at Samantha's aura he realized that although she'd been working at keeping her guards in place, the lack of sleep and worry had allowed the energy barrier to thin down to almost nothing. He spent a few moments easing the pain from her soul and pulling back some of the tight, dark cloud over her glowing energy.

Sam was a beacon for violence and needed more care than most psychics. She was an apt pupil and had come a long way, but there was still that remnant of inexperience that kept getting frazzled to the point that it was hurting her. He spent long moments easing back her ruffled edges and stroked her aura into peacefulness.

A harsh noise snapped him out of his meditation, pulling him back to Celina's living room…and slamming him back into his body.

When the doorbell rang again he managed to make it to the front door in time to stop Brandt from pushing the damn bell a third time.

"I should have mentioned that Celina is asleep."

Brandt's eyebrows shot up. "You really are looking after her, aren't you?"

Stefan nodded. "There is something beyond odd happening here. Until I can get a handle on it I can't tell if she's seriously in danger, or is a serious danger to others, or just what is going on."

He led the way to the kitchen. Brandt dropped the folder on the table. "This is the little bit I have on Joey Brown. His background is coming in from the group out canvassing. We're trying to figure out why he stabbed the women. According to Sam it was anger, but there had to be a trigger."

"And that was likely the burning pain."

"So the women were likely just in the wrong place at the wrong time?"

"Quite possible, but due diligence will need to be done to make sure he doesn't have a connection to one of these specific women."

"It's all in progress. I'll update you when I get more. At the moment it looked like the knife was there and so were the women and he just attacked."

"And that makes a sick kind of sense. I'll work on this tonight."

Brandt stayed quiet. Stefan looked up from the paperwork spread across the table. "What?"

"There is something else. The blood tests came back from the blood found on Celina's bathroom. You were right." He shook his head. "I don't know how but it's Jacob's blood."

Stefan winced.

Brandt glared at him. "Do you have an explanation? One other than Celina did this herself?"

"It wasn't Celina." Stefan leaned back. "Damn."

"Well, I know there is some freaky stuff in your world, but this is the first I've had a coma patient write notes on a bathroom wall in his own blood."

"But it's not my first time for a coma patient to do something unbelievable." Stefan frowned. He wondered if Jacob could have possessed someone else – and he hated to consider it, but if he'd taken possession of Celina – then the writing on the wall could have been hers. No. She couldn't have written so cleanly with her eyesight. Unless somehow Jacob had been able to see enough to get the job done.

He shook his head slowly from side to side. He couldn't believe it. He wouldn't believe. He knew inside it hadn't been her.

"It wasn't Celina's energy on the wall. But I have no idea if Jacob could have done this himself. Given what Lissa can do... it's not out of the realm of possibility."

"Hell." Brandt shook his head. "Well, until we figure

this out, we need to keep Celina away from Jacob and hope that Jacob wakes up and can answer a few questions for us."

"He might not remember anything," Stefan pointed out.

"No. He might not, but more to the point is let's make sure that Celina didn't either." Brandt studied Stefan's face. "I'm worried. You're in really deep with her, aren't you?"

Stefan stared back at one of the best friends he'd been lucky enough to have in his life and said in a quiet voice, "I always have been. She's always been a major part of my life. That has never changed."

CELINA OPENED HER eyes to foreign sounds. Stefan. So he was still here…and he was speaking with someone. Then she heard sounds of a door closing. She lay quietly, getting used to the idea of a watchdog. And a stranger at that. How long had it been since anyone had cared for her enough to watch over her in person? No one since Peter. He'd been so possessive and careful to make sure she was looking after herself that if she didn't he did it for her. He'd often run out to make sure there was food in the cupboard, enough of her favorite tea in stock, or any number of other little things that showed her how much he'd cared. She'd loved him to distraction.

But that possessiveness had become confining, control-ling. Enough that they'd fought over it. Enough that she'd had second thoughts…

It was so different with Stefan. With Stefan she felt safe, cared for… without that stifling possessiveness. She didn't understand why she'd trusted him as easily and as quickly as she had…but she did. He made her feel safe. Secure.

Then again it was early days yet.

Also there was no guarantee that he'd stick around for long, but she wanted what time she could have. She'd learned how dreams turned to dust, and the people she loved disappeared. Like Peter.

Somewhere along the way the pain of her loss had disappeared and she hadn't noticed. She carefully opened up that part of her psyche and took a long, in-depth look. There was a tiny ache for what might have been, but other than that there was no leftover grief. She'd passed that point a long time ago and hadn't even noticed.

She smiled. Then heard Stefan moving around in the kitchen.

And the smile dropped away.

Just because she was over one relationship didn't mean she wanted to dive into another one. She wasn't sure Stefan would give her a choice.

Feeling confused, she got up and walked into her bathroom. A shower might help. The hot water sluiced down her back in waves of comforting warmth. She stood, eyes closed, letting it pour over her. Somehow, from somewhere deep inside that she hadn't even known was there, tears started to pour.

And pour. She didn't make a sound, but the pain, the frustration, the fear. God, the crippling fear… everything she'd stuffed down oozed outward through her tears as she let the last of all she'd been holding onto slip from where she'd been keeping it all hidden. As soon as that older fear had drained, the newer fear and turmoil of the last few days rose along with the grief for her friends and their families. The bottleneck burst and suddenly she was crouched at the base of the tub, the water pounding on her spine as she sobbed.

She heard a voice a long way away say, "Easy, Celina, take it easy."

The bathtub's glass sliding door opened, letting a draft of cool air inside. She didn't have to ask who it was. Stefan's presence was warm and easily identifiable. This man cared on a level she wasn't sure she'd ever known before. But she wanted to.

And there was nothing confining about it.

The water taps squeaked in front of her and the hot stream pounding down slowed to a trickle, then stopped. Still a few more sobs came out. A towel was wrapped around her slim frame and she was picked up, still curled up into a ball.

She almost said something but was caught up by the rapt feeling of being carried. She hadn't been looking for a relationship. She wasn't now either. But in spite of that it looked like one was possibly waiting for her. If she was willing to take that step.

Quietly acquiescent, she waited, wondering what he'd do next.

STEFAN CARRIED CELINA into her bedroom, wondering at the sensations rolling through him. When she'd stayed in the bathroom for as long as she had he'd dropped his own defenses and let himself open up to her energy to see if she was okay. As her emotions rolled through him, he realized how overwhelmed she was. Some of it was easy to understand and some was not. He could feel the aged quality to many of them, and as he knew only the barest of her history he couldn't place much of it.

As long as she was dealing with them one way or another

he was good with that. Everyone had a history, including him, and whether he remembered all of his or wanted to even explore that part of himself, that was his choice. Just as she had to make her choices.

Right now the vibes were all about letting go. That was hard on anybody, but she'd be so much better for it. She just needed to know that she wasn't alone.

She'd left her bedding turned back so he set her down in the middle, efficiently stripped off the wet towel and wrapped the bedding around her as she sat waiting. With the same towel he gently dried her hair. Spying a brush on her night table, he shifted to sit behind her, picked up the brush, and gently stroked her wet hair.

She never moved. Never said a word.

But the tears had stopped. Her emotions had calmed and she was relaxed, at peace. The letting go would allow her to see more clearly.

"You're very good at this," she whispered.

"Am I?" He smiled. "That's good. I can't remember the last time I might have brushed a woman's hair." It wasn't a natural thing for him to do. But in this case she'd been like a child and in need of care.

That he could do.

"I didn't mean the hair thing as much as the looking after me." Her voice was low but peaceful.

"We all need looking after sometimes."

"Not you," she said with surprising force. "I can't see you ever needing to be looked after."

He paused, the hairbrush held midair, and thought about the many times recently where his friends had come into the ethers to find him or sat watching over his body while he'd been gone, or joined him at the children's hospital where he couldn't do what needed to be done alone. "You'd be wrong. Especially lately. There have been too many times where I did need exactly that."

She twisted around enough so she could stare toward him, making him wonder once again at what she really saw, and said in a gentle voice, "Tell me."

Not wanting to open himself up meant not giving her what she needed, and that wasn't acceptable. He thought about the various incidences and compromised by explaining about one of the times where he'd exhausted himself to the point of having to be hospitalized by splitting his energy in too many directions to keep track of many different events at one time.

She was silent for a long moment. "You can do that?"

"Yes. And much more."

"Like?"

"Like leave my body at will, or go to a place with my energetic body so I'm still in residence but can get the information I need anyway. It's not as clear and I can't do much to help at the other end, but it works well enough most of the time."

She sat quietly, listening once again with her back turned his way, not commenting. So he pushed the envelope of acceptance a little. "And I can communicate telepathically with most people."

That did it. She stiffened and turned around again, pinning him in place with that fierce blind gaze. He waited.

"I thought that was just fantasy."

"No. Dr. Maddy and I speak that way a lot. I work with many people capable of doing that."

"Ah, so you speak telepathically with others that have that same skill." She tilted her head toward the ceiling. "That almost makes sense with Dr. Maddy. While I was there with both of you there was a low-key hum sometimes, but not all the time. But it was always when no one was speaking. I thought because of the silence I could hear it more clearly." She paused, her head tilting. "That's what was actually happening, wasn't it?"

He nodded in surprise. "Yes. I had no idea there was an audible noise when I do that. Interesting."

"I think only a person with highly developed hearing would be able to tell the difference," she said. "It must be an interesting way to talk."

"It is, and it's definitely something you could learn."

"Me?" She gave a startled laugh and quick shake of her head. "No way."

He smiled at the universal answer he received from every other person he'd said that to. "Actually, you more than most. You already have an intuitive sense, psychic abilities, and are open to the concept."

"Yeah, but there is already someone in my head, remember? It's too crowded for more."

As a conversation killer, that was a good one and also brought up a valid point. "I wonder if he's telepathic and communicating that way with you but is not actually located in your head."

"I'd prefer if he was telepathic," she said, her voice thoughtful. "And yes, if he is, then I'm already communicating with him but I really don't like the concept of him being located in my head."

"If he was telepathic he wouldn't need to be. He could be anywhere depending on his abilities. Why *you* is the big question, and why the blockage would be the next big one."

"Yeah. See, now that's heading into the sci-fi arena

again," she muttered.

"Much of life is science fiction until you understand how it works." He continued to run the brush in long slow strokes through her rich, black hair. He'd met a lot of women, blondes and brunettes with every shade imaginable, but he'd not met many with jet-black hair.

Still damp, the strands were silky beneath his fingers. A wave of possessiveness surged through him. He wanted to do so much more than this but knew she wasn't ready. As she sat so perfectly comfortable nude and barely concealed by the bedding, he knew he'd have to stop soon or he wouldn't be able to control himself.

She sighed, stretching her back as the bedding dropped away, giving him a perfect view of the top of her rounded cheeks and the dimple where they joined. Slim, with her ribs and spine easily visible under her soft skin. She had an odd pattern of freckles on her left side. He smiled as his gaze caught the slightest happy face pattern amongst them. With one hand he gently traced the smile part of the face. "Did you know you have a happy face of freckles here?"

She laughed lightly. "I don't think anyone has ever said that to me."

Unable to stop himself, he leaned over and dropped a light kiss on the nose of the happy face. Then as if nothing had happened he resumed brushing her hair. She hadn't moved, relaxed, or frozen. He'd take that as a good sign.

JACOB WANDERED THE room. At first he'd been able to travel throughout the hospital, but he had never met another soul like himself. If he'd had lonely times in his life before, now it was almost impossible. He'd tried to call Lissa several times, in fact. But she hadn't returned.

He wanted to see Celina. Tell her whatever it was that was so important. But he couldn't figure out how. He thought he'd seen her before, at her apartment, sleeping, playing, but didn't know how he'd done that. If he'd done that. Maybe he'd only dreamed it. He'd tried so hard to repeat it and hadn't been able to. The longer he stayed here the harder any movement became. Depressed, he sat on the window ledge and waited.

Even a return visit from Lissa would help. Maybe then she'd give him a few more tips on how to survive this existence.

Or find a way to end it.

CHAPTER 18

CELINA FELT THE tingles move all over her body. From his kiss on her shoulder? Or had it been from something else? She could track the movement of the tingling as it moved up and down her back. Odd, and yet soothing in a way. She closed her eyes, following the sensation, then realized it was from his hands as he brushed her hair. "Wow. There is an actual energy pathway as you brush my hair. I can feel it run down my back and then back up again."

The brushing stopped for a moment then continued. "Like I said, you have a natural instinct for this."

"Ha," she snorted. "Feeling a bit of tingling is a lot different than speaking with someone through my mind."

"Which is something you already do."

Her light mood deflated. "Yes, but only with him."

"Do you want to try it with me?"

She tilted her head and considered it. "I don't think it will work."

Instantly a voice inside her head said, *Are you sure? I'm talking to you now. You can hear me as I can hear your mind buzzing over the newness of this.*

She gasped, spinning around to look at him. "Oh my God. That was you, wasn't it?"

He smiled at her and answered in her head, *Yes.*

Her gaze widened as she contemplated the significance

of that. "So my stalker guy might *not* be in my head!"

"He might not be," Stefan said out loud.

For some reason that made her feel so much better. She laughed. "That's marvelous. A telepathic asshole is so much better than a guy living in there." She shook her head, the strands of hair pulling out of his hands. "Doesn't that sound bizarre? If anyone heard us…"

"They wouldn't understand," he finished for her. "And that is too bad, because everyone is capable of so much more than they are currently doing."

She nodded. "That makes sense. How can I learn to do what you did?"

"You mean speak telepathically? That's easy. Just do it."

At her disgruntled expression he smiled. "I made it easier on you by speaking to you first. That gave you a pathway to follow back to me."

She closed her eyes. *Stefan? Can you hear me?*

Nothing.

She opened her eyes and said, "Nothing."

"Try and try again. It might not happen on the first attempt but it will happen." He smiled. "Just follow my voice home."

She laughed. "You make it sound so easy."

Then a chill settled on her skin. She gasped. "He's here."

"I'm going to try to find out what I can. Don't mention my presence to him," he warned before he went silent. She turned around on the bed, dragging the covers up and over her shoulders. She stared in Stefan's direction. She reached out to find his arm, still holding her hairbrush, was halfway up in the air. He'd frozen in place. She didn't understand what he was doing. Unable to help herself, she reached out and lowered his hand.

What are you doing?

She froze at the cruel voice in her head, then said cautiously, "I'm doing nothing."

Someone else has been here. Someone I don't think I like.

What do you mean there's been someone here? she asked, aiming for shocked puzzlement. Her mind spun with all the information that Stefan had told her. Was this man talking telepathically to her?

Someone has been here. Inside your head.

What? she exclaimed. *What are you talking about? Why would anyone be in there?*

Don't be a fool, he said, his tone turning ugly, snide. *I'm in here. And now someone else has been as well.*

She shook her head, working hard on the helplessness. *I thought you were just talking to me in some kind of telepathic way – not that you were in my head.* She took a deep breath. *How can that be?*

And the pain started. *Do not take me for a fool.*

I'm not, she cried, her hands going to clasp either side of her head. *Stop. I haven't done anything.*

You let someone in here! he roared.

How could I? If you are there then you would have seen them, she said. *You're making me crazy.*

Maybe you are crazy. He paused. *Maybe you're not just stupid and weak but also crazy.*

I'm not, she snapped defiantly. She had no idea what was going on but she wouldn't listen to this. *I didn't let anyone else inside my head. And if there had been someone there then you would have seen them. I think you are the crazy one,* she scoffed. Instantly she knew that he'd punish her for that.

And punish her he did.

The heat inside her head had her crying out. *Stop it.*

Why should I? I can do whatever I want.

Then leave, she cried. *Leave me alone.*

There was heavy silence, then he said in a thick voice, *And that's the one thing I can't do.*

And just like that he disappeared.

STEFAN WATCHED AS this silvery-black energy popped out of the blockage and vibrated at a frequency he'd never seen before, bits and pieces of energy flaring the longer it was there, and just like that it winked out. Stefan checked her mind out to make sure there were no remnants of the foreign energy there, and deciding she was safe for the moment, he slid free and went into the base of her spine with his mind. He understood what Dr. Maddy had said she'd seen but he wanted to see it for himself.

Mentally he slipped upward into Celina's neck and moved up her energetic system to her head. Inside her skull he observed the bone and brain matter. There didn't appear to be anything out of the ordinary. Then again, he wasn't a doctor. He shifted to peer into the front of her facial construction, fascinated at the energy surrounding her eyes. There really was something odd there. Not organically. Energetically. Some energy from the surgeon. There was also energy from a stranger that had zoomed in on that location for some reason. He studied it closely to be sure, but knew there was no way that this was Celina's energy.

But what he really couldn't understand was that Celina's energy held the other one almost in an embrace. She had allowed this energy to be here. Had wanted it even.

And he just didn't see how that could be.

"ERIC, HOW ARE you feeling today?"

The same doctor as always listened to his chest and his back. The same patter rumbled over his head. He sank farther into his bed, trying to ignore the looks the doctor exchanged with his mother.

They weren't listening to anything he said. They never did. He was just a kid. He didn't know anything. Monsters didn't exist. *You're just having bad dreams. A side effect of the drugs.* Well, if the drugs brought out the monsters, then why would they give the drugs to little kids? Everyone knew monsters were bad.

He stared out at the doorway, wondering if he could jump up and run away. That's what the monster kept telling him to do. He wanted to. Anything to make that nasty voice in his head stop. He knew it was the bone they'd used to rebuild his knee but he didn't care. He wanted it out. Big fat tears rolled down his cheek, but he wouldn't cry. The monster loved fear.

I want you to be afraid. Then you'll do everything I tell you to do, the monster had said.

And he would do anything if it would make this monster go away. Even jump out that window beside him. He just needed a time when his mom wasn't looking. That would stop the hateful monster.

That would make him a hero. This monster couldn't hurt anyone anymore after that.

THE MOMENTS OF clarity were getting stronger and stronger. He flexed his virtual muscles, wishing he had enough to be solid in one place instead of spread out so thin that he was many people. But considering what he'd achieved, it was damn fine indeed. Especially now that he'd figured out how to stop the problem of deteriorating further.

He needed to cut off the flow at the sources. That way he figured he could easily control the energy he currently had and become stronger as he managed to focus more. But that main artery had to be destroyed. But how? He mulled the problem over. He had done the impossible already, so this should be a piece of cake.

He'd put his impressive brain to it.

If he had one.

At that reminder he howled and his energy splintered – everywhere.

CHAPTER 19

CELINA REACHED OUT to Stefan then hesitated. She didn't know if she should touch him or if that would disturb whatever he was trying to do. He was so still. Yet wisps of air escaped through his mouth. She could hear that movement but nothing else. She moved her hand up to the sound, her fingers gently brushing the sides of his cheekbones.

Knowing she should ask permission but needing to touch, she let her fingers trail across the strong cheekbones, lean, taut jaw and on to the large forehead. In passing, her fingers slipped across eyelashes that women would die for. She sighed as her fingers found the silkiest hair she could ever imagine a man having. It went to his shoulders. She exclaimed in joy as her fingers stroked through the waves. In her mind a picture was forming close to the image she'd kept in her heart after meeting him in her dreams. She had no way to know how close it would be, but it helped her to identify with him.

His shoulders were broad, the muscles corded, lean. She wanted to stroke his skin, explore those muscles. Foolish of her. Probably what she was doing wasn't wise either. She no longer cared. Who was this man that had walked into her life like he had the right? And taken up residence daringly close to her heart. She hadn't known about him days ago, but she knew him somehow. She couldn't help her fingers stroking down his long arms, getting a sense of the breadth of him, the lean, muscled look of him. On their own accord her fingers explored upward again, coming to rest on his lips.

His lips moved beneath her fingers.

And kissed her fingertips.

She gasped and pulled her hand back.

"Don't," he murmured. "Feel free to touch."

"I'm sorry. I should have asked first."

"Why?" he asked curiously. "Is that some sort of blind etiquette thing?"

"I don't know." She laughed ruefully. "I've been very obstinate about learning anything that would help my condition. I don't want to be in this state."

"So you have resisted. That sounds normal."

She heard the hairbrush land on the bedding beside her and something in the air changed. Warmed. Reminding her that some things hadn't changed. She was still nude in her bed, under the cover of night, with a gorgeous man who was still a stranger.

Yet some crucial things had shifted. She knew that he was important to her. She was important to him. He cared. She was open to caring. And she'd let go of a lot of pain from old relationships, making room for a new one.

She smiled, the curve of her lips tilting high on one side. "Hello again."

He smiled and brushed his thumb across her lips.

His hand slipped around the back of her neck, long fingers sliding deep into her hair, and he tugged her closer.

Twisted and off balance, she fell – into his arms. He tugged her up close to his chest, her head back over his arm. She waited, again a sense of fatalism in her response. This was right. Whoever this man was, he was the right man at the right time. Now.

Just before she felt the touch of his lips against her his breath warmed her eyes, down over her nose to her lips. He whispered, "Hello."

And kissed her.

She'd been kissed before. She'd been kissed lovingly before. By a man she'd loved and who had loved her. This was different. This was a coming home. This was a realization of something she had been missing all her life – and only now just found. An awakening to something she hadn't known she'd been missing. And now that she knew, she understood the gift he was offering.

A sense of completeness.

She didn't know when the tears started to trickle. Didn't even know that they had started. Stefan lifted his head and kissed the corner of her eyes. "Tears," he said. "Why?"

"How can I answer that when I don't know?" Still, she groped for one that would satisfy. Held strong against his chest, no quiver in the muscles of his arms, she opted for the truth. If he was this strong inside, then she could be too. "The emotion is so deep right now. So momentous, there's a well opening up inside." She stopped and shrugged. "I know it sounds stupid…"

His lips touched hers, coaxing them to silence before she let the rest of her sentence out. His breath wafted gently over her skin as he whispered, "There is nothing stupid about this. About right now. It is momentous. For both of us."

And damn if huge tears didn't well up again at his words.

"Shh." He kissed the corner of her eye, his tongue gently catching the falling drop. "It's going to be fine. Just rest."

Celina's lips twitched. "I'm in bed with a gorgeous man and he says rest. Who'd believe me?"

He laughed, the sound bringing up images of deep, dark midnight dreams. She wished she could see him, but fancied that she saw him as he was inside. She had never met any man like him.

She was laid back down on the bed, the covers pulled up to her chin, with a brief but bordering-on-hot kiss before he stepped back. In bemusement she heard him walk toward the door.

"Wait."

She heard his inwardly drawn breath, sensing the stillness of his movements.

"What do you need?" he asked.

"You."

STEFAN PAUSED, HIS heart hammering against his chest. Did she realize what she was saying? Inviting? And was this what he wanted? His loins screamed yes, but his mind said it wasn't a good idea. She was vulnerable.

His heart told him to stop talking and seize what he really wanted.

He approached the bed slowly. "Are you sure?"

He studied her energy, searching for the truth. And saw what he had hoped not to see. Doubts.

"You're not ready," he said slowly, almost hating that small part of himself that needed the truth and only truth between them. That knew he had to take the high road this time. Every time.

"No," she whispered. "Maybe I'm not, but I'm not far off."

He laughed, loving her truth. "Good. I'm glad to hear that."

She patted the bed beside her. "Stay with me, please."

"Are you nervous?" He settled on the bed beside her. She rolled over, giving him her back. He stretched out, wrapped an arm around her, and tugged her up close. "Sleep. I'll look after you."

And she closed her eyes and slept.

Stefan closed his eyes and relaxed behind Celina spoon-fashion. He hadn't thought to get this far so fast with her, but when the chips were down she'd known whom to trust. He loved that. *He* was her rightful partner, but just because he said he was didn't make it so – especially not in her eyes.

And speaking of her eyes, what was going on there? He'd studied them as much as he was comfortable doing and still didn't understand. He would be sad for her if she had lost her sight completely and he'd rejoice if she hadn't. It was her life, her world that would open up more or stay as it was now.

He hoped for her sake that this could be fixed, but if not it changed nothing for him. She had the ability to see so much on other planes of existence that he knew he could help her to see more than she'd ever thought possible. It wouldn't be like before, when her eyes were healthy and strong, but it would be something.

He made a mental note to look into her accident a little further. Maybe that was the connection – to her blindness, the asshole, maybe even the other cases. And depending on what was going on and how, this could potentially only end when this asshole was stopped.

Like so many other assholes before him.

Stefan knew he should get up, but he wanted every moment he could have with her – especially like this.

His mind freewheeled through the bits and pieces of information that he'd learned this last week. Holding a mental canvas, he kept splattering the bits and pieces on the canvas, hoping to see a pattern. A connection. It wasn't easy to do, as he had many cases to sift through. Even the locations of the burning sensation that Sam had been picking up, a poison maybe, were in different parts of the body. He continued to place the pieces on his canvas, hoping that one piece would fit. Then another.

His mind spun endlessly on the possibilities. The clues were the burning heat and the fact that there were *no* similarities – that they could see. Still he understood Sam's talent, and he had no doubt the connection was there. He also believed Celina had no idea what was going on. She also knew more than she understood. Teasing it out of her would be the problem.

As Celina slept, the room had slowly filled with ghosts. He shifted his vision so he could see the energy as they floated in and around. They weren't sure what to do with his presence, but none attacked him or appeared bothered in any way. They all had very long, thin cords into Celina's energy. Cords that couldn't be released permanently until Celina let them go. No wonder she was exhausted and likely had been for a long time.

Had these guys been siphoning off her energy to keep up their existence here? It happened. And not always with malicious intent. Anyone who felt pulled in many directions with a lot of different friends could have the exact same problem. Celina would have to learn to cut the cords to gain her freedom. That way, if the ghosts wanted to stay around they could, but at the same time their presence wouldn't drain her.

Her injury also exhausted her. She probably had no idea how badly she'd been burning through her life force with her constant rejection of her blindness. Plus, this predator had become a parasite on her system. By using her abilities without protecting herself, Celina had left herself open to being taken advantage of on an energetic level, and as a result she'd become a host to many parasites.

She could change that, but as she'd given her permission for this to happen, she was the one required to make the changes. He stayed silent at her side, watching the kaleidoscope of energies filter in and out. The parasite wasn't here.

He waited, his mind slipping back in and out of his consciousness. It expanded outward, softening, accepting and open to anything. He'd learned this trick from another incredibly talented friend, Shay Lassiter, who had the ability to spread her energy so thin as to no longer exist – or rather exist – everywhere… at the DNA level. Following her lessons he spread outward and outward and outward. He had no purpose behind this exercise other than as a practice session. He was in the living room, the bathroom, the bedroom, out in the hallway, down the elevator, out in the lobby, and into the night.

His consciousness filtered down even smaller as he let himself mingle with the night.

He floated in peaceful contentment, leaving his senses wide open but relaxed as he lay there. After a few minutes he raised the level of awareness, looking for something out of the ordinary in Celina's world. Her energy pathway from her day's travels floated in faint wispy color around him. It was easy to follow her trail to Dr. Maddy's office and backwards along the pathway that she'd taken throughout the day. He could see the taxi carrying a little of Celina's energy moving throughout the rest of the afternoon, picking up other people's energy and adding it to the pile. By the time the cab itself parked that night it was a seething mass of pulsating energy.

Interesting that the cab continued to stand out as he walked through Celina's movements. Stefan studied the cab and where it had parked. It wasn't in a garage with many other cabs; it had gone to a house and parked there. It wasn't that the cab still held traces of Celina's energy, which it did, but it was so finite as to not be visible anymore. That the vehicle continue to stand out could only mean one thing – the cabby had been affected by Celina.

Stefan smiled. That would make total sense.

With something tugging at him, he turned to one of his favorite projects. The children's hospital and the wing he and Maddy had set up, similar to her other project on Maddy's Floor. He dove forward, zipping to the children's ward, pulling the tiny bits and pieces of errant energy back into alignment.

Inside the special ward, a wobble had formed on the edge at the back end. Where Eric was lying. Eric, who had been with them for only a couple of days but had managed to affect the energy field. The doctors were concerned about his mental health. He'd had surgery and had taken a violent dislike to the bone the doctors had used. What should have been an easy surgery had turned into a nightmare with the child's reaction. His medication had been changed several times and his mental state watched closely, but there'd been no improvement. Stefan zoomed in to the child's bed.

His heart hurt. Everywhere else the children slept in peaceful healing sleep. Like they were supposed to. Yet, this little boy twisted with terrible nightmares. His body couldn't heal because it couldn't rest. It couldn't rest because the boy's mind had filled with terrors.

He drifted over Eric's bed, laying a delicate blanket of healing energy over the child's body.

The small boy stiffened, his eyes flying open to stare right at Stefan. And damn if he didn't whisper, "Are you an angel?"

SAM OPENED HER eyes, pain in her leg exploding through her dreams. She kept the scream back to a whimper. She'd felt this pain before. This person's pain before. Going on instinct and dropping her training lessons, she settled deeper into the person.

And realized something else. He wasn't dead or dying — at least not yet. She dropped lower into his psyche and heard him speak. And realized it was a child. A little boy. Her heart throbbed with the pain of what was to come in his life. Yet it wasn't happening right now, and that made no sense to her.

She opened her eyes and gasped. He was talking to a spirit in energetic form.

The little boy's question echoed in the room. He'd asked the spirit if he was an angel. She took another look and smiled. The little boy was talking to Stefan.

She watched Stefan start, then lean closer, his gaze intent. He smiled and said, "No, I'm not an angel, but you have an angel watching over you."

Sam grinned. How absolutely bizarre to have her inside the boy's psyche and Stefan on the outside watching. They'd been here like this once before, but this was so different. The boy wasn't dying. He wasn't an old friend of Stefan's needing help to leave the earthly plane like last time.

And if that was the case, why was she here?

She'd never been called unless to a scene of violence.

She puzzled on it, then closed her psychic eyes and sank deeper into the boy's system. The boy was at a hospital. What had happened to the poor thing? Her heart always melted whenever she was drawn to a child. The nasty, cruel things people did to each other were amplified when they did it to a child. This child had been or was a victim of violence, she knew that for sure. As much as she wished her abilities would allow her to connect to other people for other reasons, it wasn't to be.

What she didn't know is if this boy was connected to the other weird things she'd been seeing lately. If so, the killer had either failed in his attempt, the act was going to happen immediately, or it was happening now but no one knew. Still the boy was alive, and that meant there might be a way to save him. If only she could find something that would connect this boy to the others so that she could find the killer.

She heard Stefan, understanding and comprehension in his voice, say, "What's wrong, Eric?"

Sam turned her attention back to the child. The boy had had surgery, recent surgery, but there was no air of healing. More a black wall of energy, as if a war going on in his body. The little boy whispered, "You won't believe me." He scrunched lower into his bed. "Adults never believe kids."

"But I'm not an adult," Stefan whispered. "Now tell me – what's the matter?"

And the words, so faint, so full of terror and fear broke Sam's heart. "There's a bad man inside me."

HE STRETCHED AND groaned. If he had to be here, he'd be damned if he'd do this half-existence any other way than his way. If that meant knocking off a few people, then who gave a shit?

If he could have put a stop to this a long time ago he would have. But no, it wasn't to be. So he'd taken this life and he'd owned it. Bit by bit. He wouldn't be here for too much longer – he knew that, and it was amazing how living such a good life had turned him into a man so bent on revenge and regaining his freedom that he'd toss those scruples away and become someone even he no longer recognized.

Still, it was all good. He'd have his freedom and she'd get her just end.

If he could just pull this off. He needed more power. He needed to stop the splintering process from happening even further. Better to have all those pieces blown up at once.

He froze.

Could he do that? It would make this so much easier. So much faster. And bring about a lot of chaos.

He used to hate strife and discord.

Now he'd do anything to create such hell.

CHAPTER 20

CELINA WOKE WITH a booming headache again. They'd been getting worse for weeks, but since the accident at the bar she had to wonder if she had hit her head and hadn't known. The chaos there had been seriously crazy, and it was quite possible she'd been banged up more than she thought.

She fleetingly considered contacting the doctor, then realized she'd already seen the eye surgeon and had two visits with Dr. Maddy. If there had been anything wrong surely either of those specialists would have seen it.

They had not mentioned it. Neither had Stefan. At the reminder she reached across the bed and found it empty.

An unexpected sense of loss filled her. He'd left. Then again, what had she expected? He had a life. He'd stayed with her out of compassion. There was little to keep him here.

"Feeling better?"

That deep, sensuous voice reached her from the door-way. Her insides danced. She gasped in joy. "You're still here?"

"Of course. This place isn't as comfortable as mine, but you needed looking after and as much as I want to shift you to my place, I decided this was home for you so I stayed here."

It took her a moment to digest all of that, and she realized he'd actually wanted to take her to his place. That thought filled her with an odd sense of excitement, yet also discomfort. A new place to learn to navigate.

She didn't want to be confined to her apartment, and she wasn't in the sense that she went out on a regular basis, but those trips were stressful. She'd like to avoid them altogether if she could. And that wasn't good for her. It would be too easy to become a hermit and hide away. She could even do her groceries by ordering online. She'd never have to leave again. That the suggestion was oddly appealing scared her. She didn't want to be so narrow in her focus, her world that she became that person, too scared to leave.

"I think your place must be beautiful," she said with a smile. "I'd love to see it."

"Then that answers my next question." He walked closer and placed a cup of tea on the night table beside her. "I was hoping to take you there this afternoon. It would be good for you to get out and enjoy a day's outing."

He sat down on the bed, long fingers reaching out to stroke her hair back off her forehead. "In fact, I wouldn't mind going soon."

She tilted her head, hearing an odd note in his voice. "Why the rush?"

"I have information at home that I need." He paused then confessed, "And I need to stop at the children's hospital and visit a little boy."

At the mention of the hospital she realized she'd hoped to go see Jacob. "I actually wanted to go and see Jacob at the hospital. He was injured at Chico's and has been in a coma ever since."

"Perfect. We'll do both visits then head to my place for the afternoon."

It was a great idea. And it saved her from going to the hospital alone. She gave a small laugh. "Then away with you so I can dress."

He leaned over and brushed her lips with his, startling her. Then he was gone. She heard the door whisper closed behind him. It didn't matter that she was still awestruck by that kiss. So gentle and light, but like an electric jolt. Her hormones had shot into awareness and her body had woken up big time. Even now it felt like little electric currents raced across her lips. She shook her head, determined to clear the clouds and remember the reality of her existence. She needed to enjoy having him in her life but not to get used to it. She didn't expect him to die like her parents or her fiancé had, but she did expect him to get tired of the limitations her blindness would put on them and soon pull out.

She wanted him to be different, but she hadn't seen many men who could deal with a blind partner.

Back to reality, she dressed quickly in capris and a bright-colored t-shirt. She needed to do her laundry soon. Returning to the bed, she quickly straightened out the bedding and in the process she found the hairbrush he'd used last night.

It reminded her of how she'd gone to sleep. She'd asked him to stay.

He hadn't stayed because he wanted to be here. He'd stayed because she'd specifically asked him to.

She had to remember that.

AFTER A QUICK breakfast of toast and cheese – apparently she needed to go shopping too – Stefan took her first to see Jacob. As they walked through the crowded hospital area, her hand tucked securely in Stefan's arm, she realized how much nicer it was to walk with someone. She was always so independent – specifically so as to not become dependent – that she'd forgotten the joy of just being able to relax and let go, knowing that she'd be taken care of.

She'd often wondered if there was something wrong with her. As a young teenager, after losing Caslo, then her parents, any association she made immediately became something she grasped onto so tightly she often choked the relationship – sometime to death. She hadn't realized what she was doing, of course, but she'd been very good at it. She'd also become scared of going anywhere on her own in case no one was there when she came back.

Over time, she'd lost a lot of friends and had clung a little too tightly to the rest until she was sure she wasn't going to lose them too. Eventually they had drifted away anyway. Then she'd become fiercely independent, refusing any and all assistance to the point of being stupid about it. It stopped her from being hurt when friendships broke up.

Her ghosts had helped. They were always around. In some cases there were too many around. Still, they never seemed to leave. She could send one or two away to the light, but for the most part the others stayed around all the time.

After losing her sight some problems had returned. Like the lack of self-confidence and the feeling that her friends wouldn't want to be around her now that she was blind.

It had been a rude awakening to realize that except for her co-workers at the symphony she had no friends.

Somehow she'd become isolated anyway.

At Jacob's doorway she stopped and stared in the direction of the bed. She didn't hear anything. "Is he there?" she asked Stefan in a low tone.

He squeezed her hand and led her forward. "His body is here, but it looks like he's not."

"What?" she asked, confusion coloring her voice. "Is he dead?"

"No. Not at all." Stefan pulled a chair forward and helped her into it. He then placed her hand on Jacob's warm, still one.

"Remember how you look around a room and see ghosts?" he asked.

"Yes." She frowned up at him. "And?"

"Do that now," he instructed.

With a shrug she opened her eyes to the ghosts in the room, realizing with surprise that there really was a process to it. She'd been doing it for so long it came naturally, so she hadn't seen the steps she took. With her eyes now open to the ghostly visitors in the room she cast a quick glance. There, on the other side of a long, slim rope-like thing stretching across the room to the bed she was sitting beside was a man.

She frowned, half-recognizing him, but his features were blurry. That he had distinct features at all was already unusual. Normally ghosts were blurred until she got to know them. Maybe she put their features in place so she could identify with them or be more comfortable talking to them. When a ghost appeared out of focus like this it was hard to stare at them. It actually gave her a headache, so she always brought them more into focus. And that meant adding features.

She went through the same process right now.

She gasped in joy then cried, "Jacob."

JACOB HAD LIT up at the sight of Celina and a stranger walking into his room. Finally, a visitor he'd been waiting for. He understood that only family had been allowed for a long time, but apparently that rule had been lifted.

When she'd sat down he'd wished more than anything that he could squeeze the hand holding his. He'd tried. But he'd felt nothing. Then she'd turned that wonderful gaze and looked right at him.

He'd caught his breath, that non-existent air in his chest, and hoped for something – anything – but had expected nothing.

Then she'd seen him, like actually *seen* him. And had called his name.

How could that be? He hopped off the window ledge and walked slowly toward her. He waved his hand in front of those blind eyes and laughed in disbelief when she reached out a hand to catch his. Of course her hand went right through his, but she'd actually seen it. Seen him. He wanted to laugh and scream and really wanted to cry.

He dropped to his knees beside her and laid his head on her lap. Sobs wracked his frame. Someone actually saw him.

"Jacob. This is Stefan," she said gently. "He's a friend."

Jacob lifted his head and studied the man at Celina's side. And damn if that man didn't smile at him too. "You can see me?" he asked in shock. "Both of you can?"

He turned to make sure his body was still lying separate from his soul. It was still there, so nothing had changed. He looked back to the two people watching him. "How is this possible?"

Celina laughed. "I have no idea."

"It's because the more open you are to seeing the energy vibrating at different frequencies the more able you can see what's around you."

Jacob stared at him. Who was this man who stood so possessively by Celina's side? "Who are you?"

Celina lifted a hand to grasp Stefan's hand in a lover-like way. Had he been out of real life for so long that she'd actually met someone and formed a relationship already, or had this been going on and he hadn't known? Either way, it almost made him laugh at his disgruntlement.

"I'm a friend of Celina's," Stefan answered carefully.

"A friend?" Jacob asked cautiously. He watched the corner of Stefan's lips quirk slightly. Suspicions aroused, he said, "How good a friend?"

Celina flushed and rushed to say, "Jacob, that is none of your business."

Stefan just laughed. "I'm a good friend that hopes to become a much better friend."

"At least you're honest," Jacob muttered. He stepped back to study the two of them. "Why can you both see me, talk to me, when no one else can?" Stefan remained silent, just staring back at him with a twinkle in his eye. Realizing he'd get no answers there, he turned his attention to Celina. "Celina?"

With a tiny wrinkling of her beautiful face she admitted, "I see and talk to ghosts." At his shocked look, she grinned. "I know you're not dead, and supposedly I shouldn't be able to see you, not to mention that I'm blind, but I think Stefan had something to do with that." She reached up to pat Stefan's hand on her shoulder.

"Stefan?"

"Yes?"

"You can see people like me?"

"Obviously."

Stefan didn't appear to want to discuss Jacob's state, but damn it, that's all he wanted to talk about. "Can you tell me how to get back into my body?" he asked, flinching slightly at the desperation in his tone.

"No. It's instinctive for you to leave and to go back." Stefan studied him. "Your life force is strong, your cord is healthy. Your body still needs healing time and could be in a coma for another few days."

"That's not good."

"Why?" Stefan asked.

"I..." Jacob shrugged. "There's something I was supposed to do or say. And I can't remember to whom or why." He turned to Celina and dropped back to his knees. "I think it was to you. A warning."

"A warning?" Celina reached forward to grasp his ghostly hands. "About what?"

"I don't know!" He shuddered. "I've been trying to wrack my brain about what it was but I can't remember."

"About the accident at Chico's?" Stefan asked. "Did you have something to do with the message on Celina's bathroom?"

Celina gasped in shock, her head shaking in denial. Not possible. "Surely that couldn't be?"

Stefan squeezed her shoulder. "When someone needs to send a message, the how and why they succeed is often a mystery. I had to ask."

Only Jacob's face was screwed up as if trying to remember.

"I don't know. Maybe? Yes." Jacob stood up and stared at Stefan. "Yes. A warning. About the car accident. The driver. Something..."

"Did you know him?"

Jacob frowned. "I don't know. Who was driving?"

"Owen Dugar, and he didn't survive the crash."

"Owen? Dead?" Jacob stepped back, his hands slapping to his chest even as he struggled to breathe. His hand fisted at his mouth to hold back his cries. He could see his form waver and thin. He looked longingly at his body. "My phone. He texted me. At the end. Almost at the end."

"Who is he to you?" Stefan asked urgently.

"He desperately wanted to meet Celina." Jacob stared at Celina, her blind gaze staring back at him. "I thought it would be okay."

"Yes, but who was he? Why did he want to meet me?" she asked, then suddenly understood something. "Was this your new boyfriend?"

"He was the love of my life." Jacob cried out, "And now he's dead."

Overcome with grief, Jacob disappeared.

CELINA STARED AT the drifting remains of Jacob's ghostly image and said, "Please tell me he hasn't died."

"No, he's not dead." Stefan turned her slightly and put her hand back over Jacob's hand in the bed. "He's back in his body."

He just didn't know what shape Jacob was in emotionally after that shock. It was also hard to focus on what was happening here, and now he wanted to call Brandt and set him to tracking down Jacob's cell phone. The driver of the car was important. He wished they'd fully understood why Dugar had wanted to meet Celina. That he was Jacob's partner was one thing, but he doubted it was everything.

She brightened. "That's great. Right? That's what we

want, right?"

"Absolutely. It's where he belongs. Hopefully now that he's back he'll heal."

"Goo—"

A series of alarms went off from the machines at Jacob's side.

"Oh my God, what's wrong?" she cried. "Stefan." She stood up and leaned over Jacob, her hands reaching for his face.

Running feet in the hallway were followed by a strange voice calling out, "Get back, please."

Stefan moved Celina gently but firmly off to the side. He held her close, feeling her shudder as they listened to the orders given and instructions taken as the team worked to save Jacob.

"It's all right, Celina. I can see a shift happening. He's going to be okay," he murmured against her ear. Jacob's cord was strong, glowing. "It might take a bit for his body to recover but he should heal now."

She stilled, turning her face toward him in hope. "Really? Oh, thank God."

"If you two will please step out in the hallway?"

Stefan led Celina out into the hallway at the nurse's request. Out there he ran his hands up and down her arms in a soothing motion. "There's nothing more we can do to help here. Are you okay to leave?"

She dropped her head against his chest, then lifted it to stare up at him. "Yes. I just hope he's going to be okay. That was scary."

"Maybe, but it was also very helpful in that we now have a lead to follow in that fatal crash and Jacob is back where he belongs."

Before leaving the hospital Celina took a moment to use the washroom, and Stefan took advantage of the privacy to contact Brandt. Quickly he relayed Jacob's words and association to the driver that had crashed into Chico's. *We need to find that cell phone. Jacob said he'd sent the text a few moments before the crash.*

"Which could be nothing more than a man telling his friend he's going to be late." Brandt groaned. "Why couldn't he have told us why Dugar wanted to meet Celina?"

True. It could be just that he wanted his best friends to meet. And it could be something else altogether.

Stefan smiled as people walked past him down the hallway. *For that we need Jacob to regain consciousness. In the meantime, check his phone for the messages between him and Dugar. It's probably here at the hospital. Or at the restaurant still.*

"I hope not. Chico's is still a mess."

Maybe, but it's habit to put a cell phone away immediately. Consider that he wrote the message in Celina's bathroom — that's not the action of a man who doesn't care.

"Yeah, see, I don't get that," Brandt said.

No, but he did it regardless of what we understand. That phone has to be important. He was at a crowded bar, standing around laughing and drinking. There's only so much space to put down a valuable item like that and not lose it.

The words had barely left his mouth when the hospital hallway ripped away like a curtain torn back over his mind and he could see a vision of the bar full of laughter and drinking. High-spirited calls back and forth and there, Jacob in the center. A drink in his hand and nothing else. He lifted his glass and called out, "A toast! To one of the most talented groups of people–"

"Stefan?" Celina called out, her hand rubbing his forearm. "Are you alright?"

With a jolt he brought himself back to his surroundings. Closing his eyes, he worked to ease back the edges of his control and calm his breathing. He took a shuddering breath and managed to murmur, "I'm fine. Just lost in thought. Are you ready to leave?"

At her nod he covered her hand with his and led her out the doorway. As he walked through the double doors out into the sunshine, he sent Brandt a strong telepathic message. *Find that damn phone. We need it.*

BRANDT GOT THE message the first time; he hadn't needed it slammed into his subconscious again. But Stefan was used to giving orders and having them followed. Brandt checked the report to see what items had been logged in from the crash site. Several phones, the numbers identified, and not one was registered to Jacob. He called the hospital.

There was a bag with personal items that he came in with. Yes, there was a phone there, but it had no identification on it. Brandt hung up, checked his watch, and realized he had twenty minutes to run up and check to see if it was the right cell phone and what, if anything, was on it that mattered so much.

CHAPTER 21

OUT OF THE hospital, Stefan at her side, the sunshine on her face, Celina realized how different life was from even just a week ago.

Stefan drove competently, as always. She couldn't see his hands or the look of focus on his face but she heard the engine purr under his sure touch and roar forward at his command. She doubted there was much he didn't do well. She'd gone to school with several people who just surpassed everyone naturally in a particular skill or subject. There'd been one girl in the final year who'd thought nothing of reupholstering her own furniture as a weekend project. And then did it. She'd done an incredible job.

Trusting that Stefan would take her to the next place safely, she relaxed into her seat, her mind remembering Jacob and their visit. How terrible that Jacob's love was the man who'd caused the accident. She couldn't help feeling a little guilty. He'd been coming to meet her. She hadn't known, of course, but still… She turned to Stefan. "Is Jacob really going to be okay now?"

"I don't know for sure, but he did sink back into his body. I'm thinking that is a good thing."

Such a weird concept. "It sounds bizarre."

"Only because it's new," he said. "Most people leave their bodies while they sleep."

Not something, she wanted to consider. "I don't think I ever have."

"You have." He grinned. "But like most people you don't remember the trips you've taken."

"You spoke to me in my dream once, didn't you?"

He glanced her way. "Yes. I wasn't sure you realized that was me."

"I didn't at the time because it didn't seem real." She leaned back and closed her eyes thinking about that dream. "It was real though, wasn't it?"

"Yes."

"Why did you do that?" she asked, needing to understand.

"You were having a bad nightmare. I was trying to show you how to change that to a nicer dream."

"Something about thoughts creating the atmosphere in there."

He hesitated.

Curious, she asked, "Now what?"

"It's not just in there. Our thoughts can affect the atmosphere everywhere. Everything is energy and with a little tweaking, everything can be made so much better."

"But only in our own space, right?" She frowned as she considered that information. Most people would love to make their own spaces easier to live in. If one had a tense day, being able to make it happy and peaceful would be lovely. Then she realized that Stefan hadn't answered her. "Are you saying people can affect the space around other people?"

"I did in your dream."

She wrinkled her nose at him. "And if you could do that, then presumably you can do so much more."

"Of course." But he didn't elaborate.

The engine shifted and slowed as he took a right turn, then another, and followed that with a left turn. He parked and turned off the engine.

"Where are we?"

"At the children's hospital."

Right. She'd forgotten about that. She exited the vehicle and as always, he was there beside her. Holding her hand as they walked across the parking lot. She could feel light raindrops hitting her face. The country needed the rain, but it wasn't what she'd have chosen. A light chill had settled into the air too. She tugged her sweater closer.

He responded instantly by wrapping an arm around her shoulders and tucking her up close to his chest. The man radiated heat. Waves rolled off his chest even though he appeared to be wearing a cotton shirt.

"One step up." He waited for her to step up then led her through large doors. Instantly the warmth from inside the hospital enveloped her. She smiled appreciatively. They turned to the left and kept walking.

"Stairs or elevators?" he asked. Only a bell signaled the opening of an elevator. At that moment several people brushed past her in a cloud of perfume and aftershave. And smoke. She hated the smell of smoke. At least most places were smoke-free, but the scent always took her back to her childhood. Her father and her best friend's father had smoked, often together. She'd hated the smell then and that hadn't improved. She stepped into the elevator, content to have him pick the floor.

At the seventh floor the doors slid open and she was enveloped in sensations she could barely recognize. It felt better than downstairs, and that had been good.

He led her into the ward. She first noticed the smell – it had a sterile cleanliness to it while missing the antiseptic bite. And the noises. Muted. Calm. Quiet. There were no voices. No laughing or crying. Hadn't Stefan said this was a children's ward? She couldn't remember ever having been in one, but this didn't seem quite right.

No one approached them or spoke to them as they walked. She wondered if that was unusual. Stefan wasn't a doctor. How did he have the ability to come and go in a place like this?

He slowed at another door and took a moment to do something. Head tilted, she concentrated on sorting out all of the odd noises then smiled. A card reader security system. She waited as the door clicked open and they proceeded down the hallway a little farther.

The farther they got into the new space the warmer, lighter, and softer the energy. She tried to describe it, but found it difficult considering it was really unique. It was akin to the sensation she felt taking a long, hot soak in the tub after a long day. That sense of relief, of joy, of peace as she slipped into the water. The sensation of *ahhh* as she sank into the tub and relaxed. She didn't know what to think about feeling a similar thing here. Obviously it was deliberate, if she considered his comment about creating the atmosphere one wanted. It did feel good. Special.

They were such inadequate words.

As they continued to walk she could visualize the hallway from other hospitals she'd seen before she lost her vision and realized there were likely wards on either side of her. Muted noises could be heard at certain spots, letting her know they were passing various rooms. Stefan stopped, and again the card swipe. Interesting.

He opened the door and ushered her in.

Instantly laughter and shrieks raced toward her. Happy sounds that made her heart light and brought a smile to her face. She loved it here already.

"Stefan!" Children screamed, laughed, and clamored in every way they could.

Celina laughed. "I can't see what's happening, but it sounds like a herd is racing toward us."

"You're seeing just fine, as that is ex – oomph." Stefan laughed and laughed. Celina stood in one place and let the horseplay happen. Children screamed.

"Me next."

"No – me next."

Stefan's laughter rolled all around her. Waves of joy, ripples of fun, invigorating energy bounced off her and around her to join the melee.

In the background she heard adult voices calling for order. Calling the children to return to their beds.

"Children, calm down. Let Stefan walk in."

"Aww, I didn't get a turn." Then the same voice squealed in joy, the tenor changing as he must have been lifted high in Stefan's arms.

Bemused and heartened by the children's responses, Celina didn't dare walk forward in case there were littler children underfoot. She'd hate to hurt a child. Waiting in place, she listened to the goings-on around her.

Just when she thought to clear her voice and call for Stefan, a small hand slipped into hers. She gasped softly then whispered, "Hello."

A young male answered. "Hello. Would you like to come and sit down?"

"Yes, I would." She squeezed the little hand. "Can you

take me to a place where I won't be in the way?"

Her arm was lifted and she was led forward. Not know-ing what else to do, she followed the little person. "What's your name?"

"David."

Ah, maybe this was the little boy Stefan had come to see.

"Here." Her hand was placed on the back of a chair, a little clumsy, but she appreciated the gesture. Taking her seat, she hoped to keep the boy with her. "I guess Stefan is a popular visitor."

"Stefan is the greatest." The little voice was so serious, so firm in that statement, there was no denying the truth in his voice.

"Does he come here often?"

"No," he said. "We offered him a bed but he says he can't stay here."

The plaintive tone made her giggle. "I think he has a big house to sleep in on his own."

"Then we should go to his house," David piped up. "I bet it's awesome. Maybe he has a playground too."

"I don't know what he has," Celina said with laughter in her voice. "I'm supposed to go there after this visit. Maybe I'll be lucky. Maybe he'll have a playground big enough for me."

"That would be awesome!"

Then her host disappeared, running in the opposite di-rection, laughing and screaming.

Moments later Stefan's long fingers stroked down her cheek. "How are you doing?"

"I'm fine." She smiled up at him. "Are you always greet-ed like this?"

He laughed. "More or less."

"The place feels great. I don't know what goes on here, but the energy is incredibly powerful."

"Glad you can feel it. The nurses love working here."

"I can imagine." If she had a chance to work here, she would too. "Who is it you came to see?"

He squeezed her shoulder. "Eric, but I'll spend a moment with everyone. If you're okay here for a bit…"

"I'm fine." She smiled. "Go. Take care of what you need to. I'll be fine."

"Good. You might want to open your ghost vision and see what you see."

He walked away. His heavy footsteps moving into the noise, his words hung heavy inside her mind. She opened her eyes hesitantly, half-expecting to see ghosts from deceased children. Instead, the room was alive with energy. Bright, vibrant energy. Laughing, bouncing, bubbling energy. She stared as the colors ran and raced and collided and bounced off each other in joy – all inside her mind.

At least that's what it felt like. But as she stared around the room, she could see shadows of walls. Windows. Doors. Beds and so much more. All features gray and blurry, but still there for her to see. In grayness, but there nonetheless. She strained to see more and as soon as she did, the images blurred.

She closed her eyes and rested them. Then opened them again. And saw the same vibrant colors as before and the gray surroundings.

"Amazing," she whispered and then understood.

She was seeing the color attached to the sounds the children made!

STEFAN CAST A last look back at Celina, saw the rapt look on her face, and realized she'd opened her internal vision. She'd be fine alone for a few minutes. The children, being children, hadn't been bothered by her walking stick or her unsure steps. But he needed to see how Eric was doing. And see if Eric remembered him.

He walked through the ward to a smaller room on the other side. Eric lay there, his mother ever at his side. She glanced up, saw him and immediately stood up.

"Hi," Stefan said gently. "I'm Stefan Kronos—"

"Oh I heard you'd be coming." She grinned and motioned to her son. "He's been asking for you."

Stefan nodded absently, his gaze already on Eric's huge, hollow-eyed stare.

"How are you doing, Eric?" he asked.

Eric's gaze darted to his mother and back again.

Stefan switched to speaking with him telepathically. *Any better? Is the monster still there?*

Eric's gaze grew rounder, but he answered readily enough. *I haven't heard him in a little bit.* He hesitated and said, *How can you do this?*

Stefan saw the doubt and the tinge of fear on his face and immediately soothed the young boy. *No, I'm not a monster. Remember, I'm a monster fighter. In order to fight them I have to be able to do some of their tricks.*

Eric's face lit up. Risking a look at his mother, Stefan realized that she was staring at the two of them, a frown on her face.

Eric said, "Mom, can you get me a treat from downstairs?"

Her face cleared and she hopped to her feet. "If you are okay here with Stefan alone, then I'm happy to go and find something. What would you like?"

"Milk and cookies, please."

Both males waited until she'd left, then Stefan walked over and sat down on Eric's bedside. "So no word from him?"

Eric shook his head, his face more animated than Stefan had seen yet.

"And what about bad dreams?"

"None." Eric grinned. "Did you do that? It's like there's a wall keeping the bad guys out."

"Exactly. Think of it as a castle wall that we can defend to keep you safe."

Eric relaxed. Then a whisper of worry swept across his face. "What if he comes back and climbs the wall this time?"

"Then you are going to call out to me and I'm going to come and defend that castle wall. Right?"

Eric sank deeper into the covers. "Right. You're my defender."

"And together, we'll be dragon slayers." Stefan rose as Eric's mother bustled back in with a carton of milk and a small package of cookies. Her gaze immediately went to her son and he watched as surprise, joy, and then gratitude filled her tired features. "My, don't you look better," she said as she placed the food down on the small table.

Eric grabbed the milk and had a long drink, then proceeded to tear into his cookies.

She walked over to Stefan. "Thank you. I don't know what you did, but..." she glanced back at her son, now completely focused on his food, "I've been so worried."

"With any luck he has turned a corner and will start to heal." Stefan cast another long look at the black shadow on Eric's knee and knew it wouldn't be that easy. Somehow that bone either needed to be replaced, a horrific, costly, and dangerous process, or they had to cleanse it of whatever energy was poisoning it. And given the difficulty of that, he'd likely have to bring in Dr. Maddy and have Eric actively participate when they went to take the dragon out forever.

First, they needed to know how the dragon had managed to get into this child. Then they could figure out what he wanted and how to get rid of him permanently.

BRANDT TURNED THE phone over in his hand. There were no identifying names or tags on it. Figured. He turned it on, leaning on the reception desk, the rest of Jacob's personal effects in front of him.

The phone didn't appear to be badly damaged. It was scratched up some but turned on immediately. He checked the last texts. Sure enough, they were from the dead man before he crashed.

Jacob, man, I'm not feeling good.

Ha. No deal. You wanted to meet her, you get over here.

I'm on the way. Then a second text from him. *My chest is killing me. Horrible burning. I think something is wrong.*

No.

I don't feel right. Angry. So angry. Something is wrong. No choice. I think this is it.

That was the last text. A phone call had come through just minutes before the crash, so Owen Dugar had been texting while driving, given the time frame. But what had been said in the phone call? There'd be no way to get that information, but forensics would be able to get the length of the call. That would only tell him if Jacob received it and answered it and spoke to his friend.

Would it tell him why the man had driven into the pub?

Unless like the texts implied he hadn't been feeling good and had a heart attack at the time and lost control of the car.

Nothing sinister there.

Except for that line: *Angry. So angry.* And of course the burning.

KEY. SHE WAS the key. And he needed to figure out how to turn that damn lock. He needed to find out what made her tick. He couldn't believe she was proving to be so difficult. He didn't want much. But he needed that one thing from her and she wouldn't give it to him. He hated her for that. For having power over him. He was the one that was gaining in power now. She was failing him.

He'd turn the tables soon. He just had to stay strong enough to do it. Strong enough to finally beat her. And he would. It was the one thing he was focusing on. Gaining strength for. He knew it would be the last thing he'd do, and that was fine by him as long as he got her too.

Bitch.

How dare she be stronger, better than him? Well, she could gloat for now. He'd make sure to have the last laugh – when she couldn't laugh anymore.

CHAPTER 22

CELINA WALKED INTO Stefan's house almost two hours after entering the hospital. She'd been lost in a rapt daze for the bulk of the afternoon. "Thank you for showing me the children's energies. They were the brightest, happiest things I think I have ever seen."

"I didn't show them to you. You saw them yourself."

"True. Thank you then for taking me there and suggesting I look. I was afraid initially that I'd see too many ghosts. And that would have been horrible."

"And did you?" he asked, unlocking the front door and pushing it open.

"Ghosts? Yes, a few, but they were all distant."

"As in old ghosts," he said. He led her inside and over to a place to sit, and gently pressed her into the chair. Only it was a couch made of buttery-soft leather. She couldn't resist running her fingers along the smooth cushions, almost humming with pleasure. She eased back and sighed at the fresh smell and the sunshine that drifted into the window. "Did the rain just stop?"

"Must have." But his voice held an odd note. She turned her head fully into the sun and let it bathe her eyes in the warmth and sense of peace. "Something funny?"

"No, I just find that there isn't much rain around my place all that often. The gardens need every drop, but there's something special about this location in that I get mostly sunshine here."

"Sounds like a good way to have it. You must have a wall of glass here for the sun to come inside so strong and bright."

"I do, but I also have a large deck outside and three sets of French doors along this wall opening up to the outside."

"Three sets? Most people only have one."

"I'm not most people," he said, a tinge of self-mockery in his voice.

"I believe that." She opened her eyes, wondering if she could see many energy trails here as she had at the children's ward. But it was all gray, no bright lights dancing or moving around. Disappointed, she let her gaze wander the room aimlessly until it landed on a bright pink spot somewhere in the vicinity of Stefan, but she didn't think it was him. At least it wasn't the same color energy that she'd come to associate with him. "Stefan," she said in wonderment. "I can see a big pink ball beside you."

"Ah, Lissa, say hi to Celina."

Immediately the pink ball focused into a teenager with her hair in a long ponytail, who walked over. "Hi, Celina. I love it when Stefan brings over people that can see me."

"Hi," Celina said, studying the fresh-faced girl, wondering who and what she was.

"I'm Lissa, and Stefan is a friend of my sister's and now my friend. I live here when I'm not bombing around visiting other places."

"You can travel to other places?" Celina had never met a ghost capable of even speaking the way Lissa was. Her ghosts had limited capabilities. Most lived tiny windows of experience, and most were limited to her apartment. This young girl was unlike any ghost she'd ever seen.

"She's very unusual," Stefan said, grinning, making Celina realize with a shock that she'd spoken out loud.

Lissa's light, tinkling laugh resounded around the room. She said proudly, "I'm learning to paint."

Stefan sighed. "Did you work on an empty canvas this time, or did you decide to add to one of mine again?"

"Ha! You were very specific about that." Her tone lightened as she added, "I made my own painting." Now her voice came from the far side of the room. Celina turned her head and watched as the sprite of a ghost moved through a doorway.

"If you will excuse me, Celina, I'll go see what the minx is up to."

"Not a problem," she smiled, thinking about a ghost painting and wishing she could see it. "I'll wait here."

"My guitar is beside you on the left if you want something to play with." Then he walked away. "Lissa, I'm coming."

Celina couldn't imagine a ghost that was as developed as Lissa. She herself was always trying to get her ghosts to leave the physical plane but she couldn't. They all gave her that same long, drawn-out look of disbelief that such a thing was possible. Some had managed to leave, so she knew it was possible. She needed to remind Stefan about letting Lissa go. It would be in her best interests to move on.

Curious, she reached down and picked up the guitar. She plucked a few strings, enough to know that Stefan had not scrimped on quality for his equipment. Happy to have something in her hand and not feeling quite so useless, she let her fingers drift across the strings.

"DOES SHE KNOW what she's doing?" Lissa asked.

Stefan studied her, the petulant look in her young features reminding him of her physical age.

"I'm sure she understands that she's playing the guitar," he said humorously.

"Very funny. As if you don't know what else she's doing." With a snigger she moved off slightly.

Stefan looked around this studio. "Where is your painting?

Lissa moved to the far end of the studio. She'd picked the small canvas on a tabletop easel. He was curious to see what a ghost would paint and why. He looked at her face as he walked around to see the painting for the first time. She had a moody look as if unsure what she'd painted herself. He turned to look at the picture. His eyebrows shot up. "What's this?" he asked.

Keeping his gaze on the simple, single item on the canvas, he waited for her explanation. When there wasn't one he asked, "Why this image, Lissa?"

"I don't know. It just seemed to fit."

And with that she disappeared.

"Seemed to fit?" Stefan wasn't sure what to say about that. He studied the painting for a long time then turned to return to the living room and Celina. But the crude image of a pill bottle – open, empty, thrown on the bedside, a man lying still beside it – haunted him long after.

BRANDT SAT BACK and rolled his shoulders. He'd been trying to figure out the connection between Sam's list of cases. If there was a connection. He had to admit by now that he was floundering, trying to find something. He loved

Sam to distraction, and he had the utmost respect for her ability and those that Stefan demonstrated time and time again. But why then was there nothing to be found here?

None of the cases had anything in common. And that couldn't be.

The probabilities said that wasn't to be either. The victims were both male and female. They were of all ages, from the youngest, who appeared to be Eric to the oldest, an eighty-four-year-old woman. They were all in this area or from nearby states. Thankfully he had Grant to call on once the cases crossed state lines.

He'd talk to the captain if there was anything to tell him. The captain knew about Sam. Knew of Stefan. So that wasn't a problem. But just because these two psychics were in agreement that something was going on didn't mean he had the evidence to prove the theory. He'd already pushed the limits a year ago by following the trail of a serial killer that no one else believed existed. To do it again would be an interesting experience. He normally saw patterns where others didn't, hence his trail following The Bastard, but now? What pattern was there here? None. And that bugged him.

Everything had a pattern.

He got up, cleaned off the board against his wall, and started to make a chart. Victims, age, method of death, location, and then on instinct, the type of pain Sam experienced in each case.

His phone rang about half an hour later. He checked his watch as he answered. "Grant, what's up?"

"Found a couple more cases that might be connected."

"Damn. Send them to me."

"I'm putting them into an email for you."

"Good. How many cases?"

"Three over the last year. Nothing before then."

"That fits with what Sam's been telling me. Something happened a year ago to trigger these events."

"Let me know when you find it." He hung up.

Brandt should be heading back to Sam but she was working all day at the vet hospital. Much to his pride and joy she'd been asked to get involved in the animals' patient care, helping the doctors to assess their needs with her extra senses. It was what she'd always wanted to do, to find a way to help people, not just deal with the ugly side of her talent.

He checked his watch again, waiting for Grant's email. "Ah, there it is." He printed off the three sheets, picked them up, and walked back to his chart. One more in Portland way back when, a car accident. Another about three months ago. The woman walked into heavy traffic and was killed, but also caused a hell of a car accident that injured four and killed another two people.

He stopped and stared. Then snatched up his sheets and added a second column. This time, he added in the number of other fatalities involved in each victim's death.

When he was done he sat back, feeling a heavy punch to his gut when he realized what he was looking at. In most cases, they'd taken out several other people with them.

Interesting.

Often a death was a single fatality. A heart attack. Even a car accident. But in many of these cases, even what would appear to be a suicide managed to kill several other people. Not every person had taken someone with them – but enough had to take note. He didn't have the answer, but he knew this was important.

Maybe even key.

CHAPTER 23

CELINA WOVE A colorful band of sound through the space in her head. She hoped it was wrapping around Stefan's living room and that he'd be able to see it and enjoy it. She wanted to impress him, but hated that she was still insecure enough to want that. He was a well-known and respected figure. She was a nobody. Sure, she made music, played with a well-recognized symphony, but she herself wasn't noticeable in a crowd – except for the space she took up due to her stick. Melancholic, drifting toward depression, her music changed tone and tempo, sliding into a deeper, painful rhythm that almost made her weep with the sadness.

"Why do you play such sad, depressing music?"

Celina stilled. The teenage ghost. Of course it would be her. With the typical forthrightness of her age, she hadn't heeded the sensitivity of the atmosphere and left Celina alone. Or along with most of her age group she didn't care.

"I was just feeling down," Celina said lightly, placing the guitar beside her.

"Uh-uh. I think it's more than that. Your music is very alluring, you know. Most of the time it's beautiful, then it became so sad it was painful to listen to."

Celina's eyebrows shot up. "Sorry to hear that." But she curled up with her knees tucked up beside her on the couch. Too bad she couldn't curl up into a tiny ball and pull a blanket over her head. It had been a long time since she'd been called out over something. It felt like high school all over again.

Then she laughed and realized something. Trust a teenager to make Celina regress. She'd hated high school, so Lissa was triggering all kinds of buttons. And that was just plain stupid. She smiled at the ghost. "So why do you stick around Stefan? Got a little crush on him?" she asked in a teasing tone, turning the tables on Lissa.

"Him?" Lissa snickered. "He's way too old. He's like, your age." And she disappeared.

Celina winced. "Touché," she said to the empty space where Lissa had been sitting.

"Sorry about that. Lissa has taken me on as a type of project where she wants to see me settled before she leaves."

"Settled?" Celina winced. "Sounds very old-fashioned."

"Lissa was raised with old-fashioned values."

"And I'm assuming from her dislike of me that I don't quite make the grade."

"I don't think she dislikes you at all. I think she's…" He paused to choose his words.

She twisted her lips. "Don't bother trying to make light of it. I have enough ghostly friends in this world. I certainly don't mind if this one doesn't want to be around me."

"It's not that. She's actually concerned about you."

"Concerned?" Celina said doubtfully.

"Concerned. Yes. She felt there was a lot of power in your music and she's afraid you could be…" He winced and added, "…abusing it."

Celina stared at him in shock. "Pardon?"

He shrugged. "I suggest you don't worry about it right now."

"I won't," she snapped, starting to dislike Lissa intensely. And what had looked to be an idyllic afternoon out with a nice man was starting to sound like something she'd like to cut short. "Maybe you should take me back to my apartment."

She sensed a certain stillness washing over him. She waited, wondering if she'd offended him now too. Seemed to be her day for screwing up.

And she'd hoped for just the opposite.

"I'd planned on making lunch first unless you truly want to leave. If you do, then of course I'll take you home, but please don't let Lissa be the cause."

Ouch. Was that all it took? A teenager to ruin her day out? How silly and adolescent was that of her?

"How about a cup of tea or coffee to keep away the blues?" he asked.

The air around her warmed up. She felt an almost invisible pat on her head. She frowned. Stefan or Lissa. Then deciding it wasn't an issue – she refused to let anyone else set her off again – she smiled up at Stefan and said, "Please."

She wanted to slap herself for being such a fool. What was it about being around Stefan that made her feel so insecure and incompetent? She wasn't. But he was so smooth and accomplished in everything he did, and the things he could do…wow.

Here in this place she could sense the airiness, the light. And could imagine the stone and wood that would suit him so well. Here she felt small. Unsuitable was maybe a better word, and she hated that. Maybe that's why she'd reacted badly to Lissa's words.

Music was her one great joy. Why would anyone say what Lissa had said? Unless, like she'd already guessed, Lissa was jealous of her relationship with Stefan. Not that they had much of one yet. But she could hope. He wouldn't want anything to do with her if she didn't calm down. Being blind was a handicap not everyone was suited to being around. They didn't know how to act with blind people. How to talk. Stefan had no such trouble. He acted as if she were normal. He led her around with a casual competence she had to marvel at. Either he really understood or he had a lot of experience being around people who were injured or handicapped like she was.

He seemed so assured. Everyone who she had met treated him with respect, affection, or in the case of the children, sheer idolatry. That had shown her such a different side to him. She wondered at his art. Would it be beautiful landscapes or something more like the work of the artist she'd spoken with at the gallery?

She couldn't imagine Stefan creating anything less than something completely stunning.

Footsteps sound on her left. Tilting her head slightly she sniffed the air. "Tea?" She smiled. "Thank you, it smells wonderful."

"Dragon pearls. A delicate-tasting green tea."

Of course he'd be a connoisseur of tea as well. "Is there anything you don't know or do well?"

The tray landed heavily. "Lots. Why would you think that?"

That startled a laugh out of her. "Everyone treats you with deference. I barely understand what you do with this energy work, but you are a consultant for the police and apparently a consultant with Dr. Maddy. You work at the children's hospital in some form where the staff treat you with respect and the children love you. That much was obvious."

She listened to his long-drawn exhale. "Well?" she asked.

STEFAN SAT BACK down slowly, unsure of what to say. He was admittedly learning much about himself. He preferred to give silent answers with facial and hand gestures over talking. He couldn't do that with Celina. He couldn't show her his paintings and have her understand that side of him that so few saw. In many ways he was the one that felt incapable of shining in this relationship. Partly because it mattered so much. He was the one out of his depth. Unsure of how to proceed. And for him that was unsettling. Usually he knew the step in front of him. He didn't need to know what was down the road as long as he kept his focus on the next step.

Now as he stared at the woman who'd come to mean so much and yet sat so damn far away, he had no idea how or what that next step was going to be.

He turned to gaze to his home, wondering if she'd like it. Without being able to actually see the floor-to-vaulted-ceiling river rock fireplace, the stained-glass windows that went up twenty feet. Without the visual it was hard to see how this place would suit her. She'd settled comfortably into the corner of the couch just fine, but other visitors would have wandered the place and made comments. She'd stayed in place. Even now she was still. Almost too still. Economy of movement was one thing. This…was something else altogether.

"Are you all right?"

He started. "Me? I'm fine. Just enjoying my tea."

Her lips twitched.

"Okay, and thinking about you. How you are the one

that amazes *me*. You sit with such grace, perfectly at home, not making small talk out of nerves or running on with endless conversation. You are content in the now, and that's very special."

Her brows shot up. She shook her head and said in a dry tone, "What if I'm awestruck to be in your presence?"

He spluttered the tea he'd been about to drink, then laughed and laughed. With a huge grin he said, "That's priceless. I know there's spirit in there, and I'd hate to think anything I do would ever dim it."

"Spirit?" She shook her head. "You haven't seen anything but weak, wimpy behavior. Since I met you I'm either recovering, sleeping, or in shock."

"And you've been almost killed in an accident, lost close friends, been threatened by a home invasion, shared some of your deepest secrets, learned more than you'd ever wanted to learn about the predator stalking you… and yet still you sit here calm and poised in the face of it." He knew she couldn't see, but he felt compelled to lift his cup of tea in a salute to her.

And damn if she didn't lift hers in response.

He lowered his cup and stared at her.

"How did you know to do that?"

"Do what?"

"Lift your cup in a toast type of response?"

She frowned. "I don't know. It just seemed the thing to do."

He let it go, but it was hard. There had to be something going on in there, but she didn't appear to understand herself. And neither did he. It was puzzling.

"And no, before you ask, I can't see anything." She took a sip of tea then lowered her arm, her face pensive. "Sometimes I can. A little, anyways."

"When and how much?" He sat forward and replaced his cup on the table. This might be the answer.

"Sometimes when I focus really hard I see shapes, like the world has a gray look to it. Not the real world, but a half-real world."

Interesting. And a clue to what was really happening. He said, "Does it hurt to do that?"

She nodded. "Sometimes. I get headaches. I thought it might be from straining too much."

"Have you tried to do it without straining?"

She shrugged. "I guess. If I could see like that more often it would be easier on me but because of the headaches I save it for emergencies."

"Understandable." He leaned back. "Try right now. Look around my place and tell me what you see."

Her brows furrowed. "I'm not sure I want to. The head-ache part, remember?"

"I can take care of the headache." He waited, watching the indecision whisper across her features. "It's an energy thing. I'm trying to see whether it's energy you are using to see that way or if you are actually seeing with limited visibility."

She frowned and worried away on her bottom lip.

"Not if the idea scares you."

"Of course it scares me," she said. She considered it for another long moment and took a deep breath. "Fine. But you promise you will deal with the headache."

"I will."

He sat back and watched. She closed her eyes for a long moment.

Stefan studied her energy and waited. She opened her

eyes and…he grinned. …she stood up and out of her body in a faint reflection of her normal energetic form.

She stood – looking at him from her etheric body.

That's why the gray world. That's why the headache. She was doing it consciously but separate from the rest of her. He didn't think she had any idea that she could get up and look around. As her eyes were a wonderful silvery blue now – not the silvery gray of the blind state – the look out of her eyes when she tried to see like this was almost the same, but her energy had shifted, making it something else altogether. He slipped his own energetic form free mentally and stood in front of her. She gasped and reared back. He held out his hand to her. And waited.

She lifted her arm and confirmed what he already knew. She'd lifted her etheric arm, not her physical arm. He quickly reached out and grasped her etheric hand. He laughed, a rumble of joy whispering through him, whispering through her and rolling back toward him again.

"Stefan?"

He controlled his mirth, realizing how odd this must be for her. How scary. "It's all right."

"How is this all right?" she snapped. "I can see you. Almost clearly." She sounded dazed. "I don't understand."

He pulled her close, letting his energy blend with hers in a quick hug, then with his arms still around her he said, "Look behind you."

She gave him a quick confused look, turned around and glanced back – at her body.

She shrieked and slammed back into her body.

Just as she shifted on the etheric plane Stefan thought he heard a voice say, *You will pay for this.*

SAM WALKED THROUGH to the back of the vet's office, loving to see such welcoming animals. Sure, there were a couple not happy to be here, but as she'd learned so much from Stefan and the others she could send a little calming energy to help the poor things adapt. It wasn't easy on animals or humans to have surgery, or to deal with the trauma of being in a vet office. She rolled her shoulders and stretched her neck, letting a bit of that same healing energy slip down her spine. She needed more sleep, and that was the one thing she could not seem to get. Every couple of days, narrowing to every day, there was at least one incident waking her up.

It made no sense. There were too many incidents and it was all happening too fast. Her developing senses allowed her to leave the visions before the victim died, and she worried that this was hindering her ability to learn anything useful. If she were forced to stay until the end there was a chance of gaining more information about the killer. But staying longer hurt her in many other ways, and so far she'd worked hard at getting out as fast as she could.

She had a journal full of notes on these connected cases. And as Stefan didn't need more on his plate, he was likely the one she needed to make this all stop.

Hearing a whimper behind her, she turned to watch a small pug press his flat face up against the wire mesh. His eyes were hopeful.

She grinned. "Hey, Pogo, how are you?" She reached for the latch on his door when the burning started.

She groaned. *Please, not here.*

Then she collapsed to her knees as her lower legs gave out. Her head hit the cage, then the cage no longer existed. In front of her was a kitchen counter, old-fashioned and worn though the years. Sam cried out in her vision. Her legs were burning from the inside out. She stared down at thick ankles and thicker calves encased in tight hose – support hose. There were no injuries to them. No outside flames affected her, but the woman cried out in agony as fire licked up her legs to her hips and higher.

Sam struggled against her instinctive reaction to run and the need to solve this mystery.

She closed her eyes inside the woman's energy and forced her senses to take stock. She writhed in pain as her legs kicked out in agony. The woman fell sideways to the floor, crying out for help.

Sam realized another sad truth as she heard the woman's cries. There was no one to hear her cries. And the phone on the wall was too far away. Too high to reach, and the woman too damaged to cross the short distance.

Trying to see into the woman's mind, which had been completely consumed in fear as the pain rolled upward to the woman's heart, Sam knew what was happening but she couldn't hold back that tsunami of events that would overwhelm this poor woman. For some reason Sam felt she had to stay this time. There was no rushing desire to race away. The pain was horrific, but slightly distanced from her so that she understood and suffered along with the woman.

But she couldn't leave. Only as she heard the last few whimpers of the woman's prayers to be delivered into her Savior's hands did Sam understand.

There was no one for this woman to call for help because she lived alone. And as she lived alone…Sam hadn't been able to let her die alone.

Sending her as much loving energy as she could, Sam pleaded with her to let go.

She watched as the pain receded and the old woman slumped into death. Sam lay inside the poor woman for a long moment, wondering why she wasn't being instantly snapped back to her body when she felt something odd – she felt the energy of the body lift. The release was a physical sensation. Sam stared out through the glazed eyes and recognized the woman's soul rising above her, glorious light and peace in her aura and the whispered words, "Thank you."

And she was gone.

Tears in her eyes, Sam came back to her own body, now stiff and chilled on the cold floor in the vet's office and wondered. She didn't feel the same pain and horror she so often felt after a vision. Nor the agonizing understanding of what one human had done to another. Instead, there was a sense of peace. A sense of rightness.

Did that mean the old woman had died a natural death? Sam really didn't want to start connecting with just anyone whose time had come – that would be too many visions for her to deal with.

Or was it that Sam's presence had made a difference, and she had been given a gift by seeing for the first time the aftermath of this woman's death and the rebirth of her soul to the next step?

At the end the woman had been grateful for death – then again, who wouldn't want that horror to stop? But this time it was as if she knew Sam had been keeping a watchful vigil at her side.

Keeping her company so her final moments weren't as lonely as the rest of her life.

Sam wiped away a tear and reached for her phone. Brandt needed to hear this one.

Before she could dial Stefan stepped into her mind. *Sam? Are you okay?*

HE SHIFTED THE remaining energy into a better position. What a difference now compared to when he first started. When his energy was so sprawled out, the removal of one small piece made no difference. The smaller pieces also created very little havoc – more of a damp squid of an event. Not the explosion of chaos he had envisioned.

In the past, one of his efforts – although successful – had crashed his system for days and weeks until he could recover. Now it was as if each new adjustment rippled back and forth until the other energy settled into place. A place where he felt stronger, happier, more complete.

Who knew such a thing was possible?

He almost laughed, or he would have laughed if he'd had a mouth and a voice box. But he didn't. He was endless energy. He stopped himself. No. Not quite. No longer endless. Now he could at least feel the outer edge of his existence. It still blew him away what had happened, but that didn't make him any happier to be a prisoner here.

Maybe as he continued to grow in strength he could do more. For the moment though, he had no intention of taking her out.

After all, she was responsible for this hell.

CHAPTER 24

CELINA OPENED HER eyes then slammed them shut again. She'd seen something. And that couldn't be allowed. She knew that made no sense, but to her mind…her thoughts were a jumble of confusion. A mess of contradiction and panic. Had she seen something?

She'd been attempting to demonstrate for Stefan and then what?

She gasped. She'd seen him. He'd stood up in front of her and held out his hand. She'd placed hers in his. That was when she'd realized something odd had happened, but she'd been able to see his face for the first time, and that bright clarity and color plus the rest of what had happened had shocked and overwhelmed her. Still stunned at the gray world and seeing Stefan for the first time – my God – he was…and she was lost for words. Then she'd seen her own body behind her.

She winced. Lord, she'd really screamed like a little girl and passed out. She never screamed. Never fainted. But then again, she dared the strongest out there to see what she'd just seen and not react in panic.

As expected the pain had hit right after. And the threat.

"He was just here," she whispered.

"He was." Stefan's voice rolled across her face, the gentle brush of his breath soothing the pain and easing the panic inside. "He's gone now."

She felt like she no longer understood the world she lived in. No longer knew the rules to follow, because while she'd been looking in another direction someone had changed them.

But she knew one thing. A tiny smile playing at the corner of her lips she murmured, "You're beautiful."

She felt his start of surprise, then his self-conscious laugh. "Glad to hear you could see, but I will admit there is something wrong with your eyesight."

She grinned up at him. His hands were on the couch on either side of her, holding her in place. She really didn't want to be anywhere else. "You are right there." She went silent for a moment then asked, "What just happened?"

"Several things," he said calmly. "First off, you left your physical body and stood with just your etheric body. That's an awesome trick by the way, and the more you can learn to do that willfully the more you will enjoy the sensation of not being confined by the limitations of your physical body."

She swallowed hard. "Was I like Jacob?"

"Somewhat. But he wasn't out of his body willfully. You were. You just didn't know what you were doing at the time."

"And the pain?"

"Part of the pain was your abrupt reentry to your body. That can set up a nasty vibration headache, and for some people even paralysis for a long moment until things get back to normal."

"Ugh."

"Exactly," he said, smiling. "Then there is the fact that you can see in that form and yet you can't in the physical."

She had to smile. "And for that I thank you."

"Don't thank me. You did that yourself."

"But it's never been so clear. So colorful. I could see only in muted blurry grays before. Why not this time?"

He hesitated.

"Tell me," she demanded. "The only thing different was that you were there."

He shifted so that he was sitting down beside her. "In that respect it was *because* I am here. And because I kept my hand on you."

"You helped me to see better?"

"I didn't do it on purpose, but I know that sometimes when I work with people I can help their energy to focus more. Better. Clearer."

She nodded. "In a strange way that almost makes sense."

"That is something you can learn to do on your own. As your energy learns how to fine-tune this out-of-body experience it won't need my help."

"It's all so hard to believe," she whispered.

"Yes, it is, but you are not alone. There are many of us that have these types of experiences every day."

And she suddenly knew someone else. "Dr. Maddy, right?"

"Absolutely. It's an aspect of her healing ability that allows her to make miracles happen."

Celina understood on a mental level what had happened, but on a visceral level she was still in a state of wonderment. She'd actually been able to see. For just a few moments, but for the first time in over a year she'd actually been able to see. And damn if those tears didn't start falling.

She wiped them again absently. "I want to do it again."

"No." he said, his voice strong and determined. "In all this discussion you haven't mentioned one important thing."

"Him."

"Exactly. For whatever reason, having you do this out-of-body experience makes him feel threatened. And –" now she could hear him choose his words carefully, "until I know who and what this person is doing, we can't take the chance of him trying to take over your body permanently."

She gasped. "What?"

His noisy exhale was followed by an explanation of possession that terrified her. "Surely that's not possible. How could a dead person take over a live body?"

"We don't have absolutes in this world. I can only tell you that I've seen it happen over and over again. If your cord is detached from your physical body, you will no longer have a connection. It leaves the body open for others to come in and take up residence. At the same time, if you just leave and your cord is still attached, if they are stronger than you they can take up residence and be the dominant personality inside the same body. Sometimes the two personalities fight and we end up with really sad split personality profiles. But too often the intruder is dominant – after all, look at what he managed to do – and keeps the owner of the body under his control. Often they curl up in a corner of their own mind and more or less die."

A heavy shaking made her teeth rattle and her hands tremble. She wrapped her arms around her chest. He hauled her up and over, and she suddenly found herself sitting on his lap and cuddled close to his chest.

Just where she wanted to be.

STEFAN LOVED HER acceptance of new concepts and experiences. She'd just had an incredible realization followed by a disconcerting warning. There was much she had to learn, but she'd gone down that pathway all on her own. He could help her get to a happier place, but they needed to get rid of the predator stalking her. He wasn't sure how.

She snuggled deeper into his arms. He hugged her closer. "Are you okay?"

"Sure. I mean, a blind woman who steps out of her body and suddenly sees only to find out that she shouldn't do that anymore in case a predator takes up residence while she's enjoying this experience can handle anything, right?"

His laugher rolled out. "That's the right way to look at this. Hold onto the thought that when this guy's no longer doing whatever the hell he is doing, then I can show you how to leave and protect your body while you're not in it."

She turned her face into his chest, mumbling, "That sounds so odd."

"It is, but it's also great. He can't torment you forever."

"Really?" She pushed back her hands on his chest to hold herself up. "He's been doing this for over a year now, so who says he can't?"

"I do. I won't let him." Stefan was caught by the time frame. "Did you say a year? As in exactly a year, ten months, or closer to fifteen months?"

She lowered her face slightly, her lips twisting to the side as she thought about that. "I think it's been just coming up on a year." She raised her head to look at him. "Maybe eleven and a half months."

"Did anything happen to you back then? Any particular event that might have brought this on?"

Her broken laugh made him wince. "It was three weeks after my fiance's death that I had the accident that blinded me." She winced. "I wasn't in good shape emotionally or mentally when it happened, so I have no idea how long after this guy rolled into my life – if it was days or weeks or even a month later, but there's no doubt it was close."

"Then we have to go back and look at the details of your accident. If that's when this started, then that's where we have to begin."

Stefan thought about the stack of papers he'd been going over for Brandt and realized a year ago was important for some reason. He just didn't understand why.

"Why don't I make us dinner, then afterwards we can work on a timeline? I'm consulting on another case that appears connected to yours. I don't know if the timeline works, but if it does, we might have our first real break on the case."

She sat back. "Food would be good. I'm really hungry."

"Good. Come into the kitchen with me and you can give me a hand." He stood, studying her energy. Tired and frazzled, nonetheless there was a robustness to it that would attract many sick and desperate souls. "I hate to ask as I know it's a painful issue, but when did your fiancé pass away? Was it…close to the same time?"

She paused then nodded. "Yes. He had an aneurysm in the brain, but he was brain dead soon after." She frowned and admitted, "I was pretty destroyed with his death."

"I'm sorry. Losing someone you love is tough."

"You don't have to tell me about that. I've lost everyone, starting with my best friend when I was just a young girl, to both my parents, then my fiancé." Standing up, she said in a wry tone, "For a long time I figured there was something wrong with me. That I was so unlovable everyone was dying around me to get away."

She shook her head. "It makes no sense, I know, but I

felt betrayed. Then after my accident I realized how foolish I was being. I was still alone and lonely, but not quite so desperate to be with others. In fact, I think I felt overwhelmed and began pushing people away around that time."

"Because of the blindness. You didn't want to be a burden on anyone."

She nodded. "Stupid, isn't it? From desperate to not be alone to desperate to be alone."

"Not stupid. Understandable." And now that he had an inkling of the emotions behind her actions he understood both her music and the ghosts in her life. They were connected to her emotions and sense of loss. She'd started the one and used it to attract the other. Yet she had no idea what she'd done or how to reverse the process. That's what led to her sense of being overwhelmed and why she pushed them all away. Without understanding that they'd been called to her, and until she released them they had nowhere else to go.

BRANDT PINCHED THE bridge of his nose. Sam had been devastated by this last vision. Not by the woman's death, but by the loneliness she'd felt in the old woman's energy. As if she'd been alone for a long time. There was so little Brandt could do to help her. And almost nothing to help the old woman. In true form Sam hadn't been able to get any identifying marks to help pinpoint a location so that he could even begin to find the body. Until she was found he had only Sam's word. He knew she'd be right but he might never see the result, depending on where the old woman lived. Sam's abilities were getting stronger, and her reach farther. That made his job all that much harder.

He glanced up at the huge chart he'd started earlier. It

was a vast amount of information, but again no pattern. At least not one he'd managed to determine. He stood up and added Female C – he already had Female A and B. Then entered the little bit of information he had available. The woman's legs burning was new. He double-checked and realized in no other case had Sam picked up damage to the legs. Interesting. A picture was starting to form in his head. He gave himself a headshake.

There was no way.

But when all else is wrong, what remains has to be the truth.

He stared at the answer in shock.

Someone was picking on each victim through a different body part. These victims were being chosen by the areas where Sam was feeling the burning pain.

And if that was true, how did the killer know these people had this area for him to attack? Did it need to be a weaker area? Was that what made them vulnerable to his particular form of violence?

His mind balked at the idea of a big muscular male being linked to this old woman that Sam had just connected with.

And how – if at all – did this connect to Celina? He reached for the phone. "Stefan, I think I've got something."

Assured he had Stefan's attention, he quickly explained the pattern – the fact that there was no repetition of body parts – then tossed in his hypothesis. He finished by asking if any of that fit Celina's case.

"It might. I'll call you later."

And he hung up the phone. Brandt stared in shock at the phone in his hand. He couldn't remember any time when Stefan had hung up on him.

I haven't now, but Celina was listening in. That I can't have. She's sitting on the deck now waiting for dinner. Give me that information again, Stefan said again.

Brandt quietly repeated his words to the empty room knowing Stefan could hear him. He stood in front of the chart and went over a couple of the cases out loud.

Celina's weakness is her eyes, so it makes sense that's where we'd see the energy blockage. And it's definitely connected to the asshole that is haunting her, but there's no way to know if it's the same man who's doing all the other killings.

"It's an avenue we have to consider." Brandt added, "The real question is if it is the same man who killed all of these others, then why hasn't he killed Celina? Or is she next?"

ERIC SHIFTED IN his bed. He could hear the other kids in the big room all laughing and playing. Across from him was another little boy who had just come out of surgery. He didn't look very good. His face was puffy, splotchy. His eyes closed, his breathing raspy. Eric didn't know what was wrong, but he didn't think he was going to make it. There was so much darkness around him. And that darkness would keep Eric away. He wished the other little boy had a defender. Maybe then that blackness wouldn't come closer to Eric. He hated the color black. At least now.

He glanced back at the window, happy that he no longer thought flying out that window would be a good idea. Stefan had said lots of the thoughts in his head could be the drugs or the monsters and if the thoughts weren't good ones, he was to throw them into the washing machine he'd left in the corner of Eric's mind and then they'd come out clean again.

He laughed at the idea, but if Stefan said it worked, then it worked. And that made him feel great. He eyed the blackness around the boy. Was it drifting his way?

It wasn't the same as the evil man.

It was like the blackness of some of the other sick boys.

But how could he know for sure that they didn't hear the same black man inside of them?

Eric snuck lower down under the sheets, but couldn't tear his gaze away from the cloud of evil.

CHAPTER 25

CELINA PUT HER fork down and reached for her glass of wine. She pushed her chair back slightly and sighed happily. "That was delicious. Gorgeous, capable, and a wonderful cook. Why hasn't someone snapped you up, Stefan?"

His laughter rolled out across the meadows. "Maybe I've been waiting for you all my life," he said, a warm caress in his voice.

She smiled. "No dodging the question. I almost got married and you're another what – three, four years older than me? So it's not like there would have been a lack of opportunity."

"Maybe not. But I do come with certain abilities that make some people uncomfortable."

"Oh?" She took another sip and considered. "I suppose the energy work would be as equally scary to some people as it is attractive to others."

"My art is the same. I've developed quite a name, but there is nothing nice or easy about my paintings. They are the outpourings of the worst in my soul, and that makes them difficult to gaze upon." He laughed again but it was devoid of humor. "I've seen and have been involved with a lot of seriously deranged killers and victims. It leaves a mark on your soul."

She thought about all he'd said and what he hadn't. "I'm sorry. I think you must hurt with each of the victims. It's your way." She heard the distance in the silence then felt his hand cover hers.

"Thank you for seeing that." He squeezed her hand once, then released it.

His chair pushed back and he said, "I'll clear off the table and return with the rest of the wine."

"Can I help?" She half-rose.

He pressed her back into her chair. "Relax. I have dessert to come as well."

She must have made a hum of pleasure because he laughed, dropped a kiss on her head and left, dishes clanging in his hands.

She relaxed back and thought about the man who lived and worked on ugly cases. Who slept with nightmares of the victims and still got up the next day and did it all over again. She was no longer interested in seeing his paintings as she imagined them to be torturous for him to produce, but she was happy to know he had that outlet. Like her music, they were necessary vents for the thing they called life.

Stefan returned in minutes, placing several items on the table.

"Dessert is double mocha cheesecake and I'm going to top up your wine."

She listened to the liquid splashing in the glass, and wondered at how much being here with him made her smile. Her mouth almost hurt because of it. She hadn't laughed this much in years. She said as much to him.

"What was your relationship like with your fiancé?" he asked, curiosity in his voice.

"Passionate, possessive on both sides. There was just the

two of us. No family for either of us, so we were completely wrapped up in each other. It never occurred to me until months just before his death that we were too close. Too dependent on each other."

She took another sip, her mind retracing the years. "We met, and that was it for both of us. After he died I believed there'd never be anyone else for me."

"And now?" Stefan asked, his voice as smooth as the chocolate cheesecake sliding down her throat.

"And now? I wonder if I knew what love was at all." She couldn't help the sad sigh. At the warm silence from him, she asked, "What are you thinking about so heavily? Weighing options?"

Still silence. She tried again. "Stefan, I can hear you thinking. What's going on?"

"That phone call earlier was from Detective Sutherland, who is looking into a series of killings that might be related."

"I'm sorry," she said in gentle voice. "That must be difficult." Then she got it. Her tone changed as she leaned forward and pushed her chair back to stand up. "Do you need to go to work? I know I've taken a lot of your time today."

"No. I'm not going anywhere and neither are you."

At the blank look on her face he said, "I think these cases are related to the predator you are dealing with."

She sat back down with a heavy thud. "Sorry," she said faintly. "You think this guy might be killing people? As in other people?"

"Yes, and I'm afraid he might try to kill you."

STEFAN ALMOST WINCED at the shock, horror, and instant

denial that raced across her face.

"There's no reason for him to. He wants to see something, but that's all. If he was capable, he could have killed me a long time ago if that had been his plan. It's not like I have any defenses against him."

"That's not true. We don't know how he's killing these people, or why, or even how he's picking his victims. Maybe you could tell me more about your accident, the surgery you had afterwards, and anything else that happened around the same time."

She threw up her hands. "What's to say? I was in a vehicle that was hit by a drunk driver. I don't remember any of the details, having thankfully blocked that out. I woke up in the hospital blind and was told that I was going in for more surgery." She shrugged. "I woke up a long time later with my eyes having been operated on, and this is what you see as the result. Nothing more, nothing less."

"Any other injuries?" Stefan probed gently, "Any broken bones? Deaths of other people in the vehicle? Did the drunk driver survive?"

"Ha, don't they always? He lived and was barely injured, but then he was driving some monster truck." She sighed, turning her head into the light breeze drifting across her face. "I don't have many details, mostly because I don't want many details. I talk to Gordon all the time, he used to manage the auditorium where we played, and he's never mentioned requiring any kind of continuing rehab or anything."

She winced. "Honestly, I never asked. As for my girlfriend Jillian, well, she doesn't talk much at the best of times. Then Susan moved away after the accident. I lost touch." She snorted with painful honesty. "That's not true. I was so angry. So mad that they'd walked away with no injuries that I shut them all out of my life." She lifted a trembling hand. "I'm not a nice person."

"You are." He reached over and grasped her hand. "You had a horrible shock. A terrible loss. It's a natural response to want to lash out at others who appeared to have escaped unscathed."

"Unscathed? I wonder. Do they blame themselves for my condition? I never once considered how they felt. I only let Gordon and Jillian back into my life a few months after the accident. I apologized then and we all made up. Since then I've just kept everyone else more or less away. Jacob being my closest friend – mostly because he refused to stay away."

"And he's safe because he has a male partner and is super busy so he didn't demand any more of your time than you were willing to give."

Stefan wondered what else he should tell her. He was hoping to take their relationship to the next level, but didn't think she'd appreciate hearing some hard truths from him afterwards, and it would erase all the good he'd managed up to now. But to share them with her now… yeah, she might never speak to him again. Then again, as he had no intention of letting her go home tonight after what Brandt had said. She was likely to be pretty angry. Either way he was going to be sleeping alone.

"And this is why you have no friends." She laughed. "Sorry, that just came out. It's a phrase from my childhood. But you are right. My life is stuffed to the brim and my way of coping was to keep people away."

"Sorry, I do tend to speak in truths."

"No, that's fine." She gave him a wry smile. "I prefer the truth over the alternatives. And speaking of the truth, please tell me more about the cases and how I might be connected."

As they needed to discuss this he willingly complied. "We don't know for sure, but at the moment I see the same black energy around that blockage in your head as I have around a child, Eric, who's dealing with a monster in his head, and several males in the morgue that for one reason or another are dead and managed to take out other people with them."

"Take out – how do you mean?"

"One drove his vehicle into a crowded pub a few nights ago."

"Chico's!"

"And another picked up a butcher knife and started slashing and butchering a group of women waiting to cross the road."

"Oh my God. What? You're saying the accident at Chico's is related to these poor women? I understand the connection from my attacker and Chico's, but how could he have a hand in that slashing incident?"

"He somehow managed to get the driver of that vehicle to crash into the pub and if he could do that, then it wouldn't likely be hard for him to have this other man pick up a butcher knife and starting slashing that way."

"But why?"

Stefan shook his head. "That I don't have an answer for."

"How?"

"I don't know that either."

Those silvery eyes stared toward him. "He'd have to have a way to connect to these people. Like he does me."

"True. That's why I wondered about the details of your accident."

"Are you thinking possession here? That he might have slipped into my body while I was at my weakest?"

"Or slipped into the weakest part of you at that time – your eyes."

She reared back and swallowed hard. "That's…very disturbing."

"Yes," he said. "It is."

"So he'd have had to have found a way to enter all these people while they were weak and then taken over when he wanted to and killed them – and in the process, killing others?"

"Quite possibly."

She shuddered. "I'm not sure I can do this. I need sleep tonight. How can I ever sleep again if this guy could turn me into a mass killer?"

"He won't." Stefan's voice was strong, adamant.

She didn't look convinced. "But you won't know until it happens, will you?" she said bitterly. "I could kill you in my sleep and you'd only wake up if the first blow didn't finish the job. Oh my God." She stared at him in horror. "Everyone around me is in danger."

"No, they aren't, and I'm not going to let this guy take over your body, nor am I going to let you go off under his manipulations and kill anyone."

"I hate to say this, Stefan," she said, her voice doubtful. "You might be God to some people, but I don't think this guy cares."

Stefan laughed. "He doesn't. And that's another weakness I'll be able to use against him."

She leaned forward. "This is in my head. It's not like you can reach a hand inside and pull him out."

"True enough, but only because I'm concerned about

the kind of harm he might cause you if I were to try to do that."

He shifted and spoke inside her mind. *I'm in your mind right now. Right where he is. I can see the blockage in front of me. But force is not the answer here. Knowledge is.* And he stepped back out of her mind.

She sank back into the chair, the back of her hand pressed against her mouth.

"I think I'm going to be sick."

"Uh oh." Stefan reached through her root chakra and quickly drained much of the energy churning violently and threatening to spill over.

She sat up and took a deep breath. "Thank you." She shook her head. "I think I need to go home now. Please."

"And that's where the next problem comes in." He winced. "I'm keeping you here until this is over."

She closed her eyes and leaned her head against the back of the chair. A long shaky breath escaped.

"And when will that be?" she whispered. "When we're both dead?"

VANESSA COLLER DRESSED carefully for the evening. Her first formal affair since the disaster in her life so long ago. She really loved Jhett. He was perfect for her. Twirling in front of the full-length mirror, she felt like a princess.

She spread her fingers and could almost see the diamond ring on her hand. Surely he'd ask her tonight? She twirled one more time then headed for the small makeup mirror in the bathroom. Everything had to be just right for tonight. He'd love her no matter how she looked and she was content with that, but she wanted him to be proud to be escorting her now. She looked so different after all her skin grafts and the months and months of healing. Sure, there'd been the odd weird heated twinge in her back lately, more a sense of something ready to flare, but thankfully never did.

She'd come so far…surely one more step wasn't impossible.

Tonight was that next step.

She bent over and worked on the eye shadow, her hand sure and steady. An inner calm had settled inside. She knew how to apply makeup to hide the worst of the scars. She could do this tonight. As she worked, the calm slowly broke apart from the façade it really was. She had been through a year of hell. A year of surgery after surgery. A year of needing help and helpers, of crying in pain and feeling bad for being in pain. She hated to ask for help, and this last year had pushed the limits time and time again. Bowing her head, she considered the huge ballroom formal tonight. A work event for Jhett, and afterwards he was taking her to the small exclusive dining room on the other side of the hotel. That's where he'd ask her to marry him.

At least she hoped.

SAM WANDERED THE lakeshore, loving the way the sun twinkled on the water. She'd come to love this place. Knowing it was theirs now forever made her heart swell in delight.

She stood there for a long moment and let the feelings wash over her.

And felt joy, someone else's joy, fill her. Or she filled someone else with joy? Quietly she let her mind shut down and her energy float as needed. She was humming. The wedding march. Sam would have laughed, but she was too full of happiness to do anything. This young woman was getting ready for an event – a special night. She splayed her fingers wide and Sam could see they were bare of rings and she understood.

But why was Sam here?

And could she get something to identify this woman and save her before her world exploded in pain?

She sank deeper into the vision. Letting her senses flow through the young woman, searching out the burning she knew would come.

She drifted down then spread out through the limbs. She couldn't sense anything but a woman in the prime of her life getting ready to go out for a special evening.

Her back tingled. She stilled.

Here was the problem.

And the heat was just starting. Now if only she could get something to identify this woman and save her.

CHAPTER 26

CELINA WANTED ANOTHER chance to see Stefan's face clearly. He sat on the edge of her mind the whole time he spoke. The words flowing over her. She had that one time to refer to, but having still been in shock, she hadn't been able to get such a clear look. Like black and white photo shoots, the highlights of his face had been unbelievably beautiful. With stunning cheekbones, wavy hair slightly on the long side – and damn if she didn't want to slide her fingers through it again. His eyes, a little bit of wild still in there. He'd tempered his personality, his abilities to look civilized on the surface, but something untamed, observing the outside world with a hint of …mockery perhaps…lived inside.

What he could see must give him a tainted view of the rest of the world. He lived in this world as a master, having cornered the fears and insecurities at least to the point that no one else would know what lurked on the inside. He'd carved a place for himself in society where he was looked upon with respect. So many others in his world were classed as charlatans and shysters. Stefan would never worry about others' opinion of him, as he'd found that center inside that said he was fine just the way he was.

She hadn't made it as far. It reminded her of her growing years, that "pleaser" personality so others would remain her friends. So she wouldn't have to lose anymore. So she wouldn't have to be alone.

She sighed.

"That was awfully heavy," he said quietly at her side. He'd moved the two of them to a wide lounge chair out on the deck. The sun was still high on the left, but there was little heat to it. She could feel a cool breeze running up the property and she just knew he couldn't see another house around. Whether there were trees or he just owned several acres, she understood that privacy was his solace and he'd control this space and protect it against any invasion on any level.

"I was just considering the penalty of trying to see in that world again."

"Too high," he said immediately.

"I want to see your face again," she murmured, a small smile playing at the corner of her mouth.

"You did once."

"Only for a brief second," she retorted. "When I was too shocked to take much in."

"We can't take the chance."

She wondered about that. Surely there had to be a way. She'd been able to see that way and see brilliantly with him. She wanted to see that way again.

"And why does it matter?" he asked curiously. "You don't see any other faces. So why mine?"

"Because you matter." The words hung between them. She wished she'd waited until she'd had a chance to see his face, to gauge his reaction. But that could be a long time, according to him. And she didn't want to waste time. If Stefan left as suddenly as he'd arrived, she wanted to make sure she experienced everything he had to offer first.

She knew the memories would be some of the sweetest.

She didn't recognize it at first. Then it came again, the gentlest of kisses on her cheek. Then her forehead. She smirked. "I thought I was the one that was blind, not you. But you apparently can't see where my lips–"

And her lips were taken in a long, drugging kiss, and she'd never been kissed like this before. And oh God, had she missed out. Heat raced down her spine and curled her toes. She reached up to grab his shirt and tug him closer and she kissed him back.

Sensations roiled inside as she was lifted, turned, and placed on his lap. "Perfect," she murmured and wrapped her arms around his neck.

He deepened the kiss, greedy yet contained. She was up against that control of his. She wanted him to lose it. She wanted to be the one who made him lose it, as she instinctively knew he hadn't allowed himself to with a woman before. She didn't want to be one of the women in his life – she wanted to be *the* woman for the rest of his life. She slid her hands down his chest, then came up underneath the shirt he had on. Thankfully it was something lightweight and stretchy, but as smooth as butter. Her fingers touched his skin for the first time, and she moaned. He was hard and soft, lean muscle and bone. Her fingers stroked and caressed. She couldn't get enough of him. He felt so good. Being held like this felt so wonderful, and she knew what was to come would be even better.

But he was playing with her. Worried about her. She could sense that reserve again. That indecision.

She didn't want indecision to be between them. She wanted him.

She reached up and grabbed the side of his head, pulled

back slightly and whispered, "Yes."

He hesitated.

She frowned.

"Do not be worried about me."

"It's fast. You haven't known me for long."

She heard the litany of excuses she'd have used for any other man. Not this one. He was so much more than she'd ever expected to have in her arms. She wanted it all, and she wanted it all now.

"I'm sure."

He dropped little kisses on her closed eyes, on her cheeks, then on the side of her neck, but he was thinking. It was as if she could hear the hum of the wheels turning in his head.

She smiled. "You don't believe me." She leaned back so he could see her face. "Then you need to look at my aura, my energy, and read the truth for yourself," she said simply.

There was a long moment, as if he was doing just that…and she waited.

Then his mouth closed over hers, hungry, greedy, and demanding.

For a short second she felt the fear that he'd take everything she had to give. He'd accept nothing less. If she gave him everything and then lost him…

Then she couldn't think as he deepened his kiss and took her on the ride of a lifetime.

STEFAN KNEW HE shouldn't do this. Knew he should have cleared the air first. Had intended it. Then she'd said that about her feelings, and he'd shoved all his reservations to the side and let himself take something from life that he wanted.

Had wanted for some time. Knew he'd never get tired of wanting.

She didn't see herself as he did. As a strong, valiant woman who had been dealt so many blows in life that she'd created a family of ghosts to keep herself from being alone. She'd done so well, on both an energy level and in the physical world. He didn't know too many people who would handle her stalker like she was.

Emotion had welled up. He'd intended on kissing her lightly, but her response took that control away from him and he'd ended up kissing her with all the passion and need he'd kept bottled up deep inside for so long.

Heat and longing surged up to his heart and he could no more control the response raging through him than he could pull back and put a stop to this. He didn't want it to stop. He wanted to take her to his bed and keep her there. Keep her safe forever.

Just then she lifted her head. "I don't want him to hurt you," she said fiercely.

And he realized who *he* was.

He gathered her up and strode inside. She never made a sound, just stared at him with those huge silver eyes – and that look of complete trust.

He whispered as he carried her one step at a time up to his bedroom loft, "He won't. Don't worry about that. That's never going to happen."

"He could," she whispered. "He's very capable."

Stefan knew more nasty things these entities were capable of than he wanted to know, and there was no point in lying. "He might be, but so am I."

And he had a vast network of people he could call on to help.

"Are you sure?"

"I am." Clear and definite. He glanced down at her as he walked over to the bed and lowered her to the huge duvet. "Are you?"

ERIC SLEPT BETTER these days. The relief on his mom's face when he'd told her that made him happy.

She wouldn't understand dragon slayer or monster or defending the castle. She was just Mom. Stefan knew though. Eric had felt him come by, loved hearing his voice telling him that all was well. It always made him feel safe.

He loved the idea of living in a castle. Being a dragon slayer made him grin. Stefan could teach him. Stefan was good.

The bad guy hadn't been back since Stefan secured the outside wall.

Maybe he'd never come back now.

He dropped off to sleep.

CHAPTER 27

CELINA LOOPED HER arms around Stefan's neck and tugged him down on top of her.

"Easy," he murmured, "I was going to take off a layer of clothing."

Her hands dove under his shirt even as a giggle rolled free. God, she felt good. Young, sexy, happy – carefree.

She tugged the shirt as high up as she could then gave up, letting her hands roam over the expanse of skin.

With a muffled curse he sat up, straddling her on his knees. She stretched her hands upward, following the trail of the shirt as it was yanked over his head.

"We could take our time," he muttered, coming back down on top of her.

"Next time." She smiled. "Next time slow and easy. This time there is too much need, hunger—"

His mouth covered hers. Greedy, hard – famished after a long drought, he feasted on her mouth, her lips. Shudders rippled up and down her back. She wrapped her legs around him and realized he still had his pants on. So did she.

Restless need driving her now, she couldn't remember it ever urging her on like this before. She slid her fingers inside the waistband of his pants and pushed the fabric down – only it wouldn't go over his hips. Frustrated, she stroked upward to just inside his shoulders and pushed him hard. He rolled to the side and she dove for the closure to his pants.

Her fingers immediately got sidetracked by the healthy bulge underneath. She closed her hand around him and squeezed.

He roared and rolled her down onto her back with a hard kiss she took to mean *stay there*. The mattress shifted as he got off.

"We tried it your way," he said. "Now we try it my way."

Hearing the sound of his zipper going down she bounced to her knees, crossed her arms and pulled her shirt over her head, tossing it in the vicinity of the floor to the left. Still wearing the barest of a lace bra, she scrambled to her feet and quickly disposed of her pants. She didn't recognize herself. Her eagerness. This sense of playfulness. This wasn't her. Or it hadn't been her.

Until now. Just as she straightened and kicked the cotton pants to the floor she was lifted, swung in a wide circle, shrieking and laughing so hard she could feel tears in her eyes. Then slowly, so exquisitely slowly, she was laid down on the bed.

She opened her arms and smiled her welcome. She'd thought he'd lie down as he had before. She waited, a little puzzled when he didn't. She heard him take a few steps then return.

She waited.

A heavy rose scent filled her nostrils as soft petals stroked down her skin. Her gaze widened, a gentle smile on her lips. She murmured, "Roses."

"A red rose," he answered softly. "A beautiful specimen, just like you."

The faintest warmth washed over her cheeks. "You say

the nicest things."

"You're easy to compliment. There is much to admire. To respect."

Tears collected again. She held them back. She couldn't believe this man, so strong and sure, could see anything of value in her. "I'm glad you see that, but I'm afraid you'll think less of me the better you know me. I'm no angel and have not done well by many." She frowned, hating to give voice to such talk. But her eagerness was waning. Her mood shifting.

She turned her head to face the last of the sun's rays, loving the warmth on her eyes, her cheeks.

And the lightest of chills settling on her bare skin.

Until she realized something warm and tingling was drifting up her bare legs, her hips, across her belly to rise up across her ribs and between her breasts. She covered it with her hands and found nothing there. But the heat spread outward. Not sexual, but sensual. Not hot, but warm – so deep inside she knew she need never be cold again.

"Stefan?"

"I'm here."

"What are you doing?"

"Easing your energy, helping you to relax."

"I was relaxed," she said dryly.

"Balancing your energies then."

She frowned "Why and why now?"

The smile in his voice intrigued her. "You'll see in a moment."

She relaxed again and let heat slide through her, around her, inside her darkest, coldest places. A heavy sigh worked its way up from way down below. She shuddered as a second, heavier one escaped.

And she relaxed a little further yet again.

As she lay there under his ministrations she sensed something else. It was his energy working on her energy. She could feel the intense concentration he was using. The sexual need he was holding back. She didn't know why but she had to let him do his thing. And as she felt his barely controlled hunger her own ignited.

"Stefan," she cried.

"I'm here."

"I want you with me."

"I am."

"I want you physically with me," she said.

"And I want you with me emotionally, energetically, and physically."

Emotions roiled through her but she didn't have time to sort them as a heat she never could have imagined spread out and filled her from the inside out, her very cells swelling with this energy.

"This is madness," she cried, her head turning from side to side.

She felt the weight on the bed shift, a shadow blocking the light, and then the sweetness of his lips easing the confusion – and taking control of the flame. Fire surged between them as he released the reins of his own. She sensed him there in that energy. Slightly back and slightly distant.

Her body came alive, pulsating with hunger. From his words she knew so much more was out here for her to experience. He'd shown her some. She wanted more.

So much more.

She clasped his shoulders and tugged him down on top of her. He braced himself slightly above her on his elbows. None of that. She knocked his elbow out from under him and when he stretched out full on top of her, she cried out in joy. Her hands drank greedily from the expanse of never-ending skin. She didn't need her eyesight to tell her he was gorgeous. Her fingers slid down his spine, loving the silky skin under her fingertips to the swell of his buttocks. Lean muscles rippled under her caress, his hips pressing against her pelvis. Instantly she widened her legs. He settled deeper against her.

She gasped. He froze.

She dug her nails into those sculpted buttocks.

He groaned, pressing deeper.

Celina could hardly breathe as mini fireworks rattled through her body. He shifted lower, trailing wet kisses down her throat to the top of her breasts. Using his teeth he pulled the edge of the soft, lacy bra back. She whimpered as his tongue laved the hard nipple, first on the one side and then on the second. She rolled from side to side.

"Shh," he murmured, his soothing voice penetrating the haze in her mind.

"Stefan," she cried, arching her back.

Her bra snap opened and the material was tossed to one side. When he lowered his head and suckled her nipple hard, she cried out in joy. When the other one received the same treatment she was beyond coherent thought.

She grabbed fistfuls of hair, tugged him upright and kissed him.

All the frustration blending into a greedy kiss.

He might have started with a laugh but he ended up with a groan.

Moving gently, he slid to one side, hooked onto her panties and pulled down and off.

Then he rolled back into the cradle she'd made for him.

Hearing sounds, and only dimly aware that they were coming from her, she hooked her legs around him and urged him closer.

He kissed her while his hands cupped her bottom, adjusted her hips, and plunged deep.

She cried out and stilled.

Fire licked through her. Her skin so hot she could barely stand it.

Shh, he murmured. *It's all right.*

And damn if he wasn't in her mind. The same as he was in her body.

The intimacy, the perfection, the absolute togetherness was her undoing.

The tremors started deep inside and helpless, she could only hold on for the ride. Feeling her response, Stefan lifted slightly and plunged, grinding deeper yet again. Once. Twice. Three times. Explosions wracked her slight frame and he rode her through it. Just as she didn't think she could stand any more, he shuddered above her and emptied himself into her.

And started the fireworks all over.

Hours later she curled up, her body humming in pleasure but so exhausted sleep was one breath away. And she took that breath and dropped into a deep, rejuvenating slumber.

WITH THE FEW pieces left he could feel the energy, the power surging through him. He could think so much more clearly. It felt good. No, great. Maybe he wouldn't be so quick to leave this earth yet. With this much strength he could see how this would be a possible life. An existence he wouldn't detest.

There were still a few more areas bleeding energy that he needed to plug. Then he'd be centered in just one. He sighed and stretched, loving the feeling of being so collected.

This wasn't half bad. Not perfect, but so much better.

He needed to visit her. Make sure she was still suffering. Anything less wasn't acceptable.

Bitch.

JACOB WOKE UP, his heart pounding, his head booming. He groaned as wakefulness surged through him and he opened his eyes. It took a long moment to realize he was alive. He was in a hospital, but he was back in his body.

Thank God.

That had been an experience he did not want to repeat ever again. He lay back and closed his eyes, grateful to have that nightmare over and to be awake again. His mind drifted.

Oh Lord. Immediately tears swamped his eyes. His best friend and lover was gone. And that brought the accident back to the forefront and the nightmare he'd been living ever since.

Owen. Celina. And… Stefan, her friend. He bolted upright and cried out. The room swam in front of him and he lay back down before he fell.

Where was his phone? He needed to call them.

That was his last thought as he went back under.

CHAPTER 28

CELINA MOANED, RUBBED her head against the pillow, and whimpered again. She lifted her hand to her head as the drums inside boomed and then boomed again.

The pounding changed to a sharp stabbing, a thin slice of pain directly into her eyeball. She screamed as that same knife edge came down again and again.

"Celina!"

Her shoulders were grabbed and shaken lightly. "Yeah, that helps," she snarled, twisting to free herself. "My head is ready to explode."

And she started weeping.

"Make it stop," she sobbed, curling into a tighter ball, her hands over her head.

"Is it in your eyes again?" Stefan urged. "Can you tell if it's him?"

She didn't know how to answer – the pain was too severe. She tried to marshal her thoughts and breathe through the pain but her shoulders trembled with effort. Dimly through the red and black in her head she felt Stefan's hands massaging the back of her neck and the corded ribbons across her shoulders. She moaned as his caring hands worked magic on her locked-down muscles.

She wished he could do something with the pain. He'd told her he'd be able to stop it, but it was back again and he hadn't done anything.

Angry, desperate, and hurting, she cried out silently in her head. *Help.*

And damn it if he didn't answer in her head. *Shh. I'm here. Try to stay quiet. I'm tracking him.*

STEFAN STOOD INSIDE Celina's headache, watching the blackness around her eyes pulse and vibrate with a distinctive, unholy power. He'd never seen anything like it.

He sensed the emotion. Not outside the ball but inside, driving the ball with heavy intensity. And the biggest emotion behind it all was rage.

And it was directed at Celina.

He couldn't get a reading on the soul behind this. And wished he could. There was one thing he could do though. He winced. It wouldn't be easy.

But it was necessary. He closed his eyes, spread the little bit of energy he'd used to enter Celina's mind, and rolled it out as thin as he could.

Then he spread it thinner yet again. Breathing into the energy he approached the red ball and touched it with a tiny flick of energy.

There was no reaction.

He did it again.

He needed to gain access to the energy, but in such a way that he was welcome.

The only way to do that was if the predator's energy didn't see Stefan's energy as a threat.

And that meant the predator's energy had to become used to it. Used to the feel of Stefan's energy. Accept it.

Then become one with it.

With that Stefan touched the energetic ball again, letting it blend with his energy. And merge together.

He sank deeper into the experience, emptying his mind, emptying his very cells that he could fill with this other energy and finally know what it was and why it was targeting Celina.

He pulled his consciousness back to center and deliberately opened up to the other energy and let himself be a part of it, not just merging on an energetic layer but merging consciously.

Instantly his mind was filled with hatred – black, twisted, broken thoughts wrapped and wormed through him, filling his own emotions with dark thoughts of revenge and poison.

Stefan struggled to let the emotion flow through him and out of him. To release it before it tainted his own soul. He breathed deep, letting his cells fill, then empty, always keeping them in the light of his own joy. The only way to not absorb the nastiness was to keep surrounding it in light as it moved through him.

He travelled deeper into the ball. Surely he'd be able to identify the person, the circumstances surrounding this nightmare.

Instead, he could only feel the anger. Only feel the pain. And then the determination to make Celina pay. Stefan didn't understand the other victims involved. There was no anger toward anyone else. He didn't know if that meant the person used up his anger for the victim at the time, or if he had no strong emotional ties to the others.

If that was the case, then why kill them?

Slowly, as he sat there still in the river of emotion, words and phrases slowly formed.

Bitch.

Make her pay.

Make her suffer.

Like she'd made me suffer.

She did this to me.

She was responsible.

Each new phrase matched a pulse in the ball of energy, keeping the fiery anger stoked.

Whoever was doing this had learned the power of negative emotions. But who was he and what had Celina done?

Stefan waited. Hoping for more.

Need more power, the voice whispered. *Need more. She's not suffering enough. I want her to suffer!*

More broken phrases and words, the litany a lighter fluid, but nothing new. Nothing to clarify it.

Stefan deliberately pulled a plug on the ball, giving the ravaging heat an outlet. The pulses slowed. The flashes dimmed.

No!

He widened the hole, letting more and more of the negativity and burning anger drain away. At the same time he sent cooling, healing energy to mingle with some of the energy on the far side. He didn't dare let this energy understand Stefan was there or what he was doing.

He watched the ball reduce in size, in intensity, as the trickle of energy grew to a torrent. The small gap he'd opened turned into a large fissure, draining the nasty energy from this self-contained furnace.

Stefan kept a large energetic blanket around the whole mess so that this guy's energy couldn't slide away and take up residence anywhere else.

No! What's happening? This can't happen. The energy

spiked, hitting outward into Celina's eyes.

Dimly Stefan heard her cry out. He raced to extend the healing cushion he'd placed between the energy and her eyes, something to soften the blows this asshole appeared determined to inflict. Blowing cooling colors to combat the heat, he poured soothing energy toward her eyes, protecting, healing them.

And blocking the asshole.

I need more power, the entity sobbed, the words only bits and pieces, the emotions so much more than formed sounds. *More. More. More. I need more.*

Stefan sat still and listened. *Come on,* he urged silently, *talk to me.*

There are only a few more. But that will help. Cutting them loose will be enough. They need to be enough. They must be… the energy pleaded to himself.

Stefan heard the voice that reverberated in the ball. But it was the last sentence that chilled him though.

The energy said, *Anything to make this one pay.*

And then the swiftly sinking ball of energy, quivered once, twice, then it exhaled to a deflated balloon. No movement. No heat.

No force.

The predator was gone.

SAM BOLTED UPRIGHT.

"What's happening?" she cried out, twisting in pain.

"Easy, Sam. Easy."

"No. My back. God, my back. It's burning up," she cried.

Brandt shuffled backwards in bed to see Sam's delicate

back. He flicked a light on. There was no redness. No injury. Nothing. He reached out a hand.

"Don't touch me, it's killing me." And she started weeping.

Her wording had Brandt stop, his arm midair. He moved so he could look at her face. Her eyes, dark and swirling with emotion, glared at him.

"Do something," she cried out. "Call 9-1-1. There has to be something wrong." Her tiny frame twisted and she bent over her knees, weeping.

This was not Sam.

Oh, it was Sam, but she was caught in another vision – maybe. They'd never been like this.

Taking a chance he said, "Who are you?"

"What kind of a stupid question is that? I'm Vanessa, of course."

"Sorry." He picked up the phone to show her. "I guess I don't have any practice with emergencies."

"You just have to give them my name and address," she whimpered as the pain once again had her twisting and crying.

Brandt pretended to dial. "It's ringing." Keeping up the pretense, he pretended to speak to the operator on other end. "Yes, Vanessa needs help. Her last name? Uhm…"

"Coller," she cried. "Vanessa Coller."

Brandt quickly relayed the information to the dead phone, all the while watching as his beautiful wife became someone else.

"Address. Honey, I can't remember your address." He turned back to her, his throat clenched in fear. Sam had flipped over to her stomach, now quietly weeping. But her back…Christ, it looked like it was on fire.

"334," she gasped. "Hobbard Drive."

He had a pen and wrote it down. *Please let this be close by.* Hating to ask but needing to know as much information as he could he said, "Honey, they want to know what suburb. That's a common name. A postal code, a suburb would help."

She struggle to answer. He waited. Inside his heart was breaking.

FINALLY. HE SNUCK back inside.

She slept – or was unconscious. Good. He smiled and settled back inside her head. He hated that she was resting easily now. He wanted her to suffer like he had. And she would…wait…something was different.

Smoother, softer, calmer. No. He didn't want her calm or happy or resting soundly. He wanted her tortured, tormented, grieving. What the hell had happened? He could feel the old anger rising up. The love-turned-hatred blinding his vision until he could feel the energy build inside. Enough to destroy her sleep.

He wanted to lash out, pouring his anger into the one spot in her head he had access to – the weakest part of her – her eyes. The one spot he could destroy.

He'd gotten good at that part. Only something had happened this last time. Something he didn't understand. And he had to. He couldn't afford another failure.

Nor could he afford to expend more energy trying to sort out the problem.

He gave a pained laugh, then choked it off.

He needed to save his energy – for her.

CHAPTER 29

CELINA WOKE SLOWLY. How long had she been out? Scared to move, Celina lay quiet, a thin film of sweat coating her skin. The breeze from an open window drifted across the bed, chilling her. Was it over? Or was it only over for now, and that asshole would come back to hurt her time and time again?

She knew she didn't dare risk moving in case the pain started up. After a few moments shivers rippled over her cooling body. She rolled over onto her back. "Thank God," she whispered. "The pain is gone."

"Are you okay?" he asked gently, his voice deep, dark, caring.

"Now, yes." She reached up to stoke his cheek. "That's the worst it's ever been."

"Sorry about that. Lie there and rest."

He got up and she heard water running a few minutes later. A shower would be good, but that took effort – energy she didn't have.

Moments later she almost cried out in relief as a warm washcloth stroked gently across her forehead, easing the last of the tension. "That feels wonderful," she whispered.

"It's the least I could do." Guilt twined through his voice.

"It's not your fault." She hated that he felt he'd had a

part in this.

"I didn't stop him in time before he hurt you and I said I would."

She smiled. He stroked the washcloth down over her breast, sending shivers across her sensitized skin and making her gasp. After a night of heavy lovemaking followed by the horrific pain she'd just survived, her body should have been too exhausted for anything else. Replete and complete. Until now.

Her body uncurled slowly and turned toward him.

His slow strokes slid down lower and lower, drawing lazy circles on her ribs, across her stomach, and down the V of her legs. She lifted her hips toward him, wishing, hoping, pleading.

She rolled closer and cried out when Stefan kissed her hipbone, trailing moist kisses across her flat belly.

Still trembling with the memory of the recent pain, her body willing fell under the spell of Stefan's ministrations, letting the peacefulness of being here together with him draw her away from all that horror into the sweetness of his embrace.

Yet the fear persisted. Stefan reared up and she sensed him looking deep into her gaze. Tired and worn out, but needing what only he could give, she opened up and welcomed him into her heat.

Still warm from their recent lovemaking, he settled into place and loved her. Slowly, carefully, as if she was the most precious thing in his world, he proved to her with the drugging kisses, his clever fingers, with the complete possession of her body that she was his.

She wouldn't have it any other way.

BRANDT DROVE TO the address Sam had given. If Sam was correct, Vanessa hadn't died yet and maybe… maybe there was something they could do for her. And maybe she could tell Brandt something about her attacker.

There were already two cop cars and the flashing lights signaled an ambulance off to the side. Damn it, he was too late.

He strode up to the first group of officers milling around and flashed his ID. They willingly shared the story. The young girl's back has been badly burned but she was going to make it. They still had no idea what had caused the injury, but weren't looking for an attacker in this case – at least not according to the victim.

Brandt nodded then saw the gurney coming out the house with a young girl, a woman who appeared to be her mother walking at her side. Brandt wondered at the wisdom of speaking with her.

He walked closer, showed his ID to the mother and asked her, "Do you know what happened?"

She shook her head, tears in her eyes. "Nothing we could see. She's been fine for a long time. We thought it was all over with. Then this…"

"Thought what was all over with?"

"My daughter was in a bad accident. She was burnt on twenty percent of her body. She'd been through so many skin grafts and dealt with so much pain. Her back looked perfect. The scars were minimal. Earlier today she said her back was unnaturally warm. But this was a big evening for her, so she ignored it then out of the blue, she said it started burning up." She shrugged helplessly. "I don't know what to say. There's no reason for this to have happened."

"I didn't do anything," Vanessa whispered, her voice

slow and heavy. The drugs must have kicked in. "For no reason my back got really hot really fast. There was no warning. It felt like I was in another accident."

Brandt looked over at the paramedic and said, "And the physical damage?"

"Bad," the paramedic said.

Brandt nodded and stepped back to give the men room. He would ask the couple of uniforms if there was any damage to her bedroom – with that kind of heat there must have been.

Her mother wrapped her arms around her chest as they both watched Vanessa being loaded into the back of the ambulance. As Vanessa's mother went to join her she whispered, "She hated her recovery. It was horribly painful. I hope she doesn't have to go through all that again."

"She's going to have to," he said quietly, but the mother had gotten into the ambulance with her daughter and didn't hear his words.

He opened his phone and made a call. When Dr. Maddy answered he said, "I need a favor. It's related to the same case that involves Stefan's Celina."

"Tell me."

HE SHUDDERED IN the darkness. Shivering from shock, he felt a fear he hadn't had a chance to experience before slide through him. Where was that killer anger, that burning heat that warmed him and kept him on the edge of clarity? That conscious thought he desperately needed to make this all happen?

He finally admitted that this was moving too fast. He'd set something in motion that he probably shouldn't have – at least not with the speed with which he'd gone at it. Something had happened that he didn't understand. Likely wouldn't have time to understand.

What had he done? He wasn't quite ready to die yet, and for the first time he had to wonder if he really wanted to any longer.

Besides, if this wasn't death, what was death? That it could be nothing – that he'd cease to exist completely terrified him now. Now that his consciousness was functioning again, now that fear was working its way through him.

Before the fear, anger, the justified anger had been easy to utilize to finish his project. Now he wondered if he wanted it finished. He now had a glimpse of a life he could live here – limited, but possible.

Did he want that? Not really, but the alternative completely destroyed him. Fear, now that it had raised its ugly head, threatened his plans.

If he could stay here he'd need to keep his strongest connection. That would have to be Celina.

Could he stay a part of her forever? If he pulled all his energy completely home to just her physical form? Would he be strong enough to take her over and stay there – possibly always in control, or possibly only sometimes? If he couldn't, would he want that?

He almost laughed. If that attempt didn't work then it wouldn't make any difference anyway – he'd do what he'd planned to do in the beginning.

Take her out – permanently.

DR. MADDY SETTLED into her favorite yoga position and slipped free of her body. She stretched out her arms and rolled her head back. A huge sigh of relief welled up and floated free.

She needed this. She couldn't imagine all those people staying in their bodies all the time when her soul craved this freedom. She gave a happy sigh then connected to the burn center, a place she'd had reason to go too many times in the last year now that her name was starting to spread.

She floated gently above the admissions desk. The center was quiet, busy but under control. She watched the intake being done on a patient until she realized it wasn't who she was looking for. She carried on through the new admission areas, looking for the girl Brandt had told her about.

There was no sign of her until a new ambulance unloaded a gurney. She floated closer, seeing a beautiful young woman, her aura thin, flat against her body, anguish and pain rippling down her sheet-covered form. The energy worker in Maddy understood the trauma had already affected the woman's psyche. The shock, the pain, and something akin to despair. She didn't understand the full story yet as she'd only gotten the little bit Brandt had to offer.

The sheet had been tented over the woman's back. As it was pulled back Maddy gasped. Poor girl. It was one thing to hear the details, but quite another to see the actual damage. She couldn't help herself. She immediately poured cooling, healing energy down the woman's spine on the inside, sending the energy to the underside of the injury to stop it from burning through the underlying tissues.

The girl moaned but was no longer in agony. Instead, there was a teary gratefulness to the sound. The girl's mother reached out to clasp the girl's hand.

"Vanessa?"

"It feels so good," she whispered. "I don't know what it is but it's helping."

Her mother frowned and stared at the several nurses working on her. A doctor came over to assess the damage.

Maddy laughed. It was the same young doctor who'd asked her to consult on a case last week. She smiled and whispered inside the doctor's head, *Hello, Dr. Vitner.*

The doctor jerked, looked around then smiled. "Vanessa, this just might be your lucky day." To the nurses she said, "Let's get the treatment started."

She turned to the mother. "I'm so sorry. As you've been here before, you know the routine."

"I'd hoped to stay…" Her voice trailed off at the doctor's head shake.

"Sorry. This is a tough stage for your daughter." She led the mother to the doorway. "We'll let you know when it's done."

Maddy whispered in the doctor's mind, *Let me help.*

Dr. Vitner looked over the nurses. "I'll handle the beginning of this."

Surprised, they nodded and backed away. "Do you want us to stay or go and start on the next stage?"

"Go and set up for the next stage. I want to take a closer look at this case. The police are going to be involved in this one as well."

They nodded, understanding in their eyes. With sympathetic glances to the young woman now lying blissful on the bed they left the room.

"I hope I've done the right thing and that's really you," Dr. Vitner said.

Maddy laughed. *It's me. Let me take a look.*

The doctor walked closer. "This doesn't make any sense.

The burns stopped and started with distinct lines as if a sheet of burning metal had been placed on her back."

Where were the original skin grafts?

Maddy could see many grafts and the energy from before, but there was also that same damn blackness she'd been seeing on too many sad cases.

"They were all over the place, really." She motioned to many of the areas so Maddy could see. "Some took better than others. Some became almost invisible, but some – there were a few that didn't graft as nice." She took a deep breath. "We replaced the initial grafts as soon as we could with her own skin as per normal treatment."

Maddy pulsed more cooling energy through the woman's back, easy and healing as she sent the energy upward through the bone and tissue to heal from the inside out. She considered Dr. Vitner's comment. Had the original skin donor been the origin of the black energy? If so, why was it still here? That would have been months ago, and the original skin would have been removed – thus removing the black energy – and been replaced with Vanessa's own skin.

Could the original skin – the remnants of the energy from that donor – have blended into Vanessa's tissues? Healing and growing stronger. Would that have been enough to have allowed the energy to stay? Or was something else going on?

Dr. Vitner frowned. She studied the woman's back. "I don't understand how this kind of damage could have happened."

I might. And she did. Unfortunately Dr. Maddy was starting to really understand. And the tracking and finding of any and all other potential victims could be almost impossible.

As far as she could see the grafts that had been damaged were beyond repair, and she didn't dare heal them if they were the ones causing the trouble. The last thing she dared to do was let the asshole behind this know of her existence – or what she could do.

I'll work from the inside up. You can work from the outside in. I'll see how far up I dare go.

"Dare go?" the doctor asked.

Yes. And Maddy left it at that. How could she explain that she was afraid the donor of that original skin graft might just be alive – living an energetic existence – and killing people?

Especially when skin donors were usually dead.

CHAPTER 30

C ELINA WALKED OUT onto Stefan's balcony and tilted her face to the sun. It was a beautiful warm morning. She'd have brought a change of clothes if she'd had any idea that she'd be spending the night. There was such a sense of peace here. She loved it. Going home to her cozy apartment where everything had a place seemed confining all of a sudden.

She smiled as Stefan slipped his arms around her shoulders and tugged her gently back against his chest.

"Okay?"

"Better than okay." With a happy sigh she reached up to clasp his hands. "Thank you."

She felt his start of surprise.

She laughed. "No, not for the night of wonderful sex, but more for the level of acceptance. And for showing me how much more there is to learn out there. When I lost my sight I closed off inside, thinking I needed to focus on controlling my world to keep safe. My life became very limited. An end to so much. I hadn't realized how much. I'd figured learning 'out there' was over, and how the only learning I was ever going to do was how to survive as a blind person in a visual world."

He hugged her gently and rested his chin on her head. "A natural reaction. I've crawled inside at various points in my life, just to be able to heal. When life became too much or a hurt too great. By doing that we narrow our focus to control what we can when our life is out of control. Then, when we regain confidence, we widen that circle of experience at a rate we believe we can handle."

She laughed. "I'm not sure I've made it to that point. It widened without my permission."

In a serious voice he said, "Everything happens for a reason. Sometimes it seems as if we've become victims, but it's a chance to get out of victim status and take charge again. From where I stand you did a wonderful job."

She turned her head so his heart pounded against her ear.

"And I am grateful that you let me into your inner circle," He said in a deep caring voice.

"I'm not sure I had much choice there either," she teased.

"You always had the choice. Some rules, even personal ones and energetic or karmic ones, just *have* to be obeyed." His voice deepened. "Whether we like it or not."

Sensing something deeper, darker, she twisted slightly to see him, an instinctive reaction she couldn't stop even after a year. "What do you—"

The phone rang in his pocket.

He hesitated as if he wanted to say something, but she knew how many different things he had going on. She stepped back slightly. "Answer it. Maybe it has something to do with this nasty predator."

"True." He pulled his phone out of his pocket. "Hello, Maddy. What's happening?"

Celina bumped up against the railing at her back. She turned and stared blankly out over his property. She didn't want to eavesdrop but the tiny snippets were worrisome.

"Right. It would have to be someone very close to her," Stefan said.

Celina wondered if she was the "her" in question. Stefan ended the conversation and said nothing for a long moment. She could feel questions as if they were actual items floating on the air.

"What do you need to know?" she asked, trying for a light tone of voice but failing. Her stomach clenched with nerves. He reached over and stroked her back gently.

"A few questions have arisen. One, you said you've lost everyone in your life. Can you give me a list?'

Surprised but willing she said, "Caslo, both parents, and my fiancé – in that order. There might have been others, but those were the ones I was extremely close to." She frowned, remembering some of his confusing discussion about dead entities and possession. She shook her head. "Don't even think that they could possibly be involved in any of this. For one, they're dead. All of them."

"Are they?" he murmured. She sensed more than saw that he quirked his lips.

"Yes," she said sharply. "I see ghosts, remember? I haven't seen any of them ever." She stopped, remembering Caslo, and sighed. "Okay, so that's not quite true."

"Which part?"

"Caslo. He was an old friend. My best friend. I had thought he'd become so much more, but he was taken away to a special institute when I was like twelve." She instinctively slipped her hand into her pocket to hold the soothing rock that Caslo had given her. "He had some weird things he could do – honestly I can't even remember the specifics, but this place was supposed to help him. I'd hoped I'd hear from him, I prayed every night that he'd be able to contact me – somehow – to say he was okay and would come home one day."

She wrapped her arms around her chest. "I loved him. God, I loved him. Losing him was my first lesson that life wasn't fair. And about the perfidy of humans. I'd asked his parents over and over again where he was and when he was finally coming home. They always gave me this pitying look and said 'maybe soon.' He never came home. They moved away soon after and I lost touch. Then years later I'd almost forgotten about him, but every once in a while he was there in the back of my mind."

She gave him a tremulous smile. "One day, he came to me in ghost form. He was the first ghost I knowingly recognized. I was delirious with joy and yet horrified for him. For me. I wanted him back in my life, but never as a ghost. I couldn't send him to the light for the longest time, then finally I realized he was stuck here on Earth because of me. And I couldn't have that. I loved him so much I had to let him go. So I sent him away. It wasn't my finest hour, as he didn't take it very well, but I finally had to tell him to never come back."

Even the memory hurt. She bowed her head and sniffled back the tears. "God, I regretted that the minute he was gone, but I couldn't call him back. It was for his own good."

"I wonder about all the ills in the world committed because it was for someone else's own good," Stefan said, his voice pensive, deep.

She barely heard him. Then he said, "And your parents?"

"They were travelling in Mexico and were involved in a horrific vehicle accident. It was bad. There were no bodies to bring home. It made it easier and so much more difficult."

She sighed. "My aunt went down to deal with the official stuff. I couldn't. There was no way I wanted anything to do with that country. I can't ever see wanting to go there."

"Interesting."

"What, my reaction? Their death, or that there were no bodies to recover?"

"All of it." His voice was so noncommittal she was immediately suspicious. "And your fiancé? What happened there?"

"He died from an aneurysm in his brain. I lost him so fast." She tilted her face, wishing the sun was still out. But along with the conversation the weather had chilled. "There was no preparation. He was here one day and then gone."

She swallowed the tears back and said, "Anything else you need to know?"

"How was your relationship with him up to the end?"

"Outside of the fight that night, mostly wonderful. We both fell so hard that we were locked up in our own world. Probably too much, as I said before." She winced. "Looking back, it was definitely too much. He was possessive. Then again, so was Caslo. I'd promised Caslo that I'd always be there for him before he left, but obviously that was a lie," she said bitterly. "And I promised Peter I'd never leave him. He'd said the same – many times. He was really big on promises." She closed her eyes in pain at the broken memories. "If you made a promise, then it was forever, he said." She turned slightly to face him. "Another promise I couldn't keep."

"He died," Stefan said quietly. "That's not your fault."

She shrugged. "It felt like it was. God, you should have seen us. We did everything together, even dressed the same half the time. It was really stupid."

"How is that stupid? You loved him."

She winced. "And I guess that's where I slid. I wondered if I did love him. I wondered if I gave all my love to Caslo and then had nothing left for anyone else."

He stroked her back. "Love doesn't work that way."

"No. By the time Peter came into my life I was desperate to not be alone anymore. I wanted someone in my life who cared. I was just as possessive as he was because I *needed* someone to love me. I was so tired of being alone. And so afraid of being alone forever. He felt like my only choice, my last chance to have someone love me." Her voice broke, and damn if those tears didn't start to fall again.

She wiped them away, furious at herself for letting all that out. "God, I'm pathetic."

"No." He tugged her into his arms. "You aren't. I understand loneliness. Most of us do."

"Then why do I feel so guilty? I did everything I could afterwards to lock myself in and away. People like Jacob wouldn't let me stay locked away. But I was always afraid he'd die too, just like everyone else that got close to me. And look what happened to him!" Her voice rose and broke at the end.

"Shh," he said against her hair. "He's going to be okay. It's going to be okay."

"No," she whispered. "It's never going to be okay again."

STEFAN STRUGGLED WITH the information he was getting and the information he was intuiting. He didn't know how much to ask her because he didn't know how much she could handle. There were several major truths ahead of her. All at once was too much. So which were the easiest or most important right now?

Taking a deep breath, he asked the one question that had to be asked. "What happened to your fiancé's remains?"

She stiffened. Then stepped back. Her voice cold she said, "I was the one in charge of that. As he was brain dead at the hospital I donated his body. Once the decision was made and I knew that's what he'd wanted, I signed the forms for the doctors to recover what they could."

Her eyes were glassy but defiant.

"What kinds of body parts were donated?" He deliberately kept his voice mild, curious. She didn't have to know everything all at once. "Do you know?"

She waved her hands around. "Some. I was thrilled to know they could use as much as they did. Heart, kidneys, lungs, veins, even skin." She beamed. "It helped a lot to know that even in death Peter had gone on to give so much to other people."

Stefan nodded, then remembering she couldn't see he said, "Good. I've heard that from other donor families, that it brought them much satisfaction in helping others in need." He turned her to the kitchen. "Now, how about some lunch?"

He mentally contacted both Brandt and Dr. Maddy at the same time and passed on the information. *We need to see if any or all of these victims received donor organs and if they came from Peter, her fiancé.*

The dual shocked responses were immediate.

Dr. Maddy said, *That would make a horrific sense.*

Brandt said, *I'm on it. I'd just gone down that road myself. It might not have been her fiancé though – it's quite likely that all the organs came from the same body. God, it really makes you rethink that whole process.*

Stefan sat Celina down on the island stool. "How about a big salad?"

As if the conversation had been processing through her mind and she had an inkling of what was to come she said, "Anything that's not from a dead animal."

BRANDT MOVED TO the computer and started clicking the keys, bringing up the information, or as much of it as he could get a hold of. He hadn't printed off a file for himself as he had for Stefan, preferring to work electronically. But right now he wished he had. He shifted closer to his chart and slowly pulled the bits and pieces from the files. When he came to the trucker who'd had the heart attack while driving the fuel truck, Brandt noted he'd had bypass surgery many months before his final action.

That could be one. The old woman with the burning legs could have had veins donated to repair hers. But he was guessing. Getting ahead of himself.

He checked the girl and her burning back, already knowing she'd had skin grafts, but when was that and was there a way to track from whom? Not in this file. Not deterred, he carried on until one by one he'd found what he needed. Two of the cases he had little to no information on their physical health and more digging would be required. For most, they'd been through a traumatic injury or health crisis and had indeed received donor organs. At least the big organs. He had no ideas how many body parts could be used to help others. Like the skin stuff. He had a lot to learn. He picked up the phone and called the local hospital to see how the process worked.

That led him to the donor center. And more questions

and more phone calls and more questions.

He sat after the last call and wondered. Could it be? Really?

Stefan mentally answered. *I'm very much afraid it is.*

Holy shit.

HE SHUDDERED. NOTHING felt right. Or good. Something was wrong. He didn't know how to fix it. His energy was failing rapidly. The time to do something was now. In fact, the time was past. He had to make a decision. Doing this took too much energy. He needed a big surge to center in just one place. But he had to make sure he ended up at the right place. That was the trick. He had to cut off everything but the one he wanted. And he had to do it fast.

An idea formed in the back of his mind. Was there a way to take that huge mess of little parts and pieces and finish them for good? Most were collected at one place – at least from what he could sense.

Focusing was getting harder. He was so out of time. If only he could find the answer for one last push.

Had someone interfered in his process? He wasn't sure what else it could be. He wasn't doing a great job lately – he'd thought the last one should have been a shoo-in, but there appeared to be a tiny little bit of him left there. As if the job had only been partially completed.

That shouldn't have been possible. The aftermath should have finished the rest.

And somehow it hadn't.

That couldn't be allowed, but someone had stopped the burn. He could sense that bit of himself still there but it was fading quickly. Something had happened. Some*one* had happened.

He needed to cut out one of the biggest drains now. He'd held off, thinking the kid might be an alternate landing spot. But it wasn't to be.

And now he needed to fix that one and fast.

He had to have all the power he could find for that final blow.

ERIC SAT UP in bed and waited for the lady to put his food in front of him. He sniffed the air experimentally and brightened. Burgers? He was starving. There was something that looked like a pudding. His stomach settled lower and some of his appetite waned.

His mother stood up from where she'd been sitting at his side. In an overly bright voice, she said, "Lunchtime. Open it, it smells great."

"It smells terrible," he muttered. He took the lid off and a half grin popped back up again. It was a burger. Just a little dull, flat, burger – but it was a burger. And fries. Now he smiled. Lifting one, he happily bit off the other end. "Hey, it's pretty good."

"Great. So maybe you'll eat today?" she asked hopefully.

Eric nodded. "I'm hungry."

"Oh, that's wonderful." She sat back in her chair and watched him as he worked his way through the burger and fries. By the time he got to the pudding he was hitting his stride. Too quickly it was all gone. He frowned as he checked over the tray. "Mom, do you think they have any more?"

She gasped in happy surprise. "Why don't I go and look?" She almost ran out of his room.

He pushed the small mobile table away to lean back. He

wanted to go home. He hated it here. Hated the stuff he'd been through. He wanted it over.

Too bad. It's never going to be over for you.

Eric froze.

"What are you doing here? I thought you were gone," he whispered. Oh no. His gaze darted around the room. He needed the dragon slayer.

"Stefan?" he managed to croak out. "Stefan," he cried louder. But only silence was his answer.

Until the dragon in his mind started to laugh. *Say good-bye, little one. This time no one will be there to help you.*

The scream that ripped from Eric's mouth echoed throughout the hallway of the hospital. In the background he vaguely heard the sound of running footsteps.

Then he heard nothing more.

CHAPTER 31

"THIS IS DELICIOUS." Celina ate slowly, savoring the novelty of having someone else make her a meal. She enjoyed cooking but this was a treat.

"Thank you." She loved the smile in his voice. "After lunch I'd like to see if Jacob is awake. I'd like to go visit him if he is."

"Sure. He's doing much better now, so maybe this afternoon we can head over there."

Enjoying the food, she took another bite and froze as Stefan took a harsh gasp of air. Then his arm hit the table with a thud and the fork clattered onto the plate. "Stefan? Are you okay?" No answer. And she thought she knew. "Are you having another vision?" she asked hurriedly. "Is there anything I can do?"

"Worse. Back soon."

But he sat in front of her, frozen in place. She reached across and covered his hand with hers. He didn't need her. She needed him.

"You shouldn't touch him when he's in a vision."

Celina snatched her hand before she realized she was taking instructions from a ghost. A teenage ghost at that. "Lissa?"

"Yes. Stefan has gone to help someone."

"How can you tell?"

"His energy raced off almost in a panic. He does everything for everyone. No one does much for him."

Celina tilted her head. "He's very self-sufficient. I think most people imagine he doesn't need anyone. Or they might not know how to help him."

"And you – where do you sit?" Lissa challenged.

Ah. Time to embrace this. "Why don't you like me, Lissa? There are few ghosts that I've met who have your abrasive personality."

Lissa laughed. "I'm only abrasive with you."

Bewildered, Celina said, "Why? I didn't even know you before yesterday."

"No, you didn't, but I recognize what you're doing and I don't like it. I don't imagine any ghost does."

Anger rose up. "Look, you don't have to like me. That's fine, but if you've got a problem with me tell me."

"You think you can talk to ghosts."

"I do talk to ghosts," Celina snapped. "Otherwise I wouldn't be having this conversation with you."

"And you have a lot of ghosts in your world, right? Been there for a long time."

"Too many of them, yes. But it's a gift I can't refuse. If I can help them, then I try to help them. They should be crossing into the light. You should be crossing into the light. Not sitting here and haunting Stefan."

Lissa sucked in a deep breath.

God, what a conversation. "Look, I'm sorry. I understand that Stefan is special for you and that you…" Celina waved her hand helpfully, "evolved somehow. That is seriously cool. But just as I try to help my ghost friends to cross into the light to continue their journey, I feel I have to tell you to do the same thing."

"I can leave anytime," Lissa snapped. "Can you say the same thing about all the ghosts in your world?"

Celina sat back. There was something edgy in Lissa's voice. Something brewing. Something important. She really wished she could see her cleanly, but the edges of her form waffled and sparked as if from the emotion pouring through her. Whatever she was bothered about was really upsetting her.

"Yes. They are all free. I don't keep them with me." She waved her arms around. "There aren't any here with me now. They come and go as they please. I presume they come to me because I can see them and because I can help them." Celina kept her voice gentle, calm. Realizing how cocky that sounded, she quickly amended her words. "I can help some of them."

"Only you don't. You call them to you with your music, with the promise of being able to talk to you, and then you bind them to keep them at your side." Lissa spat out the last words. "Forever."

STEFAN DOVE INTO Eric's energy system. The screams of terror had brought everyone within hearing distance into the little boy's room. That was only going to make Stefan's job harder.

The predator was there.

And not there.

Stefan raced to the injured site, to the tiny cadaver bone, and studied the depth of the blackness. It went right through. The best answer would be for that bone to be removed. Eric was correct there.

But they didn't have time to make that happen right

now.

He needed the predator's energy to be separated from that piece. As he stared at the heat level rising from the actual organic material, he finally realized that's exactly what this predator was doing. He was killing off the bone and the boy with it, by raising the temperature of the surrounding areas, the membrane, the walls of the veins melting, letting the boy bleed out.

He was killing off the bits and pieces of himself that had been given to other people to help them live.

Why he'd do that Stefan had no idea.

He wished he could communicate with the man.

You can, but it won't help you save the boy, the predator snapped. *And who the hell are you?*

Stefan ignored the question, asking his own instead. *Why would you kill him?*

Stefan couldn't see any one specific soul to communicate with so he sent out his thoughts in a surround-sound pattern. At the same time he pulled one of Dr. Maddy's tricks and slipped a tiny bit of energy inside the actual bone. And carefully, with as little pressure as he could, he let the cool healing energy work its way into the bone at the DNA level.

Dimly in the outside he could hear nurses and doctors working on Eric, but Stefan knew the real battle was right here. Right now.

He needed to know why this asshole was doing this.

Connected as they were, Stefan heard the harsh laughter in his head.

I had no choice. You try living like this. Splintered. Fractured. In a million tiny pieces waiting to be transplanted so other people can be healed.

So other people can live better lives, Stefan murmured.

What about my life? What about my horrible existence?

Stefan slipped more and more energy into the damaged bone. Fighting for possession of something long dead made no sense. The doctors would say the cadaver bone was just a tool to help rebuild Eric's leg.

But there was life in that bone long past the point there should have been. Somehow, this man had continued to exist in the various parts and pieces as his body was dissected and used in organ transplants. Just the thought made Stefan's stomach heave. God, what a horrible existence.

Damn right, the other man said bitterly. *I can't do this. Then I realized that several of my 'pieces' had more consciousness than others. I started to gain in strength a little bit at a time. Maybe enough of me had been transplanted out that they could all find each other here – wherever here is. Do you know how lonely this has been? To think of this going on for decades and decades? I couldn't do it.*

Until? Stefan prompted. He poured more and more energy into the bone, filling the cells and slowly moving out the blackness. Replaced it with light, healing blue. He worked from the very center out, gently pushing the other's energy to the edge. He didn't try to shove it completely out yet – he needed the bone to be full of vibrant energy before he made that last transition. The blackness appeared to contain a residue left in it. Or rather, someone left in it. Used pieces parceled out to others in need. Which then made him more victim than anyone could know.

God, that sounded horrible.

It is horrible.

More energy poured and pulsed. A light-blue core glowed deep inside. More energy. Feverish, and knowing the predator – and how could he call him that – would under-stand what he'd done soon enough.

The blue glow brightened, swelling outward and filling the bone. A glow lit up behind the blackness. Stefan didn't want to envelop the black energy. He needed it to disappear completely, but he didn't know how to do that…unless the man could separate on his own. And he'd have to have damn good reason to do that.

What's happening? the man cried. *It's not supposed to do that. Is that you? What are you doing?*

I'm healing the bone so the little boy can live, Stefan admit-ted. *You can detach and go to wherever it is you need to go.*

No, I need the energy from here, he cried.

For what?

For her. To make her pay.

Stefan's heart froze. *Pay for what? How?*

For killing me! For forcing me into a lifetime of tortured existence. He laughed, but it was harsh, pained, agonizing for Stefan to hear. *Imagine how I felt when my consciousness had collected together enough to understand what had happened and by whose hand. I want her to see me. To know what she did to me.*

She couldn't have known that you would be conscious through this process. Hell, who could know?

She must have, he snapped. *I was perfectly healthy and I was with her, then nothing. She killed me. I will kill her. But not yet. Not until I've made her suffer first.* That same laugh ricocheted in the air. *Then I'll take her out – but leave her as a shell to be cut into a million pieces forever.*

Christ.

Stefan shook off his restraint and poured as much energy into the blue volcano as he could. The temperature was rising as this asshole turned up the heat. That's how he'd managed to kill off his separate organs – by utilizing his anger, his hatred, to focus on one spot, and that rage had created enough heat that he could destroy the tiny piece of himself. And like any rage it was always looking for an outlet. Hence, the need to take out as many people as he could while killing off himself. And if the organ recipient had any rage for him to draw on, it made him that much more powerful.

Stefan still needed answers. He had to save Celina.

You won't save her, the predator screamed, rage flowing through him, but Stefan was stronger and the more rage the man sent out the more loving energy Stefan poured in to protect Eric.

No, the predator screamed. *I will win.*

Then it was as if a bomb went off inside the child's leg.

The final massive blast shocked through Stefan. Frantically he poured more energy and realized it was no longer his energy. Dr. Maddy was there, calmly securing the rest of the child's leg from the damaging rays and systematically, with the loving touch she was so well known for, wrapping up the last bits of heated energy and cooling them down.

It was over.

Eric was safe.

Stefan collapsed.

BRANDT PICKED UP the phone for what had to be the fiftieth time this morning – as soon as he'd exited his meeting with the captain. That had been a hard sell. Yet the look on his face as if something crawled over his skin when he'd understood – priceless.

God, how horrible.

He knew that the chance of getting the information he needed without a warrant wasn't good, but he'd also found this morning that Dr. Maddy's name opened doors, windows, and probably safes if he tried. He shook his head and waited for the clerk on the other end of the line to answer.

"Yes, we have records in that name. Tissues were collected on June seventeenth – almost a year ago."

"That's a match. Is there any chance that any of that tissue is still here? I understand you are always short, but just thought I'd ask."

"No, sorry. Some of it was deemed not viable when it was taken for transplant, and the rest was used about ten months ago for a Vanessa Coller."

"Perfect, thanks. That matches my records."

He hung up the phone and realized it all lined up. A horrible, nasty line that made him reconsider the possibility of something like that happening again. He had the organ donor system set up in case anything happened to him, but the last thing he wanted was to wake up fractured like that into an existence of only time and space – and endless awareness.

He shuddered.

Now to check with the organ bank. Maybe it was a good thing that there was always a shortage on organ donors, as it would mean all this man's body parts had been placed in people already. According to the chart on the wall, most were dead too. The few he knew to still be alive were Eric and Vanessa. Thankfully. But what he couldn't do was connect Celina to the same man. Then again, he hadn't been able to get any information from her eye surgeon either. He'd contacted Dr. Maddy for that.

If she could confirm that it would be perfect.

But he'd learned a long time ago that nothing in life was perfect. And as he looked at what this man had gone through he realized death was no final answer either.

DR. MADDY GOT off the phone and considered the information she had on file with the information Dr. Jorgensen had provided. Both matched and provided little that was new. The car accident had broken several of the occipital bones around Celina's eyes and there'd been some damage to the surrounding tissue from the swelling. One optic nerve had partially detached and was successfully reattached. Even then she should have had vision in the other eye. Instead, she was blind in both.

The bottom line was that Celina had never had a transplant.

That surprised Dr. Maddy. She'd been sure that something of the predator had been given to Celina. But apparently not. The surgery had been simple and shouldn't have affected her eyesight at all. She'd had poor eyesight going in, but after the surgery, when the swelling had gone down her sight should have returned.

So they were still missing that one bit of information.

Why her eyes? Why had the predator settled in her eyes?

And that deep into her system. Unless it was someone she'd loved. Who'd once loved her. Who was in her heart chakra already.

Because she'd loved him.

Because he'd loved her.

And why her eyes?

She realized it was likely very simple.

Because he could.

She'd been injured, but the facial injuries had been the worst. Therefore the weakness.

Giving him more power. More control.

The accident gave him an opening and he took it. Settling into the one area he, with his stronger energy, could dominate.

And once he'd grabbed hold he'd been able to control everything – except what was around her.

Because she couldn't see.

Now, at least, Dr. Maddy knew why she couldn't.

CHAPTER 32

CELINA HEARD STEFAN'S loud groan as if from a long
way away. Then again, she'd been in a fog herself since
Lissa had delivered her hefty blow. It certainly explained
Lissa's animosity towards her, but nothing in that explanation made Celina feel any better about herself. Was she
trapping ghosts? Was she so lonely, so unstable, that she'd
had to trap people who didn't want to be here beside her so
she wouldn't be alone anymore?

She leaned back, her mind consumed with the number
of ghosts she'd kept just out of reach. Had she brought them
in only to push them away? Chained to her at her own
convenience?

Was she such a pathetic, horrible person? Just then she
heard an odd sound. "Stefan?"

"I'm here. Give me a moment." His voice strengthened
to the point that it sounded almost normal at the end. "That
was quite the trip."

"What happened? Lissa said you'd gone off to save a little boy. Was that Eric?"

"Yes. The predator went to kill off the part of himself
that was inside Eric's body. Given his methodology that
would likely mean killing the donor recipient at the same
time."

"A part of him was inside Eric? Donor recipients?" Fear

seized her heart and squeezed. "Oh please, no. Please don't tell me this predator, this nasty parasite, is my dead fiancé?" She shook her head as an awful panic swept through her. It was too horrible to consider. "No, I won't believe it. That's so wrong."

"Why don't you believe it?"

She shook her head. "Because he wasn't like that," she cried. "Peter was gentle. Besides, being an organ donor was something we were talking about. I was only fulfilling his wishes. Why attack those people? Why me?"

"Your eyes."

She reached up to her eyes. "My eyes. So?" she asked in confusion. "What does that have to do with him?"

"That's where he's centered. The weakest part of your body. The easiest place to set up control. And the best location to kill you – given his options."

She stared at him, uncomprehending. "What? That's not possible. He loved me."

"And that's something else we have to get to the bottom of – and fast. He may have loved you at one time but he hates you now."

She started to shake. The tremors began inside her body and slowly worked outward. "It can't be Peter then. He loved me. If anyone would hate me it would be Caslo," she whispered. "I sent him away. Locked him out of my life. He loved me. And I treated him like that."

"Why?"

There was an odd note in Stefan's voice, but she was too tortured to sort through it all. "Because it's what he needed. And I loved him too much to keep him chained to my side."

Her own wording brought tears to her eyes. She refused to let them fall. She'd done enough crying these last days.

After a moment, dry eyed and hanging onto the threads of her control, she said, "And Lissa was right. After losing Caslo, my parents, and then my fiancé, I couldn't let them go anymore. Let anyone go anymore. I was so lonely." Tears threatened. "God, I'm horrible. I was keeping the ghosts around so I wouldn't have to lose them too." She shuddered then cried out, "I didn't know that I was doing that!"

She heard a chair being moved back, then felt her own chair being turned. Stefan wrapped his arms around her. "What you did was instinctive and out of pain. You didn't mean to hurt anyone. You just were trying to survive."

"Yes." She burst into tears and buried her face against his shoulder. She cried for the last few years of roller-coaster emotions and despair, of loss and grief and death and ghosts. When the storm abated she pulled back slightly and looked into his face, wishing she could see the expression in his eyes. Because she couldn't she had to ask, "Do you hate me?" Her voice was tremulous and low but she got the words out.

"No, Celina. I love you. I always have."

She frowned. "Always. You've known me what, a couple of d–"

And the predator attacked.

She screamed and fell awkwardly to the floor. Stefan caught her and laid her down on the wood surface. She clasped both hands over her eyes and sobbed once. Then screamed, rage and anger and betrayal spilling over. "Is that you, Peter? Are you the one doing this to me?"

The answer came in through her mind. *Yes. It's me. Finally, you know.*

"You could have told me. Why do you hate me so much? What did I ever do to you?" Was there any pain like finding out the greatest love in your life was a fraud, and that instead of loving you he only wanted to possess you?

You killed me, and then not being satisfied with that you had me cut up into little pieces to live in endless torment.

What? she cried. *I did not kill you. We signed those donor cards together. I never would have killed you. You died from a brain aneurysm.*

I remember. And I also remember that you pulled the plug, he snapped, something ugly in his voice.

Whatever he was doing, he tightened the screw more. Her body twisted in agony.

I remember you screaming at me. You wanted me dead.

We were having an argument at the restaurant. I never wanted you dead. She didn't know how to make him listen. *We were at Chico's, remember? We were at the same damn place you had that poor man drive through the restaurant. Were you trying to kill me then too?*

No! But if it had happened then I would have been okay with that. Of course I knew what the location meant. But he was coming to thank you. You gave him my heart! I was afraid you'd know it was me behind this. I didn't want that. I wanted you to suffer. Like I suffered.

"I didn't kill you," she said, sadly, desperately. *We got you to the hospital right away, but you went into a coma and they said you were brain dead.* Owen Dugar, the others, had all died because of him. Poor Owen. Poor Jacob. Oh dear God. All that pain… She said, still disbelieving, *The doctors said you were dead.*

Silence.

Then in that horrible, nasty voice he said, *Guess what —* *they were wrong. My body was sectioned off into as many usable parts as they could take, and I could only watch helplessly. I blanked out there and only came to a few months ago — actually,*

I don't know when I first regained consciousness, because there is no time in that existence. There is nothing but endless space. But I could sense more of me out there.

He gave a vicious laugh. *And I woke up inside you. A captive inside the woman who'd killed me. And took my eyes. Talk about nasty. But it gave me an idea of what to do.*

She couldn't stop crying, but his voice pounded at her through her tears. *I never held you captive. I don't have your eyes or any part of you. I loved you.*

He snorted. *Lies. As a few of the recipients had died, I started to understand what was happening. As these people died, they ceased to be a drain on me, and I gained in strength. And I knew what I had to do. But it took time. And a lot of energy. Finally, I'm here.*

Am I the last one? she asked painfully. *Have you killed all those people whose lives were enriched because of the donation of your organs? Because I kept your memory in my heart.*

I am all here now. There are a few tiny sparks of life out there, but they're too small for me to grab onto. They are just wisps, like a memory I can't quite reach out and touch. You might have tried to keep me trapped in your perfidious heart, but I escaped – and went to your weakness where I could tighten the screw.

Celina didn't know what to say. She could sense Stefan in her mind, listening in, but he was exhausted from saving Eric. Peter would kill him too if he could. Or at least burn out Stefan in the fight to take out Celina.

I can't believe this, she whispered. *Who could even know that this was possible?*

I've lived this reality for too long. I'm not planning on killing you – at least not for a while, but I do plan on making sure you suffer for as long as I can. If I get a year, a month, or a week, it's all a bonus. I'd wondered if I could have taken over your body permanently, but my energy is decaying. Slowly dying without something new to infuse it. I've tried so much and nothing changes, so as death was my ultimate wish, death is what I'll get – but not until you have suffered for what you did to me.

She didn't dare repeat that she'd done nothing. Her own guilt over the ghosts already plagued her. She'd been so happy with the organ donation she'd done everything she could to make sure they took everything. And now most of the recipients were dead. And that guilt was hers too.

No, Stefan whispered. *That is not yours to own. That was his.*

She didn't want Peter to understand that Stefan was here.

She wished she could turn time back and enjoy the gifts she'd been given, to have taken a different path with so many people in her life. Now at this moment in time grief for Caslo overwhelmed her. Talk about useless.

Maybe not, Stefan said. *Love is the answer here, sweetheart. If you have a love for Caslo locked away inside your heart it's time to let it out.*

It's not love but guilt, she cried painfully.

Or is the guilt hiding the love? Stopping it from coming out?

She wondered. She had to grow past it. She didn't have to worry about calling Caslo to her – he was dead, but she'd stopped acknowledging the special bond they'd had all that time ago and – Stefan was right – the love they'd shared. She smiled, remembering the days they'd been inseparable. The plans they'd made. The stories they'd shared and their hopes and dreams. She'd been so lost, so broken when he was gone.

Now she could release the pain of what she'd done – for

all the right reasons. And release the love to warm her heart and rejoice the time she'd been touched by his. He'd been special to her.

Her fingers once again clutched at the rock she still carried in her pocket. It had once been heart shaped and cracked in two. Her fingers stroked the broken edge.

Now love flowed. Flowed and poured outward from her heart.

Stefan whispered, *Direct the love upward, honey. Send it to yourself, yes. But also to him. He's lived a cold, endless life with no dawn and it's warped his energy. He needs the light as much as you need the love.*

Tears flowing, she followed Stefan's instructions blindly. She waited for Peter to howl in rage and pain, but he didn't. She sensed him there in the back of her eyes and sure enough, her eyes started to heat up.

But she was blind anyway. There was nothing more he could do without damaging the physical body he was now inhabiting. Maybe if she infused him with her own loving energy he'd feel the pain he inflicted on her. And that would be his own pain. She almost smiled, loving the thought of him getting a dose of his own medicine. He'd caused so many people pain, and here he was about to get his own. But she knew instinctively that was the wrong path to follow. She'd never have done this to the Peter she'd known. She hated that he'd suffered. Would have done anything to save him from such a fate.

What are you doing? Peter asked sharply. *Stop that. It's too late to save yourself.*

Really? Well, now you are a part of me, so if you hurt me it will hurt you too, Peter.

So what do I care? I have been suffering already for a long time.

So have I, she whispered, her own heart opening up as she released the energy she'd clutched onto so tightly. Released the restraints she'd used to hold him close. So scared of being alone, of losing someone else, she'd hung on well past the time of letting go.

Easy. Keep up the love, Stefan said quietly. *Don't slide into pain or fear. He feeds on it and uses it to empower himself.*

That made so much sense. Well, she'd had enough of being afraid. She'd had enough of being a victim. She had Stefan now, and she desperately wanted to explore the path that he'd opened up. She deserved it. She had so many broken dreams and crushed hopes littering her past. She wanted to start fresh and create something special. With someone special.

With him? Not likely, Peter scoffed. *I'll kill you now before you get to experience that kind of happiness.*

And I forgive you for thinking that way. I forgive you for feeling that way. I forgive you for all the bad things you've done because I understand how hard this last year must have been. I'm so sorry. I didn't know it would hurt you. No one could. She took a deep breath. *I love you and forgive you and…I let you go.*

Doing what she'd done to Caslo so long ago, she encapsulated his energy and booted him from her space. She immediately filled up the gaping hole in her head with as much loving abundant energy as she could. The last thing she heard was Peter's long, lingering cry of *Noooo.*

Then she knew no more.

WHEN CELINA WOKE, it was to find herself pinned to the

floor.

"Stefan?"

No answer. She could feel his breath against her cheek, but it wasn't warm, active. Instead, like the rest of him, the air wafted out on the faintest of efforts. Panicked, she rolled over, crying out, "Stefan?"

"He's lost."

Celina glared at Lissa. This wasn't funny. "What do you mean lost?"

"His soul is out on the ethers. Lost."

"He goes into the ethers all the time. How can he be lost? He owns that space."

Lissa laughed but there was a bitter edge to it. "Yes, he does. Or did. But he was trying to stop your asshole boy-friend from killing you, so he used his energy as a buffer between you two. In such a way that when you kicked him out, that part of Stefan – hanging on so tightly to the asshole – went too."

"So what, you're saying this is my fault?" Damn that ghost. She'd be happy to never see another ghost if this one would just be like the other ones. But she wasn't. And would never be.

"It's your fault if you don't save him."

Celina scrambled to her knees. "And how do I do that?"

"Call to him with your music, with your colors. Show him the way back to you."

"No. You said that will cage him. I can't do that to Stef-an."

"All psychic energy is determined by intention. If you don't intend to cage Stefan then you won't. But if you call to him because you are alone and afraid and fearful, then you will draw him to you to fill that void. You have to call Stefan with love and show him the way back to here."

Celina winced. "And if I don't love him? I've hardly even had a chance to get to know him."

"You know him. More than you think, but once again," she snapped in exasperation, "you won't see."

"See what?" Celina almost screamed in frustration.

"Let me try to bring it to you."

And Lissa blinked out of sight.

Celina shook her head, bewildered, but the ghost was gone. She stared toward Stefan's prone body. Maybe if she did what Stefan had shown her how to do it would work. She may not be sure of how she felt about him, but she really didn't want him to die on her. She wanted time to explore what they had.

She slid her hand down his shoulders and arms to snatch up his hand and hold him in her lap as she knelt at his side. She started by calling to him, knowing it was useless but unable to stop herself. She had to consider Lissa's suggestion. She'd do anything to avoid caging Stefan to her, but she had to bring him home.

Why weren't his other psychic friends here to help? Then again, from the sounds of it they were all busy helping others.

It was up to her.

She opened her eyes hoping for some change in her sight. But there was only gray. As usual. And a deep ache, a burn. She closed her eyes again. Gently she replaced her hand on his chest, thought how to reorient herself in this place, and crawled forward to where she thought the guitar was. It took several moments before she found it. Snatching it up, she scooched back to sit beside him. She plucked a couple of chords. How could she play with the necessary emotion when panic tightened her throat and cramped her fingers? She rippled her practice notes by habit, feeling them relax against one of her favorite instruments. Where would she have been in all these months of darkness without music to lead her way?

That thought made her wince. She'd been a light in the never-ending darkness for the ghosts out there too.

She lifted her head, thinking about that. Music led her down the path and Stefan was a painter, so in theory he could follow the colors she'd paint home. And how could she paint a pathway for him? Slowly her mind, half-absorbed in thought, she watched the twisting fronds of color rise up and twine sadly in the air in front of her. She grimaced. That was likely to lead to his funeral, not a happy homecoming. Closing her eyes so she could see the colors easier, she added a lighter note, then another so there was a happy jig dancing, but realized that wasn't going to work either.

"Don't think about it – just do it," Lissa urged.

Good advice. She pressed her fingers flat against the strings for a long moment, then thought about Stefan, calling out to him. Calling to him from a place of home – of heart. She smiled. "I might not love you yet, but I'm so on the edge I'll be there in a nanosecond."

She almost laughed as the words resonated with the haunting tune. She continued to weave all the reasons why he should return to her. All the reasons to come back to this life, to this reality, to what they were together. She didn't realize there were tears in her eyes until they dropped down onto her hands.

"Ah, Stefan," she whispered. "See what you do to me?"

She rejoiced in the joy of what they had, what they could have. The notes swelled with passion. She watched as vibrant colors braided into a strong, tight cord in front of her. She mentally pulled it back, winding it up so tight that it would launch as soon as she released it. She held it close in her mind's eye, filling it with love and joy and peace and need. Need for him to return. Need for him to come back to her that they might be together again.

Then she let it fly, laugher bursting free as the rope flew out of her sight, out of the house, and heading toward her love.

Her fingers danced and stroked and kicked up the tempo, keeping the colorful road rippling forward. "Come back to me, Stefan, come back!"

For a long moment there was nothing, just the power of the music pouring from her heart.

Finally, in the distance the faintest of whispers drifted toward her.

Celina.

Yes, she cried, *follow the path. I'm right here at the end of the road.*

She played as if her heart were dying, her fingers moving so fast she was afraid the slightest thing would trip them up and the music – the pathway – would be broken.

Then suddenly he stood in front of her, his form glowing golden, vibrant and strong.

"I'm here. You can stop playing."

"No, I can't. You might disappear if I do." Then the briefest touch of his lips brushed against hers and her fingers clanged together, the music jarring to a stop.

She gasped. "Stefan."

And damn if he didn't reach over and grab her hand physically and squeeze. "I'm here."

She burst into tears. She leaned over and was crushed in

his embrace. After a moment she felt something hard, small, and round between them. She lifted up slightly, her hand grasping the cold object. "What's this?"

"You're welcome," Lissa said from the side, but there was no condescension in her voice this time. In fact, if Celina wasn't correct, there just might have been tears clogging the teenager's throat.

"You are some special ghost, you know that?" Celina straightened, her heart full and happy.

"I'll admit you're turning out to be not too bad after all yourself."

Celina beamed. Peace with Stefan's ghost. Just about perfect.

Her fingers played with the object, a frown on her face as she tried to identify it. After a couple of moments she realized there was only silence from Stefan.

"Stefan?"

"I'm here," he murmured, his voice the barest of whispers.

She sagged with relief.

"Lissa brought this." She held up the object. "It's the first I've known of a ghost that could move objects."

"Some do," he said quietly. "Lissa is getting more adept."

She tilted her head and smiled, a tiny quirk to her lips. "So what is this?"

"Why don't you tell me?"

The edge of one side of the object caught her attention. Her heart froze. She couldn't breathe. Her mind was too shocked to make any sense of what just happened.

"It can't be," she whispered. She shifted so she could put her hand into her pocket and withdrew her precious Caslo rock that she'd been holding so much today. Hands shaking, she carefully lined the two up and felt them settle into place. "Caslo," she whispered. "Is it really you?"

"Why don't see for yourself?"

See? As in, if the predator was gone could she really see? "I tried earlier but there was just grayness."

"Try again." Stefan's voice held a hint of amusement. She frowned at him. But fingers whispered across her closed eyes just then. He said, "It takes something else – belief."

Scared to try and terrified not to, Celina opened her eyes and saw Stefan, as in *really* saw Stefan. For a long moment a vision of Caslo's younger self from her memory banks settled over the top, adjusted, then lined up with the Stefan she knew today.

And she could see *him* for the first time.

The boyfriend of her childhood, the best friend of her heart, the beautiful youth she'd loved forever, the same one she'd sent away permanently – lay on the floor watching her, a little wary, a little uncertain, and just as she'd last seen him, always full of love – for her.

As she'd always loved him.

Caslo!

AN HOUR LATER a cool cloth over her eyes to ease the burning from the bright lights, and curled up against the one man she'd thought never to see again, Celina realized she'd be happy to never move again.

He cuddled her closer.

There should have been no tears left, she didn't want to cry any more, but a few snuck out the corner of her eye to trickle down her cheek. Tears of relief at having the predator gone. She couldn't even begin to digest that it had been her fiancé. Right now all she wanted to focus on was having Caslo back. And then there was the miracle of her vision, her eyes that could actually see now.

"You okay?"

"I'm just fine," she whispered, tilting her head to look at him, "now."

He grinned. She'd never get tired of looking at him. He was stunning. He'd been a pretty youth and had grown into those dynamic looks so well. She sighed with pleasure. "I'm glad I couldn't see you at the beginning." At his raised eyebrows, she explained, "I'd have been so distracted by your good looks."

"You used to say I was as pretty as a girl," he accused, but the twinkle in his voice belied the words.

She grinned. "And you were. I was terribly jealous."

"Ha. You were always stunning."

She waited a moment. "Why?"

"Why did I leave and not come back?"

She nodded, almost hating to hear the answer.

"Partly because you sent me away. Partly because you were determined to believe I was a ghost, and partly because there are laws in the universe and when I had to step back to that extent, I had to stay out of your way until the timing was right."

She pondered that. "I really thought you were a ghost. I couldn't possibly have imagined that you could leave your body and appear as yourself." She shifted. "And then there is your name…"

"Ah, yes. You see, that place I was taken to was for 'special people' so I could get help. But it was more of an institute for those beyond help." His voice was wry, pensive as he added, "When I escaped it was imperative to change my name. To keep from being discovered and hauled back. I'd learned a very big lesson there. One I wasn't going to forget again." He laughed, a boisterous laugh that made her sigh happily. "Besides, Stefan is my name. Stefan Caslo Kronos."

"And your parents?"

"They were foster parents, and I think they were quite happy to wash their hands of me. Many years during that time are a complete blank. As such, it's hard for me to even identify with my old self." He hugged her close. "It was hard to always appear in the form you would recognize. And then after you sent me away…"

"I'm so sorry," she whispered. "I hated to do it, but I thought it was for your own good."

"If I'd been a ghost, it would have been, yes." He stroked away a tear. "You needed time to understand. You couldn't have understood what I could do, to see me in my many forms. To be with me. You had to grow too. To learn and to remember the love inside."

"But I didn't, so I sent away the one person in my life that I loved." She rubbed her hand across his chest. The bright light still hurt her eyes, so she just looked through her lashes, loving the gift she had back. To have been blind and now to see… was priceless.

She said out loud, "To have back someone I thought was dead…"

He was silent for a moment then said, his voice low and solemn, "And the reverse is also true."

Something in his voice had her pushing back to stare at him. "Is that comment directed at something specific?"

He opened his eyes and said, "While you were blind you

lost track of reality on some levels."

Frowning, she sat up and stared at him through her lowered lashes. "On a lot of levels. Which are you talking about?"

He stared at her, reached up, and caressed her cheeks. "Jillian and Gordon?"

"My friends?" She frowned. "What about them? I haven't seen Gordon since the hospital." Her face cleared and she smiled. "But you were there with me, weren't you?"

"I was, but Gordon was there in spirit only. As was Jillian in your apartment."

She gasped. "Gordon is dead?" Another shock to her system. Another shock to her reality. How had she not known? She thought of all the conversations with Gordon. He'd been dead all this time, and yet there for her.

Jillian, her friend, saying yes to tea and never drinking any. Damn. How could she have not seen it? And that was of course the problem. She'd been living in the dark and assuming that her friends were there in the flesh. She didn't know what to say or how to feel. She was sad for them, but as she'd stayed in touch with them over the last year it just felt…odd. Distant. "How could I not know?"

"When you lost your sight you saw energy in different depths and easily confused the physical entities with ghostly ones. Reality was also easier on you this way."

She shook her head. "You must have thought I'd lost it."

"What I thought was that you were the most beautiful woman in the world and the only one for me. The rest were issues that could be dealt with. You'd had a tough couple of years, but nothing you couldn't recover from."

"And now?" she whispered.

"Now? Now I'm just happy to be back in your life." He

tilted her head and kissed her. "I have never stopped loving you."

Once again tears misted her eyes. She burrowed close against him and whispered, "And I love you. I always have."

This concludes Book 7 of Psychic Visions: Eyes to the Soul. Read the first Chapter of Now You See Her: Psychic Visions, Book 8

Now You See Her: Psychic Visions
(Book #8)

Energy is the life-force of inherent good…and the vigor of unnatural evil. Which is stronger?

When she was young, Tia was forced into a prison, studied and tortured, because of her special talent. The chance for escape led her to run as far away as she could…but she quickly discovered there is nowhere she can hide that they can't find her. Stefan Kronos, a psychic who's formed a community of those like her, is the only person she believes can help her. When she begs him to help her, she awakens from a coma six weeks later. Her problems have only just begun, chief among them that she's still being hunted.

Now you see her…

Dean is moonlighting as a guard at the hospital Tia finds herself in upon rousing from unconsciousness. Between a rock and a hard place, Dean has met Tia, a woman he can't forget…and equally can't believe the insane things she's telling him – until there's absolutely no other choice. What's at stake becomes only too clear when Tia's problems become Dean's, entwining them so neither knows where one stops and the other starts. If she runs again, how can he find someone of her unbelievable talents?

Now you don't…

Book 8 is available now!
To find out more visit Dale Mayer's website.
https://geni.us/dmnowyouseeher

PSYCHIC VISIONS: NOW YOU SEE HER (BOOK #8)
CHAPTER 1

"OKAY TIA. IT'S now or never."

"Never." That was her vote. Besides, what was she saying? She always voted with her feet. Who needed to talk things over? It made no difference. She pushed the long strands of hair back off her face and stared out the window over the sink.

"You're at a crossroads." Simone stood up from the kitchen table and walked over to Tia. Her long arms reached out to grasp Tia's crossed arms. "You can't keep going like this."

"Sure I can," Tia muttered. "I always have."

"But you're not sixteen anymore. In fact, in the last decade you were supposed to have learned something," Simone said in exasperation.

"And I have," Tia replied, turning to face her. "But one thing that never changes is that instinct that says *go. Run. Hide.* It's kept me alive all these years."

Simone, a fine dusting of gray hair at her temples, nodded. "I understand. I'd always hoped something in your life would break and you'd be free of him." Her tone turned sad.

"In a different way than my Mandy is now free."

Tia couldn't help the wince. Mandy hadn't survived childhood after being struck down with a rare cancer. "Never going to happen. Once he realized what I could do – I was done."

"But you've been safe for a long time now. How did he find you? What changed?"

Tia turned to stare out the window again, the ageless sheers hanging cheerfully off to the side. What could she say? She had no idea what had changed. She was tired of this. More tired than she ever had been. She might have to take the one step she had avoided all these years. And accept the help from the one person who cared. Who'd offered to help years ago.

She had no real reason for not accepting Stefan Kronos' help. She couldn't even formulate an answer as to why she hadn't accepted his offer – except an ingrained fear of not knowing who to trust and trusting the wrong person.

She liked to think she was capable of doing this without help. She was independent. Stiff-necked stubborn more likely. She could handle this. She'd been handling it since forever.

Until now.

Until enough years had gone by and she'd let that hard edge of awareness dull down to something much more comfortable to wear. She slept at night again. Could stop and enjoy a cup of tea without seeing bad guys behind the bushes and villains in the woods.

She'd softened. Become more accepting. She'd become complacent.

She sighed and slowly rotated her head, trying to ease the tension. What she'd done was become stupid.

And that had to stop. Before this asshole stopped her.

She knew what he wanted. Knew what he'd hoped to get from her. She couldn't let him learn her energy techniques. She didn't know if he could imitate them or not, but she didn't dare let him try. The world was so not ready for that. She stared at the thin bracelet one of her fellow inmates had given her a long time ago. She'd kept it all these years as a reminder of how being a captive had defined who she was today. That she was in charge of who she was going to be from here on in. And of a memory of someone special now lost to her.

But as she stared down the long lean years of hiding, the years that had formed her early adulthood, the loneliness, the pain, she didn't think she could go back to the person she'd been. She couldn't go back to that lifestyle. She'd let that go when she finally found herself safe for the first time.

No…she couldn't go back to that stage of her life, she wouldn't. It wasn't possible.

Neither was it required.

She reached for the phone.

Without giving the other person a chance to respond, she said, "Stefan, I need help."

THE DUSK HAD settled, giving an odd light to the various pedestrians walking down the sidewalk. But there was no mistaking the woman across the street. There she was. Finally within his grasp. Tia. He smiled. Time had been a blessing in many ways. She was stunning. Good. And she wouldn't recognize him. Too bad. She'd doted on him back then. Of course she didn't know who he really was. She'd always called the boss The Bastard. And he was. But that boss was the old bastard. Now he was the New Bastard.

He grinned. He wasn't really one of course. His family had very high connections. His birth was well documented. Maybe he deserved the name for other reasons. But his reasons had always been to benefit Tia and the others. To help them be the best they could be.

A homeless man, curled up on the newspaper in the corner, whimpered. The New Bastard turned to face the homeless man. "Leave. Now."

The homeless man's gaze widened. He opened his mouth as if to say something then snapped it shut. He nodded meekly. Grabbing up his sparse belongings, he scurried backward down the alley.

Run, little mouse, run.

The Bastard turned and stared across the street where Tia leaned so casually. As if there wasn't a care in the world. His mood darkened. Bitch. Princess. All she'd put him through. All she'd cost him. He'd been searching for her for years. But finally, she'd come home. Well, it was time for her to pay up. They'd tried all sorts of things to make her do what they wanted her to do. Tried everything they could think of.

Kept her isolated at the end. But when he'd gone back for her…somehow she'd escaped.

Now look at her. She was so defiant. Independent. Stubborn. Always had been. Too bad for her. He needed something she had. And he was going to get it.

Tonight.

He fingered the small balls in his pocket as he watched her. He'd done everything he could to make her show her true self and she'd always resisted. Well, no more.

Several people walked by staring at her, but she ignored

them.

Typical of her.

Still, she was hardly someone anyone could ignore. Not the way she stood out. With her chameleon abilities, she didn't have to stand out right now. She could blend right in if she wanted to.

So she wanted to be seen.

Therefore, she was waiting for someone.

He'd have to wait. See who it was.

But energy vibrated through his fingers. Anger. Hate. He had a lot of reasons for not liking this stage of his life. Especially knowing the answer – the ability to fix all that had gone wrong – was right across the street.

Only he didn't want to wait. He wanted action. Now.

He turned his head and stared back toward the alley. And smiled.

TIA, HER LEATHER jacket tugged up high on her neck, her long hair pulled into a high ponytail, leaned against the brick wall at the city park. She hadn't been back in Portland in years, and this area was new to her. She wasn't afraid but found it hard to settle comfortably into her surroundings. She didn't fear the night or the others in the world, just the one man and the organization that pandered to his every whim. Combined they were a deadly force. One she'd like nothing to do with ever again.

As far as she could see, she was alone. A cop walked the other side of the street. A few single women scurried through the almost empty area. A couple of men strode confidently along. The profile of one caught her eye, but she couldn't get a clear glimpse of him. She kept an eye on him but he walked past. She didn't feel safe but neither did she sense imminent danger.

That spidey sense of hers was not accurate in all situations and she hadn't figured out why, but the thought that the predator might have a new tool to help knock her spidey sense out of commission had kept her senses turned on and humming in the background – for years.

Now…such a different life.

Her ribs ached, the old faded scars quivering with long submerged memories of life before her escape. She'd survived those long years, barely. And only because of Simone.

Simone hadn't been able to turn Tia away.

Thank God.

From such things great friendships were born.

She owed Simone her life. And her very sanity. She'd seen things when working on Tia that no one had ever seen. That no one would ever know or suspect were possible. And she'd kept quiet, protecting her.

Tia knew that damn asshole still wanted her, still searched for her to take her back to his lab. Rat that he was.

And she'd do a lot to avoid his cage.

A couple strolled by, holding hands, heads together wrapped up in an aura of new love. Behind them, slower and not as wrapped up, was an older couple strolling by, still holding hands after decades of marriage, still in love.

The thought made her smile. Then she remembered where she was and why. How anyone could stay innocent of the evil in the world she had no idea.

Still, like a movie on the big screen, it was a nice bit of fantasy.

The sky was eerie in the moonlight with the clouds drifting in and out. She thought she recognized a man across the street. As he stepped into the lamplight, she realized it was a stranger.

She leaned her head back and closed her eyes. She'd promised Simone she'd return to her house at ten if her meeting didn't happen.

Stefan had better show. She needed him.

The street light across the road flickered.

She tensed.

And closed her eyes. She reached out with her spidey sense to see what was disturbing the energy of the lamp.

And found…nothing.

She frowned. It could have just been a flicker in the power grid from the city center. Dirty power being an issue in many cities. But here? Not so much. At least it hadn't been a problem ten years ago. She'd left soon after and was surprised at the sprawling mess the city had become. Either it had grown or her memories had shrunk. Either way it wasn't great.

She'd become a small town girl. There, she could be who she wanted to be and ditch the personas she had to create every time she picked up and started over.

And if she told herself that often enough she might believe it, because in truth it sucked. You had to remember the lies that were the flavor of the week and over time the lies grew and had to be built upon until you started to believe some of them yourself. After all there wasn't much of a choice once you started down that path.

It was also lonely. She always had to play a part. She could never be herself. Only with Simone. But it was dangerous to stay close to her. And she'd do anything to keep her safe. She was the only person in Tia's life who cared about her.

At least until she'd ended up at Land's Edge, a small town close to the Canadian border. She'd figured that if she was found there, she might be able to slip across the border and get lost in the northern wilderness. Instead, she'd found a place to call home. At least temporarily.

It was a place of misfits. Travelers. People who'd arrived in the town and ended up staying, putting down roots. Probably thinking along the same lines she had.

Tia had parents somewhere, but when her talents had shown up they had taken her from doctor to doctor to "fix" her.

Only there'd never been anything wrong, nothing to "fix."

Her parents had taken a hard line and their actions at that point forever divided her from them. Her baby brother had arrived soon after. Her parents, wanting the taint to stay contained with her, isolated her from him while they tried to deal with Tia's problems.

Of course the problem never was resolved so she never got a chance to get to know her little brother. A decade younger than her, she wouldn't be surprised if her parents had erased her existence from his memory. An easy thing to do in one so young. Especially after they put her in that program.

She shifted restlessly as the evening cooled down. The bricks were uncomfortable on her back. She deliberately removed some of the energy from her shoulder blades, minimizing their ability to scream in pain.

The lights flickered again.

Shit.

She tensed and slid a little further down the wall. Deeper into the shadows.

He'd found her.

No, she argued silently. He couldn't have. No one knew. Just Stefan, and he'd never tell. Not the Stefan she'd heard so much about. He had almost a cult-like following. People loved him.

But that didn't mean he didn't accidentally tell someone.

Maybe his phone line was bugged.

Maybe his own security had been breached.

All things were possible.

But not likely.

She closed her eyes as pain suddenly slammed into her heart. There was only one other person who'd known where she was coming and when.

Simone.

Shit. Shit. *Shit.*

Had something happened to her? She slid her cell phone out of her pocket, and shielding the light from the screen, she checked for messages.

There was one from Simone. *Someone broke in tonight. Run.*

The hair on her skin rose up straight and her breath caught up in her chest.

Her instinct said to pick up her feet and go. And keep running. She took a deep breath and fought against the urge. She'd been at this point too many times in her life. No more. When did this ever stop?

She texted Simone. *Protect yourself.*

The danger, whatever it was and whatever form it was taking, approached from the left. She slipped her phone into her pocket, closed her eyes and went still. Very still.

As in sinking her bony frame into the hard bricks. As in letting the sensation of her feet sinking into cracked cement become real. Becoming one with her surroundings. Being one with the universe. Old energy at her feet. Newer energy at her back. Fresh energy in front of her from those who passed by in the last day. This was an old area. She frowned, hating the fear that spiked. Had she been set up?

Old energy was one thing. Ancient energy was something else altogether. She couldn't do ancient. Yet inside she knew she should be able to. Energy was energy, supposedly. It could be used for good and bad. That rule at least applied to most energy.

As she stood still sinking in sensation, her foot trembled. She shuddered.

No, this couldn't be happening. It wasn't supposed to be like this.

It couldn't be.

She tried to lift her foot, tried to step away, but tentacles, faint tendrils of energy lifting and sliding up over her shoe stopped her. She couldn't move it.

She hadn't had time to react. But knew inside it didn't matter. This force of the ancient earth had already taken place. She'd felt it before, once.

She'd escaped that energy – once.

The energy moved up her ankle.

She was caught.

Damn right you're caught, bitch.

She shuddered as panic overwhelmed her. This shouldn't be happening. She couldn't be imprisoned like this. She wouldn't be. Her life couldn't happen in this way. Not again.

She needed help.

She'd never be a lab rat again.

Never be a test subject for them to work on.

She'd die first.

And if that happened now, at this moment, fine. She had no life worth missing. No friends to love. Nobody to miss her if she were gone. Only Simone. And if this asshole had hurt Simone…

Death was the best answer.

But instinct just didn't give way to passive nothing. Her will to live didn't just roll over and wait for death.

Her body still fought for survival, still fought to survive this horrible scenario.

She couldn't go out this way.

How completely undignified.

How completely ironic that she who dealt in energy was going to die by an older and more skilled energy.

A cosmic joke.

Go.

A new voice slammed into her brain, making her groan out loud. She had no idea where it came from or who it was.

Still, she tried to fight the restraints on her feet. She struggled, hearing a horrible laughter in front of her. She didn't know who was laughing.

Now. I said go.

Damn it, I can't, she screamed at the intruder in her head. *I'm caught.* But they obviously didn't understand what was going on. She couldn't "go" anywhere. *Who are you?*

Stefan. And you are not caught. You can't be caught.

I am a prisoner. My feet are stuck. She trembled with panic as the binds holding her fast to the ground climbed higher and higher up her legs. Her feet were cold and numb, but the leading edge of that horrible energy burned hot, scalding her with the heat of its moment. *I'm chained to the earth, I can't get free.*

The volume of the voice rose to the point it pounded at a pitch she couldn't stand.

Go, I said, he roared. *Now!*

She screamed back. *I can't.*

Of course she can't, she's mine now. I don't know who the hell you are, but get lost.

Tia froze, the bile rising up her throat, and she knew she was done. This was it. There was only a small ball of regret. For the things she hadn't done. For the pet she hadn't been able to have. The friends she'd never know. The family she could never have.

Do you want a future? Stefan asked. *Or do you want to give up and die?*

Damn it, she cried out. *I don't have a choice, can't you see that?*

I see an exquisitely powerful woman who has no idea what she can do and right now, if she doesn't do something, she's going to die. Or worse. Stefan's voice hardened. *She's going to wish she were dead.*

She closed her eyes again at his words, her body buffeted by a weird sensation. That creeping feeling of having been caught in a spider's web. That horrible sensation of being spun into a cocoon saved for a better day.

Only there were two people here.

Who was the spider and who was her rescuer?

Or were they both out to get her?

She couldn't tell friend from foe.

Of course not, you don't know me, Stefan said in her head. *But what are you going to do about it. Will you believe me when the vehicle pulls up and they throw you, now fully paralyzed into it? Or will you have to wake in a padded room, tied down to a metal bedpost to realize what's happened?*

She groaned, her body trembling in fear, that horrible burning edge of paralysis climbing higher and higher. *I can't live that way again.* She pulled at her legs desperately to lift them, desperate to get away.

That's your future if you don't move, Stefan urged. *Now.*

I'm trying, she cried out. *I can't. The energy is too strong. Too old. Don't you get it? I'm not stuck here by any normal energy, this is ancient energy. I can't…move.*

Stefan gave a heavy sigh. *Die then.*

There was a horrible sound, a burning in her gut, then a horrible flash of heat as her spine turned to burning ash.

What's happening she screamed. She twisted and twisted but couldn't escape from the pain. She was going to die. *I'm so sorry,* she sobbed. *I don't know what I've done to deserve this but if there is anything – anything I can do to get away then help me. Please.*

Damn it. Stefan's voice whispered through her.

She almost laughed then cried. Stefan hadn't left her.

Sure he has. You're all alone. You've always been all alone. That hated evilness twisted through her mind, its poisonous tone dominating her thoughts.

"Miss, are you okay?" A strange voice penetrated through the mess in her head, his voice dark mysterious. "Can I help you?"

She groaned. No, please not an innocent bystander. He wouldn't understand. "No," she whispered. "Run or you'll get hurt too."

"What?"

In the background there was more noise. The stranger spoke to someone. Dimly she understood he was calling for an ambulance. Oh Lord, he was going to get hurt. She couldn't have another death on her conscience.

But overriding the worry of the stranger wove the hated

voice of her nightmares. Too Late. *You were promised to me years ago. It might have taken this long to corner you, but I'm not going to lose out on my best test subject. I've waited a long time to have you come back to me.* He laughed. *But don't worry, I'll make sure you live a long and healthy life.*

"No," she cried out loud. "I'd rather die."

Yes. Stefan spoke up again. *That's exactly right, finally. Do it. Die.*

"Whoa," the stranger crouched beside her called out. "Take it easy. Help is coming."

The help was too late for her. It had always been too late for her.

And it's too late for him. This innocent stranger you've sucked into this mess. I'm going to kill him too.

She couldn't let that happen. She reached out to save the man trying to help her. He needed to disconnect from her. From this. Or he'd be lost.

Only she couldn't feel him. Or see him, but she was connected…somehow. She reached out a hand and drove a bolt of energy at him, trying to cut him loose. To push him away from her. To remove his hand on her wrist. Then it was too late. Too late to wonder…to worry. She finally gave up on it and gave into the paralysis, the pain, the torment and she relaxed her grip on her life.

And passed peacefully. Screams from her tormentor echoed *No* in her head as she slowly, one tiny fragment at a time – died.

Free from him at last.

Book 8 is available now!

To find out more visit Dale Mayer's website.

https://geni.us/dmnowyouseeher

Simon Says... Hide: Kate Morgan (Book #1)

Welcome to a new thriller series from *USA Today* Best-Selling Author Dale Mayer. Set in Vancouver, BC, the team of Detective Kate Morgan and Simon St. Laurant, an unwilling psychic, marries all the elements of Dale's work that you've come to love, plus so much more.

Detective Kate Morgan, newly promoted to the Vancouver PD Homicide Department, stands for the victims in her world. She was once a victim herself, just as her mother had been a victim, and then her brother—an unsolved missing child's case—was yet another victim. She can't stand those who take advantage of others, and the worst ones are those who prey on the hopes of desperate people to line their own pockets.

So, when she finds a connection between more than a half-dozen cold cases to a current case, where a child's life hangs in the balance, Kate would make a deal with the devil himself to find the culprit and to save the child.

Simon St. Laurant's grandmother had the Sight and had warned him that, once he used it, he could never walk away. Until now, her caution had made it easy to avoid that first step. But, when nightmares of his own past are triggered, Simon can't stand back and watch child after child be abused. Not without offering his help to those chasing the monsters.

Even if it means dealing with the cranky and critical Detective Kate Morgan …

Find Simon Says… Hide here!
To find out more visit Dale Mayer's website.
https://geni.us/DMSSHideUniversal

Author's Note

Thank you for reading Eyes to the Soul: Psychic Visions, Book 7! If you enjoyed the book, please take a moment and leave a short review.

Dear reader,

I love to hear from readers, and you can contact me at my website: www.dalemayer.com or at my Facebook author page. To be informed of new releases and special offers, sign up for my newsletter or follow me on BookBub. And if you are interested in joining Dale Mayer's Reader Group, here is the Facebook sign up page.
http://geni.us/DaleMayerFBGroup

Cheers,
Dale Mayer

About the Author

Dale Mayer is a *USA Today* best-selling author, best known for her SEALs military romances, her Psychic Visions series, and her Lovely Lethal Garden cozy series. Her contemporary romances are raw and full of passion and emotion (Broken But … Mending, Hathaway House series). Her thrillers will keep you guessing (Kate Morgan, By Death series), and her romantic comedies will keep you giggling (*It's a Dog's Life*, a stand-alone novella; and the Broken Protocols series, starring Charming Marvin, the cat).

Dale honors the stories that come to her—and some of them are crazy, break all the rules and cross multiple genres!

To go with her fiction, she also writes nonfiction in many different fields, with books available on résumé writing, companion gardening, and the US mortgage system. All her books are available in print and ebook format.

Connect with Dale Mayer Online

Dale's Website – www.dalemayer.com

Twitter – @DaleMayer

Facebook Page – geni.us/DaleMayerFBFanPage

Facebook Group – geni.us/DaleMayerFBGroup

BookBub – geni.us/DaleMayerBookbub

Instagram – geni.us/DaleMayerInstagram

Goodreads – geni.us/DaleMayerGoodreads

Newsletter – geni.us/DaleNews

Also by Dale Mayer

Published Adult Books:

Shadow Recon
Magnus, Book 1

Bullard's Battle
Ryland's Reach, Book 1
Cain's Cross, Book 2
Eton's Escape, Book 3
Garret's Gambit, Book 4
Kano's Keep, Book 5
Fallon's Flaw, Book 6
Quinn's Quest, Book 7
Bullard's Beauty, Book 8
Bullard's Best, Book 9
Bullard's Battle, Books 1–2
Bullard's Battle, Books 3–4
Bullard's Battle, Books 5–6
Bullard's Battle, Books 7–8

Terkel's Team
Damon's Deal, Book 1
Wade's War, Book 2
Gage's Goal, Book 3

Calum's Contact, Book 4

Rick's Road, Book 5

Kate Morgan

Simon Says… Hide, Book 1

Simon Says… Jump, Book 2

Simon Says… Ride, Book 3

Simon Says… Scream, Book 4

Simon Says… Run, Book 5

Hathaway House

Aaron, Book 1

Brock, Book 2

Cole, Book 3

Denton, Book 4

Elliot, Book 5

Finn, Book 6

Gregory, Book 7

Heath, Book 8

Iain, Book 9

Jaden, Book 10

Keith, Book 11

Lance, Book 12

Melissa, Book 13

Nash, Book 14

Owen, Book 15

Percy, Book 16

Quinton, Book 17

Hathaway House, Books 1–3

Hathaway House, Books 4–6

Hathaway House, Books 7–9

The K9 Files

Ethan, Book 1

Pierce, Book 2

Zane, Book 3

Blaze, Book 4

Lucas, Book 5

Parker, Book 6

Carter, Book 7

Weston, Book 8

Greyson, Book 9

Rowan, Book 10

Caleb, Book 11

Kurt, Book 12

Tucker, Book 13

Harley, Book 14

Kyron, Book 15

Jenner, Book 16

The K9 Files, Books 1–2

The K9 Files, Books 3–4

The K9 Files, Books 5–6

The K9 Files, Books 7–8

The K9 Files, Books 9–10

The K9 Files, Books 11–12

Lovely Lethal Gardens

Arsenic in the Azaleas, Book 1

Bones in the Begonias, Book 2

Corpse in the Carnations, Book 3

Daggers in the Dahlias, Book 4

Evidence in the Echinacea, Book 5

Footprints in the Ferns, Book 6

Gun in the Gardenias, Book 7

Handcuffs in the Heather, Book 8

Ice Pick in the Ivy, Book 9

Jewels in the Juniper, Book 10

Killer in the Kiwis, Book 11

Lifeless in the Lilies, Book 12

Murder in the Marigolds, Book 13

Nabbed in the Nasturtiums, Book 14

Offed in the Orchids, Book 15

Poison in the Pansies, Book 16

Quarry in the Quince, Book 17

Revenge in the Roses, Book 18

Lovely Lethal Gardens, Books 1–2

Lovely Lethal Gardens, Books 3–4

Lovely Lethal Gardens, Books 5–6

Lovely Lethal Gardens, Books 7–8

Lovely Lethal Gardens, Books 9–10

Psychic Vision Series

Tuesday's Child

Hide 'n Go Seek

Maddy's Floor

Garden of Sorrow

Knock Knock...

Rare Find
Eyes to the Soul
Now You See Her
Shattered
Into the Abyss
Seeds of Malice
Eye of the Falcon
Itsy-Bitsy Spider
Unmasked
Deep Beneath
From the Ashes
Stroke of Death
Ice Maiden
Snap, Crackle…
What If…
Talking Bones
Psychic Visions Books 1–3
Psychic Visions Books 4–6
Psychic Visions Books 7–9

By Death Series
Touched by Death
Haunted by Death
Chilled by Death
By Death Books 1–3

Broken Protocols – Romantic Comedy Series
Cat's Meow
Cat's Pajamas

Cat's Cradle

Cat's Claus

Broken Protocols 1-4

Broken and... Mending

Skin

Scars

Scales (of Justice)

Broken but... Mending 1-3

Glory

Genesis

Tori

Celeste

Glory Trilogy

Biker Blues

Morgan: Biker Blues, Volume 1

Cash: Biker Blues, Volume 2

SEALs of Honor

Mason: SEALs of Honor, Book 1

Hawk: SEALs of Honor, Book 2

Dane: SEALs of Honor, Book 3

Swede: SEALs of Honor, Book 4

Shadow: SEALs of Honor, Book 5

Cooper: SEALs of Honor, Book 6

Markus: SEALs of Honor, Book 7

Evan: SEALs of Honor, Book 8

Mason's Wish: SEALs of Honor, Book 9

Chase: SEALs of Honor, Book 10

Brett: SEALs of Honor, Book 11

Devlin: SEALs of Honor, Book 12

Easton: SEALs of Honor, Book 13

Ryder: SEALs of Honor, Book 14

Macklin: SEALs of Honor, Book 15

Corey: SEALs of Honor, Book 16

Warrick: SEALs of Honor, Book 17

Tanner: SEALs of Honor, Book 18

Jackson: SEALs of Honor, Book 19

Kanen: SEALs of Honor, Book 20

Nelson: SEALs of Honor, Book 21

Taylor: SEALs of Honor, Book 22

Colton: SEALs of Honor, Book 23

Troy: SEALs of Honor, Book 24

Axel: SEALs of Honor, Book 25

Baylor: SEALs of Honor, Book 26

Hudson: SEALs of Honor, Book 27

Lachlan: SEALs of Honor, Book 28

Paxton: SEALs of Honor, Book 29

SEALs of Honor, Books 1–3

SEALs of Honor, Books 4–6

SEALs of Honor, Books 7–10

SEALs of Honor, Books 11–13

SEALs of Honor, Books 14–16

SEALs of Honor, Books 17–19

SEALs of Honor, Books 20–22

SEALs of Honor, Books 23–25

Heroes for Hire

Levi's Legend: Heroes for Hire, Book 1

Stone's Surrender: Heroes for Hire, Book 2

Merk's Mistake: Heroes for Hire, Book 3

Rhodes's Reward: Heroes for Hire, Book 4

Flynn's Firecracker: Heroes for Hire, Book 5

Logan's Light: Heroes for Hire, Book 6

Harrison's Heart: Heroes for Hire, Book 7

Saul's Sweetheart: Heroes for Hire, Book 8

Dakota's Delight: Heroes for Hire, Book 9

Tyson's Treasure: Heroes for Hire, Book 10

Jace's Jewel: Heroes for Hire, Book 11

Rory's Rose: Heroes for Hire, Book 12

Brandon's Bliss: Heroes for Hire, Book 13

Liam's Lily: Heroes for Hire, Book 14

North's Nikki: Heroes for Hire, Book 15

Anders's Angel: Heroes for Hire, Book 16

Reyes's Raina: Heroes for Hire, Book 17

Dezi's Diamond: Heroes for Hire, Book 18

Vince's Vixen: Heroes for Hire, Book 19

Ice's Icing: Heroes for Hire, Book 20

Johan's Joy: Heroes for Hire, Book 21

Galen's Gemma: Heroes for Hire, Book 22

Zack's Zest: Heroes for Hire, Book 23

Bonaparte's Belle: Heroes for Hire, Book 24

Noah's Nemesis: Heroes for Hire, Book 25

Tomas's Trials: Heroes for Hire, Book 26

Heroes for Hire, Books 1–3

Heroes for Hire, Books 4–6

Heroes for Hire, Books 7–9

Heroes for Hire, Books 10–12

Heroes for Hire, Books 13–15

Heroes for Hire, Books 16–18

Heroes for Hire, Books 19–21

Heroes for Hire, Books 22–24

SEALs of Steel

Badger: SEALs of Steel, Book 1

Erick: SEALs of Steel, Book 2

Cade: SEALs of Steel, Book 3

Talon: SEALs of Steel, Book 4

Laszlo: SEALs of Steel, Book 5

Geir: SEALs of Steel, Book 6

Jager: SEALs of Steel, Book 7

The Final Reveal: SEALs of Steel, Book 8

SEALs of Steel, Books 1–4

SEALs of Steel, Books 5–8

SEALs of Steel, Books 1–8

The Mavericks

Kerrick, Book 1

Griffin, Book 2

Jax, Book 3

Beau, Book 4

Asher, Book 5

Ryker, Book 6

Miles, Book 7

Nico, Book 8

Keane, Book 9

Lennox, Book 10

Gavin, Book 11

Shane, Book 12

Diesel, Book 13

Jerricho, Book 14

Killian, Book 15

Hatch, Book 16

Corbin, Book 17

Aiden, Book 18

The Mavericks, Books 1–2

The Mavericks, Books 3–4

The Mavericks, Books 5–6

The Mavericks, Books 7–8

The Mavericks, Books 9–10

The Mavericks, Books 11–12

Collections

Dare to Be You…

Dare to Love…

Dare to be Strong…

RomanceX3

Standalone Novellas

It's a Dog's Life

Riana's Revenge

Second Chances

Published Young Adult Books:

Family Blood Ties Series

Vampire in Denial

Vampire in Distress

Vampire in Design

Vampire in Deceit

Vampire in Defiance

Vampire in Conflict

Vampire in Chaos

Vampire in Crisis

Vampire in Control

Vampire in Charge

Family Blood Ties Set 1–3

Family Blood Ties Set 1–5

Family Blood Ties Set 4–6

Family Blood Ties Set 7–9

Sian's Solution, A Family Blood Ties Series Prequel
    Novelette

Design series

Dangerous Designs

Deadly Designs

Darkest Designs

Design Series Trilogy

Standalone

In Cassie's Corner

Gem Stone (a Gemma Stone Mystery)

Published Non-Fiction Books:

Career Essentials

Career Essentials: The Résumé

Career Essentials: The Cover Letter

Career Essentials: The Interview

Career Essentials: 3 in 1